Determination

Mary Kingswood

Sutors Publishing

Published by Sutors Publishing

V0

ISBN: 978-1-912167-57-9 (paperback)

Cover design by: Shayne Rutherford of Darkmoon Graphics

 This is a work of fiction.

Author's note:

this book is written using historic British terminology, so *saloon* instead of *salon*, *chaperon* instead of *chaperone* and so on. I follow Jane Austen's example and refer to a group of sisters as the Miss Wintertons.

Contents

About the series

One man with a secret. A family torn apart by the consequences.

Mr Bertram Atherton has one foot in the Ancient World, emerging from his library only to eat and sleep. But when the chaplain of his uncle, the Earl of Rennington, is brutally murdered, it is revealed that he was never ordained and so the earl's marriage was invalid, and his children rendered illegitimate. Bertram's father is now the heir to the earldom, and Bertram after him. It's a horrifying change of circumstances for a man only interested in intellectual pursuits.

Miss Beatrice Franklyn is shocked to discover that her betrothed, the earl's eldest son, has been disinherited and can't make her a countess. But his cousin Bertram will inherit now, and he'll do, won't he? Bea sets her sights on a second betrothal, and she usually gets her way. How can unworldly Bertram resist her feminine wiles? But no matter how many tricks she tries and how determined she is to lure him into matrimony, she finds that Bertram is equally determined not to be lured. Which of them will win the battle of wills?

This is a complete story with a happy ever after. A traditional Regency romance, drawing room rather than bedroom. Book 2 of a 6 book series.

Isn't that what's-his-name? Occasionally characters from an earlier series pop up, or are mentioned. Lady Esther Franklyn's father, the Duke of Camberley, approved the marriage of his daughter, the Lady Grace Bucknell, to George Skelton, the Earl of Brackenwood's heir, in *The Governess.* Lady Esther's brother, the Marquess of Ramsey, had a tumultuous romance in *The Betrothed*. Lady Harbottle, in *The Widow*, and the Duchess of Orrisdale, in *The Duke,* were also Bucknells before their marriages.

About the series*:*

Book 0: The Chaplain: a man adrift, dreaming of a home *(a novella, free to mailing list subscribers).*

Book 1: Disinheritance: a man freed, looking for a new purpose in life

Book 2: Determination: a man pursued, forced to outwit his adversary

Book 3: Anger: a woman alone, trying to choose a different path in life

Book 4: Secrecy: a woman neglected, scheming to secure her own happiness

Book 5: Loyalty: a man of dreams, torn between the past and the future

Book 6: Ambition: a woman thwarted, unswervingly set on making a brilliant debut in society

Want to be the first to hear about new releases? Sign up for my mailing list at https://marykingswood.co.uk.

Principal Characters

The Atherton family of Corland Castle, North Riding of Yorkshire:

Charles, 11th Earl of Rennington (55)

Caroline, Countess of Rennington (50)

Their children:

Walter, Viscount Birtwell (29)

Mr Eustace Atherton (27), living on his own estate nearby, Welwood-on-the-Hill

Josie (Josephine), Lady Woodridge (26), married to Viscount Woodridge; they have two sons

Izzy (Isabel), Lady Farramont (24); married to Ian, Viscount Farramont (35); they have two daughters

Mr Kent Atherton (22)

Lady Olivia Atherton (18)

The earl's blind sister: Lady Alice Nicholson (48)

Her husband, the earl's chaplain: Mr Arthur Nicholson (55, deceased)

Their daughter, Miss Tess (Teresa) Nicholson (20)

The George Atherton family of Westwick Heights, North Riding of Yorkshire:

The earl's younger brother: Mr George Atherton (50)

Mrs Atherton (Jane, 45)

Their children:

Mr Bertram Atherton (25), a Latin scholar

Mr Lucas Atherton (23)

Miss Julia Atherton (20), betrothed to Mr Webster

Miss Emily Atherton (18)

Miss Penelope Atherton (16)

Master Philip Atherton (6)

The Strong Family of Birchall House, North Riding of Yorkshire:

Sir Hubert Strong, baronet (53)

Kitty, Lady Strong

Their children:

Miss Winifred Strong (24)

Hebe (22), married to Mr William Plaister of Pickering

Their daughter: Prudence (1)

Mabel (19), married to Mr Charles Danby of Knaresborough

Miss Lily Strong (17)

Master Harris Strong (15)

Master Lionel Strong (12)

Mr Alfred Strong (48), unmarried

Aunt Minna (46), married to Mr John Wilton of York, with many children

Aunt Sofia (42), married to Mr Edmund Blackwood of Westminster, London; 1 son

The Franklyn Family of Highwood Place, North Riding of Yorkshire:

Mr John Franklyn (46)

Lady Esther Franklyn (33), daughter of the Duke of Camberley

His daughter from his first marriage:

Miss Beatrice Franklyn (21)

The children from his second marriage:

Master Henry Franklyn (7)

Master Charles Franklyn (3)

The Murder Investigators:

Captain Michael Edgerton (37), formerly of the East India Company Army

Mrs Edgerton (Luce, née Willerton-Forbes, 30)

Mr Pettigrew Willerton-Forbes (38), a lawyer

Mr James Neate, a lawyer masquerading as a footman

Mr Alexander Grant Saxby (Sandy, 25), now known as Mr Alexander

Miss Peach, a former governess

1: A Meeting At Corland Castle

WESTWICK HEIGHTS: JUNE

Sometime around noon, Mr Bertram Atherton opened his well-worn copy of Virgil's *Aeneid* and began to read.

'Ast ego, quae divom incedo regina, Iovisque et soror et coniunx, una cum gente tot annos bella gero! Et quisquam numen Iunonis adoret praeterea, aut supplex aris imponet honorem?'

The clock struck four. Bertram emerged, blinking, from Carthage, and laid aside his book. It was time for his glass of Canary. He rose and crossed to the sideboard where resided the decanters, poured himself a modest amount, then took his customary tour of the library. *His* library, as he liked to think of it. Not literally, not yet, but one day all of Westwick Heights would be his, and since no one else in the family was in the least bookish, the library had become his particular domain. There was something peculiarly satisfying about the shelves filled with volumes, the unique smell of musty paper and ancient leather bindings, and the exhilarating possibilities to be found within them. If ever he became crotchety or unsettled in any way, the library could always restore his equanimity.

With a sigh of pure pleasure, he settled back into his chair and set his glass down on a side table. Adjusting his spectacles more firmly on his nose, he picked up his book.

'Talia flammato secum dea corde volutans nimborum in patriam, loca feta furentibus austris, Aeoliam venit. Hic vasto rex Aeolus antro luctantes ventos ...'

And he was gone, lost in a world of long ago, the prosaic nineteenth century vanished in a burst of poetic Latin. There was nothing like Virgil to weave a magical tale. For an unknown length of time he was immersed, quite unaware of his surroundings.

A loud cough drew Bertram back into the modern world. "Oh... what is it, Carter?"

"Beg pardon for disturbing you, sir, but this has just arrived from Corland... from his lordship."

Bertram glanced at the letter on the salver. "It is addressed to my father."

"Yes, sir, but the master is not in his study, not in the house at all, and the groom who brought this insisted it was very urgent."

"Is an answer expected?"

"No, sir. The groom has already left, but it is very important, he was quite clear about that."

Bertram frowned, considering. "I think my father might be in the stables. Greatheart was heated in one fetlock yesterday, and Whyte was going to apply a poultice. Let me see if I can find him."

"Thank you, sir. I should be most grateful, sir. The groom was most insistent."

Bertram carefully marked his place in *The Aeneid*, took the letter and set off for the stables. It was just like his father to disappear there merely because one of the horses had a minor injury. To Bertram's mind, that was the purpose of grooms, to see to such matters, but to his father, every horse was treated as if it were a precious child, to be cosseted and fussed over. No, that was not even an appropriate comparison, for he had always been relaxed about his children's well-being. Bertram and his brother Lucas had had the freedom to do very much as they pleased, and although Mother flew into a panic at the least sniffle or sign of fever, no one minded their scrapes and tumbles and the mischief that all boys get into. Mother's health and Father's horses — these were the real causes of alarm at Westwick Heights.

As he had expected, his father was in the stables, together with Morton, the head groom, and Whyte, the youngest of the grooms. Whyte had grown up in the village smithy and farriery, so he had lived his whole life with horses and had a great skill, even though Morton still distrusted anyone so young. The three of them were leaning over the rail of Greatheart's stall, deep in discussion, looking up only when Bertram was almost within touching distance.

"Ah, Bertram," his father said, his expression vaguely puzzled, as if seeing his eldest son and heir was a surprising event. "Going somewhere?"

"Shall I saddle Catullus, sir?" Whyte said.

"No, I came in search of you, Father, not a horse. There is an urgent note for you from the castle."

"Urgent?" The frown deepened as he took the letter, turning it over and over in his hands, but he nodded, gave his final instructions to the grooms and followed Bertram out of the stables.

"Any idea what this is about?" he said as they walked back to the house.

"None, sir. The groom who brought it was most insistent that it is a matter of great importance."

"We had better know the worst at once, then."

They were close to the small summer house, so they went inside and sat. While his father broke the seal and read the letter, Bertram admired, as he always did, the fine view of the house. Westwick Heights was not a large building, but it was elegantly constructed from the local honey-coloured stone, and looked as if it had grown naturally on the small eminence which gave it its name. From where he sat, he could see down the hill to the village of Birchall, and the chimneys of the estate on the far side, half hidden by sheltering trees. If he craned his neck, he could see the road meandering down to the town of Helmsley. Bertram spent most of his life mentally travelling the Ancient World in Latin, or occasionally Greek, but if he had to be in the modern world, this was where he would always choose.

"What do you make of that?" his father said, passing him the letter.

'To Mr George Atherton, Westwick Heights, North Riding. George, A family matter has arisen which must be addressed. Pray be at the castle tomorrow at noon, and bring Jane and Bertram with you. This is very important, so do not fail me and do not be late! Rennington.'

"A family matter? Involving us?"

"Yes, it is odd, is it not? Yet my brother would not write in such terms unless it were so. He is not in the least fanciful. What do you think it can be about?"

"Surely it must be regarding Nicholson. It is three weeks since he was murdered, so perhaps the villain has been caught."

Bertram hardly liked to think about the murder. He read about death and war and unspeakable horrors every day, but they were safely in the past, distanced from real life by thousands of years, and most of what he read was mere fanciful mythology, not even real. It was another matter entirely when a man one had known well, an uncle by marriage, died by violence. Arthur Nicholson had been chaplain to the Earl of Rennington for many years, and was married to the earl's sister, Lady Alice — a genial, inoffensive man, Bertram would have said. Yet someone had taken an axe to the room where he slept and hacked him to death. It was too dreadful for words.

His father clicked his tongue. "But how can that affect the family... or us? Unless... surely it cannot be one of the family? No, that would be unthinkable. It cannot be anything to do with the murder."

"Well, scandal, perhaps? Money troubles? The castle is about to fall down and they all want to come and live here?"

His father laughed. "You are right, of course. It is futile to speculate. Most likely it is some legal matter. He went haring off to York last week, remember, so perhaps he saw the lawyers. Whatever it is, we shall learn of it soon enough. Let us go and tell your mother."

Futile as it might be to speculate, nevertheless that was all the family did for the rest of the day. First his parents invaded Bertram's library, then his brother Lucas, and then his sisters drifted in. It needed only his little brother Philip to arrive from the nursery, and there would be a veritable party in progress.

By the time they assembled in the drawing room before dinner, they each had their favoured theory. Lucas had settled on financial woes — Lord Rennington was in the basket and wanted their father's fortune to bail him out. Julia, with all the wisdom of her twenty years, thought it was some fresh scandal involving their cousin, the earl's heir.

"Birtwell has got himself into some mess or other, you may be sure. A girl, most likely, and Uncle Charles is looking to us to help him patch it up. Or Bertram, perhaps."

"Nonsense," their father said tersely. "Birtwell has never been one to get into *that* sort of mess."

"George, please," Mother said. "This is hardly a fit topic of conversation in front of the girls."

"Julia started it," Lucas said.

"And she should not have done," Mother said, lips pursed. "Most unladylike. Depend upon it, this is to do with the Dowager Countess. She must be on her deathbed at last, and how she has lasted as long as she has is more than I can fathom."

"That would merely be a letter to inform us of her death, not this odd summons," Father said.

Penelope, who at sixteen thought everything related to marriage and romance, said, "Perhaps the earl wishes to arrange a match for Bertram."

"Ooh, good idea," Julia said. "But with whom? Not Olivia!"

The three girls collapsed in giggles.

"Olivia will make a great match," Mother said. "An earl's daughter with a good dowry and as pretty a face as hers will marry into the nobility, you may be sure. She will certainly not marry her own cousin."

"Tess Nicholson, then," Penelope said. "Her father left her a fortune, so she is quite a catch now."

"She will be in mourning for her father for quite some time," Mother said. "Really, girls, you are too fanciful by half."

"We shall find out what this is all about soon enough," Father said.

***

The carriage was ordered in plenty of time, for it would never do to be late for such a meeting. Besides, Bertram and his parents were agog with curiosity by the time they arrived at Corland Castle, the principal seat of the Earl of Rennington. The castle was a monstrously ugly building, in Bertram's view, for although it was newly built, it was very much in the heavy style of the Normans, with four corner towers linked by uncompromisingly solid façades. The interior was austere, and festooned with collections of swords, pikes, maces and a multitude of other sharp, malevolent objects whose sole function was to kill in as unpleasant a manner as human ingenuity could contrive. The whole place made Bertram heartily glad he was born in a less warlike and more enlightened age. He liked his violence strictly between the pages of a book.

Simpson and Wellum, the butler and under-butler, greeted them in the echoing entrance hall, its stone floor and marble statuary chilling the air, despite the summer heat outside.

"Good day, sir, madam. Good day, sir. You are in excellent time."

"What is this all about, Simpson?" Father said, as Wellum collected hats and gloves and canes.

"I couldn't say, sir. His lordship has not taken me into his confidence. Lord Birtwell is already in the study with Lord Rennington, and the others are gathering in the library."

"The others? Who else is summoned?"

"Lady Rennington, the Lady Alice Nicholson and Miss Nicholson, Mr Kent and the Lady Olivia are already here. Mr Eustace has not yet arrived."

"That boy is always late," Father muttered.

Simpson showed them into the library, where the door to the earl's study was resolutely closed.

Mother went at once to Aunt Alice, the earl's blind sister, who sat beside the countess, her back rigidly straight.

"How are you, dear?" Mother said, in the special voice she reserved for the sick or newly bereaved. "Bearing up bravely, I am sure. I hope you are taking a little beef tea every day. It is just the thing to stop you falling into a melancholy."

As they talked, Bertram was struck by Lady Rennington's face. His aunt was normally the most imperturbable person, but today her face was grey. This was serious, then.

Bertram and his father gravitated to the other side of the room, where Bertram's cousin Olivia sat.

"Olivia? Are you well, dear?" Mr Atherton said gently.

Olivia was dark haired with a rounded figure which suited her striking beauty admirably. She was given to bursts of histrionics, however, and although she was nothing like so bad as her older sister Izzy, she was still trying company and Bertram avoided her as much as possible.

Today she had decided to be lachrymose, a handkerchief pressed to her face. "How can I be well, Uncle, with this... this *thing* hanging over me?"

"What thing is that?" he said kindly.

"Whatever it is Papa wishes to tell us. It is bound to be horrid, and if it means that my come-out has to be put off *again*, well... life will be insupportable. I want to be *out,* Uncle."

"You are already out, are you not? You attend the assemblies at York and Harrogate and —"

"That is not *out!*" she said scornfully. "Out is Almack's and being presented at court and everyone knowing who one is."

"We are called in," Bertram said, nodding towards the door of the study, which now stood open.

The others moved forward, but Bertram hung back, waiting for Tess, the daughter of Lady Alice and the murdered chaplain. She was a dark, slight creature, always hiding in shadowy corners as if she did not want to be observed, but Bertram could not help feeling sorry for the girl.

"How are you, cousin?" he said gently.

"Quite well, thank you," she said in her soft voice, as if surprised he had asked. Without another word, she followed the others into the room.

The study was crowded, for it was not a large room, being situated in one of the circular tower rooms that sat at each corner of the castle. Chairs were found for the ladies and for a few minutes, as they settled themselves, all seemed perfectly normal. Just another family meeting. Only the grey faces of the earl and countess suggested something unusual. And had the countess been crying? That was a bad sign.

Bertram looked at his cousin Walter, Lord Birtwell, the heir to the earldom, and then he knew something terrible was afoot. Walter looked dazed... shocked, as if he had suffered a great loss. It must surely be another death, for what else could grieve the family so? Izzy, perhaps, or the eldest of the girls, Josie. One of the Lochmaben family, maybe. Or something of import to the nation — the King or Queen? The Prince of Wales? An invasion by the upstart Corsican?

"No Eustace?" the earl said, frowning. "Where is that boy?"

"Charles, must we wait for him?" the countess said fretfully. "Can we not just get this over with?"

The earl would not start without Eustace, however, so they waited until, a full twenty minutes after the designated hour, Eustace strolled in. Then at last they all turned to the earl in trepidation.

He licked his lips nervously, gazing around at their expectant faces. "Something terrible has occurred... has been discovered. Nicholson..." He took a deep breath, fixed his gaze on a point on the opposite wall and then rushed on. "Nicholson was never ordained as a clergyman, so the marriages he conducted are not valid. The countess and I are not legally married, and all our children are illegitimate. Birtwell... Walter cannot inherit. None of my sons can inherit. George, you are my heir now, and Bertram after you."

Bertram felt as if someone had punched him in the stomach. Birtwell disinherited? The title, the estates... *everything*, passing to his own father, and then to him? He would be the Earl of Rennington one day!

And in that moment, his placid future of books and ancient kingdoms and long-dead warriors vanished like smoke. Even his home, lovely Westwick, would be lost to him, and he would have to live in this mausoleum of a castle. His life would be filled with stewards and attorneys and land management and government bills and the wretched Season every year, he would have to marry suitably and there would be no peace to be found anywhere.

Nothing would ever be the same again.

2: Expectations

Bertram's mother burst into tears. He exchanged a look with his father, seeing the same disbelief written there as he felt himself. This could not be true!

"Is it certain, my lord?" Bertram said. "Is there no possibility of a mistake... a misunderstanding?"

The earl shook his head. "None. I have discussed the matter with the Archbishop of York, and he is quite sure of it. Nicholson was not ordained, and a marriage is only valid if conducted by a Church of England clergyman, that is absolute."

"Then Izzy...?" someone said. "Nicholson married her and Farramont."

"Yes, Izzy's marriage is invalid, too, and her two daughters rendered illegitimate. Thank God she has no sons to be disinherited, as Birtwell... Walter has been."

"But Josie is safe, one assumes?"

"She had some archdeacon fellow to marry her — someone from Woodridge's family. Yes, she is safe, for although she is illegitimate, that no longer matters now that she is married."

The questions went on, but Bertram heard little of it. His own fears buzzed in his head so loudly that nothing else penetrated. He was heir to an earldom... There were men who would relish such a change in their fortunes, but he was not one of them. *An earl!* And he would have to marry, that was the worst of it. He would have to go to town and caper about in ballrooms and do the pretty to well-connected but dull females, instead of mouldering in his library for the rest of his life. He had two younger brothers, after all, to do what was necessary to continue the family line. Not that he was against the idea on principle, but the only woman he could imagine letting into his life would be someone as bookish as he was. If a wife would sit quietly in the library, as engrossed in her reading as he was, then he would have no objection, but as he had never met such a creature, he remained unwed.

But after a while, as he looked round the room, he realised that others were far worse off than he was. Walter, for instance, had lost his entire inheritance. The rest of the cousins were rendered illegitimate. Lady Rennington was not even a wife any longer! That was a quite undeserved punishment when they had done nothing wrong... *none* of them had done anything wrong, yet they were all cast down, and Bertram and his father unexpectedly uplifted. He should not be ungrateful... but he was, for all that. No one was pleased by this turn of events.

The room eventually fell into a deep silence, broken only by the occasional sob from Bertram's mother. Everyone had run out of questions, it seemed.

After some time, Eustace said, "I suppose you will have to give up Miss Franklyn, Walter."

Bertram had forgotten Bea Franklyn. She and Walter had been betrothed for the best part of a year, awaiting a favourable moment to marry. She was an odd, forward sort of girl, who had set her cap at Walter almost from the moment she had moved into the parish. Walter had been amused by her persistent assault, but she had forty thousand pounds and some very distinguished connections, so he had yielded gracefully in the end.

But now, even if the marriage were to go ahead as planned, the Franklyns needed to be informed of the change in Walter's circumstances. He was dispatched to deliver the news, and everyone else was bundled out of the room, the ladies to see the ailing Dowager Countess, and the men presumably to congregate in corners of the library and discuss the disastrous turn of events at inordinate length.

"We will talk more of this later," the earl said. "Pray leave me now. George, you and Bertram may stay."

Olivia was about to leave the room, but now she stopped. "Does that mean Izzy is not Lady Farramont?" she said, wide-eyed. "Is she Lady Isabel again?"

"No, because she is illegitimate," Eustace said, his voice harsh. "She is merely Miss Isabel Atherton, you are Miss Olivia Atherton and I am not even an Honourable any more. We are all stripped of our titles, little sister, just like Walter, so you had better get used to it."

She burst into tears, and raced from the room.

"That was unkind, cousin," Bertram said to Eustace.

He had the grace to look a little ashamed. "You are right, but... it is such a shock, and coming after the business with Nicholson... it is hard to be rational when one has lost everything. And what did I say that was untrue?

We must all grow accustomed to our new place in society. You must not be too severe on us, you whose station in life is so immeasurably improved."

"Has it?" Bertram said, astonished. "You think I want this?"

"To be rich? To wield great power? To hold a rank which commands respect from the entire world? Why would you not want it? Anyone would."

"I had sooner be respected for my character and my achievements than for something that came to me only by an accident of birth, cousin."

Eustace laughed and shook his head. "What an unnatural creature you are, to be sure. Yes, yes, Father, I am going."

The door closed behind him with a soft thunk, and then Bertram was alone with his father and his uncle.

"Brandy," Father said. "You need a brandy, Charles, and so do I, God knows. Bertram, will you do the honours? Lord, this is far worse than any of us could have dreamt. Our imaginations were well exercised by your letter, but nothing we thought of came close to the truth. This is appalling, Charles."

The earl sighed. "It is not quite as bad as it seems. The marriage vows can be made again, so Caroline may be comfortable. For the children, Walter is the worst affected, but at least he is engaged to be married already. He will have Miss Franklyn's fortune to support the life of a gentleman, and I will honour my side of the settlements, naturally — the house, and an increased allowance. I shall not cut him adrift. Eustace has his own estate and independence, Josie and Izzy are married, and Kent and Olivia are young enough to make a recover from this blow, as we all shall, in time."

"You might, but what of us?" Father said. "I shall do my duty, of course, as your brother, and accept the burden when it falls to me, as I was raised to do, but do consider Bertram's plight. By the time he was born, you already had two sons. He has never had the least expectation of succeeding to the title. It is a great upheaval for him."

"True, but a good one, surely?" the earl said. "Look at the opportunities that will now open to him — no longer merely the son of a country gentleman, but a future heir to an earldom. He will have the world at his feet, and may take his pick of eligible young ladies. If he comes to town with us next spring—"

"No," Father said firmly. "I will not have him hounded to make a suitable match, as I was — and as you were, Charles. Lord, the so-called eligible young ladies who were paraded under our noses! It was dreadful, and I will not have Bertram pressed in that way. He has never shown the least interest in females, and that has never mattered to me because I have two other sons. Lucas is already showing signs that he will want to marry sooner rather than later. You may take *him* to town with you if you wish, but not Bertram."

"You let your children run rings round you, brother," the earl said, but with a glimmer of a smile. "Very well, it shall be as you wish, but nevertheless he is now second in line for the title and estates, and I should like him — both of you, in fact — to have some idea of what you will be taking on in the future."

"Well, if we must," Father said dubiously. "Clarke takes care of everything for you, does he not? Good fellow, Clarke."

"An excellent man, although I never wanted him. I thought to leave Nicholson to handle everything, as he used to do for my father, but when the estates passed to me, the lawyers thought it better to have someone from outside the family. The awkwardness if there were any mistakes in the accounts, you see."

"Oh, quite," Father said. "We will have a word with Clarke, then, and he can explain it to us. Not that we need to. I am sure your affairs are in good order, and you will be with us for many more years yet, God willing."

"Will tomorrow suit you — about twelve, say? I shall look out the account books."

They agreed to it, although not with much enthusiasm. Bertram's father had married a wealthy woman and lived comfortably on her fortune without ever needing to think about money, and so Bertram had never had to think about it, either. Their modest estate and a sum in the four percents did not require much in the way of management. The prospect of, one day, being responsible for the earl's numerous holdings and investments sank them in gloom.

As they waited in the entrance hall for the carriage to be brought round, Bertram said quietly to his father, "Thank you for protecting me from the Marriage Mart. I appreciate it."

His father chuckled. "Bertram, you are five and twenty years old, and sensible enough to know your own mind. If ever you feel the desire to take a wife, you can manage the business perfectly well without any help from me or anyone else. Even with this great burden thrust upon you, I would never want you to feel obliged to marry to ensure the succession. It is hardly necessary. Just as my father had more than one son, so did I, and failing that, we have a multitude of cousins. The succession lies in no danger."

"You are very good," Bertram said, with the utmost sincerity. He had encountered many young men, both at Harrow and at Cambridge, whose fathers beat them or expected the impossible or even ignored them entirely. He was singularly fortunate in having a father with whom he seldom disagreed, and with whom he could not quarrel even if he tried. His mother was more of a trial, but so long as he displayed no signs of incipient illness, she, too, was undemanding.

As they drove home to Westwick, his mother kept up a never-ending patter of concern for the Dowager Countess, for any issue of health, even one that merely marked the end of a long and fruitful life, was of inexhaustible interest to her. The two men remained silent.

Lucas and the girls were waiting for them when they arrived, and were told the story in the baldest of terms.

"Will you have a title, Papa?" Penelope said.

"No, only the direct heir has a title, and I am only the heir presumptive. If... *when* I become the earl, then Bertram will be Viscount Birtwell, just as Walter is... was."

"But why, Papa? That is most unfair! You should have a title of your own, so that we could all be called Lady, or at least Honourable. I should very much like to be Lady Penelope."

"And I should like that, too, my dear, but unfortunately, that is not how it works. The titles only work from father to son... or daughter, and with very good reason. Walter had a title of his own because nothing could stand between him and the earldom. Any other sons his father had would be younger. But I cannot have the title of Viscount Birtwell because there is always the possibility that the earl could father another son... a legitimate one, that is, and he would have the right to the title."

"Aunt Caroline is too old to have more children," Julia said scornfully.

"True, but if she were to die and the earl were to marry a younger woman, he could father any number of sons... legitimate sons."

"So he could," Mother said softly.

"Yes, that would let us off the hook very prettily," Father said with a wry smile. "Happily for the countess, she is exceedingly healthy."

"Never mind titles," Lucas said impatiently. "Who cares about titles? Will we have to move to Corland Castle?"

"Not immediately," Father said. "We can stay here until Lord Rennington dies, but your mother and I will have to move there eventually. It is the earl's principal seat, after all."

"I give you due notice, George," Mother said, a set look to her mouth, "that I shall never live at Corland Castle, never."

"But the castle is so much more spacious than Westwick," Lucas said. "I should love to live there."

"You are not attached to Westwick, Lucas?" Father said.

"Not especially."

"That is good, because once the dust settles on this business, I intend to offer Westwick to Walter and Miss Franklyn as their marital home, since he has been deprived of his rightful inheritance."

Mother burst into tears again.

***

Miss Beatrice Franklyn sat on the terrace in front of her easel, paintbrush suspended in hand. She was supposed to be painting the flowers spilling over the edge of a stone urn, but she had long since lost interest and sat motionless, gazing out at the park. The trees were still small and protected by fences, but the ha-ha was in place and deer roamed freely. Surrounding her was the bright new stone of the terrace balustrade, punctuated by the giant flower-filled urns. Below, several gardeners laboured to plant box hedging around the *parterre en broderie*. Highwood Place had been a modest country house when they had moved there five years ago, but a vast new frontage had tripled its size, and now her stepmother's plans for the garden were reaching fruition.

A shifting of the breeze brought a sudden scent to Bea's nose, something earthy and herbal and oddly familiar. Instantly her mind was thrown back to a different time and place — the cosy little back garden of the Newcastle house, when Papa had still been an attorney. Not much had grown there, only a few ancient apple and pear trees, and the tubs of herbs that Aunt Betty used. Above the herbs and between the trees hung a hammock, and there Bea had passed endless summer afternoons with her books, reading, always reading. At dinner, Papa had quizzed her on what she had learnt and so they talked of people long dead or lands far away, of new ideas and old, and a myriad different subjects.

But that time was long past, before Papa inherited his great fortune, before the move to a much grander house, before he had married the Lady Esther Bucknell and become a gentleman. Before Lady Esther had set about turning Bea into a lady. It was a dull business, being a lady, but Lady Esther had assured her that if she practised diligently, then she and her dowry of forty thousand pounds would be able to marry into the nobility, and so it had proved. Bea was betrothed to the Earl of Rennington's heir, and sometime in the future she was going to live at Corland Castle and be the Countess of Rennington, and she would never have to paint flowers again.

"How is your painting progressing, Beatrice? I confess to having a little trouble with the geranium — that particular shade of pink is hard to capture. It is almost red, and yet with a hint of purple. Very challenging. Do you not agree?"

"Yes, Mama."

Thus prodded, Bea turned her attention back to her watercolours, which was exactly as her stepmother intended. How dreary a way to pass the time! There must be a thousand more interesting things to do. Even looking through her wedding clothes once more would be more exciting than trying to paint a flower. Not that Bea was particularly enamoured of clothes, but a great many had been made up in town in preparation for her wedding. In the end, Walter could not leave his ailing grandmother, who was likely to die at any moment, so it had not happened. Still, her stepmother had dreamt up an even better scheme, for them to be married at Marshfields, the Duke of Camberley's seat. Now *that* would be something!

Walter had jibbed at that, too, but she had no doubt she would persuade him in time. He was so easy to steer in whatever direction she chose. However much he shied away at first, she could twist him round her thumb. Walter was essential to her plans, for he was going to take her away from this bleak life of submission to her stepmother. Lady Esther Franklyn was a daughter of the Duke of Camberley and thought herself far grander than a mere gentleman's daughter. But one day, very soon now, Bea would marry Walter and be Viscountess Birtwell and then no one, absolutely no one, would tell her what to do.

Hobbs appeared and bowed to Lady Esther. "The master asks if you and Miss Franklyn would be so good as to join him in the library, my lady. He has Lord Birtwell with him."

Bea bounced to her feet so abruptly that the easel wobbled. "Excellent! He has come to set a date for the wedding, I imagine."

"Gently, Beatrice," her stepmother said. "Pray moderate your actions to move with graceful deportment."

Lady Esther wiped her brushes without haste, then rose to proceed into the house with the graceful deportment she had tried but failed to instil into her stepdaughter. Bea sighed as she followed, as demurely as she could manage.

The library was in the new part of the house, a large and much ornamented room. Bea was not fond of excessively large rooms, although there was something breathtaking about the gallery on the floor above. Its pillared grandeur was one hundred and eighty feet from end to end, and one could never complain about a room large enough to house a ball. It was reputed to be the largest gallery in the North Riding, outranking Corland's paltry one hundred and ten feet by a large margin. But then Mama always had to have everything bigger, and had been mortified after the plans for the new wing had been settled to discover that Highwood would not, after all, be larger or have more rooms than Corland. Only the size of the gallery and a more imposing entrance hall outclassed the castle.

Walter looked more serious than usual, and greeted her without so much as a smile. Such treatment always put her on her mettle, so she slipped one arm through his, smiling up at him.

"Why did you not join us on the terrace, Walter, instead of calling us into the stuffy library? There is a most refreshing breeze outside."

"There is some information to impart to you, Bea," her father said, and he was not smiling either. That was a worrying sign! "Atherton?" he said, turning to Walter expectantly.

Atherton! That was not his name, yet Papa was always so correct.

Walter said nothing, so Father went on, "Bea, there has been a change in the circumstances of your future husband. It transpires that the earl and countess were married by Mr Nicholson, who was not in fact ordained at the time. That means that their marriage is not valid, and all their children have been rendered illegitimate. This does not materially affect their standing with their friends, naturally, and the earl will continue to treat his sons and daughters exactly as before, but it means that he has no legitimate heir, and Mr Atherton is not Lord Birtwell and cannot now inherit."

"So he will not be an earl?" Bea said, grasping the important point.

"No, but that need not affect your plans," Mr Franklyn said. "Lord Rennington and I are of one mind on that, and you need not worry about money, Bea. Your settlement will not be any the worse for this change in Mr Atherton's circumstances."

"What about the castle? He will have that, surely?"

"It is entailed, Bea," Walter said. "Almost everything is entailed. Not Langley Villa, fortunately, so we shall still have a place to live."

"But you are still your father's eldest son. He cannot cut you out completely."

"Lord Rennington has no choice, my dear," Papa said. "When property is entailed, then, like the title, it can only go to the eldest legitimate son."

She frowned. "So... Eustace gets it?"

"He is illegitimate, too," Walter said. "We are all illegitimate, Bea. Father has no legitimate children, no heirs. We are all disinherited. The title and estates will go to Father's younger brother, Uncle George."

"And then Bertram," she cried triumphantly. "Very well, I shall marry Bertram instead."

It was a blow, of course, for now she would have to begin all over again, but Bertram would do just as well.

"Bea!" her father said, shocked. "Surely you cannot... there is no need... were you only ever interested in Walter for his title, then?"

"Oh no, for he is much better looking than Bertram, but I should very much like to be a countess, Papa. I certainly will not marry a man who is not even a proper son and cannot inherit. I have forty thousand pounds, after all, so I am entitled to marry into the peerage, or at least a baronet.

Even Sir Hubert's wife is Lady Strong, and I want to be a proper lady, too. If Walter cannot do that for me, then I will not marry him. May I go now?"

Papa made no protest, and she made haste out of the room, for she had plans to make. She had a new betrothal to arrange, with Bertram Atherton.

3: Miss Franklyn Pays A Morning Call

'To Mr Bertram Atherton, Westwick Heights. Sir, My daughter has ended her betrothal to Mr Walter Atherton since he is not now to become an earl. As it appears that you stand in line to inherit, she has decided to marry you instead. Please be assured that it would delight me beyond measure to have you as my son-in-law, but if the prospect appals you, as I fear may be the case, you may need to resort to a priest's hole. Failing that, I recommend that you leave the country at once, while you still may. New Holland may possibly be far enough away to deter her. Yours in friendship, John Franklyn.'

***

DETERMINATION

The family was still gathered in Bertram's library discussing in exhaustive detail the implications of their new circumstances when Carter brought in the letter from Mr Franklyn, so Bertram read it out loud.

"Oh, poor Walter!" Mother cried. "To lose his inheritance and his future bride in the same day — the poor boy!"

"That is hard indeed," Father said. "But the loss of his inheritance must be the greater loss, I should think. His whole life has been spent in preparation for acceding to his father's honours and estates, and now all that is snatched away from him and tossed into my unworthy lap. As to his attachment to Miss Franklyn, it never seemed to me to be very great, and it seems hers was no more so. It is the title she wants, it would appear, and so you are to be the man to lead her to the altar, Bertram. I congratulate you, my son. Forty thousand pounds is a very pretty dowry."

"I shall not be marrying Miss Franklyn, Father, as you know perfectly well," Bertram said, laughing at his father's teasing tone.

"What a pity we have no priest's hole," Lucas said. "It will have to be New Holland."

"No, no, we can hide him in the attics," Penelope said. "There is so much lumber up there that even Bea Franklyn could not discover him."

"The dressing-up box!" Julia said. "We could cover him with a mountain of damask hoop dresses and moth-eaten fur tippets."

"The cellar would be better," Lucas said. "Somewhere between the pipes of port and the apple barrels. There are plenty of dark corners there, and he is not large, so he can squeeze into a small space. You are not afraid of a few spiders, are you, brother?"

"Very droll," Bertram said, joining in the general merriment. "I am not afraid of Bea Franklyn, certainly."

"Perhaps you should be," his father said wryly. "She is a very single-minded young lady. Look how she wound Walter around her thumb."

"He must have had some affection for her," Bertram said. "A man cannot be forced to marry where he has no inclination for it, after all."

"Can he not?" his father said dryly. "You could always run away to your Aunt Lochmaben."

"Scotland is not far enough to keep Bea Franklyn at bay," Lucas said at once.

Their wit flowed for some time on the subject, until Carter entered again.

"The Lady Esther Franklyn and Miss Franklyn have called, madam," he said.

The girls shrieked with laughter, but Mother said placidly, "Show them into the drawing room, Carter."

"I have already taken the liberty of doing so, madam."

"Well, Bertram?" Mother said, with a wry smile. "The girls and I will receive them, but you need not, if you are not so inclined."

"I would not miss it for the world," Bertram said, smiling.

"We will protect you, brother," Emily whispered to him. "She shall not harass you."

"Thank you, sister," he whispered back gravely. Emily was such a timid creature that forthright females like Bea Franklyn terrified her. Bertram was tolerably confident that no female, no matter how forthright, could puncture his masculine defences.

They all trooped out of the library into the hall, the girls still giggling and being shushed by Mother, and thence into the drawing room. Lady Esther stood regally in the centre of the room, her manner as composed as if this were nothing but a routine morning call.

"My dear Mrs Atherton... Mr Atherton... we came at once to congratulate you on your unexpected good fortune."

"We do not regard it as a matter for congratulations," Mother said sharply. "It is a piece of *ill* fortune for all concerned, as far as I can see. The earl has lost his wife, his children are all rendered illegitimate, Walter has lost his inheritance *and* his future wife—" Here she paused to glare at Bea. "—and all *we* have acquired is a burden we never wanted. Pray be seated, Lady Esther. May I offer you some refreshment?"

"Thank you. Most kind. My dear Mrs Atherton, the earldom may seem like a great burden, but it is also a great honour, is it not?" She frowned a little, her aristocratic forehead wrinkling ever so slightly. "*My* family have always regarded it so. An honour and a privilege, although of course the circumstances in this case are most distressing, naturally. How do the family at Corland bear up under this blow?"

The two ladies sat and fell into the sort of restrained conversation typical of two near neighbours who have little in common. Bertram's mother came from the sort of gentry stock more at ease with the local parson than a scion of a ducal family, and although she could move with ease through any level of society, there was something of reserve in Lady Esther's manner that prevented real intimacy.

Bertram chose to remain standing, but near the door so that he could beat a retreat if the occasion demanded it. Lucas chose a seat by the window, watching the drama unfolding with a little smile on his face, while their father stood beside the fireplace. The three girls, very much in protective mode, waited until Miss Franklyn sat down, then immediately surrounded her. That did not deter her in the least. To Bertram's amusement, she watched him steadily for two or three minutes, then rose and crossed the room to stand beside him.

"Well, Mr Atherton, I am very sorry for Walter and all his family, but this is a fine thing for you."

"Is it?" he said. "I cannot see it, myself. There is distress on all sides, and no one can be happy about that."

"No, it is very sad indeed, but you will be an earl one day. Surely you must be at least a little gratified by that."

"Why should I be? My life was planned out, Miss Franklyn, and I was contented with the future before me. Now those plans are in disarray, and I do not know quite what will replace them." He hesitated, wondering how much he dared to say, but with Bea Franklyn, there was no point in subtlety. "On one matter only am I sure of my future, and that is that marriage will have no part in it. I have two younger brothers and a whole platoon of cousins, and therefore have no need to marry to secure the succession."

She smiled at him. "You are quite sure of that, are you?"

"Quite sure, Miss Franklyn. I tell you this so that there will be no misunderstanding between us. Your father wrote to me, you see, to tell me that you had jilted Walter now that he cannot be earl, and were set on marrying me instead. I should not like you to waste any effort on trying to get me to the altar, for you are doomed to fail."

Her smile widened, and she whispered, "I relish a challenge, Mr Atherton."

There was no dealing with such obstinacy. He made her a small bow. "You will excuse me, I am sure. I have an awkward passage of Horace to transcribe."

And so saying, he made his escape to the library, empty now and an oasis of tranquillity. With a sigh of relief, he sat down at his desk, opened his copy of Horace and set to work. He was so engrossed, he did not hear the door open or soft footsteps approaching him.

"So this is where you are hiding," Miss Franklyn said in her clear voice, right in his ear.

He jumped half out of his skin and dropped his pen, splattering ink all over the page. "Pft! Now look what you have made me do! I shall have to begin again."

"I am very sorry," she said, not sounding at all contrite. "I do not know why you did not hear me, for I was not at all creeping up on you or trying to be quiet."

"It is of no consequence," he said resignedly. "What are you doing in here, Miss Franklyn? Did you wish to find a book?"

"I wondered what you were doing, that is all."

"As I mentioned before, I am transcribing Horace."

"Yes, but why?"

"It is for a treatise I am to present—" He realised abruptly how skilfully he was being drawn in. Here they were, alone in the library, and the door was closed, he now noted, and she was keeping him talking. What interest had she in Horace? Not the least in the world! "You should not be in here without a chaperon, Miss Franklyn. Allow me to escort you back to your mother."

Before he could do so, the door opened and first Carter and then Bertram's three sisters came in at a rush.

"There you are, Bea!" Julia said brightly. "We wanted to show you the new morning gowns in the *Lady's Magazine*. They are quite ravishing — do come!"

Bea laughed, perfectly aware of the deception, but allowed herself to be shepherded away with only a single backward glance at Bertram.

"I beg your pardon, sir," Carter said, looking flustered. "I left William to watch the hall, but he was obliged to step downstairs for a moment, and the lady slipped past unnoticed. It will not happen again, I assure you."

"Thank you, Carter. I appreciate your concern on my behalf, but it is quite unnecessary."

"If you say so, sir," the butler said, but he sounded unconvinced.

Bertram returned to Horace, and remained undisturbed until the dressing bell.

***

As the carriage made its ponderous way back to Highwood Place, Bea told her stepmother all that Bertram had said.

"I do think it is too bad of Papa to write to him in that way, as if I were *jilting* Walter! As if I could possibly marry him after his circumstances have so materially altered. You do not think I am wrong to aim for Bertram instead, do you?"

"It is never wrong to aim as high as you can, Beatrice, and an earl is an excellent match for you, with your attractions. I confess I was disappointed that nothing came of your first three seasons in town, apart from the usual array of younger sons and other fortune hunters. You always said that Lord Birtwell was the most likely prospect, and you were proved right about that. But no, I do not advise you to marry an illegitimate son. That would be a sad come-down for a girl in your advantageous position. However, I have to say that Mr Bertram Atherton is likely to be a tougher nut to crack. Nor is he as promising a specimen, to my mind. He is not at all handsome."

"Do you think so?" Bea said. "It is true that Walter is handsomer and more... more manly, perhaps, but there is something rather appealing about Bertram, especially when he removes his spectacles. Do you think he meant what he said, about never marrying? Perhaps I should try for Lucas instead."

"No, no, no! Never accept a younger brother when the elder is unwed... or at all, frankly. It is far too uncertain. Besides, all men say that they will never marry, right up to the point when they propose. Mr Bertram Atherton is certainly your best hope here, but perhaps you would like to cast your net more widely? Not the season again, for there are far too many Honourables and Lady this and that for you ever to shine there, fortune or no fortune, not to mention a few outstanding beauties who attract all the attention. It is a pity about your nose... and those excessive curls, and black, too. If only you had been fair! Golden hair does stand out in a crowd. But you have a trim little figure and are not at all shy, which is fatal with gentlemen. Nor have you ever been so foolish as to fall in love."

"I should hope not, Mama!"

Her stepmother laughed. "No, indeed. That can only end in tears and regrets. But perhaps we should look to my family for a solution to the difficulty. Charity quite took you under her wing this spring, and she invited us to Brandlebury, did she not? Or at least... I am sure I can persuade her to invite us. Should you like that?"

Bea considered for a moment, but she was reluctant to abandon all possibility of securing Bertram. "Lord and Lady Ramsey are still in town at the moment, I believe, and Charity did not know where they would go after that. Let me see what I can do with Bertram, and if I make no progress, then perhaps we can go to Brandlebury in the autumn."

"Very well, dear. That sounds like a sensible plan."

Having thus reached an accord, the two ladies settled down to discuss the abominably provincial fashions of Mrs George Atherton and her daughters.

***

Bertram and his father went the following morning, as arranged, to see the earl and examine the accounts. Bertram's mother decided at the last minute to accompany them.

"I shall sit with Caroline for a while, and perhaps look in on the Dowager, if she is awake."

"Very well, dear," his father said peaceably. "You might see Alice, too, while you are there. My poor sister is having a dreadful time — not only has her husband been killed, but now she discovers that he was a fraud all these years."

They found the earl in a towering rage, fulminating against young women in general and Bea Franklyn in particular.

"To throw him over, just because he will not be an earl! It is a great deal too bad of her. He is the same man, after all, and a fine, upstanding specimen of his sex, as well. Any woman would be glad to have him, I am sure, but not Bea Franklyn, oh no! She thinks herself too grand for him now, just because her stepmother is a duke's daughter, but her father was nobody before he inherited all that money — a mere attorney, and not a very good one, by all accounts."

"Now, now, Charles, I am sure Franklyn was a perfectly competent attorney," Bertram's father said, laughingly. "I am very sorry for Walter if his attachment was a strong one, but he will find someone else, you may be sure."

"That is all very well, but he should have been married long since. Twenty-nine, George! Almost thirty! I was married with four children in the nursery at that age. We knew our duty in those days."

"Three."

"What?"

"Three children in the nursery. At thirty, you only had Walter, Eustace and Josie, but not Izzy."

"Oh... pft. You know what I mean. Now he has to start all over again."

"But imagine if he had been already married, with a whole string of children deprived of their inheritance, too. He is a personable young man, and will not have the slightest difficulty finding a wife, just as soon as he sets his mind to it. But what is he to do with himself, Charles? Eustace has his independence and Kent has always needed to make his way in the world, but Walter has never had to think about a career."

"Nor does he now," the earl said sharply. "He is my eldest son, and I shall not cast him adrift."

"I can help there," Father said. "If Bertram is to inherit Corland, then he has no need of Westwick. I should be happy to leave it to Walter, when the time comes."

"Westwick? Leave Westwick to Walter? My dear brother, it is not to be thought of."

"It is only equitable, Charles. Since Walter has been deprived of his rightful inheritance by Bertram and me, it is fitting that we should surrender our inheritance to him."

"No, no, no! Westwick is Jane's, and only came to you by marriage. It should be kept within her family. You have two other sons, after all. Let Lucas have Westwick. No, I shall take care of Walter, as a father should. I will make Langley Villa over to him and a sum of money... enough for him to support a wife, if he has a mind to. In time, perhaps. I am not sure quite how I am placed just at present. I shall have to ask Clarke. Ha! In all the upheaval, I forgot to tell him to come today."

"We shall see him sometime," Father said easily. "But you cannot be short of money, Charles, not with an income of eight thousand a year."

"No, I am sure... Although after Father died, things were left... No, I cannot be short of money, but Clarke is so stuffy, sometimes. When Nicholson ran things for Father, he had only to ask, and Nicholson would say, *'Of course, my friend. Let me take care of it.'* And he did, whereas Clarke just sucks his teeth, you know how he does, and says, *'Perhaps next quarter, my lord, if the weather is favourable for the harvest.'* And every time he shows me the figures, I am worth a little bit more than the last time, so I suppose his way is best. But he makes me feel guilty, sometimes, for asking for my own money."

"This needs looking into, Charles. You cannot allow your land steward to oppress you."

"You are right, brother." The earl heaved a sigh. "I suppose I ought to take more interest myself. Very well, since three heads will be better than one, we shall all pore diligently over the accounts, and attempt to make some sense of them."

4: A Proposal Of Marriage

Bea was practising rather laboriously on the pianoforte, for Mama insisted on an hour a day to improve her skills, when her father came into the music room.

"Papa!" Bea cried, spinning round on the stool and clapping her hands excitedly. "Have you come to listen to me play?"

"Beatrice, a lady does not break off in the midst of a performance," her stepmother said in her well-modulated voice. "She brings the piece gracefully to a conclusion."

"I believe this is a matter worthy of interruption, just this once," he said. "A proposal is surely important enough to warrant it, would you not agree, Lady Esther?"

"Is it Bertram?" Bea said, suddenly dizzy with happiness. So soon! She had not expected—

"It is not Mr Bertram Atherton, no. It is Mr *Eustace* Atherton."

Bea groaned in dismay, and Lady Esther said sharply, "Not again!"

"You would censure him for returning a third time," Papa said, "but for myself, I find such devotion pleasing. It speaks to a sincere attachment."

"His only attachment is to my forty thousand pounds, Papa," Bea said.

"There is nothing wrong with a man seeking to better his position. It is not as if he were penniless himself, for he has a very pretty estate at Welwood, and an income of fourteen hundred a year."

"Welwood is so old-fashioned!"

"That is hardly an insuperable problem. Besides, it is not the house that matters, Bea. Eustace Atherton is a man of impeccable lineage, and even if the unfortunate circumstances of his father's marriage have rendered him illegitimate, he is still an earl's son, and a gentleman of independent means. With your fortune—"

"I cannot marry Eustace."

"Why not?"

"He has no title, and is not likely ever to get one."

"Bea, this obsession with a title at all costs is most unbecoming. Neither title nor wealth nor blood is any guarantee of good character. A title will not make you happy."

"*Marriage* will not make me happy, Papa, for it is merely to exchange one form of servitude for another. The lowliest washer-woman or labourer's wife may be a Mrs, but I can be a Lady, and I shall, too. Bertram will make me Lady Rennington, Papa, and how can Mrs Eustace Atherton compare with that?"

He sighed. "Very well. I shall send Atherton away."

"No, no. I shall see him myself. It is only civil to allow a man the opportunity to make his speech."

"Very well, but be kind to him, Bea."

"Of course. I am always kind to my rejected suitors."

Which was a grand parting remark, and allowed her to leave the room with her head held high, but it was sheer bluster, for all that. How many suitors had ever reached the point of a proposal? Eustace, twice — three times, now. That cheeky brewer's son. A younger son destined for the church and a stammering honourable in her first season. And that was all. No one at all in her second or third season, except for the usual fortune hunters sent packing by Papa. Even Walter had had to be pushed into it — in fact, she had all but proposed to him.

And here was Eustace again, another fortune hunter, but not one who could be easily turned off by Papa. Well, she had no intention of accepting him, but she did not intend to turn him off, either.

He looked rather smart, his boots polished to a high shine and his neck cloth arranged just so. The Atherton men were generally careless of their appearance, but Eustace always made an effort.

"Miss Franklyn."

So, he was choosing to be formal. He bowed, she curtsied and then, to encourage him just a little, she gave him her hand. He raised it to his lips and dipped the lightest of kisses on it. That was prettily done!

"Here I am again," he said, with a little laugh. "I thought my goose was cooked after the last time, and naturally I was very happy for Walter when you accepted him but... everything has changed. He has lost everything he expected to inherit and since you are free again, I thought this might be an opportune moment to remind you of my own circumstances, which have not changed. I still have my house. I still have my estate. I still have a good income, more than enough to support a wife. In fact, it has increased somewhat since the last time I approached you. I flatter myself my circumstances are such as to make the offer of my hand not disgusting to you. Bea, I have the sincerest and deepest attachment to you, and that has not diminished over the years. Will you not make me the happiest of men and become my wif e?"

"You are very kind, Eustace. I am flattered and honoured, but these are difficult times for me. When you approached me before, I felt I was too young to make such a momentous decision. Then there was Walter and I felt obliged to accept such a good offer. Now, I am all at sea. My future appeared to be settled, and I have not yet come to terms with the very great change that has been wrought. It is a great comfort to me that your feelings towards me remain unchanged — the one constant in my life at present! Yet I cannot but feel it is too soon to make any decision about my future. I need time to come to terms with all that has occurred. Do you understand?"

"Of course, and I would not for the world importune you. I shall withdraw for the present, but be assured that my offer stands, and you may call on me at any time, whenever you feel ready. I bid you good day, Miss Franklyn. Accept my good wishes for your future, wherever it may lie, and pray convey my regards to Lady Esther."

He bowed and was gone, leaving Bea to reflect with satisfaction on the interview. Not that she had the least intention of marrying him, oh, the delight of a proper offer! It was a balm to her soul to have such a persistent admirer.

***

Bertram's days had become rather full. The time was rapidly approaching when he would depart for Landerby Manor in Lincolnshire to present his paper on Horace, and it was as yet only half written.

Worse, he had not even completed his reading and formulated his conclusions. Yet he could not deny his father his company, if nothing more, on his mission to discover the state of the earl's financial affairs. Each day they rode together to Corland Castle, and sat in the study while the earl looked bemused and Clarke, the land steward, waved his hands vaguely in the air and tried to explain about sheep farming or coal mining or the ownership of canals, while the earl, his brother and his nephew attempted to make sense of it without falling asleep. Bertram had been used to think of himself as a reasonably intelligent man, but Clarke made him feel inexpressibly stupid.

"Why is this so hard?" he said to his father one day, as they rode away from Corland in the now familiar fog of ignorance.

Mr Atherton chuckled. "Imagine yourself explaining the intricacies of... oh, *The Aeneid*, say, to someone unfamiliar with it. Clarke understands his work very well, but it is so ingrained in him that he finds it difficult to explain. What we need is someone with a more methodical approach to make it simple for us."

"I suppose we cannot simply leave Clarke to get on with it?" Bertram said. "Do we need to know about sheep farming?"

"We need to know enough to know that Clarke is doing what he should, that is all," Mr Atherton said. "In the old earl's day, it was all left to Nicholson and... well, no one knew what was going on. When your uncle inherited, the lawyers insisted on Clarke, and on your uncle taking an interest in his affairs."

Bertram's eyebrows rose. "Was there a suspicion that Nicholson was lining his own pockets?"

His father chuckled. "That was precisely the problem, no one knew what he was doing, or whether it was all correct or not. Most of what went on was in his head. At least with Clarke, it is all written down. Or mostly, anyway."

After three days, however, they were summoned to the old schoolroom, where the investigation into Mr Nicholson's murder was proceeding. There they were introduced to a lawyer by the name of Willerton-Forbes, a fearsomely fashionable man in the London style, who reminded Bertram of Mr Franklyn, another dandy. Willerton-Forbes, being at a loose end, offered his services to disentangle the earl's financial affairs, and since his first words were, "Let us make a complete list of all his lordship's holdings, with all that is known of them, shall we?", Bertram's father fell on his neck with delight. In no time, sheets of paper filled in the lawyer's neat hand grew to a sizeable pile, and Bertram's father's frown lifted somewhat.

With his father somewhat happier, Bertram felt easy about returning to the delights of Horace or, for light relief, Virgil. The disadvantage of this plan was soon discovered, when Carter crept into the library and coughed discreetly.

"The Lady Esther Franklyn and Miss Franklyn have called, sir."

Bertram, writing furiously in a notebook, chose not to reply.

Carter coughed again. "The mistress and the young ladies are entertaining her ladyship and Miss Franklyn in the drawing room, sir."

With the sentence in his head satisfactorily set down on paper, Bertram sighed, laid aside his pen and removed his spectacles. "And this is of interest to me in what way, Carter?"

"Her ladyship asked for you most particularly, sir."

Another sigh. He had had a great-uncle once who dealt with intrusions by ordering his butler to, *'Tell him he may go to the devil for all I care. I am busy.'* And the butler would relay this uncompromising message word for word to the hapless caller. Bertram wished with all his heart that he could do the same. One day, perhaps, when he was old and, he hoped, famous throughout the land for the intellectual rigour of his work, he would perhaps do so, but at the age of twenty-five, and still living under his parents' roof, the tug of good manners was too strong.

He sighed yet again, rose and donned his coat before making his way to the drawing room. Miss Franklyn bounced across the room before he had even completed his courtesies to Lady Esther. Tucking her arm in his, she said cheerfully, "There you are, Bertram! At last you are at home when we call! Were you hiding away from me?"

"Not at all," he said politely. "I have been much engaged with my father at the castle."

"Preparing for when you are an earl, I dare say. Well, you are here now, so let us sit and talk. We will get a refreshing stream of air from that window, so we shall sit there."

She towed him across the room to a window seat just wide enough for two, sat at one side of it and patted the seat invitingly. How was a man supposed to deal with such forward behaviour? He could hardly snub her outright, not in his mother's drawing room, and if Lady Esther saw no need to reprimand her stepdaughter for her unbecoming manners, it was not for him to do so. He glanced at the clock. Ten minutes he would allow her, then he would return to Horace.

"Now then, Bertram," she said, taking his arm again so decisively that he did not feel he could well disentangle himself, "tell me all about it. Is the earl teaching you how to wear your coronet and robes? How to bow to the king?"

"Nothing of the sort!" he said, discomfort at her closeness making him speak more sharply than he intended. "The earl has invited my father and me to learn about his estates and investments."

Her eyes visibly became glassy. "Oh, *money!* How horrid! And very dull, I should think."

"Not dull, but... complicated."

"Oh yes, because he must be vastly rich, of course. Eight thousand a year, is it not? Although that is not so very much for an earl, is it? Papa has far more than that. How is Lord Rennington? He has sent Lady Rennington away, I hear, poor lady. She must be very sad."

"I do not think he has sent her away," Bertram said. "She has gone to stay with her sister, I believe."

"Oh, Lady Tarvin? Is that where she has gone? I did not know. Mama was wondering about it only this morning as we drove here." She raised her voice to carry across the room. "Mama? Mama! Did you hear that? Lady Rennington has gone to Lady Tarvin at Harfield."

Lady Esther winced at the raised voice and nodded an acknowledgement, but declined to conduct a conversation across the full width of the room.

For a little while, Bea seemed content to talk about the inhabitants of Corland Castle, as Bertram surreptitiously watched the hands of the clock marching slowly onwards to the time when he might consider duty done and withdraw.

But then Bea said, "Mama is planning an evening entertainment — dinner, music, a little dancing and so on. You will come, I hope?"

"It depends when it is."

"Early next week. Tuesday, I believe."

"I shall still be here then, so—"

"You are going away?" Her voice rose to a squeak. "When? Where? For how long?"

He could not help laughing at the astonishment in her face. "I do have friends who invite me to stay occasionally, you know. I shall be going to Landerby Manor in Lincolnshire in two weeks, to stay for a month."

"*A month!* Two weeks! Goodness! That does not give me much time."

"To do what, Miss Franklyn?"

"Why, persuade you to marry me, of course."

He shook his head in bemusement. "I do wish you would give up this idea, ma'am. I am not at all minded to marry at present... perhaps never. I should not like you to waste your time. Why not try Lucas? He would be far more amenable to your charms, being less distracted by poets dead for two thousand years."

"Horace, you mean? I asked my father about him, and he found me a book about him in the library, but it is mostly dry stuff. I liked some of his writings, though. The translation, that is, for I cannot read the Latin."

"You read Horace?" Bertram said, diverted.

"Why should I not? He is very funny sometimes. But that is nothing to the point. Lucas will not do, for he will not become the Earl of Rennington — not unless you die, of course, and I should not like that."

"Neither should I," he said, with the faintest quiver in his voice.

"Quite so. It must be you, and in all honesty, Bertram, what could be more sensible? We are old friends, after all, and I have forty thousand pounds, which is a great sum for you to bring into the estate, and if you marry me, it saves you all the bother of trying to find a wife for yourself. Men make such a great fuss about the business, and dither and dawdle over it, and you would not enjoy the season, I am sure. This way, you will have a wife without the least trouble, and think how convenient that will be. I shall not rush you to the altar, you may be sure. The autumn, perhaps, or even next spring if you should prefer it, but we should become betrothed before you go away to... wherever it is."

"Landerby Manor, in Lincolnshire."

"Who lives there?"

"It is one of the homes of the Duke and Duchess of Wedhampton, but they will not be present. One of his brothers, Lord Thomas Medhurst, hosts a gathering of friends from Cambridge every summer, who sit about and discuss long-dead poets. It is great fun, and I look forward to it all year."

"Heavens! You have a curious idea of fun. Are they all as clever as you are?"

"Now how am I to answer that?" he said, amused. "Whether I say yes they are, or no they are not, I sound abominably conceited. Let me say only that we all have a great interest in the Latin poets, and some are cleverer than others."

"And are there ladies in the company?"

He frowned, for it was something of a sore point. "The original intention was to keep it entirely a male gathering, the better to focus on our subject of interest. However, there were those right from the start who proposed that female company would provide an agreeable diversion from intellectual pursuits, and several of our number have now married and wish their wives to accompany them. Last year, several unmarried ladies attended, too — sisters and cousins and such like. Such a mingling of the sexes does indeed change the atmosphere of our gatherings, but not all would agree that the change is for the better."

"Do the ladies discuss Latin poets with the gentlemen?"

"I never came across one who did so. Very few ladies know Latin, I fear. Mostly they keep to their feminine pursuits during the day, leaving the men to their Latin, and the sexes mingle again in the evening."

"And is there music in the evenings? Dancing? Theatrical performances?"

"No theatrical performances, but the ladies like to perform on their various instruments, and sing for us, and there are cards, naturally. Last year, three of the ladies created a tableau of a scene from Julius Caesar, which they thought would amuse the gentlemen. Unfortunately, they based their work on Shakespeare, and several of our members took issue with the details. Mr Shakespeare may have been a brilliant dramatist, but his grasp of history was shaky at times. Oh... are you leaving?"

Lady Esther had risen, and was making her refined farewells around the room. Bea jumped to her feet too, and curtsied demurely to Bertram. "Good day to you, Bertram. We shall meet again very soon, no doubt." Then, leaning forward, she whispered in his ear, "Since I have only two weeks."

5: Schemes And Gossip

"You did very well, Beatrice," Lady Esther said complacently, smoothing her gloves, as the carriage wended its way homewards. "He is by no means so easy a target as Walter was, but I am not unhopeful. You kept him well enough entertained today that he did not run away, and that is a very good sign. He will come to our little evening party, I trust?"

"He did not say he would not, but—"

"Excellent. You will have ample opportunity to advance your campaign."

"But Mama, he still says he will not marry me, and he is going away in two weeks, for a whole month!"

Lady Esther turned sharply. "A month? That is very bad... oh, I recall now, he does so every year. Some gentlemen's affair. And by the time he returns, we shall be beginning our autumn round of visits, by November we shall be snowed up and he will not go to town in the spring. This is very bad, Beatrice. It means we must move rather more precipitately in the two weeks allowed us. We cannot afford to delay."

"I can win him round in time, Mama," Bea said. "I managed it with Walter, after all. It is merely a matter of persistence."

"Walter was a far easier fish to catch. You had him on your hook early, and could take your time in reeling him in. Bertram is set against you from the start, and will be far more of a challenge. Perhaps we should give up the idea altogether, and concentrate on Marshfields... or Brandlebury. What do you say to Lord Hector, perhaps? He seemed interested and you would be Lady Hector immediately, instead of Lady Rennington at some time in the distant future. Does the idea appeal to you?"

"Not really. Lord Hector is so... *cold,* somehow. Bertram is not so imposing a figure as Walter, it is true, but there is something rather sweet about him. Besides, I know him well and he is not starchy, like some of the nobility. They look down on me because my father was only an attorney."

"And the fortune from iron foundries," Lady Esther said slowly. "It is true that you have not been received into my circle with the enthusiasm that one might have hoped for, and that will only be worse now. The problem is, Beatrice, that everyone now knows that your primary interest is a title. With Walter your single-minded approach was easily mistaken for love, but that fiction can no longer be sustained. Nor have you the advantages of great beauty or breeding that would naturally attract suitors. I have done my best with you, as you know — your accent is perfectly acceptable, most of the time, and your deportment and manners are... adequate. But there is that forwardness in your behaviour that deters some men. It will stand you in very good stead when you are married, but it does make it a touch more difficult to attain that state. Besides that, you are one and twenty already, and perilously close to being on the shelf. One does not wish to appear desperate." She was silent for some time, lost in thought, but then she rallied. "So I believe we cannot wait, and must resort to a degree of subt erfuge."

"Mama, I do not want to *trap* Bertram into marriage if he is set against it," Bea said unhappily. "It would be quite horrid if he resents me afterwards."

"Nonsense!" her stepmother said robustly. "Men never know what they want until they have it. Once you are safely married, you will be able to ensure that your husband is completely happy. I shall teach you how to achieve that. Your papa is happy, is he not?"

"But you did not trap him into it," Bea said. "He was already thinking of marrying again before he met you."

"So he was, but I had to put myself in his way to ensure that those thoughts became focused on me. A lady has many weapons in her arsenal with which to ensure the correct outcome."

"You make it sound like a war."

"And so it is, in a way, and although we may lose a battle here and there, nevertheless, we always win the war, if we set our minds to it. In your case, putting yourself in Bertram's way will not do, nor will resolution. He does not strike me as a man who will simply surrender. But he is an honourable man, and so we will arrange for him to behave in an honourable way."

"Mama, what are you planning?"

"No need for you to worry about that. So long as you do what I say — *precisely* as I say, mark you — all will be well, and we shall have Mr Bertram Atherton in your pocket in no time."

And nothing more could she be induced to say about it, leaving Bea uneasy in the extreme.

***

'Mr Bertram Atherton, Westwick Heights, Birchall, North Riding. My friend, I am the bearer of bad news, I fear. Wedhampton has taken it into his head to host our little gathering this year, or rather Her Grace has. Having suffered the restrictions of a confinement and a multitude of bereavements which have kept her at home these past two or three years, she is determined to enjoy herself a little at last, and inflict the same enjoyment on the rest of us, whether we wish it or not. What is worse, she is bringing her two cod-faced cousins with her, with the object of finding husbands for them, and we are all bidden to bring spinsters of our own to Landerby so that Her Grace may exercise her match-making skills to greatest effect. It sounds appalling, but I know you have sisters, so you may wish to bring one or two of them along. Wedhampton is a good fellow, however, so the talks are to go ahead as planned, and we are all looking forward to your paper. Optationes optimas ad te, Thomas Medhurst.'

***

"What, send the girls off to mix with your Cambridge friends?" Bertram's mother shook her head decisively, as she paused in pouring the tea that evening. "No, no, a thousand times no. Julia is already betrothed, Penelope is too young for such raffish company, and Emily would not enjoy it, even if I could spare the time to take her. Can you not take Lucas? He would enjoy it, I am sure."

Lucas looked up hopefully, but Bertram shook his head. "The Duchess has particularly requested unmarried young ladies," he said, slightly bemused by the description of his scholarly friends as *'raffish'*. "The place will be awash with male company as it is."

"One does not like to disoblige a duchess..." his father began, but his mother waved a hand imperiously.

"It is impossible. There is no question of it, Bertram, you must see that."

"Of course, Mother. It was only an idea, a way of introducing Emily into a wider society without all the fuss of a season."

"Emily will do very well at Harrogate, and perhaps York. Nothing too demanding... an assembly here, a musical evening there. Nothing so dissipated as to risk her health. There is no need to go to London, none at all. Look at Julia — betrothed without ever leaving Yorkshire. When do you leave for Landerby, dear?"

"Late next week, Mother. Thursday, most probably. Father, may I take Whyte with me this year to look after my riding horse? He is more than capable now of managing on his own, and that will leave you Morton for the coach, for Mother's comfort."

"Thank you, dear, that is most thoughtful. I much prefer Morton," Mother said. "Such a careful driver! One always dreads an overturning, and the dire consequences that inevitably follow. Remember Milly Dewar who was thrown from the gig, and seemed perfectly unharmed? Dead within a week! Will you call Emily from the instrument now? She plays very well, but her fingers will be worn to the bone and she must be at her best for tomorrow night." She heaved a sigh. "This has been such a pleasant evening — a quiet, family evening, just as I most enjoy."

"You need not go to Highwood tomorrow if you dislike it, my dear," her husband said. "Bertram, Lucas and I can look after the girls perfectly well. It will be a very starchy affair, I am sure, and I know how such entertainments wear you down. I can make your excuses for you."

"I do not like these evening engagements," Mother said plaintively. "The night air is so injurious to one's health, if one is not very careful. However, if the girls wrap up well in the carriage and stay away from any windows that have been recklessly thrown open, they may escape without taking a chill. Besides, one must make the effort for a neighbour, although I always end the evening with my head aching abominably, and my face numb from too much smiling. Lady Esther always makes me feel... inadequate, in some way."

"She just likes to show off her grand new house and her army of footmen," Father said. "Such ostentatious display is quite unnecessary. We all know she is a duke's daughter, so there is no need for her to rub our noses in it. To my mind it would be more becoming in her to keep her entertainments simple when she is in the North Riding, and save all the display for town, when she has a credulous audience more willing to be impressed by it."

"For the son of an earl, and perhaps a future earl, you are very hard on a fellow scion of the nobility," Bertram said. "I imagine it is only what she is used to."

"Very likely. All the dukes are very grand, as you must be aware, considering who your friends are. One must maintain appearances, and ensure the world knows one's exalted rank. I have always been very thankful to be a second son, and spared the necessity to live my life as anything other than a country gentleman."

"But that will change now, will it not?" Bertram said. "There will come a time when you will have to assume an exalted rank yourself."

"Maybe not," his father said complacently. "My brother is to take a new wife."

This announcement naturally caused a sensation, and for a few minutes he was so bombarded with questions that he could not speak at all, but eventually he hushed them enough to say, "It is all your mother's doing, persuading Lady Rennington to stand aside."

"I did no such thing!" Mother said indignantly. "I merely asked if she had considered the idea, and she took it up at once. She needed no persuading, I assure you. She has been greatly distressed by the rendering of her own children illegitimate, and she is past the age when she might hope for more children herself. As soon as I mentioned it, she said at once that it was the very thing for Charles and would I draw up a list of suitable candidates, so that he need not suffer the indignity of the London season."

"How will he meet these candidates?" Bertram said.

Mother went slightly pink. "Well… I shall invite them to stay with me here, so that Charles may meet them discreetly."

"So that is why Lady Rennington has gone away," Bertram said.

"Poor lady," Emily said softly. "It must be very hard to be cast aside after so many years."

"Thirty years," Julia said, her eyes wide with shock. "Walter is twenty-nine so it must be thirty, at least."

"Caroline is doing what every wife and mother must do," their father said, "and that is her duty. She is no longer married to the earl, so she is stepping aside to allow him to marry a younger woman who will give him sons."

"More sons," Julia said.

"*Legitimate* sons," her father said firmly. "And we must all be very thankful for it. I shall never have to assume the heavy burden of the peerage, your mother will not be obliged to leave her beloved home, and Bertram is spared a most unexpected inheritance."

"Let us hope this second marriage is fruitful, then," Julia said acidly. "Just imagine if Aunt Caroline makes this noble sacrifice, and all that happens is that the nursery at Corland fills up with girls… or perhaps no children at all. How bitter that would be!"

"There is never any bitterness in sacrifice," her mother said complacently. "Caroline is doing the right thing to secure the succession, and may draw satisfaction from that."

"And if her sacrifice is in vain, then Papa will be ready to step into the breach," Penelope said, beaming at him.

"There is no need to look so gleeful, young lady," Father said. "I shall do my duty, as we all must, but I cannot suppress a feeling of relief that it may not be necessary. However, this scheme is all very much in the air, so none of you must say a word to anyone about it. No doubt it will become known soon enough, but for the present say only that Lady Rennington is staying with her sister for a while, and nothing about the rest of it, or poor Charles will be besieged with hopeful maidens wishful to become a countess."

6: An Evening At Highwood Place

Bertram had not thought at all about the evening party at Highwood Place until the time came to change and he found Bayley had laid out his silk knee breeches.

"Oh, Lord! Must I?"

"Her ladyship is very particular as to attire, sir," Bayley said. "The mistress told me herself what you are to wear tonight."

Bertram sighed, but resigned himself to the inevitable. At home, his evenings could be spent buried in a book, or he might even retreat to his library and carry on with his work, for his family understood him. No one asked him to sit and listen to the girls' playing and singing, or insisted he make up a four at whist. He could disappear after dinner, and someone would bring him tea later. Sometimes, if the words were flowing, he would work on into the night. But he knew his duty. Tonight he must clear his head of all Latin, and be a good guest, dancing or playing cards or whatever was asked of him. It was only one night, after all.

He was in the second carriage with Julia and Lucas, and since the two of them bickered gently together, as brothers and sisters so often do, Bertram was left to his own thoughts. Sometimes he wished that he had been a second son, like his father. Lucas, with his sociable disposition, was far better suited to be the heir, to marry well and take on the stewardship of Westwick, while Bertram was only suited to his books. If he could have stayed at Cambridge and become a Fellow and later a Professor, he would have been perfectly happy. Not that he was precisely unhappy at home, but this business of perhaps inheriting the earldom was a complication he could well do without. And yet, he could not quite approve of the present earl marrying again, purely to get sons — that did not seem right! It was s o difficult...

The carriage drive at Highwood Place was decorated with a multitude of coloured lanterns, which were not lit when they arrived, for it was still full daylight, but they looked very pretty. A small army of footmen materialised from the house to help them alight from the carriages, Bertram's father and mother, Emily and Penelope from the first, and Bertram, Julia and Lucas from the second. Mr Franklyn, Lady Esther and Bea were waiting in the hall to greet them, but Bertram was relieved to find that Bea neither said nor did anything untoward. He bowed and bade her good evening, she curtsied demurely and bade him welcome, and he was permitted to move into the saloon. Or rather, the Gold Saloon, for the newly extended Highwood Place now boasted several drawing rooms and saloons.

The room bore an overpowering scent of roses, for there were vases and bowls of them on every surface, in the fireplace and arranged in tiers in the corners. The Strongs and Cathcarts were already there, deep in conversations, so Bertram loitered on the outskirts until the last guests arrived, the party from the castle. Bertram had not expected to see any of them, but although the earl had not come, Kent and Olivia were there, accompanied by Mr Willerton-Forbes, the fashionable lawyer from London, and several others Bertram did not recognise.

Kent, the youngest of the earl's three sons, immediately crossed the room to stand beside Bertram.

"Evening, cousin. Well, this is amusing, is it not? An excellent attendance."

"Who are the three with Willerton-Forbes? The team investigating Nicholson's murder, I imagine."

"Exactly so. The little fellow with the military bearing is the leader. Captain Edgerton of the East India Company Army. No doubt we will hear some of his tall tales at dinner. The elegant lady is his wife, and the big blond fellow eyeing up Olivia is a Scotsman by the name of Alexander. A strange crowd. There is an elderly spinster, too — some kind of companion to Mrs Edgerton, but she does not go into society. Goodness me, these flowers are making me want to sneeze. Lady Esther always puts on a splendid show. There is to be dancing later, I understand, and all manner of delights. Shall you dance, do you think?"

"I imagine it will be unavoidable," Bertram said.

"For you, yes." He lowered his voice conspiratorially, drawing Bertram a little aside from the chattering groups. "Bea Franklyn will undoubtedly insist on it. Another chance for her to get her claws into you, now that she has thrown Walter over."

"Is he upset about that?" Bertram said curiously. "I have not seen him since that day we were all told the news."

Kent shrugged easily. "He does not seem unduly upset about any of it. You know he has gone off to town now? He is to take up a government post, seemingly, with Alfred Strong. Winnie has gone with them."

"Winnie?" Bertram looked vaguely round the room, not having noticed Winnie Strong's absence. She was not a person who stood out in company. "Well, that will be a pleasant little holiday for her. She deserves a treat. But how are you all at the castle? I did not expect to see you here tonight."

"That is Olivia, not me. You know how she is wild to be out in society, and now it is all up in the air. She cannot be presented at court, not as a bastard. She wanted to come tonight to prove that she is still a person of consequence in her own county, and Mother is away, so Mrs Edgerton had to be invited to chaperon her, and that meant Edgerton and the whole crowd. Still, Edgerton is amusing, the Scotsman will charm the ladies and the lawyer will dazzle us all with his tales of the Duke of This and the Marquess of That."

Lady Esther came across to them with her polite smile. "We shall be going in to dinner shortly. Mr Bertram, may I call upon you to escort my daughter, as the highest ranking young gentleman present?"

"I?" Bertram said, startled, throwing a glance at Kent, who smiled and shook his head. "Oh... oh... of course, Lady Esther. Delighted, naturally."

When she had moved on, he whispered to Kent, "Are you truly to lose all precedence because of this? You are still the son of an earl, after all, and I am only a nephew."

"But you are legitimate, and the son of the heir presumptive, while I am nobody. Poor Olivia! She will not like it one bit."

Bertram saw the truth of this remark as the dinner procession began to form. Lady Esther, being a duke's daughter, was highly conscious of her exalted station, so the company lined up precisely in rank order, although Bertram was surprised to see the fashionable lawyer and Mrs Edgerton among the first. Kent and Olivia as well as the various Cathcarts were of so little consequence they had not even been assigned partners.

Poor Olivia indeed! As the Lady Olivia Atherton, legitimate daughter of an earl, she had always taken her place high in any gathering, but as Miss Olivia Atherton, without rank or title, she was no one. Her head was lowered as the little procession filed past her, as she tried very hard not to show how much she minded the snub.

Bertram's heart was wrung. He stopped, and everyone behind him had to stop, too.

"Olivia?" He held out his spare arm to her. "Will you not honour me with your company, too?"

Her head shot up, pleasure written all over her face. "Why, thank you, cousin. That would be most agreeable."

And so he walked into the dining room with a lady on each arm, in defiance of Lady Esther, who was too well-bred to show the slightest displeasure at this breach of protocol. Bertram was rewarded for his chivalry, for the two ladies set out to exert their charms on him. Olivia was always lively company, and was delighted to have achieved a higher station than her new rank merited, and Bea... well, Bea was just Bea, good-humoured and boisterous as always. But with such dinner partners, Bertram had no need to struggle for conversation, and if he puzzled over the contents of a particular dish, Bea was able to explain that it had once been quail or a lamb's head or a leveret, before Lady Esther's expensive cook had smothered it in unidentifiable sauce.

When the ladies withdrew and the gentlemen gathered around Mr Franklyn, Bertram was glad to yield his higher place to Kent and Captain

Edgerton, and sit with the Cathcart boys where he could listen but had no need to participate. Politics, country sports and horses held no interest for him, and Mr Franklyn never allowed any discussion of a ribald nature, so he prepared to be bored for a half hour or so. However, Captain Edgerton would not allow boredom to take hold in any company he was in, and his two friends, the handsome Scotsman and the fashionable London lawyer, were almost as full of amusing anecdotes as he was. After an hour, the butler sidled in to remind Mr Franklyn that the ladies were expecting them.

The old dining room in the original house, now refurbished and renamed as the Red Saloon, was the appointed place for dancing. The carpets had been rolled up, and the elegant sofas and tables removed, leaving only chairs and a few large cabinets around the perimeter. Mrs Dewar, the vicar's wife, was already ensconced at the pianoforte, preparing to play, with a couple of men with fiddles for support. The windows and the door that led out onto the terrace already stood open, as Bertram's mother fought a spirited but unsuccessful campaign to have them all closed again.

"Come, girls," she said to Julia, Emily and Penelope. "Let us place ourselves as far as possible from unwholesome draughts. Keep your shawls wrapped tightly about you, except when you are dancing. One must not take the least risk of a chill, or else it will settle on the lungs and any inflammation there is invariably fatal. One cannot be too careful in such matters."

"Yes, Mama," they chorused, making a show of tightening their shawls over bare arms, to be loosened the instant their mama looked elsewhere.

Where she was only taking notice of the windows, they were assessing the gentlemen as they arrived, their hopeful expressions settling into resignation, for even Julia's lack of skill with numbers could not disguise the fact that there were considerably more young ladies than gentlemen willing or able to dance. Bertram could see at once that he was not going to be able to evade his duty. There would be no escaping to the card room this evening. The one bright spot was that he would only be obliged to dance with Bea Franklyn once. He looked around for her, planning to get this chore out of the way early, only to see her with her hand already resting proprietorially on Mr Alexander's arm. As the music started up, he looked around quickly, and spotting Bridget Dewar nearby, held out his hand to her.

There was a great deal of pleasure to be had from such dancing. It was certainly not impromptu, and nothing under Lady Esther's aegis could ever be described as informal, but there was not the rigidity of a regular ball. The older generation joined in just as enthusiastically as the younger, young ladies without partners stood up together and nobody minded much when anyone went wrong or toes were stepped on. Bertram had danced with Olivia, Alice Dewar and Lily Strong, when he was accosted by Bea Franklyn.

"Your turn to dance with me, Bertram," she said cheerfully.

"It would be my pleasure," he said politely.

"Shall we wait near the windows? It is so hot in here, do you not find? I declare, if I do not get a little air, I am sure I shall melt away altogether. Shall we step onto the terrace for a moment?"

Rather alarmed by her high colour, he agreed to it at once. The terrace was certainly cooler, delicately lit by lines of coloured paper lanterns which cast soft light over Bea's gown, turning the pale silk to gentle shades of blue and pink and orange. A slight breeze ruffled the dark curls framing her face, pressing her skirts closer about her legs. She looked remarkably pretty, was his surprised thought.

She crossed the terrace swiftly, resting her hands on the stone balustrade and gazing out into the garden. The little pools of light made no impression on the darkness beyond, and to Bertram, it felt very like standing at the rail of a ship gazing into the black ocean.

"I should like—" she began, and then stopped, her breathing rather rapid.

"What should you like?" he said gently. "May I fetch something for you? A cool drink, perhaps?"

"No... no... I merely thought... perhaps..." Again her breath came very fast, but Bertram could see no cause for her agitation.

"Miss Franklyn?" he murmured, but she made no response.

Then, from behind them, came a voice high with distress. "Miss Franklyn! Miss Franklyn! Do come back inside, I beg you. The night air... so very injurious... I could not forgive myself..." Bertram's mother materialised in a flurry of alarm, throwing a thick woollen shawl about Bea's shoulders. "Bertram, what are you about, to be taking Miss Franklyn *outside!* At night, too, and when she is excessively heated from dancing. How many times must I tell you that one cannot be too careful in such matters? My dear Miss Franklyn, will you not come back into the safety of the house before you catch a chill?"

"Yes... yes, of course," Bea said, laughing suddenly, and allowing herself to be steered back to the house. "I am so very sorry to alarm you, Mrs Atherton. But do not blame Bertram, for it was entirely my doing. I was so hot."

"No, no! He should have prevented you. He ought to know better. Come now, you will be much better inside. Deploy your fan with vigour, and Bertram will fetch you a glass of lemonade... or an ice, if you promise to eat it very slowly. Too much icy cold food consumed in haste is just as fatal for the constitution as too much hot food. There now, here is your mother, who will feel just as I do, I am sure. No harm done, Lady Esther, for I believe I covered her with the shawl before her blood could be chilled."

"You are all kindness, Mrs Atherton, I am sure," Lady Esther said frostily, "but Bea hardly needs such coddling. You will have her overheating in this heavy wrap. I know you mean well, but I believe I understand my daughter's constitution better than you do."

"Oh... of course... a thousand apologies, my lady."

Bertram followed them back into the house, his mother distressed, Lady Esther regally in charge and Bea... Bea was giggling, as if it were all a great joke. She was a strange girl, sometimes.

7: Bertram Has An Idea

In the Red Saloon, the dance Bertram and Bea were supposed to be a part of was going on without them. Lady Esther swept regally through the room, neatly dispatching Bertram's mother to her vigilance by the windows and ordering Bertram to follow. Her exact words were, "Would you be so good as to bear my daughter company while she recovers her composure, Mr Atherton?" but it felt very like an order to Bertram.

Lady Esther found two seats for them in the room set aside for refreshments, and summoned a footman to bring two glasses of wine. "There, you will go on perfectly well now, Beatrice, and Mr Atherton will take good care of you while I return to my duties as hostess." So saying, she sailed out of the room without a backwards glance. The few others also seeking refreshments there watched her go, then turned back to their own conversations.

"You must not mind her," Bea said. "She's so used to people jumping at her every word that she's come to expect it, but she means no harm by it, none at all. I'm sure you understand that. Oh... our wine... thank you, James." She took a large gulp, then went on , "I do hope your mother is not offended."

"No, I am sure—"

"It was so kind of her to come out with the shawl for me, so very kind. So very timely... just at the right time, and I'm so very grateful..." Another gulp of wine. "I like your mother very much."

"So do—"

"Yes, a lovely lady, quite lovely, and so very kind. How thoughtful of her to rush out like that when..." An even larger gulp of wine. "...when she must fear the night air so much on her own account. So very brave!"

She raised the glass to her lips again, but Bertram reached out and took it from her, setting it down on the table beside them. "You might wish to drink a shade more slowly, Miss Franklyn."

She giggled and put one hand over her mouth, but her eyes were laughing up at him. Then, abruptly, her mood changed. Settling her hands demurely in her lap, she said more soberly, "I am very sorry, Bertram. Whatever must you think of me? I have been babbling, have I not?"

"I like your babbling. Do you realise that your accent develops more than a hint of your Newcastle origins when you are excited?"

Her eyes widened. "Oh, *pray* do not say so to Mama! The hours she has spent teaching me to speak properly - you would not believe it. I was not a very apt pupil, and I still struggle to talk correctly, as you have observed."

"I find it rather charming," he said. "You may take another sip of wine now — just a small one, mind."

"You are very kind — kinder than I deserve," she said in a subdued voice, taking a tiny sip and carefully setting the glass down again.

"Are you quite well, Miss Franklyn?" he said teasingly. "This meek tone is not at all what I have come to expect from you."

"No. You think me mannerless, I dare say," she said. "Brash. Bumptious. Thoroughly obnoxious."

"Full of energy," he said. "Enthusiastic. Animated, and let me tell you, that is a great deal better than being spiritless and drooping, like so many fashionable young ladies."

"Oh." She looked up at him with a hint of a smile. "Then you do not hate me?"

"Hate you? Heavens, no! Why on earth should I?"

"Because I almost— Well, never mind. But you dislike me?"

"Not at all."

She lowered her voice and leaned towards him. "Then are you going to be so obliging as to offer for me?"

He lowered his voice too. "I am not, Miss Franklyn. Sorry as I am to disappoint you, marriage has no part to play in my future."

"What a pity," she said in her normal voice, "when we get along so admirably, too." But then she laughed. "Nevertheless, I do not yet despair of changing your mind on the subject. Shall we have that dance now?"

He laughed, too, and held out his hand to her. It was impossible to be cross with such a good-humoured girl for very long.

When Bertram had finally abandoned Bea and was looking about for his next partner, he saw Miss Parish sitting quietly in a corner, watching the newly formed set avidly. She was a cousin to the Cathcarts, and recently orphaned.

"Well, Miss Parish," he said, taking the seat beside her, "what do you think of the dancing so far? Are we not an energetic lot?"

"Oh, yes," she said in her soft voice, blushing fiercely.

"Who do you think is the best dancer?"

"I... I cannot say."

"Very diplomatic. I would say my cousin Olivia is the most graceful of the ladies, but for the gentlemen, and it pains me to say so, the palm must go to Mr Franklyn. I never saw a man of his age dance so well. He quite outshines the rest of us." He paused, but when she said nothing, he went on, "I know you are still in black gloves for your father, but in a setting such as this, amongst friends, it would not be improper for you to dance, surely? May I have the honour?"

"Oh... no, no! Indeed, no." Then, after a long pause she whispered, "Thank you."

"Then I shall stay and enjoy your company, Miss Parish."

"No, no, you must not... look there, Aveline... Miss Cathcart..."

He looked where she indicated and saw Aveline Cathcart watching him hopefully. With a smile, therefore, he rose, bowed, and went to claim his designated partner. At least she could talk sensibly, unlike Miss Parish.

"She does not dance," Aveline said, as they waited for the musicians to begin.

"The black gloves—?"

"No, she has never learnt. She plays divinely, but she does not dance at all."

"I know her mother died young, but surely her father had her educated?" Bertram said.

"If one could call it education. She knows all about engines and spinning machinery and the cost of flax, and she darns stockings admirably, but she cannot paint or embroider, and she thanks the servants for doing their work."

"Such good manners are refreshing," Bertram said, offended on Miss Parish's behalf.

"There is no accounting for taste," Aveline said, with a curl of the lip.

Bertram had nothing else to say to her, and they remained silent for the rest of the dance. He noted, almost without thinking, that Julia and Penelope were dancing but Emily was not. She sat in a corner with Mother, watching surreptitiously, but averting her eyes with a blush whenever a man looked her way. Shyness was a terrible affliction, and Bertram might have been no better, had not several years at Harrow and then Cambridge knocked it out of him.

When released from Miss Cathcart's sneering company, he ambled over to Emily and led her across the room to where Miss Parish sat. They had met before, in that they had been introduced and occasionally spent some time in the same room, but they had never before had an opportunity to talk to each other. Being so similar in age and temper, he was not surprised to see them soon chatting comfortably together.

As he turned his attention to his next partner, and wondered if he might escape to the card room now, he found Kent by his side, a mischievous grin on his face. "Have you escaped unscathed from Bea Franklyn's clutches, cousin? Or are you even now preparing to return tomorrow for the necessary interview with her father?"

"No interview, cousin," Bertram said, with an easy laugh. "I am not so easily caught."

"And yet she contrived to get you outside, did she not? If you had been discovered kissing her in the garden—"

"There was no kissing and we were not in the garden," Bertram said sharply. "We were on the terrace in full view of anyone near the windows. Indeed, Mother saw us and rushed out to swathe Miss Franklyn in a shawl, lest she fall ill with some putrid fever after five minutes out of doors."

"Aunt Jane saw you and rushed out to ensure you were not compromised, you mean," Kent said, with a wry grin. "Take care, cousin, or you will be leg-shackled yet."

With a languid wave, he ambled away, leaving Bertram in an odd mixture of fury and chagrin. Had he been naive? Had Bea led him out onto the terrace in order to compromise him? It was an unsettling thought, and her behaviour at the time and afterwards — her obvious agitation, the babbling, her unusual nervousness — all suggested it. And yet she had *not* proposed anything improper. There had been no attempt to kiss him, nor to lead him down into the darkness of the garden, and it was malicious of Kent to suggest otherwise.

When the Athertons left, there was a rearrangement, such that Bertram's sisters and brother travelled together in the second carriage, and Bertram was in the first with his parents. Barely had the horses begun to move before his mother said, "I was a little concerned this evening, Bertram."

"Were you, Mother? In what regard?"

"Regarding Bea Franklyn. She is a mischievous creature, and I should hate to see you taken in by her wiles."

"Mother, I know you mean well, but Miss Franklyn is as good-hearted a girl as ever breathed, and I will not hear her impugned in this way. Far from being wily, she has been utterly straightforward in all her dealings with me. She has told me openly that she intends to persuade me to the altar, and I have told her openly that she will not succeed in that objective."

"But she is so very enticing, dear."

"Just because we stood up for one dance does not mean that there is enticement going on. I am perfectly capable of resisting the charms of a young lady, you know. I have been doing it for years, after all."

"Bertram, dear, few men are proof against a truly obstinate woman. Look at Walter, after all... or his father, come to that. He was looking in quite a different direction when Caroline got her claws into him. All men have their weaknesses and a woman like Bea Franklyn will always seek them out."

"You make her sound like a manipulative harpy, full of schemes and devices."

"And is she not full of schemes?" his mother said in her gentle way. "Inveigling you out onto the terrace in that underhanded manner! If I had not gone out after you—"

"She was hot and wanted some air," Bertram said huffily. "You refine too much upon a perfectly innocent event."

"Very well, dear," she said calmly.

Bertram was cross the whole way home.

***

Bea prepared for bed, but did not attempt to sleep. Instead, she wrapped herself in a robe, lit several candles and waited for the inevitable visit from her stepmother.

It was half an hour before she came, arrayed in an extremely expensive lace confection under her silk wrap, with a matching nightcap. "Oh good, you are still awake, because we must put our heads together and see how we may redeem the situation. Goodness, but I could have slapped that interfering Jane Atherton, poking her nose in where it is not at all wanted, and when all was progressing so advantageously. You did so well to get him out onto the terrace, and in another moment you would have been down the steps and into the garden, and then we should have had him well and truly caught in our web."

"That is horrid!" Bea said. "I am not a spider, and Bertram is not a fly — he is a man who ought to have a free choice in who he marries, or if he marries at all."

"Where would we be if every man took it into his head to choose where he marries?" Lady Esther said, with an airy wave of her hand. "It is very much in Bertram's own interests to marry you, as he will realise once you are safely wed. But we are very short of time, and I cannot arrange another evening party, not at such short notice. It will have to be an afternoon affair — a Venetian breakfast, perhaps."

"Mama..."

"The weather might be a problem, but so long as you can get him outside and wandering here and there, our plan can still work. Such a pity the maze is not well grown enough to provide concealment, but the shrubbery will do very well, and if it *should* come on to rain, why then you will have the perfect excuse to seek shelter in the Grecian Temple... or even better, the Grotto. Yes, that should work. We shall not let him slip through our fingers again. Good night, Beatrice."

***

Bertram woke abruptly, with a line of his friend's letter running through his head.

'We are all bidden to bring spinsters of our own to Landerby so that Her Grace may exercise her match-making skills'.

He leapt out of bed, and raced across the room to his writing desk, pulling the paper out from the receptacle for letters still to be answered, and scanned it carefully once more. Spinsters... Her Grace the Duchess of Wedhampton wanted spinsters, and it was very possible that Bertram could oblige her. Landerby Manor would be stuffed to its ancient, worm-eaten rafters with scions of the nobility — he counted three amongst his own particular friends — which would provide plenty of opportunity for Bea to climb the ladder of society, and if her grace was to be there, even Lady Esther could not object.

At breakfast, therefore, he said to his mother, "When are you planning to call at Highwood Place to thank Lady Esther for her hospitality?"

"Today, I thought. It was not a ball, so one does not absolutely need to call the very next day, but neither was it a mere dinner engagement. It would be a pleasing attention to a neighbour to call sooner rather than later. Why do you ask?"

"I shall come with you, if I may. I can sit on the box, so that you will not be crushed inside."

"Oh... as to that, I shall only take Julia. Emily should rest after the exertions of last night, and Penelope is in disgrace for dancing three times with that Scottish fellow. He may be excessively handsome and charming and so forth, but he is neither betrothed to her nor likely to be, given his lack of fortune, and therefore not to be danced with more than twice, or better still, only once. It is not as if there had been any shortage of partners, and you are only sixteen, Penelope, and not even properly out yet."

"Oh pooh," Penelope said. "At an informal evening like that, no one counts dances, and besides, his cousin is a baron, he told me, so he is very eligible."

"Your mother counted," her father said, "and if Mr Alexander were himself a baron with an estate in good order and were to apply for your hand in... oh, two or three years, say, perhaps I might consider his suit, but until then, you will not dance with him or any other young man more than once. Bertram, why this ardour to call at Highwood? Has Miss Franklyn managed to infiltrate your heart?"

Bertram laughed. "Certainly not! However, her persistence is becoming annoying. It occurred to me that her objectives and mine might both be secured if I can obtain an invitation for her to Landerby Manor."

"Where you will both be living under the same roof," his mother said waspishly, "and she will be able to chip away at your resolve every hour of the day. It is madness, Bertram."

"Give me credit for a little sense, Mother. She will have to agree to quit her pursuit of me before any invitations are issued."

"She will agree to anything if it brings her closer to her aim," his mother said darkly.

His father set down his coffee cup with a snap. "I am of Bertram's mind in this, Jane. Bea Franklyn is not a perfect lady, by any means, but she has never struck me as sly or underhanded in any way. Let Bertram talk to her and see what may be achieved."

***

B

ea and Lady Esther had risen indulgently late, and so had only just begun the work of planning the Venetian breakfast when Hobbs came into their parlour.

"Beg pardon, my lady, but Mrs George Atherton is here, together with Miss Atherton and Mr Bertram Atherton. Are you at home?"

"Bertram?" Bea squeaked in astonishment.

"Naturally we are at home," her stepmother said, with no more than a blink of surprise. "The terrace, I think, Hobbs. The *eastern* terrace. The view over the shrubbery is so pleasantly green at this time of year. Bring suitable refreshments." As soon as the butler had withdrawn, she turned to Bea excitedly. "This is a very good sign, Beatrice. You must be sure to capitalise on it this time. You will propose a walk in the gardens, and then lead him away from the house and into the shrubbery. I will come after you in a little while. Come, let us greet our guests."

Bea said nothing. She was very happy to see Bertram, naturally, for what could be more pleasing than a man who pays a duty call at the very first opportunity? But a sleepless night and the prodding of her conscience had led her to the conclusion that she could never be comfortable trapping a man into marriage. She would pursue Bertram with every fibre of her being, but there would be no disappearing into the shrubbery to trick him into a compromising kiss.

They met their visitors in the hall, and then out onto the terrace, where Father emerged from his study to join them. There was a slight breeze, and at first Mrs Atherton baulked at being out of doors at all, but Hobbs brought shawls for Bea and her stepmother, and the Atherton ladies were well-clad in stout pelisses, so it was deemed safe to venture forth.

For a while they all sat about decorously making polite conversation. The events of the evening before were gone over, congratulations offered and accepted for the success of the party, and there was a general air of complacency that so many people had gathered in one spot and yet no disaster had befallen them. Bea and Bertram were seated side by side, but said little, until Bertram said into a lull in the conversation, "Shall we all stroll about a little? What do you say, Miss Franklyn?"

That was a surprise indeed! Bea could only nod, while, one by one, the others demurred. "We shall admire your energy from our comfortable seats," her father said, reaching for his wine glass.

Now Bea could not be comfortable. She knew perfectly well what her stepmother expected of her, but she could not... she absolutely could not do it. How unfair it would be to Bertram and what a dreadful start to married life to secure him by treachery. So they walked here and there, and he talked easily about nothing in particular, and she began to feel that in another minute or two she could profess to be feeling chilled and ask to return to the house.

But then he startled her even more. "Shall we sit? That bench over there, perhaps... it is quite sheltered from the wind, but still in clear view of my mother, who is watching us anxiously from the terrace."

"Is she? But why?"

"In case I thoughtlessly allow you to grow chilled, for that leads to inflammation of the lungs, you see, and then a putrid fever, whereupon you will certainly be dead within three days. A cool breeze is invariably fatal in Mother's eyes. So we will not stretch her nerves for too long, but there is something I should like to talk about."

"Oh. Not an offer, I suppose?" she said teasingly, as she sat on the bench he indicated.

He settled himself beside her, his long legs stretched out before him. "I am afraid not, but it is on that subject, in a way. I should like to understand your mind fully. When you set out to marry first Walter and then me, is it the particular title to which we are heir that attracts you, or would another title do as well? Or is it Corland Castle that entices you?"

This was plain speaking indeed, but she very much liked such a direct approach. "Not the castle, no — such a great echoing place, and so cold! Highwood is not exactly cosy, but at least one is not chilled to the bone all year round. And I do not care about that title in particular."

"So you would be happy with another title... any title? You want to be noble?"

"I want to be a *Lady*, Bertram. I am so tired of being plain Miss Franklyn whose father was an attorney and whose fortune came from iron foundries. There is something terribly dispiriting and... well, *industrial* about iron foundries, do you not think?"

"What does it matter where the money came from?" he said.

"Oh, believe me, it matters! When Papa inherited all his money, all our friends in Newcastle drew away from us. They thought we were too far above them now. So when Papa married Mama, I thought we would find a level amongst her people. But no, they are too grand to admit the likes of us to their ranks. They not only despise Papa and me, they despise Mama, too, because she married beneath her. She married a commoner, you see. So I decided that I would marry a nobleman and then they would *have* to acknowledge me and treat me with respect. And when we moved here, you... all the Athertons were kind to us, and never made us feel inferior. So that is why I chose Walter first, and then you, because you don't despise me and will make me a Lady."

"Suppose," he said, slowly, smiling his gentle smile, "that I could find you another nobleman to marry? One who could make you a Lady straight away and not at some indeterminate point in the future?"

"Can you do that?"

"I can try. I shall be spending a month at Landerby Manor, which will be full of noblemen, particular friends of mine, and two of them at least I know for a fact are looking to marry."

"Truly? And they already have titles?"

"They do. The brother of a duke, and a viscount. And, as an outside possibility, what would you say to the heir to a dukedom? Should you like to be a duchess?"

Her heart beat a little faster. "Oh, Bertram!" she whispered. "I should outrank Mama."

He laughed. "So you would. How very gratifying that would be, and I can ensure that you are invited to Landerby, but there is one condition."

"Ah. I knew there would be a catch."

"You must promise me you will stop pursuing me, and not just at Landerby — forever, Bea."

"But nothing may come of it."

"Then I shall find some other way to help you achieve your ambition, but I have no intention of marrying, and I do not wish you to waste your time on a project doomed to failure. Will you promise? If I obtain an invitation for you to Landerby, you will leave me alone forthwith?"

"I will."

"Then let us go and put the idea to your mama."

8: On The Road To Lincolnshire

The Franklyns were two days on the road to Landerby Manor in Lincolnshire, and with every mile that passed Lady Esther's smile widened a fraction. An invitation from the Duchess of Wedhampton was exactly calculated to set her in a benign mood, for she was returning to her rightful place amongst the nobility.

Bea's father, who had elected to join them on the visit, was not of noble blood, but he looked so very much the part that he might as well have been. His well-fitting, expensive clothes and patrician air were impressive, and he was still fit and active, despite being beyond forty years of age.

Only Bea herself was out of place, for she was neither elegant nor especially ladylike. Her stepmother reprimanded her at regular intervals for her slouching deportment or excessive boisterousness. "A lady is restrained at all times," she said loftily. But Bea preferred to remember the way Bertram had described her. *'Full of energy. Enthusiastic. Animated, and let me tell you, that is a great deal better than being spiritless and drooping, like so many fashionable young ladies.'* Spiritless and drooping! How dreadful that sounded. So even as she obediently straightened her back and lowered her head and suppressed her instinct to point out every landmark they passed, she kept the flame of her enthusiasm burning within her.

She had not enlightened her stepmother about the real reason for this visit. Bertram had said only that the Duchess of Wedhampton had asked them all to bring young ladies along, to lighten the otherwise heavily male atmosphere of the gathering, and he had thought it might amuse Bea. Lady Esther had agreed to it instantly, added herself and Papa to the invitation, and set a date, the whole being decided within no more than ten minutes. But nothing at all had been said about finding a suitor for her, or about her pact with Bertram.

Bertram... she could not make up her mind about him. On the one hand, his immovable resistance to the very idea of marriage was disappointing, but on the other, he had very kindly arranged this visit so that she might meet other, less reluctant, gentlemen. Two of his friends, he had said, were actively looking to marry, both able to give her the place in society she craved. Perhaps she would never fly so high as her stepmother, but no one could sneer at her if she were a Lady... not openly, at least.

Mama was always slow in dressing in the mornings, so Bea and her father waited patiently in their parlour at the George Inn at Selby. Her father had buried himself in a local newspaper, but Bea sat by the window, her legs tucked under her, gazing down at the market square below. There was no market today, but there were a few carts selling fresh vegetables and cheese, wagons and riders passing by, a bustle of people scurrying about and a fine view of Selby Abbey. After the emptiness surrounding Highwood

Place, it was delightful to watch the endless motion and ever-changing sights of town.

Her father laid down his newspaper and folded it neatly. "Have you heard anything of how Walter Atherton is going on in London?"

Without turning away from the window, Bea said, "No. Why should I have?"

"I should have thought it a matter of interest to you. After all, you almost married him. Had his grandmother not been so ill, you would have been married by now."

She looked at him, then said with a sigh, "I suppose I should have asked. I saw Lady Strong not two days since, and she would have known. No doubt Winnie is an assiduous correspondent. But his name was not mentioned, and I did not think to ask." Another sigh, and she turned fully to face him, swinging her legs to the floor. "You think me unfeeling, I am sure, and perhaps I am. Did you expect me to go into a decline? Or to marry him anyway, even though he is not the man I betrothed myself to?"

"I expected you to show some sign of distress, yes," he said. "After all, you showed a marked preference for him right from the start, and that was five years ago. Can all of that be set aside so easily? Surely you must feel some... not regret, perhaps, but pangs of loss. He was a fine young man, after all — handsome, charming, well-mannered."

"And entirely indifferent to me, Papa," she said, with a sudden spurt of anger. "He made it very clear that he cared as little for me as I did for him. It was a matter of convenience to both of us. He got himself a wealthy wife without exerting himself in the slightest, and I—"

"You got a title," he said softly.

"*Yes!* Lady Birtwell, and eventually Lady Rennington, but without that, Walter is just another lazy, arrogant aristocrat. If he has to work for a living now, it will do him a great deal of good and perhaps teach him a little humility."

Her father's eyebrows arched a fraction. "If you despise him so much, I wonder you wished to marry him at all, title or no."

"I do not despise him, I merely see him as he is, Papa. Would you think better of me if I had been in love with him? What good would that have done?"

"Love is not a prerequisite for a contented marriage," her father said slowly. "Not love... but one must at the very least *respect* one's partner in life, and if you did not respect Mr Walter Atherton, it is better that you should not marry him. And if you do not respect Mr Bertram Atherton, you should not marry him, either. Marriage is a bond for life, Bea, and that can be a very long time with a spouse for whom you feel nothing but contempt."

"I shall respect my husband well enough when I have his ring on my finger, you may be sure," she said with a gurgle of laughter. "I understand the rules of the game, Papa. You have taught me well that I must marry for advantage above all else."

He shifted uneasily. "It is true that both my marriages were advantageous, the first for my career and the second socially, but that was not the reason for them... not the *sole* reason. I had an affection for both my wives before I married them."

"And would you have married either of them if they had not been advantageous?" Bea said.

"Certainly! Well... possibly... who can say? The situation did not arise. My principal reason for marrying was to provide myself with the comfort of my own family. For a man, female companionship and a pleasant home are powerful inducements. For a woman... well, you have no need to marry at all, Bea. I understand why you refused Walter Atherton in the end, but this rush to replace him, and with a member of the nobility at all costs…" He shifted again, folding and then unfolding his arms. "I do not interfere with how you and your mother address your marital prospects. My task is only to ensure that the man you choose is financially sound and not a scoundrel. However, I hope you will not marry without the most careful thought. A hasty marriage…" He paused, looking at her thoughtfully. "Well, I do not wish you to regret it, that is all I have to say on the matter." He pulled out his pocket watch. "Time is passing. I shall go and see what is delaying Lady Esther. Ah, here she is at last!" The relief in his voice was palpable. "Now we shall be soon on the road again."

Bea was glad to be on her way again, too. A whole evening confined to an inn parlour with her parents reminded her forcibly of the long-ago time when her father was a mere attorney and the two of them lived in perfect contentment, sitting one each side of the fire with their books after dinner, not needing the company of any third person. Or so she had thought.

Then her father had unexpectedly inherited his fortune, bought a larger house, become a man of fashion and set out to distance himself from his humble roots. Lady Esther had come into their lives soon afterwards, and although Bea was very glad of the wider society the daughter of a duke could offer, she could not but regret the loss of those long, companionable evenings. Books were set aside now in favour of elegant embroidery or tapestry or music, and if she were allowed to read at all, it must be an improving work suitable for young ladies. Nor was she left to read even such dull material in peace, but was exhorted to read certain passages aloud, or questioned closely to ensure she had understood the moral. It was all very well for her father to advise her not to marry in haste, but another summer under her stepmother's tutelage would surely have her fit only for the asylum.

Of course she must marry! And soon, for she was one and twenty already, practically an old maid. There was an urgency about the matter that had not been there before. Three seasons in London with the humiliation of no betrothal... not even a sensible offer. But Walter had always been there, always in her orbit, just waiting for her to bring him to the point. And when one is only seventeen... eighteen... nineteen, oh, there is all the time in the world.

No longer. She must find herself a husband and a title before the winter, or she would have failed utterly. But if Eustace and Walter would not do, and Bertram would not surrender, then she must take whatever opportunities presented themselves. She had a month to find a husband from amongst Bertram's noble friends.

Here she quailed a little. A month! So little time to find the right one and bring him around her thumb. How would she know? With the Atherton men, she had known them now for several years and had a very good idea of their characters. How could she meet a man for the first time and decide instantly whether he would do or not?

But then she reminded herself that the men she would meet at Landerby Manor were aristocratic, and therefore they would all be gentlemen. They were not like some of the men she had met in London, whose only interest was in her fortune, or those in Newcastle who had unwelcome designs on her person. A gentleman had no need of her fortune and would respect her person, so she need only find one who appeared responsive to her overtures. Surely she had decision and will enough to bring this off? She would be betrothed within the month or her name was not Beatrice Franklyn.

***

Nothing occurred to delay the journey and by the middle of the afternoon the Franklyns' two carriages turned aside from the turnpike onto a narrow, badly rutted track. Two small villages came and went, children and geese and dogs scattering before the horses and then running excitedly after the carriages until exhaustion or boredom or the clouds of dust overcame them. Bea let down the window, leaned out and waved enthusiastically to them, until her mama chided her.

They came to a long, moss-covered wall, crumbling in places, and eventually two stone gate posts, one of them leaning slightly. The gates stood wide open, so they drove through at a smart pace onto a carriage drive liberally coated with weeds, and shaded by elderly lime trees in rigid lines. The avenue was short, and very soon they reached the house. Bea had seen many imposing houses while visiting her stepmother's relations, but there was something unspeakably sad about the decaying splendour of Landerby Manor. The stonework was stained from overflowing rainwater pipes, the high mullioned windows showed cracked panes stuffed with sacking, and monstrous untrimmed shrubs loomed menacingly over the lower windows. And yet beneath the neglect lay a fine Tudor house.

Lady Esther sniffed. "I hope the interior is in better condition, or we shall be most uncomfortable."

The great wooden front doors, bleached almost white by the sun, slowly opened and a stream of liveried footmen poured down the steps, supervised by a most superior butler. Lady Esther's face brightened. Barely had they decanted from the carriage than a small figure, dwarfed by the great doors, emerged from within and raced down the steps, holding her skirts high enough to reveal shapely ankles.

"Lady Esther! Lady Esther!" the figure cried, slithering to a halt so late that she almost crashed into them. "I cannot tell you how grateful I am to you for coming. I doubt you remember me, but we met several times in town three years ago, and I so admired your elegance… your deportment… oh, everything about you! Of course you will not remember, for I was merely Lady George Medhurst then, and George had no expectation of the title. Why, no one ever thought of it, least of all me! But here we are, and here I am with not the least idea how to go on, and no mother-in-law to advise me, and my own mother simply throws up her hands and says *she* knows nothing about it, but you were brought up in a ducal household, you see. Oh, is this your daughter? So pretty! Such lovely hair you have, my dear. Are those curls natural? How lucky you are! And Mr Franklyn — welcome, sir, welcome! You are all welcome."

She paused for breath, and Lady Esther, who had long since made her curtsy, now said in faint tones, with just the hint of a question at the end, "Your Grace."

Bea was trying very hard not to laugh at this most unregal duchess. She caught her father's eye, and saw the unholy amusement therein, and that almost undid her. Fortunately, she managed to turn her laugh into a cough, and Lady Esther, never over-endowed with a sense of humour and certainly not when it involved a duchess, had taken charge of the situation.

"We are honoured to be here, Your Grace. Such a fine residence! So imposing. Shall we go inside?"

"Oh… yes, yes, of course. Do mind the steps, Lady Esther, for some flags are cracked. Landerby may be imposing, but the late duke neglected it terribly. Not that I mean any disrespect to my father-in-law, naturally, for

I am sure he had many other calls on his purse, but it does seem a shame. We have thrown an army of servants at it this past month, so I hope you will not— Oh, careful, Miss Franklyn! The steps are so worn. Do take the greatest care. Now just down here is the Great Hall. I had hoped, Lady Esther, to house you and Mr Franklyn in the Great Chamber, but sadly the damp could not be got out of it, despite weeks of blazing fires. We have men on the roof mending all the leaks. This way, if you please. Do mind these steps, they are so uneven. Miss Franklyn, pray hold the rail. This way! Thi s way!"

Passing through great echoing chambers, their stone floors only partially covered by threadbare carpets, the damp air chilling even now, in the height of summer, Bea thought it would take more than an army of servants to bring Landerby Manor to any degree of comfort. It needed a small fortune spent on it. But then the Duke of Wedhampton was reputed to have a very large fortune, the late duke having been reluctant to spend so much as a single unnecessary farthing if he could possibly help it, or, even better, if he could persuade someone else to spend it on his behalf. But that was how the rich became even richer, she supposed, by hanging on to their farthings.

They ascended a staircase lit by newly cleaned windows, which only revealed in starker detail the cracked stonework and dust in the air. Their feet threw up clouds of it as they passed by, and a scattering of half-filled buckets here and there suggested that the men on the roof would be kept busy for some time.

"Here we are," the duchess said, throwing open a door. "This is for you, Lady Esther, and there is a dressing room beside it. And Miss Franklyn, your room is just through here."

It was not large, but it was a corner room with windows on two sides, coloured buttercup yellow by the afternoon sun. One window had a view over lawns to a church and a line of trees that perhaps marked a stream, and the other overlooked the stable yard, where their carriages were just arriving. As she watched, grooms moved forward to unhitch the horses for the postilions to return them to the last staging post.

"Do you think you will be comfortable here?" the duchess said anxiously, following Bea into the room. "We have contrived as best we may, but the house is in such a state of decay I scarcely know what to do about it. I hope Lady Esther will advise me, for I have not the least idea how to go on. I was never intended to be a duchess."

"It was all very sudden, was it not?" Bea said sympathetically.

The duchess nodded, sitting down with a sigh on the bed. Next door, the thumps and huffs and grunts suggested that trunks were arriving. Lady Esther's imperious voice could be heard giving instructions. Bea sat down beside the duchess.

"When I married George, he was the second son of a second son, Miss Franklyn, with four people ahead of him in the succession. No one cared who he married, and I was only a lowly squire's daughter... not even an eldest daughter! Youngest of five, and not a bean to my name. But Henry and George both offered for me... Henry was George's elder brother, you see, but he never expected to inherit, either, so it was left up to me to choose which of them I wanted... or neither!"

"How did you choose?" Bea said, for the question of choosing a husband was much on her mind.

The duchess roared with laughter. "I kissed them! At least, Henry kissed me, and that was pleasant enough but it did not set me on fire, if you understand me. Have you ever been kissed, Miss Franklyn?"

"No, never."

"Oh, then you will not know, but with the right man, something magical happens when you kiss. So having kissed Henry, I wanted to kiss George, too, and so I did and I knew... I just knew. And so did he. If ever you want to know about a man, what kind of man he is, then you must kiss him, Miss Franklyn, then you will know."

"So you kissed Lord George," Bea breathed, enchanted with the story, "and you just *knew.*"

"Yes, and so we were married, and we had our sweet little house and our sweet baby came along and we were so happy. And then... it was dreadful! So many deaths! First George's father, and then his uncle and cousin, one after the other. And then poor Henry was the heir and he rushed out and got himself married, and then he died too! And bless me, but the old duke went and died straight after. I was so terrified that George would die, too. It was quite horrid, as if we were being punished for something. But then we were in a dreadful state because Louisa... Henry's wife, that is... his widow, poor girl. Can you imagine, only married a month and then widowed? Anyway, she was with child and so was I, so we all had to wait to see if she had a son who would be the new duke, but she had a girl, poor thing, so it was all for nothing. Although she is still at Rodmersham, for George has not the heart to ask her to remove to the Dower House. And in the end, I was the one who had a son, and so the succession is secure... for the moment. But Thomas... he is George's younger brother, you see, and everyone is wild for him to marry soon, and start producing more sons."

"Lord Thomas... he is here, is he not?"

"Oh yes, but how much we will see of him I cannot say, for he is one of these learned men talking Latin to each other. But two of my cousins are here — you will like them, I am sure. Several other young ladies, too. We shall find much to amuse us, shall we not? Do you ride, Miss Franklyn?"

"I do. My horse is being brought here in easy stages."

"Excellent. This is supposed to be good riding country, although I have not had time to explore myself. Oh good, here are your boxes at last, and this is Peggy, who will unpack for you. Do you have a maid with you?"

"My stepmother's maid will see to both of us."

"Of course, but send for Peggy if ever you need any additional help. The ladies tend to gather in the State Saloon in the afternoons. Ask a footman to direct you. There are no bell pulls here, just hand bells and footmen everywhere — you cannot go far without finding one. And there are names on all the occupied rooms, so that you don't wander into one of the gentlemen's bedrooms by mistake. I shall see you later, Miss Franklyn."

And in a flurry of muslin skirts, she was gone, leaving Bea amused, if a little breathless.

9: Landerby Manor

Bertram was surprised to find himself looking forward to Bea's arrival. The presence of the Duke and Duchess of Wedhampton changed the atmosphere of the gathering, although not in themselves, for they were mild-mannered by nature and not at all high in the instep. In addition to the title, however, they had inherited all the old duke's vast retinue of very grand servants, starting with a house steward, comptroller, three secretaries, chaplain, butler and housekeeper, and not forgetting the team of six cooks and man-cooks who contrived to lade the dinner table with a cornucopia of delights. There were, it seemed, certain traditions that must be followed in order to ensure the dignity and honour of the ducal family.

All the comfort of the relaxed meeting of intellectuals, where scarcely a word of English was spoken for the entire month, was lost in the increased size of the company. Several of the participants now had wives with them, and the wives brought sisters and cousins and even their mothers, occasionally, and now the duchess had invited her cousins and several other young ladies. Having made a successful and happy match herself, she was determined to bestow the same happiness on everyone else within her orbit, whether they wished for it or not.

Into this tiresome setting, the Franklyns arrived with all the charm and familiarity of home. When Bertram and his fellows streamed out of their meeting and entered the faded grandeur of the State Saloon, almost the first sight he saw was Bea's smiling face across the room, her black curls bouncing merrily as she waved to him.

Seeing that Lady Esther and Mr Franklyn were absorbed into the crowd around the duchess, he weaved his way across the room and executed a more than usually jaunty bow.

"Miss Franklyn, what a pleasure to see you here, and precisely at the appointed hour. May I take it then that you had an untroubled journey?"

"Oh yes, not the least trouble in the world. Is this not an amazing house? We got lost just coming down from our rooms, for although the building appears to be symmetrically arranged around the courtyard, there are so many rooms and oddly shaped passageways that we could not work it out at all. First of all we came down the same stairs we had gone up to find our rooms, but then we could not recognise anything and we ended up in a long open passage with columns, but quite in a different part of the building, and Papa would not go back or ask the footman we passed at the foot of the stairs, and Mama got very cross with him. In the end, she made us walk across the courtyard to the Great Hall and there was a footman by the front door, so she asked him how to find the saloon. But it was so amusing! Fancy being in a house large enough to get lost in!"

"It is confusing, that is true," Bertram said, and he could not help smiling at her laughing face. "The fact is, the house may look symmetrical, but it is not at all. Should you like to know how it works? If you understand it, you will be able to lead your mama and papa about without anybody getting cross."

Her face lit up with excitement. "Ooh, yes please! I should like that very much."

Offering her his arm, he led her through the saloon, ignoring the speculative glances sent their way, and out into the eastern stairwell.

"Here is the first irregularity," he said. "There are staircases on both the side wings, but this one is on the inside, overlooking the courtyard, and the western stair is on the outside, overlooking the stable yard. Come into the courtyard, for the whole building is easy to understand from there. You see those two towers, one on each corner of the southern wing? Fix those in your mind and you cannot go wrong. With the towers at your back, you are facing the Great Hall. On your right is the formal wing with the state apartments, facing the gardens, such as they are, and on your left, the family wing, facing the stables. Behind you is—"

"The columns!"

"Exactly. It is called the colonnade. Let us go in, and I can show you the chapel, which is where we hold our meetings."

"In the chapel?" she cried, sounding shocked. "Is that not... disrespectful? To talk about the pagan Romans in a church?"

"Possibly, but when we first came here, it was the only room large enough that was still usable. Most of the state rooms had been filled with anything not wanted elsewhere — furniture, pictures, vases, boxes and boxes full of old clothes, no fewer than three rocking horses, statues, books—"

"Statues? My goodness!"

"Oh, you cannot imagine! But the chapel had remained empty. Here we are." He threw open the door and ushered her in, watching her face as the excitement faded. "Disappointing, do you not agree?"

She nodded. "No altar, no pews, not even a single cross, and even the candles are plain."

He watched her taking in the simple wooden lectern, the rows of seats and the worn rugs on the floor. Was she shivering? The room was never very warm, even at this time of year.

"Come and see the gallery," he said, drawing her shawl a little higher over her shoulders.

He took her up the spiral stair inside the tower, letting her go ahead of him, so that she came out into the long gallery first. With windows on both sides, it was flooded with light, bathing the paintings, massive lacquered urns and busts of bewigged ancestors in a golden glow. Bea's mouth made an 'O' of surprise.

"A long gallery! How wonderful!"

"I agree entirely. Look at this fine fellow — is that not a splendid coat he wears? All that gold braid!"

"Oh but his hat! So dreadful — did men truly wear such appalling creations? Oh, I like this one. He has such a mischievous smile."

They walked about for a while, admiring the paintings, but then Bertram ushered her to a window seat. "While I have you alone, we should talk about strategy."

"Strategy, Bertram?"

"For finding you a titled husband, Bea. I have made you a list... here." He pushed a paper into her hand.

"How kind you are, Bertram," she said, unfolding it. "Just the three... oh, the Marquess of Embleton? Tell me about him."

"Ah, straight for the biggest prize, I see," he said, smiling at her. "Thirty years old, heir to the Duke of Bridgeworth but he has four... or is it five... younger brothers, at least two of them married, so nobody much minds whether he marries or not. I will be honest with you, Bea, I cannot claim to know him very well. He has always been around my crowd, but he is so quiet and unassuming that one tends to forget about him. I have no idea what sort of woman would catch his eye, but no one could be displeased with you, so you may be lucky."

"Oh! What a pretty compliment, Bertram, and entirely untrue, since you yourself are displeased with me."

"Not in the least, I assure you. If I were looking to marry, I should be very tempted by you, but at present I prefer my books."

"You could have books *and* a wife," she said, looking up at him in wide-eyed mock innocence. "There is no law against it, I believe."

"Now, now, you promised I would be off the hook if I got you this invitation, so do not tease me, Bea. The second name on the list is Viscount Brockscombe, and that is a real title, not a courtesy one. He is seven and twenty, a jolly sort. He always has some jape or other under way, so your liveliness might be the very thing to catch his eye. His mother is pestering him to set up his nursery, too, so your timing is perfect."

"What about the last one... Lord Thomas Medhurst?"

"The same age as I am, five and twenty, brother to the Duke of Wedhampton and very keen to marry, given the excessive number of deaths in the family over the last few years. He has been my very good friend since we met on our first day at Eton, and he is the best of good fellows, but I will tell you at once that he is very swayed by a woman's face. Show him a line of potential partners at a ball and he will invariably move directly towards the most beautiful."

"Oh." Her face fell. "I shall stand no chance, then. I might pass for tolerable in a darkened room."

"Nonsense!" he said briskly. "You are very well looking, and you must not let anyone tell you otherwise. It is true that you have not that perfection of feature that some women can boast, but that merely makes you more interesting. Beautiful women are the dullest creatures on earth."

Her expression lightened, with a hint of a smile. "Are they truly dull? I had never noticed."

"It is easy to be distracted by beauty, but believe me, most of them have not a sensible thought in their pretty heads," he said.

"And I am more interesting, am I?" she said, shaking her head, so that her black curls tossed about. "You are very full of compliments today, Bertram. If I did not know you better, I might think you were flirting with me."

"I would not know how," he said with perfect truth.

"Quite so. I cannot thank you enough for your help, and if I succeed in finding a husband here, I shall name my first child after you in gratitude."

"Let us hope your first-born is a boy, then," he said, and that set her giggling so hard that any sensible conversation was at an end, and he judged it best to take her back to the saloon.

***

Bea had dressed for the evening in the gown and hair ornaments selected by her stepmother, and was reading an ancient book of philosophy she had found in a cupboard in her bedroom, when her mama entered the room.

"Good, you are ready in excellent time, Beatrice. Gentlemen so like punctuality."

"It would be discourteous to our hosts to be late," Bea said, rising to make her curtsy.

"That too," Lady Esther said calmly. "You look very presentable this evening, quite a credit to your father and me. I must say, my dear, everything is coming along very well. I noticed how Mr Bertram Atherton singled you out the moment he entered the saloon, and lost no time in taking you away. Where did you go to?"

"He wished to show me around the house, Mama, but we only went to the chapel, the colonnade and the long gallery. Was that wrong? Should I have refused? Or taken a chaperon?"

"In this case, it is perfectly acceptable... you were never anywhere other than public places, and you are as good as engaged."

"Mama, I do not think—" Bea began in some alarm.

"One should never be over confident, naturally, but the signs are unmistakable."

Bea did not wish to explain her arrangement to her stepmother, but neither did she wish Bertram to be bounced into an engagement. "You do not plan to... to trick him?" she said anxiously.

"Trick him? Goodness, Beatrice, you make me sound like such a scheming mama! Gentlemen sometimes need a delicate nudge to ensure they do the right thing, that is all — a little encouragement, a sign of ladylike affection."

"A kiss?" Bea said tentatively, her mind still on the duchess's words.

Lady Esther chuckled. "Certainly a chaste kiss can do the trick."

Bea had no idea what a chaste kiss was, but it sounded rather agreeable. "That would not be too forward?"

"Naturally, one does not distribute kisses to all and sundry, but with a gentleman, it is perfectly safe. No true gentleman would take advantage of a little enthusiasm from a lady, and it can be a most effective device for bringing him to the point. However, Mr Atherton seems to be proceeding along the correct path all by himself, so I believe we need not intervene. We have a whole month, after all, so we may sit back and allow matters to take their course. As for being alone with him now and then, in a private party of this nature and overseen by a duke and duchess, there is not the least harm in it. Walking in the long gallery, for instance, or in the gardens in daylight hours, can occasion not the smallest comment. Mr Atherton is a gentleman to the core, and would never do anything to put a lady to the bl ush."

"And the others here... they are gentlemen also, are they not?"

"Certainly, my dear. Even those who are not nobility are gentlemen, or the duke and duchess would not have invited them. Shall we see if Mr Franklyn is ready to go down yet?"

With her list safely tucked into her reticule, Bea meekly followed her parents down to the saloon, where the company was gathering for the evening. She did not need her stepmother's hissed warning of *'Marshfields rules!'* as they entered to remind her to be on her best behaviour. Anywhere the nobility congregated in large numbers invoked Marshfields rules in Lady Esther's eyes. This included the ballrooms and saloons of London, but principally Marshfields itself, where her very haughty relations gathered to squabble gently and reassure themselves of their unimpeachable heredity. Bea always felt very small and provincially insignificant there, where only breeding mattered and no fortune, however large, could compensate for the lack of a title.

Landerby Manor, she devoutly hoped, would be different, not least because the presiding duke and duchess were not crusty relics of a bygone age. The duchess could not be less intimidating, and her husband was cut from the same cloth, a quietly-spoken man who beamed genially at Bea, talking to her at some length about her Newcastle home and what she missed about it. It was a difficult question to answer, since the truth, that she missed almost everything, was hardly flattering to her father and stepmother. But she could not go back to those simpler times, and if she had to move in the much grander society of her stepmother, she would play the game and obey the rules until her marriage set her free.

As the saloon filled with guests, all arrayed in their most splendid evening finery in compliment to the duke and duchess, Bea soon discovered she had several rivals. She counted eight other young ladies, most of them younger than her, and two uncommonly pretty. That was disheartening. There was one advantage of so many young ladies, however, and that was that she easily discovered the most eligible gentleman in the room.

"Who is that man over there?" she whispered to the duke, when his questions about Newcastle had finally trickled to a halt. "The one almost hidden by the bevy of eager young ladies."

The duke chuckled. "That is Embleton, poor fellow. I thank God that I was already married before it seemed likely I would inherit, or I should have been besieged, too."

"The Marquess of Embleton," Bea said musingly. "Heir to a dukedom."

"Quite so, but if you fancy becoming a duchess, Miss Franklyn, I had better warn you that Embleton is not much in the petticoat line."

"He looks quite bewildered by the attention," Bea said.

"One would imagine him to be used to it by now, for he has been the heir since birth. Unlike me, he has never had a period of blessed anonymity. Yet somehow it always takes him by surprise when ladies take an interest in him. They are wasting their time, sadly, and would be better advised to turn their attention elsewhere. Now there is one who is definitely a man with an eye for the ladies — over there, talking to my wife, the very handsome fellow with the diamond pin in his cravat."

He was indeed very handsome, with a mane of golden hair, a patrician brow and a hint of permanent amusement about his lips. Bea liked him at once. Was he perhaps one of those on her list?

"I have not yet been introduced to him," she said. "Who is he?"

"That is Grayling... Lord Grayling, that is."

A lord! But not on Bertram's list, which was curious.

"Is he married?"

The duke laughed, and turned to her with eyebrows raised. "Oho, is that a certain interest I detect? No, he is not married. Should you like to meet him?"

"I shall be very happy to make the acquaintance of all your guests," Bea said demurely, but she could not help blushing a little. Lord Grayling was indeed very handsome, the sort of splendid figure of a man that any girl would dream of in a husband.

The duke laughed again, and led her across the room. "Grayling, here is someone who wishes to meet you. Miss Franklyn, may I present to you Lord Grayling of Melton Mowbray. Grayling, Miss Franklyn is from Newcastle. Excuse me... I must... um..."

He bowed, tucked the duchess's arm in his and led her away, leaving Bea gazing in some awe at Lord Grayling. If she had been asked to describe her ideal specimen of manhood, the example before her would have come very close. He was imposingly tall, with broad shoulders that strained his coat to such an extent that she wondered how his valet had ever wrestled him into it. His legs were shapely too, and he dressed in a manner which was fashionable and at the same time not in the least ostentatious.

He executed an elegant bow. "Newcastle, eh? A fine city, I believe, although I have never been there. For what is it famous?" His tone was languid, not very interested in Newcastle or, very likely, Bea herself.

"Coal, sir. A vast deal of coal goes out from Newcastle to London and elsewhere. But I no longer live in Newcastle. My father's estate is in the North Riding, which is famous for sheep, wool and extensive moorland. But tell me of Melton Mowbray. I have never heard of it, but I am sure it is famous for something."

His eyes turned fully on her, a little surprised at so robust a response. "I imagine so, but whatever it is, I cannot tell you. My estate is five miles outside Melton, and I rarely go there."

"For shame, sir! Are the inhabitants to be deprived of the sight of one of their most distinguished residents? What dreadful crime have they committed to inflict this dire punishment on their heads?"

His lips twitched. "I am sure they are as upright as the residents of any other English town, Miss Franklyn, but, as towns go, it is rather small and not well endowed with such facilities as banks and attorneys and shops. I tend to go to Leicester instead, and since I feel sure you are about to ask, it is famous for the manufacture of stockings."

"Ah, stockings! How useful. It must be a fascinating place if it is wholly given over to the manufacture of stockings. I adore stockings and should very much like to visit a town filled with them."

He chuckled. "I do believe there are one or two other enterprises carried on there, apart from the manufacture of stockings. But if we may speak of the county as a whole, then for those of my own class, it is not stockings but hunting which is the principal attraction. Leicestershire boasts the finest hunting country in England."

"And you are so fortunate as to live there. How glad your friends must be!"

He laughed out loud at that. "Yes, indeed, I am excessively popular during the hunting season. How is it that you have never been in town, Miss Franklyn? I am certain I should have remembered you if we had ever met."

"You are mistaken, sir, in supposing me a stranger to the Metropolis, but you are quite right — we have never met. I too am confident I should have remembered such an event."

She had his full attention by this time. "I imagine that you have been constrained to attend only such wholesome places as Almack's. Very dull stuff, Almack's."

"So it is, but I was also so fortunate as to attend the occasional card party with octogenarians, to drive through Hyde Park in a barouche and to visit the theatre, although only when works were performed of a nature suitable for demure maidens. I have been gay almost to dissipation, I do assure you."

He laughed again, his eyes twinkling in an alarmingly attractive way. "What a pity I was not in charge of devising your entertainment, Miss Franklyn. I should have offered you a far more interesting time of it."

"What would you suggest for my entertainment, Lord Grayling?"

"Have you ever attended a masquerade ball? They are the most astonishing fun, and one may be quite anonymous. And then there are places where cards are played more excitingly than with your octogenarians."

"Ooh, that sounds most amusing! But are such places not... dangerous? I have heard that one may lose a fortune in the turn of a card or the throw of a die."

"But that is what makes them so exciting," he said, leaning close to whisper in her ear. "You would be quite safe with me, Miss Franklyn."

Bea could feel his breath tickling her neck. She was conscious of a warmth that had nothing to do with the lingering heat of a summer afternoon or the crowded room. His closeness made her feel almost dizzy. Only an insistent tapping on her hand drew her out of her strange absorption in h im.

"*Miss Franklyn!*"

"Bertram?" she said, turning to him in bewilderment. "Whatever is it?"

"*If* Lord Grayling will excuse me for taking you away, there is someone I should like you to meet." His tone was curt, as if he had been trying to attract her attention for some time.

"Pray do not let me monopolise you, Miss Franklyn," Lord Grayling said, with another elegant bow. "We shall have plenty of other opportunities to get to know each other better."

"I look forward to it very much, Lord Grayling," she said, curtsying. Rather disgruntled, she allowed Bertram to tow her away.

10: Dinner At Landerby

"What are you doing?" Bertram hissed, as they weaved through the crowds filling the saloon. "He is not on the list!"

"He is a lord and unmarried," Bea hissed back.

"But not on the list." He drew her aside into a quieter corner of the room. "Trust me, Lord Grayling is not looking for a wife."

"Mama says that no man ever is, right up to the point he proposes. Besides, the duke said he has an eye for the ladies, so that means—"

"Bea, if we are to succeed in our objective, you must listen to my advice. Grayling is not hanging out for a wife, and if you persist in flirting with him so outrageously—"

"I was not flirting with him!"

"Well... allowing him to flirt with you, then, you will not only be wasting your time, you will put off the ones who *are* on the list. No man likes to know that he is a woman's second choice. Come and meet Medhurst and Brockscombe, and get to know them before you start homing in on a particular target. But no flirting, mind — just be yourself."

Before they reached them, however, a slender man with dark hair jumped in front of them. "Atherton! Is this the neighbour you told us about? Won't you introduce me?" His accent was marked, but Bea could not quite place it — somewhere in the south of England was all she could say for certain.

"Of course," Bertram said, but the tone was clipped. "Miss Franklyn, allow me to present *Mr* Herbert Fielding, the newly installed parson of... where is it?"

"Higher Brinford in Brinshire... somewhere between Staffordshire and Shropshire, and I'm not installed yet. The wheels turn very slowly in ecclesiastical matters. How do you do, Miss Franklyn. Delighted to make your acquaintance, quite delighted. I hope you're pleased with Landerby Manor?"

Before Bea could answer, Bertram cut in impatiently, "Yes, yes, but I have promised to introduce Medhurst and Brockscombe to Miss Franklyn, and you are holding us up, Fielding."

"We shall have plenty of opportunities to talk, Mr Fielding," Bea said kindly, even as Bertram tugged at her arm, and muttered, "Come *along!*"

Lord Thomas Medhurst was a pleasantly-featured man who smiled benignly at her but his eyes often slid past her to gaze about the room. Viscount Brockscombe was far more attentive, a tall, well-built man with a jolly face and booming voice, who paid her florid compliments while busily exercising his wit at the expense of others in the room, then laughing at his own humour. Since Mr Fielding had followed them, and joined in with his own more subtle style of wit, Bea was kept well entertained until they were summoned to dinner.

This was held in the echoing Great Hall, the stone floor and great height of the ceiling making it feel cool after the crowded and overheated saloon. Bea found herself with Lord Thomas on one side of her and Lord Brockscombe on the other, which she suspected was exactly as Bertram had intended. He was directly opposite her, with one of the duchess's plain cousins on either side of him. Mr Fielding was on that side, too, waving cheerfully at her as he took his place. The marquess, still looking bewildered as if he was not sure quite what he was doing there, was seated beside the duchess, with one of the very pretty girls on his other side, smiling winsomely at him and throwing triumphant glances at some of the other girls less fortunately situated. Her eye fell on Bea, hesitated momentarily, then passed on, uninterested.

The meal passed slowly. Lord Thomas spent most of it ogling the very pretty girl beside the marquess, who tossed her blonde curls and laughed every time the poor fellow opened his mouth. Viscount Brockscombe was better company, for he teased Bea unmercifully with every tired jest about Yorkshire that he could think of, but at least he was attentive, and very willing to fetch her this and that dish to try. When she could divert his mind into other channels, he was helpful in identifying the other guests.

"Who is the blonde girl beside the marquess?" she asked him in a low voice.

"That is Grayling's sister, the Honourable Miss Grayling. Did you not meet her in town this spring? She has just made her come out."

"I never saw her, that I can remember. We move in different circles."

"Yes, that would be it. She never got vouchers for Almack's, and Grayling was outraged by that, positively snarling about the Patronesses, but one has to behave to be admitted there. Since Grayling has been reviling them all over town for years for excluding his older sister, it was not very likely that they would take the younger to their bosoms, is it? She failed to take, too, which was another crime to set at their door, apparently."

"I did not take either," Bea said uncomfortably. "Not everyone does."

"Oh, indeed. Or wants to, I dare say," Lord Brockscombe said easily, not at all discomfited. "But Grayling had been touting it that she was bound to make a great match the instant she set foot in town, so it was a blow to his pride that she did not."

"She is so pretty," Bea sighed. "I cannot imagine why she did not have suitors three deep around her."

The viscount laughed, and raised an eyebrow. "You think men only look for beauty in a wife, do you? Hmm." He glanced at his friend, whose eyes were still fixed on Miss Grayling. "Well, some do, perhaps, but most of us are more sensible, and look for other qualities — a large fortune, for instance. A hundred thousand pounds trumps a pretty face any day of the week."

He laughed at his joke, or at least Bea hoped it was a joke. And yet, was that any different from her own attitude? She was attempting to trade her forty thousand pounds for a title, and as high a rank as possible, so she could hardly blame a man who bore a title for looking for a wealthy wife. That was the way of the world, but it left an unpleasant taste in the mouth, nevertheless. For the first time, she wondered at her own ruthlessness. Was it really so important to be Lady Something? Would it not be just as wonderful to be Mrs Something, so long as he was a gentleman? It was the man attached to the name that mattered, surely? Was it not?

And yet, if it were all about character, how was she to judge? It was all so difficult!

***

The evening at Landerby Manor drifted gradually to an end. The ladies retired soon after midnight, and although some of the men were still playing cards and seemed to be settling in for the night, Bertram and his friends took the opportunity to retreat to their bedchamber. In the early days of their gatherings, when only the dozen or so enthusiasts had attended, Landerby Manor had been so neglected that they had been obliged to squeeze into the few weatherproof rooms. The chapel had served as study, dining room and saloon, and three large bedrooms in the east wing acted as dormitories. The habit had stuck, and even though many more rooms had been made habitable, Bertram, Medhurst, Brockscombe and Fielding still shared a room, comfortably provided with ancient and patched old chairs and a tray of decanters. With brandy poured, they settled down to discuss the evening.

"So tell us more about Miss Franklyn," Fielding said eagerly. "Her father is here, I noticed."

"And her stepmother, Lady Esther," Bertram said. "Daughter of the Duke of Camberley. What do you want to know about Miss Franklyn?"

"Why isn't she married?" Fielding said, which made the others laugh.

"She is not very pretty," Medhurst said, pulling a face. "Almost as bad as that fish-faced heiress... what was her name?"

"Miss Hutchison, and you're far too fastidious," Fielding said. "Miss Franklyn has far more interesting qualities — liveliness, for instance. Atherton, did you get a single word out of those two inanimate objects sitting beside you at dinner?"

"The Miss Pikesleys are not strong conversationalists, it is true," Bertram said with a shrug. "They are restful dinner companions, however."

"Who wants restfulness when one could have Miss Franklyn?" Fielding said. "Give me a girl with a bit of life in her any day, and she has such a sweet smile. Don't you agree, Atherton?"

"I have never thought about it before, but… yes, she does," Bertram said, rather surprised by the discovery.

"So why is she not married?"

"She was betrothed to my cousin Walter for some time, but that fell through so—"

"Wait — which is Walter? The middle one?"

"No, the eldest. That fell through, as I say, and so Miss Franklyn was at rather a loose end and I invited her here to make some new acquaintances."

"Why did it fall through?"

"Does it matter?" Bertram said testily. "Circumstances change, that is all."

"I believe it does matter," Fielding said, sipping his brandy thoughtfully. "I should not want to waste my time pursuing her if she is a flighty minx who will lead me on and then drop me without notice, but I believe she would suit me very well, and now that I have a living and six hundred a year—"

"My good friend, I am very sorry to disillusion you, but Miss Franklyn has forty thousand pounds and is not destined for a country parsonage, I assure you."

Fielding's face fell. "Ah, what a pity. Still, I may enjoy that lovely smile for the next month, even if not thereafter. But she would do for one of you fellows, with a fortune like that. Medhurst, as a younger son, such a sum would be very useful."

"It certainly would."

"Does that make her a little prettier?" Fielding said mischievously.

Medhurst had the grace to look a little ashamed. "I can certainly allow her to have a sweet smile under such circumstances. Oh, to have a fortune of my own, and be able to marry where I please!"

"Which would be Miss Grayling, no doubt," Bertram said. "What is her portion?"

"Five thousand!" Medhurst said in despairing tones. "A mere trifle, and not enough for me, even if she could take her eyes off Embleton for long enough to notice me."

"Ah, the trials of a young man contemplating matrimony," Bertram said lightly. "Take my advice and steer clear of the wedded state. It is far better for one's peace of mind."

"It is all very well for you, Atherton," Medhurst said. "You need not whistle for funds, and you have never been in the petticoat line, so you remain above the fray. But for those of us who value the opposite sex and would like nothing better than to share our lives with one, it is far too difficult to find one who has the appropriate combination of rank, fortune and appearance."

"You make such heavy weather of it," Brockscombe said. "It is obvious how we should proceed. Medhurst, you must marry Miss Hutchison and her hundred thousand pounds, a sum which will easily compensate for any lack of beauty, and Fielding may marry Miss Grayling, whose modest portion is well suited to a parson's wife."

"And what about you?" Fielding said.

"Why, I am going to marry Miss Franklyn, of course," Brockscombe said.

He grinned at them, and Fielding and Medhurst railed at his choices with great fluency until the brandy decanter ran dry. Only Bertram was silent, unaccountably unsettled by all this discussion of Bea. This was what he had wanted, after all, for her to marry one of his friends. So why did he now feel so uneasy about it?

***

Bea woke early, restless and discontented. Even the weather was downcast that morning, for rain fell steadily, blurring the panes so that the view from the windows was reduced to muted shades of brown and green, with no distinguishing features. She paced about her room until Harper came to dress her, and then went down to breakfast with her parents.

Her stepmother was deep in conversation with the duchess for the whole meal. The gentlemen rose to leave one by one, her father amongst them, and other ladies came and went, but the two remained side by side, their voices a low murmur. From what Bea could hear, it was all domestic matters — sheets and coals and the dinner, and something about musicians. That was promising! Perhaps there would be dancing.

"Mama, shall I—?"

"Oh!" Her stepmother looked up, startled. "Are you still here, Beatrice? I shall be occupied with her grace for some time yet. You can find something with which to occupy yourself, I am sure. Your tapestry, perhaps."

"Might I take some exercise in the Long Gallery, Mama?"

"An excellent idea, but do not overtire yourself. The other ladies will be in the saloon when you have finished."

Eagerly she rose, and, knowing now how to find her way about, made her way to the gallery. It was rather a beautiful room, she decided, divided into three by sets of elegant pillars and with a prettily decorated ceiling. Without the glorious afternoon sun, the room was less magical but it was easier to admire the little lacquered cabinets and Chinese vases that were dotted about. In front of the hearth was an intricately carved wooden fire screen and a dusty harp stood forlornly in a corner.

She had made four circuits and was about to begin a fifth when a burst of male laughter drew her notice. Where had that come from? The eastern end of the gallery, she thought. With hasty steps, she made her way there but all was quiet again… no, she could dimly discern a voice, just one this time. But another burst of laughter told the story — the noise emanated from behind the door at the furthest end of the gallery.

Creeping nearer, she tentatively turned the knob. It squeaked violently, but another burst of noise concealed it. She pushed, it opened, and immediately the noise was all around her. Or rather, *below* her, for she was in a little gallery above the chapel. Tiptoeing further in, she could look down on the rows of chairs and the tops of the men's heads. They were facing forwards, towards where the altar should be, where Mr Fielding was declaiming with great spirit — in Latin. Now and then, someone from the audience would make a remark, also in Latin, and the crowd would laugh or jeer or murmur approving noises. And sometimes Mr Fielding would say something which brought on the laughter.

And oh, what fun it looked! How she longed to know what they were saying, and why it was funny or sometimes not funny at all. Occasionally she caught a familiar word — *'Caesar'* was mentioned several times, and she knew all about him! Or rather, them, for were there not several Caesars? And quite a few words sounded like they had come from one of her Italian songs. Not that she knew any Italian, for Mama had made her learn the songs by rote, but she recognised the words, even if she had no idea what they meant.

There were several dusty chairs in the little gallery, so she cleaned one with her handkerchief and sat down to listen, mesmerised, as the ancient words rolled about in the air. Very foreign to her ears, but some of the gentlemen put a lilt to them that reminded her of the Italian singers she had heard perform in London or, once, at Marshfields. The signora had stayed for several days, performing each evening but eating with the family, and her accent, even when she spoke English, had had just that cadence. No, that was not quite right. Some of the words sounded vaguely familiar, but the rhythm was different. It was intriguing! How she wished she understood it.

One voice rose above the others, authoritative and commanding, so that the room fell silent. Bertram! He started to speak... no, to *recite,* for it was clearly poetry of some sort, even she could tell that from the rhythm and tone. But oh, such beautiful poetry! The words rose from his lips and filled the air with a kind of music, weaving itself around the pillars that fringed the chapel and over the heads of his silent audience, rising to enfold Bea in its majesty. Such power in his voice! Such glorious balladry that held her transfixed and enchanted.

Eventually the recitation came to an end, and the audience erupted in cheers and foot-stamping, and many cries of appreciation. Amongst the rattle of words, she caught a familiar one — *'Horatius'*. Horace! The very man whose writings she had been reading, although not like this... nothing like this! The translation, however elegantly worded, could surely not compete with the unearthly beauty of the Latin.

The gentlemen settled down, and Mr Fielding began to speak again, although now he was reading from papers, and it sounded dull by comparison with Bertram's melodious cadences. The audience was quieter, listening attentively, she supposed, for every now and then there was a low murmur of approval, but nothing more.

She began to lose interest, and after a while, since nothing more exciting offered in the chapel, she crept away and set off to explore the rest of the house.

11: Rumour And Supposition

Bertram was enjoying himself hugely. For several hours each day, he was immersed in the world of several thousand years ago, speaking and thinking and even dreaming in Latin, his head filled with the vivid imagery of the Roman poets. When he was forced back into the modern world by the presence of the ladies, he no longer resented the intrusion, as he had in previous years, for he had a serious project to occupy him, that of finding a titled husband for Bea.

By the middle of each afternoon, when the gentlemen had wearied of Cicero, Tacitus and Ovid, and even Fielding's obsession with the Caesars had receded marginally, they joined the ladies in the saloon, followed by gentle rides about the estate or walks in the overgrown garden on fine days, or parlour games and general conversation otherwise. Bertram generally sought out Bea and his friends, and watched as she exerted her charms on them. Not that she flirted — Bea was not that kind of girl. But she was lively and vibrant and *fun.* She had them all laughing, and she never flagged, her high spirits carrying them through dinner and then cards afterwards, until Lady Esther came to take her away.

"Time for us to retire, Beatrice," she would say.

Then Bea would look up, startled. "So soon? But I am enjoying myself so much."

Bertram could see his friends melt under such delightful treatment. Brockscombe had been willing to be beguiled from the start, but even Medhurst's eyes drifted less often towards the beautiful Miss Grayling. As for Fielding, he was already more than half way to being in love with her. And amusingly, Lady Esther clearly still supposed that Bea was chasing Bertram, for she smiled benignly on him whenever he was with Bea.

Bertram himself was not at first a target for any of the young ladies. He said nothing of the changed circumstances of his family, which might see him inherit an earldom one day, so at first he remained merely the heir to a modest estate. With so many titles and scions of wealthy families at Landerby Manor, and one who would be a duke in the fullness of time, a man worth no more than three thousand pounds a year was of little interest.

After a few days, however, he became aware of a change in their manner towards him. None of them were as open as Bea about their intentions, for they were as subtle and scheming as snakes, and their behaviour towards him did not visibly alter. Yet somehow they contrived to draw him into their toils. Miss Hutchison loitered near him as dinner was announced so that he would be obliged to escort her in. Miss Grayling invited him to make up a four for whist, and since she already had two other players organised, she effectively excluded Bea. Amusingly, Lady Esther sank that promising scheme by requesting the duchess, one of Miss Grayling's four, to join her own table. The duchess, no doubt entirely in Lady Esther's confidence regarding her hopes for Bertram, rose at once and called upon Bea to take her place.

It was Miss Hutchison who asked Bertram directly, wriggling to insert her bony body between him and Medhurst as they walked in the garden one afternoon. "I have heard a strange rumour about your uncle, Lord Rennington, Mr Atherton. I am sure it cannot be true..."

She paused, perhaps hoping he would intervene to rescue her from the unladylike act of repeating gossip, but he merely raised an enquiring eyebrow.

With an arch look, she went on, "No, it cannot be."

She tittered, in an irritating way that made him want to slap her. Why were so many women incapable of talking sensibly, saying what they meant without prevarication, and by all the gods, not giggling? If only they were all so straightforward as Bea!

"But then it came from my aunt," she persevered, "whose neighbour is a very great friend of Lady Rennington, so it must have *some* truth in it, would you not agree?"

"Since you have not yet told me what it is, I can hardly comment," he said.

"Why, that the earl's marriage is invalid and all the children are disinherited."

"Ah, that rumour."

"So... it is not true? Is that what you are saying?"

"I have not said anything of the sort."

"Then it is true? You are confirming it?"

"I have not said that, either. I merely said, *'That rumour'*. I am confirming that I have heard the rumour, that is all."

An ugly scowl crossed her face, and she stamped her foot. "Really, Mr Atherton! You play with words to belittle me."

"No, only to encourage you not to listen to gossip, Miss Hutchison. There is no profit in it, I assure you."

With a huff of annoyance, she swirled about and stamped away to find more promising ground for her attentions.

Bertram and Medhurst walked on in silence for some minutes, their feet marching in step on the gravel path. Ahead of them, Bea's clear voice drifted back to them, along with the lower rumbles of Brockscombe and the excitable tenor of Fielding, but the height of the untrimmed shrubs hid them from view. The gardeners had made a start on cleaning up the paths for the visitors, but had not yet tackled the wilderness beyond.

"If Birtwell and the younger boys were disinherited," Medhurst mused, "that would make your father the heir. Title, castle and vast income included. And you after him."

Bertram said nothing.

"It does explain, of course, the sudden interest. Miss H has it in mind to trade her fortune — a hundred thousand, is it not? — for an earldom."

"There is no guarantee it will ever come to me," Bertram said.

"Oh, but—?" Medhurst stopped, working it out. "How old is your uncle?"

"Five and fifty."

"Oh." He laughed suddenly. "Perhaps you should tell Miss H that. And Miss G, as well, for she has been hovering around you, too, of late. Have you any idea how annoying that is, Atherton?" He laughed again, and shook his head. "Here I am, quite prepared to be swept off my feet by the lovely Miss Grayling — Sarah," he added with a sigh. "But will she so much as look at me? She will not. She prefers to be a duchess, seemingly. Or failing that, since Embleton is clearly a hopeless case, a countess would do. You, with your possible great elevation, could take your pick — the beauty or the fortune. Both of them are eating out of your hand at the moment. And yet, they might as well be invisible, for all the interest you have in either of them. I truly think the only way either of them would attract your attention would be to speak to you in Latin. You are a hopeless case, Atherton, even worse than Embleton, and I cannot imagine why I remain on friendly terms with you."

"Because I correct your deponent verbs, that is why."

"Ah! Very true. And subjunctives, too. Lord, that passage from Cicero! I thought I would never get it straight. Very well, you remain the very best of good fellows, for now, but if you marry Miss Grayling, then all amity between us is at an end, and you become my mortal enemy unto death."

"Not Miss Hutchison?"

He pulled a face, and whispered in Bertram's ear, "You may have her and her hundred thousand pounds with my goodwill. Encroaching little baggage."

And Bertram whispered back, "I do not want her."

"Even if she speaks to you in Latin, in Alcaic metre?"

"Not even then... although... that would be interesting, for a while. It might get a little wearing at the breakfast table, however."

For the rest of the walk, they amused themselves by inventing verses suitable for such an occasion, and wondering what the Roman equivalent for Bath buns might be.

***

Bea could not remember so pleasurable a visit, or at least, not since Papa had married Mama. For the first time in years, she was not under the constant supervision of her stepmother, for Lady Esther had a new interest, one of far more importance than the marriage of her stepdaughter — she had a duchess to guide in her new rôle. The Duchess of Wedhampton was gratifyingly eager for Lady Esther's advice, for as the daughter of a duke and raised in a ducal family since birth, naturally Lady Esther knew precisely how a duchess should behave at all times, and how to manage a great house. From breakfast until they retired at night, the two ladies were almost constantly together, and Bea was left free to pursue her own interests. So long as she appeared to be continuing her pursuit of Bertram, her stepmother left her in peace.

It was gloriously freeing. She could wander at will around the house or gardens, with no need to sit decorously with a hated piece of embroidery in her lap. The formal gardens were like a wild kind of maze, with long-neglected shrubs towering over the paths. Within five minutes of leaving the house, one could be entirely out of sight, and Bea delighted in finding stone benches tucked away in odd corners where she could sit and contemplate her progress.

Or lack of progress, it might be said. Bertram very kindly took pains to ensure that she spent a great deal of time with his friends, but no matter how many games of whist she played with them, she could not feel she knew them well. Not well enough, at any event, to make a decision about marrying one of them. How difficult it was!

When she watched the Latin speeches, occasionally the decorous atmosphere dissolved into something more lively — calls from the audience, cheers and jeers, bursts of laughter, and a kind of verbal sparring between the speaker and another, rather like the cut and thrust of a fencing match.

Even though she could not understand the Latin nor recognise most of the speakers from her high perch, she could detect the real emotion behind the words. Seeing the raw and open way the gentlemen behaved in such situations, and comparing it to the painfully restrained and polite way they behaved when amongst ladies was both a revelation and a frustration.

How could she ever come to understand the characters of the three names on her list when they showed her only bland civility? She wanted to see the real men behind the guarded appearance they presented in her company. They could be themselves with other men, so why not with her?

Only one man in the whole company was not bland, and that was Lord Grayling. Despite Bertram's warning that he was not looking for a wife, he seemed very drawn to the ladies, bestowing his attentions on all the unmarried ones in turn. Nor was it merely her imagination that suggested he was more drawn to Bea than to any of the others. After dinner, when the gentlemen returned to the saloon, he was always one of the first, would pass a few words with one or two of the others, but would then make his way steadily towards Bea and settle beside her until the card tables came out. At that point he would disengage, for he always played in the same four, but Bea could not mistake his interest in her.

She found him much easier company than the men on Bertram's list. He teased her gently, as a friend would, and laughed when she paid him back in his own coin. She felt she knew him well, and since he was a baron, she had no doubt at all that she would accept him in a heartbeat if he should offer for her. So while she allowed Bertram to steer her towards his friends, she kept Lord Grayling in her eye and in her mind, and nurtured her hopes.

There was only one of the names on Bertram's list that she had not got to know at all, and that was the Marquess of Embleton. When she had been introduced to him, he had made her an awkward bow. He had not the distinguished appearance which would befit his exalted rank, for he was small in height and slight in stature, his face pale and unmemorable. When she addressed him, he replied, "P-p-pleased to m-m-make your acquaintance, M-M-M... *Miss* F-F-Franklyn."

Oh dear. She smiled, and addressed two or three questions to him, to which he replied with the minimum of words, as might be expected for a man with such a defect in his speech. He was speedily reclaimed by Miss Grayling, who helpfully rushed in to guess each word he struggled with in a patronising manner which set Bea's teeth on edge. She wondered how the marquess bore it so patiently, but perhaps he was used to people treating him like an imbecile.

Since then, she had never had occasion to speak to him. He was a distant figure glimpsed at dinner or in the saloon, and although she thought he attended the Latin meetings, she never saw him speak. But one day, as she explored a new corner of the garden, a sudden turn in the path brought her face to face with him. He was sitting alone, deep in contemplation, on a marble bench facing a statue of a goddess or nymph of some kind. Perhaps it had once been part of a fountain, for there was a deep stone bowl surrounding it, but now the bowl was half filled with rotted leaves and weeds.

The marquess jumped up as she approached, and bowed. She curtsied, and would have walked past him at once, but the way beyond the bench was blocked by a fallen branch.

"What a peaceful spot!" she said. "I shall leave you to enjoy it in solitude."

She turned, intending to walk back the way she had come, but he said quickly, "Stay!"

"Do you want some company?" When he nodded, she went on, "I should have thought you would be glad to find yourself alone for once."

"Your c-c-company... welcome."

"How very kind of you to say so. I shall sit with you for a little while, and chatter away, because I always do. I cannot seem to help it. There is no need for you to speak unless you wish to, you know. I am quite capable of chattering for both of us." She settled herself on the bench and he sat beside her, smiling. "Of course, if you prefer me to be silent, I can try, I suppose, but I am not very good at it."

He laughed at that. "P-p-please... chatter away."

So she did, and although he said very little — in fact, she could not recall him uttering a word — he smiled a great deal and laughed occasionally, and altogether seemed not displeased. After a while, she heard distant voices. Having no wish to be found alone with him, for such a thing would cause endless speculation, she rose, curtsied, thanked him for his company and set off down the path. But whenever she saw him after that, he smiled at her and waved, even if there was no opportunity to speak.

12: A Latin Primer

One afternoon, the Latin meeting ended at an earlier time than usual. Bertram's friends planned a ride despite damp weather, but Bertram was not minded for exercise. He had received a letter from his mother with interesting news, which he was sure that Bea would want to know. He made his way to the saloon, but there was no sign of her or her stepmother. Mr Franklyn was there, however, deep in a game of chess with the duke. He looked up at Bertram with a knowing smile.

"Looking for Bea, Atherton?"

"I was, in fact. She is usually here at this time of day."

Franklyn's smile widened. "I have not seen her since breakfast, but I do know that she planned to stay indoors today. She is not a great one for getting wet."

"Ah. I shall look for her, then."

He started in the few formal rooms where guests congregated in the afternoons, but without success. His next thought was the Long Gallery, in case she was taking her exercise there. When he found it empty, he checked the little gallery above the chapel. She was not there, either, so he made his way to the bedrooms assigned to the Franklyns. He was not quite sure which room was hers, for three rooms bore the label *'Franklyn'*, but by knocking and calling at each in turn, he found a surprised maid, who confirmed that Bea was not there, but also that she had not taken any of her outdoor clothing.

She was definitely in the house, then. That narrowed the possibilities. Now it was a tedious matter of working his way through each wing in turn, calling out *'Miss Franklyn?'* at regular intervals. He was on the third floor of the west wing, the windows grimy from years of accumulated dirt, when a head appeared from a door.

"What is it? Am I wanted? Oh, Bertram, it is you! What is the matter? Is Mama looking for me? Or Papa?"

"No, nothing of that nature. I wondered where you had hidden yourself, that is all. What are you doing up here?"

She grinned at him. "It is the old schoolroom. Come and see."

It was so dusty that he could clearly see footprints on the floor. Great cobwebs hung from the ceiling and across the windows, and a hobby horse was so caked in dust that it looked black. But in the centre of the room was a table and chair which had been thoroughly cleaned, and here a book lay open, with a slate and a box of chalks beside it.

"You are working on your copybook, I see," he said. "What a good schoolroom miss you are. Your governess would be proud of— Oh!" He picked up the book in astonishment, turning it over to read the spine. *'A Schoolboy's First Latin Primer'*, read the inscription in faded gold letters. "You are learning Latin?"

"There is no need to sound *quite* so astonished," she said. "We females do have brains, too, you know."

"Of course, but... Latin?" He picked up the slate and laughed as he read from it. "'*Ubi sunt nautae.*'"

"Oh, is *that* how it is pronounced? '*Ubi sunt nautae. Nautae in taberna sunt. In tabernis non puellae sunt.*' Did I get that right?"

"*Ita vero.*"

"That means yes, does it? *Ita vero. Ita vero.* What would no be?"

"*Non ita.* Do you truly plan to learn Latin, Bea?"

"Why not? It is by far more exciting than embroidery. I have been listening to all of you chattering away in Latin for more than a week now, and some of it is lovely. Whatever it was you read out at Mr Fielding's talk last week — that was so beautiful and melodic and poetic."

"Horace, the third book, Ode number nine. '*Donec gratus eram tibi nec quisquam potior bracchia candidae cervici iuvenis dabat, Persarum vigui rege beatior.*'"

"Ohhh," she breathed. "Yes! That was it. What does it mean?"

"Let me see... I might translate it thus. '*As long as I was agreeable to you, and no one more favoured put his arms around your white neck, I was happier than the Persian monarch.*'"

"Oh. He is writing to a lady, then? It is quite pretty, although it sounds better in Latin," she said disappointedly. "You must teach me the words... although I dare say I can find the book. Horace, third book, Ode number nine. I can teach myself to recite it by rote, but I should so like to *understand* it. I thought if I learn the language, then next year I shall be able to listen to all your talks and understand what is said."

"Bea, I started learning Latin when I was six, I think, and intensively by the age of eight. It took me ten years, perhaps, to reach this level of fluency."

"Ten years... then I shall be fluent by the time I am one and thirty." He laughed out loud at her insouciance. "Oh, you think I cannot do it? Let me tell you, Bertram Atherton, that I always succeed at whatever I set my mind to, no matter how long it takes. I succeeded with Walter, did I not?"

"But you have not, and *will* not, succeed with me."

"Only because you have given me an acceptable alternative," she said smugly. "Lord Thomas Medhurst, Viscount Brockscombe or the Marquess of Embleton. Although... I am not getting on very well."

"No?" he said teasingly. "I should have said you were making excellent progress."

"But I cannot tell whether they would suit me or not," she burst out. "How can I possibly know? They are all perfectly agreeable and gentlemanlike, but I cannot tell what their characters are. I sit beside them at dinner, I play cards with them, we talk about... well, nothing at all. How may I know which of them would be faithful or not? Which might prove to be extravagant or frugal or downright penny-pinching? Or which might explode with jealousy if I so much as look at another man? With Walter, I had known him long enough to understand him. You, too, are no mystery to me. But your friends... it is an impossible task. I have a month, Bertram... a single month in which to decide the whole course of my future life, and I have no idea how to do it."

He was silent, quite unable to answer her satisfactorily. Having never looked for a wife himself, he had never had to make such calls of judgement, and had no idea how it might be done.

"The duchess said—" she went on, stopping abruptly with a quick laugh. "I dare say it is all nonsense, but it is how she chose her own husband."

"Did she go out at dawn and throw a silver sixpence down the well?" Bertram said teasingly. "Or make a wish while stirring the plum pudding? Or was it a Romany prophecy?"

She tutted at him. "No, silly! She kissed them, that was how she decided. And when she kissed the duke, she just knew... and so did he. Do you think if I kissed the three men on my list—"

"Bea, that is the most ridiculous thing I have ever heard," Bertram said. "As if you could simply kiss a man — several men! — without consequences. If you were caught, you would be obliged to marry, whether you wanted to or not."

"I should not be caught. It is not like—" She looked embarrassed. "It is not like that evening at Highwood when we went out onto the terrace... do you remember?"

"When my mother rushed out after us with a shawl for you?"

"Yes! And I was very glad of it, I assure you, for Mama had devised this cunning scheme... I was to take you out into the garden and get you to kiss me... well, it hardly mattered whether you did or not, for Mama planned to find us out there and make a fuss so that you would be obliged to offer for me, being a man of honour and so on. But I found I could not do it, in the end. I was so relieved when your mama rescued me. It was a dreadful thing to do, and I should never have countenanced the idea, not for a moment, but Mama... well, she is quite immovable sometimes, and there is no help for it but to go along with whatever devious plot she has dreamt up."

"You are not much of a plotter, are you?" he said, with an unexpected rush of affection for this odd girl, so different from anyone else he knew. "Your nature is too straightforward, too honest."

"I hope so," she said, sounding dubious. "I told Walter exactly what I was about, and the same with you. But your friends... I do not know them well enough to say, *'Delighted to meet you and by the way, I plan to marry one of you.'* That would take more brazenness than even I can summon."

He chuckled. "There is no need for brazenness. They are looking to marry already, and they are well aware of your attractions, I assure you."

"My forty thousand pounds, you mean," she said gloomily. "Do you know, Bertram, I would trade the whole of it any day for even half of Miss Grayling's beauty. Those blonde curls, and great big blue eyes — would it not be glorious to be so lovely?"

Impulsively, he took her hand, raising it to his lips and kissing it, and because in that moment he sincerely felt for her, he kissed it properly, not the almost kiss that politeness decreed. "Bea, even if you were the greatest antidote in the kingdom, and you are very far from that, believe me, you should know by now that beauty is not everything. Being open and kind and warm-hearted — these are far more important, and you are all of those."

"You are very good to say such things, but it is not true. If I were better looking, I should have had men falling over themselves to wed me, including lords. I should have been married long since, with my great house and a carriage with a crest on it. Or if I could flirt, perhaps, like Miss Hutchison — that thing she does with her eyes, looking up through her lashes. It must be very beguiling to a man, because so many of them cluster around her. No one clusters around *me*, except your friends and that is only to oblige you. I am destined to end up an old maid, like Winnie Strong."

"Stuff and nonsense, Bea. You are very well looking, and never let anyone suggest otherwise, and as for flirting, sensible men detest a flirt. You are certainly not likely to end up an old maid, like— Oh, that reminds me," Bertram said excitedly. "Mother wrote to me, and Lady Strong told her that Winnie has a suitor — a serious one, seemingly. Someone she met down in London. She was attacked by pickpockets and this man rescued her and was instantly smitten, and now they are in daily expectation of a proposal."

"*Winnie Strong?* But she must be twenty-five if she is a day."

"She is four and twenty, Bea, and her aunt was well into her middle years when she married, if you remember."

"Oh, yes, almost forty! And Mama was twenty-six when she set her cap at Papa, and I do *not* want to be still unwed at that age, Bertram. It would be utter failure. Forty thousand pounds, and I still cannot find a nobleman willing to marry me. It is humiliating, and I must not allow it to continue. You have given me this opportunity, for which I am exceedingly grateful, and I am set on making the most of it. Three men... two, I suppose, for the marquess is not an option — a future duke is bound to look amongst his fellow peers for a wife. So two possibilities, but how to choose? And I only have two more weeks. I must force the issue, I think. I shall kiss each one in turn, and that will tell me which of them I should marry."

"You cannot be serious," he said. "Think of what your stepmother would say."

"She would be all in favour of it. She wanted me to kiss you, if you recall."

"Bea, I strongly advise against it," Bertram said in alarm.

"Because we might be discovered? Pooh, I shall take good care not to be."

"No, because..."

He stopped, wondering just how much to elaborate. Bea was certainly very forward in her behaviour, but she was still a total innocent and he did not wish to spoil that innocence by warning her of rakes. There were one or two, the charming Lord Grayling amongst them, who might take advantage of Bea's naivety. They were dangerous. But his own friends... none of them would do so. She could safely kiss Medhurst or Brockscombe with no fear that they would misunderstand, or try to take things further.

"Just be careful," he ended lamely. "Make sure you are not discovered."

"Of course," she said happily.

"But where will you start? Medhurst or Brockscombe?"

"Yes, it is difficult, is it not? And I have never been kissed before, so I have no point of comparison. I think I should kiss some neutral party first, just to see what a kiss without any expectations might be like."

Bertram laughed. "And where will you find such a person?" Then he understood the expression on her face, and his stomach turned over in the most alarming fashion. "Oh, no, no, no, Bea! You must not look at me like that."

Slowly he backed away from her, but just as implacably she pursued him, laughing. Step by step he retreated, hands raised in defence. Step by step she followed, until he was backed up against the wall and could retreat no further. Then, still chuckling, she placed her hands on his shoulders.

"It is only a kiss, Bertram. What are you so afraid of?"

His resistance crumbled. She was right — what was there to fear? It was only a kiss, only Bea, only an old friend asking a modest favour. Where was the harm?

Slowly his hands dropped and he allowed her to move nearer, to press herself against him. His head inched towards hers. There was a moment's awkwardness as they worked out how to arrange their noses, and then... then...

The warmth! Surprise that Bea threw herself into kissing with the same enthusiasm as everything else in life. Astonishment that it was not at all how he had imagined it.

That was his last rational thought before his brain melted into nothingness. But he could still *feel*...

He felt the weight of her body leaning against his. He felt a wisp of her hair tickling his nose. He felt the softness of her muslin gown as his hands crept round her waist, the fabric bunching under his fingers. He felt her chest rising and falling, heard his own blood drumming in his ears, his heart racing, a strange noise at the back of throat.

He was drowning, lost in a thousand unfamiliar sensations, and yet he wanted more of them. He wanted — *needed* — to hold her this way, to kiss her, to taste her sweetness, to hold her against him for ever. He adored her with a passion so intense he could not understand why he did not burst into flames.

Abruptly, she pulled away. "Can't... breathe..." she whispered.

He was crushing her against him, he realised, squeezing the breath out of her. "Sorry... so sorry..."

At once he released her, but for a moment she stood immobile, staring up at him. She took a breath, odd and uneven, then another, her eyes a deep, mysterious blue. Then, without a word, she turned and fled.

Bertram's legs would not hold him up a moment longer. He slid down the wall to land with a plop on the floor, oblivious of the dirt coating it. What on earth had happened?

For a long time he sat, quite incapable of a single coherent thought, living again through that all-consuming kiss, while the fires within him slowly became less intense, and the churning emotions subsided into something more recognisable... more manageable. A state where he began to feel as if he were slowly coming back to earth.

But not coming to himself... or at least, not himself as he had been. He would never be that Bertram again. This was a new, altered Bertram, one who knew passion and exultation and joy in the company of a woman. His life was divided by that kiss — the time before, grey and dreary, and the time after, alive and colourful and vibrant.

As his logical mind finally emerged, shaking, from the storm, only one question arose — how was he ever to exist from now on without more of those kisses... and of Bea?

13: Experiments In Kissing

Bea ran. There were no words, nothing she could say without revealing how shocked she was. Dear heavens, were all kisses so earth-shattering? And Bertram was a dear friend, but there was no love between them. Indeed, he was entirely indifferent to her, yet if his kiss could reduce her to this quivering heap of turmoil, what would a kiss from her future husband be like?

She fled to her room, but Harper was there sorting out stockings, so she ran on, first to the Long Gallery and then to the little gallery above the chapel. The room below was empty now, and the gallery deserted. She closed the door, and succumbed to a bout of near-hysterical weeping.

However, she was not one for giving way to her feelings, and within a few minutes common sense reasserted itself. Her reaction was merely the shock of her first kiss, no more than that. When females were brought up in almost complete isolation from males, and even when grown mingled with them only under the most circumscribed situations, the intimacy of kissing was bound to give rise to tremendous agitation. Now it was over, and she had the point of comparison she had desired.

Within a few minutes, she began to plan — how might she contrive to get Lord Thomas Medhurst and Lord Brockscombe alone, and how should she convince them it was necessary? She was all for openly asking each one to kiss her, but what reason could she give? She could hardly tell either of them that she wanted to choose which one to marry. It was decidedly awkward.

For the rest of the afternoon, she pondered the question. All through dinner she was preoccupied, so that Mr Fielding, who sat beside her, asked increasingly pointed questions about her health. But after dinner, she was granted the opportunity she sought. The drizzle prevailing all day had given way to a fine evening, and since they dined early, there was a general wish to take the air before it grew dark. Bea found Viscount Brockscombe looming over her as she arrived in the entrance hall, clad for the outdoors.

"May I offer you my arm, Miss Franklyn?"

She looked round at her stepmother, who raised an eyebrow but nodded encouragingly, so she smiled at the viscount, and placed her hand on his sleeve.

More than a dozen walkers set off into the gardens, but within five minutes the overgrown shrubs hid them all from sight. At first, voices could be heard and boots crunching on the gravel, but before long even those sounds died away, and they might have been the only two people in the garden.

Rather nervous now, Bea had found her voice again, and chattered on unstoppably, while the viscount said very little. Occasionally, he laughed at one of her little jokes, and sometimes he would say, *'Yes, it is so at Brockscombe Hall, too,'* or perhaps, *'My aunt has experienced the same thing,'* but otherwise he seemed content to listen.

Eventually, by some means, she could not say how, they came to the marble bench facing the nymph statue. "Shall we sit for a while?" Lord Brockscombe said.

So they did, and it turned out that she did not have to contrive at all, for it seemed that the gentleman was of very much the same mind as she was. As soon as she settled on the bench, he sat beside her, rather closer than was seemly, and slid an arm around her waist.

"Ah, Miss Franklyn, how delightful you are. So delightful, in fact, that I am very tempted to kiss you."

"Oh!" How easy it was! All she had to do was to lean a little towards him and—

His lips touched hers. No, that was not right. Surely there was something amiss? Where was the warmth, the *glory* of it? His lips were—

She pulled back sharply.

At once he released her, his expression horrified. "I have mistaken you. Pray forgive me, I did not mean— I cannot apologise enough— Miss Franklyn, I am the world's greatest fool. You would be quite within your rights to banish me from your sight henceforth."

"No, no! It is quite all right. I was surprised, that is all."

"Then you can find it in your heart to forgive me?"

"Most readily, sir. In fact, if you would care to begin again, I should not be surprised a second time, and we might get on a little better."

He laughed out loud. "Miss Franklyn, you are the sweetest creature alive, I swear it."

Leaning nearer to her, again his arm crept around her waist, and again his lips found hers. She was not surprised this time, but she was... *disappointed.* That was the only word for it. There was no fire, no sensation of falling, falling into... she could not even describe it. There were no words in her vocabulary for the way Bertram's kiss had made her feel.

No... she had a word. Alive. Vibrant. Desired. That was three words. Passionate. Protected. Cherished. Six words. What else? She had felt like a woman. Full of life and hope and energy and joy and some kind of fizzing, bubbling, light-filled sensation that had no name at all.

She felt none of that with the viscount. It was pleasant enough, she supposed, but nothing more. Eventually, he had had enough and drew back, to her relief. He was laughing, light-hearted, exhilarated. She had to force the smile to her face.

As she rose, a lock of hair abruptly came free and dangled annoyingly on one shoulder. She raised a hand to it, puzzled. "Oh! I must have lost a hairpin."

His guilty expression told its own story.

"Lord Brockscombe? Did you... *tamper* with my hair?"

Sheepishly, he held up a single hairpin. "I collect them, you see. Souvenirs of a pleasant interlude."

A pleasant interlude? Was that all she was to him, a few moments of pleasure and a stolen hairpin? That was humiliating.

"How many such souvenirs do you possess?" she said coldly.

"A few... a dozen, perhaps... no more than two dozen perhaps. Not *many* more. Yours will have a treasured place in my collection, you may be sure, Miss Franklyn."

They walked slowly back to the house, and this time, he was the one who talked and talked, while she was almost silent in seething resentment.

In the entrance hall, she made some excuse to retreat to her room, where she sat, staring unseeingly out of the window, her anger at Lord Brockscombe draining away as she remembered another, very different, kiss. Even the memory warmed her inside and made her smile. But what on earth did it mean?

***

Bertram inched his way back to some state of normality as the evening progressed. Perhaps not normality — that was not quite the word for it, but he could function again. If addressed, he could answer with at least the appearance of coherence. He was barely aware of what was said or what he ate or drank, but he hoped his disordered mind was not too obvious.

He was acutely aware of Bea, however. Even without looking, he knew precisely where she was. He knew when she entered the saloon, watched as Fielding escorted her into dinner, heard her voice amongst the babble of chatter around the table. It was odd, for she spoke no more loudly than anyone else, but her voice was instantly identifiable to him. There was some resonance to which he was acutely attuned.

When he returned to the saloon, he was immediately conscious of her, sitting quietly beside her stepmother who was talking to the duchess. He longed to go to her, and yet dared not. Would she be embarrassed if he approached her? And what could he possibly say to her? He could not bring himself to talk about the weather after such a momentous event in his life.

Naturally he saw her jump up as soon as the idea of a walk was mooted. Bertram rose, too — perhaps he could walk with her? But Brockscombe put paid to that idea, and Bertram suffered the anguish of seeing Bea walk away happily with his friend. Would she find an opportunity to kiss him? Surely she would, and how could he resist? No man could resist Bea at her most open and artless.

Why did that distress him so much? It was an odd thing, but he felt extraordinarily proprietorial towards her now. That kiss had made her his in some strange way, even though she was destined to marry elsewhere, even though there was no attachment between them beyond the gentle affection of friendship. As he wandered aimlessly about the gardens, the thought that she might at that very moment be wrapped in Brockscombe's unworthy arms gave him extraordinary pain.

Abruptly, he spun on his heel and strode back to the house, unable to endure even one second more of the evening. He retreated to his room and buried himself in Horace until the light grew too dim to see the page. He cast the book to the floor in disgust, stretched out his legs on the window seat and leaned his head against the pane. Tomorrow... he would be better tomorrow. This strange excess of sensibility would leave him and he would be well again.

His friends returned shortly before midnight, Brockscombe in buoyant mood, Medhurst thoughtful, Fielding sullen. The latter said accusingly to Brockscombe, "You kissed her!"

Brockscombe looked sheepish. "How do you know that?"

"Wait! There has been kissing? Who? Not Miss Franklyn!" Medhurst said.

"Of course Miss Franklyn. There is no one else here worth kissing, after all. See? I have here the proof." He drew forth a hairpin and waved it around in glee.

"You and your hairpins," Fielding said in disgusted tones.

"Yes, I wish you would not do that," Medhurst said. "It is disrespectful to the lady to inflict yourself upon her person merely to steal a hairpin. How did you get her alone? This garden, I suppose. It is a wilderness."

Brockscombe chuckled. "Most conveniently overgrown. It is all too easy to hide away. I thought we were very discreet, but somehow Fielding knows all my secrets. How did you manage it?"

"I followed you, naturally. It is the sworn duty of a younger son to learn to creep about unnoticed, the better to spy on one's older brothers, and such a talent never deserts one. I followed you all the way to your private little nook, watched you try and fail to kiss her, saw you finally get it right, and then hid in the bushes as you passed me by on your return."

"You sneaky little—"

"Never mind that," Fielding said. "Does this mean you are courting her seriously, Brockscombe? I suppose you will expect us all to stand aside for you now."

"Well, I—"

"No need for that," Bertram said quickly. "Until there is a proposal accepted, Miss Franklyn is as free as a bird, and any of us may try to attach her."

"Who are you to be the arbiter?" Brockscombe said testily. "You have no interest in that direction yourself, so you have no right to interfere. Fielding is right — he should stand aside. She let me kiss her and that is a sign — it means she will accept me if I offer for her."

"If?" Fielding said, snatching at the most hopeful part of this. "Then you have not yet decided?"

"Well... not entirely, no. It is a momentous decision to take, and one must be absolutely sure. But I do not think we should be falling out over this. I have made the most progress with her, so I should have the first shot at her."

"I do not see that at all," Medhurst said. "Suppose she dislikes you, and would prefer me... or even Fielding here, for some unfathomable reason. Why should we step aside? She might think we have no interest in her, and accept you merely because yours is the only offer she receives. We should give her the widest possible choice."

"I have no intention of stepping aside," Fielding said, lifting his chin a little. "I already have her father's approval to court her."

Three faces turned on him in astonishment. "You have talked to her *father?*" Brockscombe said incredulously. "Already?"

"You are not even eligible to marry a lady with forty thousand pounds," Medhurst said.

Fielding shrugged. "That is what I thought at first, but when I considered a little more deeply, it does not seem to me that my situation is so very ineligible. I may be a younger son, but my family is perfectly respectable and not poor or wrapped in scandal or anything of that nature. I have a very comfortable income... No, no, it is not vast, but six hundred a year is not negligible, and I shall have another two hundred a year from my great-uncle. I can well afford to marry, and even to install a curate if my wife should not care for the parsonage. So I asked Mr Franklyn what he thought. Is anyone ever going to pour the brandy? Atherton, you are unaffected by these deliberations. Will you do the honours?"

Silently, Bertram poured and handed round glasses, hoping the others would not notice how badly his hands shook. What was the matter with him?

"So what did Franklyn say? He did not show you the door, presumably," Brockscombe said.

"Not a bit of it. He said he could hardly object since my family is more respectable than he is — his words, not mine. He was an attorney before he inherited his fortune, did you know that? And it all came from iron foundries, so for all his fine clothes, he is only a hairsbreadth away from trade. Then he said that Miss Franklyn was a lady of decided views and would choose for herself who to marry, so he would do nothing either to promote or to hinder my suit, but for himself, he wished me well with the endeavour. So you see..."

"That means that any of us may try for her, kisses or no kisses," Medhurst said. "I wonder if she would kiss *me*, if I asked. She might, for she is an amiable little creature, and as cosy an armful as any man could wish for. I should very much like to put it to the test."

"And so should I, indeed I should!" Fielding said. "I must say, it is too bad of you fellows to barge your way in like this when you know perfectly well I liked her the moment I set eyes on her."

"But why would she want a clergyman when she could have a viscount?" Brockscombe said loftily.

"Or be part of a ducal family," Medhurst put in.

"Stop it, stop it, stop it!" Bertram cried. "Stop *squabbling* over her, and talking about taking a shot at her, as if she were a pheasant or... or a rabbit. To hear you, no one would imagine you were talking about a lady you hope to elevate above all others and share your life with. It is quite horrid, and I am ashamed of all of you. I wish I had never brought her here now."

They all turned and stared at him, surprise written on their faces, as if they had forgotten his existence.

"Atherton? Are you quite well?" Fielding said. "I have never heard you raise your voice before."

"No, I am *not* well. I am heartily sick of you treating my good friend as a mere object, to be sold to the highest bidder. She is the sweetest, most agreeable girl in the world and she deserves more respect from you — all of you. I do not want to hear another word from any of you about her. Fielding, have a look and see if my man is outside, will you? I am going to b ed."

***

Bea had no idea what to make of it all. One kiss that made her melt inside and one that did not. Even without the hairpin, Lord Brockscombe had displeased her. She needed to kiss Lord Thomas before she could make a final judgement, but for several days there was no opportunity. A spell of fine weather encouraged the duchess to organise outings for the ladies each day which returned only in time to dress for dinner, and the arrival of musicians brought dancing every evening, which was enjoyable but did nothing to advance her purpose. So she gave up any hope of secretive walks in the garden and abandoned herself to the pleasures of the dance.

She decided that the marquess, surprisingly, was the best dancer. Mr Fielding seemed hazy about where his feet should be, Lord Brockscombe was energetic but inaccurate, and Lord Thomas was perpetually half a beat behind everyone else, an anxious expression on his face.

Bertram she already knew to be a skilled dancer, but for some reason he seemed disinclined to offer his hand to her. Perhaps it was because he already saw a great deal of her, for he had begun to help her learn Latin. He had arrived at the schoolroom one morning before breakfast with a paper in his hand, having compiled for her a list of simple phrases to learn. It amused her to greet his friends at breakfast with, "*Salvete! Valetisne?*" and hear them respond in chorus, "*Salve! Valemus! Et tu?*".

At first all she could say was that yes, she was well, too, but they were happy to join in the game, and give her the words for plate or ham or salt, so that she could ask them to pass her this or that. Her father raised his eyebrows, but said nothing, occasionally joining in the game, too. But it was Bertram who sat with her for hour after hour, reading passages for her to repeat or to translate, and helping her perfect her accent.

So she was not surprised if, in the evenings, he avoided her company, confining his attentions to the other young ladies who clustered around him. His new-found popularity was soon explained — word of Lord Rennington's difficulties had spread, and as Bertram was now the heir to an earldom, he rapidly became a person of the greatest interest to the unmarried young ladies. Her stepmother fretted over this new rivalry for Bertram's hand, as she saw it, and urged Bea to secure him as soon as she could.

"He is halfway there, to be sure," she said to Bea, "but you do not want someone to steal him from under your nose. Nasty, grasping harpies, these girls, throwing their caps at him in the most unbecoming way."

Bea could not blame them for that. After all, was it not what she herself was doing? It was also what her stepmother had done. Someone like Winnie Strong might be content to wait until a chance meeting brought a suitor into view, but Bea was all for reaching out to grab a husband whenever an opportunity offered. Not for her a life spent meekly sitting in the drawing room waiting to be chosen. She would do the choosing, thank you very much.

Although if she were to be totally honest, she was not having much success at present. She knew perfectly well how to pursue a man she wanted, and wear down his resistance until he surrendered to her greater will. It had worked with Walter, and perhaps, if she had persevered, it would have worked with Bertram too, and although he was not nearly so handsome as Walter, there was a sweet, gentle air about him that she rather liked. And there was that astonishing kiss, which she would like very much to repeat, possibly on a daily basis, even if it reduced her to a quivering wreck every time.

Now, though, she had agreed to let him go in exchange for this month at Landerby Manor — a month, that was all! Four weeks to select the man who would best suit her and bring him to heel, and she was floundering. Bertram was out of bounds, and Lord Brockscombe was out of favour, but there was still Lord Thomas.

It was the dancing which finally gave her the opportunity for her next kiss. The Great Hall had been given over to the enterprise, the furniture moved aside, and the ancient stone floor providing a secure base for their feet. All the windows had been thrown open in a manner which would horrify Bertram's mother, and the door to the courtyard stood wide open. At the fourth or fifth dance, Lord Thomas approached her and she stood up willingly enough, although the heat was oppressive.

"Oh. Another reel," she said with a sigh, as soon as the musicians struck the first notes. "Her grace does so love a reel."

"Should you prefer to sit out this dance, Miss Franklyn? Or we might take a turn about the courtyard, if your Mama permits?"

The courtyard! That had possibilities...

Mama did permit, but even then, Bea was not optimistic of a private moment. The courtyard was well lit, and a few small groups stood or strolled about, enjoying the fresh air. Lord Thomas gave her his arm, and they perambulated slowly around. Eventually they arrived at the colonnade at the far end, which she guessed now had been his objective all along, for he led her directly into the deep shadows, where they could not be observed.

She was not minded to protest. It was what she wanted, after all, to kiss him and thereby compare him against the rather dull kiss of Lord Brockscombe. Yet somehow, she was affronted. Had he talked to the viscount, learnt of the kiss and now decided she was easy prey? Had he simply seen her disappear with him, and presumed? Did he—?

He grabbed her, there was no other way to describe it. Taking her by the shoulders, he pushed her against the solid stone of one of the pillars and clamped his mouth onto hers. She may have made a squeak of protest, but she supposed, since she had gone willingly into the shadows with him, he felt entitled to a kiss. Still, it was a distinctly unpleasant experience.

Fortunately, it did not last long. He soon broke away, gasping for breath but laughing, too. "What a darling you are, Miss Franklyn. That was delicious — thank you!"

Delicious? Her eyebrows rose. "Shall we return to the Great Hall?" she said coldly.

Still laughing in the most irritating manner, he offered her his arm, but she ignored him, stalking away, head high, still seething. Irritating man! How could she possibly marry a man who simply took what he wanted without even asking if she minded? That would never do! She did not expect her husband to fawn over her in a supine manner, but she demanded a certain amount of respect.

But it was all very awkward. Of Bertram's three candidates, one was disappointing and the other took liberties, while the marquess, she felt, might be a dear, but seemed entirely uninterested in marrying at all. Besides, she dared not aspire to such a rank. Bertram himself was adamant that he did not want to marry, and she had promised she would not pursue h im.

What on earth was she to do?

Still, there was one other who might do. Lord Grayling continued to be attentive. He was a lord, which was the main thing, but he was also handsome and amusing company. What would a kiss from him be like?

She was smiling again as she entered the Great Hall.

14: Thoughts Of Marriage

Bertram was utterly disgusted when he saw Medhurst whisk Bea out of the Great Hall. Now *he* was going to kiss her, too! And when he returned with a smug expression on his face, Bertram could hardly contain his ire. Bea was smiling, too, although she was not hanging on Medhurst's arm, which was something. Had she chosen? Perhaps she had chosen, and it was to be Brockscombe.

Bea returned to her mother's side, while Medhurst ambled across the room to where Bertram stood with his friends.

"What a pleasant evening this is," Medhurst said, still grinning.

Fielding glowered at him. "You too!" he hissed. "Traitor!"

"We agreed," Medhurst said. "No one is obliged to stand aside. You are just jealous."

"Of course I am! I wish you would all stop kissing the lady I hope to marry."

Medhurst tutted at him. "Can I help it if she is a good-natured and affectionate little creature, who bestows her favours widely?"

"You take advantage of her — you both do," Fielding muttered. "You should not kiss a girl unless you intend to marry her."

A rumble of masculine laughter from nearby caused them all to turn, where they saw Lord Grayling's handsome countenance wreathed in smiles.

"Good Lord, Fielding, the world would be a very dull place if we were all bound by such conventions," he drawled. "I thank heavens I am not, or I should have a hundred wives, at least."

"That is nothing to boast about," Fielding said hotly. "I should be ashamed to admit to such behaviour."

"I doubt you have anything to admit to," Grayling said, still amused. "How very virtuous you are. Unlike myself, or your friends, seemingly. Or the amusing Miss Franklyn, who bestows her favours so widely. I wonder if she would bestow them in my direction?"

"Now that is not fair, Grayling, when you have not the least intention of marrying her," Fielding said in outraged tones.

"Marrying her? Oh no, I do not intend *that.*"

Still smirking, he wandered away, leaving Bertram smouldering with suppressed rage.

"Does he mean what I think he means?" Fielding said, his face ashen. "He would not... would he?"

But several of the ladies came near just then to solicit support for a riding expedition the next day, and nothing further could be said. It was not until the four friends retired to their room at the end of the evening that Fielding finally exploded.

"If that scoundrel harms so much as a single hair of Miss Franklyn's head, I shall... I shall... well, I shall not be responsible for my actions. If he thinks that just because she has a warm heart, she is fair game—! I am almost minded to call the fellow out. The abominable arrogance of the man! I have always disliked him, and now—!"

"He is only trying to provoke you," Brockscombe said, passing around the brandy glasses. "It amuses him, no doubt, to say such things and see your outrage, but he would not disrespect Miss Franklyn, you may be sure of that."

"I am not sure of it — not in the slightest bit sure," Fielding said. "He has such a dreadful reputation, and there is always a mistress or two in his keeping, you know that."

"He is a libertine, it is true, but he does not seduce the daughters of gentlemen," Brockscombe said soothingly. "Opera dancers and the like, that is where he finds his ladybirds."

Bertram listened to them in silence, having nothing to contribute to the discussion. Spending little time in town, he knew Grayling only from Cambridge and the Latin meetings. Although the baron was noted as a rake, Bertram neither knew nor cared about the details. So long as he left Bea alone, that was all that mattered.

He was encouraged by Brockscombe's reassurances. Besides, Bea was at Landerby with her father and stepmother so she was hardly unprotected, and in another ten days or so, she would be safely back in the North Riding and far away from the charms of Lord Grayling.

"Miss Franklyn knows not to look towards Grayling," he said. "I have warned her that he is not the marrying type, and she is too shrewd to entangle herself there."

"She is female, so entangling herself with the wrong sort of man is just the sort of thing she would do," Fielding muttered.

"A fine opinion you have of the lady you want to marry," Bertram said indignantly. "She is cleverer than you give her credit for."

"Why, because she has learnt a few Latin phrases? That is merely book learning, and anyone may do as much, even a woman, but there is not a female alive who has an ounce of sense where the male sex is concerned. A female needs to be guided, to ensure her footsteps remain on the correct path."

Bertram burst out laughing. "I wish you good fortune with *that* idea where Miss Franklyn is concerned. She is a lady who knows her own mind, and pursues her own objectives with the utmost resolution, and if you think that any man, even you, is able to stop her, you are entirely wrong, I assure you. Indeed, I should very much like to see you try it, and watch how ill you manage the business."

"What is the matter with you, Atherton?" Fielding cried. "Anyone would think you want the girl for yourself, given the excessively high opinion you have of her. She is a darling, but she is as weak and foolish as any other female. Look at the way she throws herself at Brockscombe and Medhurst, with not a thought for me, who truly cares for her. She sees the titles and is dazzled, as all females are. You have only to see how they sniff around Embleton, poor fellow — and you, now they think you might be an earl one day. They ignore you for weeks, but at the slightest hint of a rumour that you are in line for a title, there they are, gazing worshipfully at you and hanging on your every word."

"Miss Franklyn has forty thousand pounds, my friend," Bertram said uncomfortably, for that was close to home. "Why should she not aim for a title, if that would please her?"

"Because a title is no guarantee of good character, that is why," Fielding said. "Look at Grayling, if you doubt it. And mark my words, Miss Franklyn is not as sensible as you imagine. She has been flirting with Grayling since she arrived, and who can blame her? Not I! He is every woman's dream, is he not? Handsome, charming, rich and a baron — how can a mere clergyman, without good looks or address or fortune, compete with that? How can any of us? We are all deficient in one way or another, while he has everything a woman could desire in a man. Atherton, you get along better with her than any of us — if you want to save her from Grayling's clutches, maybe you should offer for her yourself."

"I have no wish to marry her," Bertram said in a low voice. Was that true? He was too confused to say.

"Then perhaps you should stop berating those of us who do. Ack, what is the use? She will never look at me. I am going to bed. Try not to snore so much tonight, Brockscombe."

***

Bertram's sleep was troubled that night. He woke several times with Bea's face in his mind, and then lay fretfully awake. At first, he occupied himself with envisaging her happily married to one or other of his friends, but in every case the result displeased him. Brockscombe was a frivolous coxcomb, Medhurst would be distracted by every passing pretty face and as for Fielding, surely Bea deserved a better fate than to be a clergyman's wife.

Then there was Lord Grayling... and that was another matter. It was all very well for Bertram to say confidently that Bea was too sensible to be taken in by the smooth words of a snake, but she certainly seemed to enjoy his company. It was worrying.

What was the matter with him? *Anyone would think you want the girl for yourself, given the excessively high opinion you have of her.* So Fielding had said, but was he right? What would it be like to marry Bea? At once an image filled his mind of the two of them at the breakfast table, speaking in fluent Latin, just as he had talked about to Medhurst. What fun that would be! And yet... married? Was he ready to surrender his freedom?

He rose as soon as there was enough light to see by, dressed in clothes old and unfashionable enough to be donned without his valet's aid, and went down to the stables. John Whyte, his groom, was already up and sweeping. Was there never any end to the need to sweep out the stable yard?

"Morning, sir," Whyte called out cheerfully. "Saddle Catullus for you, shall I?"

"Thank you, yes, and I shall want him again this afternoon. The ladies are getting up an expedition, seemingly."

"So I heard, sir. Such a sight it will be to see all the fine ladies riding out! Tis a pity your sisters ride so seldom, sir, if you don't mind my saying so. A lady never looks so pretty as aback a horse after a good ride. Proper puts colour in their cheeks, it does."

Bertram laughed and agreed to it, though he had never noticed it.

He did not ride far, not wanting to overtax Catullus with two long outings on one day, and although the exercise was good for his body, it did nothing to soothe his troubled mind. Still, the hour was now sufficiently advanced that he could summon Bayley to dress him for the day, and then make his way to the old schoolroom.

These visits had become a secret delight to him. He had begun the very day after that devastating kiss, horribly torn about it, but bound by his promise to help Bea to learn Latin, or so he told himself. He was not sure how he could face her… or whether she would even want to see him. Surely it would be dreadfully embarrassing for both of them? But he had the happy idea of arming himself with a written list of some common Latin phrases, and although Bea coloured up and would not look him in the eye just at first, the list had given them something to talk about. Within a very few minutes, they were again on the easiest of terms, and no one to see them together would guess that she had reduced him to a quivering wreck just the day before.

Each morning before breakfast, therefore, they met in the schoolroom, and studied the Latin primer. Bertram read passages from the book for Bea to repeat, and then to translate, and sometimes he dictated while she wrote it down, the scratching of chalk on the slate taking him straight back to his childhood. Today she was there before him, already hard at work.

"How are you progressing with those declensions?"

She pulled a face. "Will you help me with this passage? It is by Caesar, and I am finding it difficult. It reads, *'Caesar, exposito exercitu et loco castris idoneo capto…'*. What is *'idoneo'?*"

"Suitable."

"Ah. A suitable position for the camp. But this part, *'ubi ex captivis cognovit…'*. The sentence seems too convoluted."

"It is a little awkward to the English ear. So, 'Caesar, having landed the army and captured… found, perhaps, a suitable position for camp, when he learned from prisoners…'"

"Why does he write about himself that way… *he* did, *he* learned? Why not I did, I learned?"

Bertram smiled. "Julius Caesar was a genius. He could write however he liked."

"I suppose in a way it reads better," she said thoughtfully, her head tipped to one side like a bird. "It makes it less personal, more of a historical record. Now, this line here..."

Bertram sat beside her, as they both bent over the book. The print was quite small, so it was necessary to lean close to her to read it. Her arm rested barely an inch from his, a curl of her hair tickled his ear and he could see her chest rise and fall as she breathed. For himself, it was hard to breathe at all. He was painfully aware of her closeness, the whiteness of her finger resting on the page, her voice soft in his ear, the rustle of her gown as she moved. Her scent — something he could not identify — wreathed itself around him. So hard to *think...*

"Bertram? Are you quite well?"

"Um..."

"*Valesne?*"

That forced a little burst of laughter from him. "*Ita... ita... valeo. Ignosce mihi.*"

"Admit it, you were wool gathering," she said, laughing up at him, eyes twinkling. "This must be so dull for you, this basic work and my beginner mistakes. I expect you are planning for your talk to your friends. When is it to be?"

"Oh... let me see... tomorrow, I think. Yes, tomorrow."

"*Cras.*"

"*Ita. Cras. Hodie... loquor pro Embleton.*"

"Oh. Today Lord Embleton speaks? No... *pro*, so you speak for Lord Embleton? He has written a paper, but it would be difficult for him to read, so you read it for him, is that the way of it?"

"It is, except that he writes poetry, not research papers."

"Original poetry? His own composition?"

Bertram nodded. "It is excellent stuff. If you like Horace, you should come along and listen. I know you lurk in the gallery sometimes, but you could sit with everyone else if you wish to."

Her face lit up. "May I? Your friends would not mind?"

"Mind having an attractive young lady in their midst? Of course not! But I shall not be able to translate for you, since I shall be reading the poems, and all the discussion will be in Latin."

"Oh, I just like to listen. If I need any translation, I am sure Lord Brockscombe or Lord Thomas would be happy to help."

No! She is mine!

Bertram was shocked by his visceral response to Bea's artless comment. Now he would be forced to stand at the front of the room while she was surrounded by his ever-helpful friends, and no doubt Fielding would be hovering around her too. Yet was that not precisely what he had wanted? Was it not the very reason he had invited her to Landerby Manor, so that she could attract the attention of suitors? So why did the thought of it distress him so much?

Fielding's words echoed in his head. *'What is the matter with you? Anyone would think you want the girl for yourself.'*

What *was* the matter with him? How foolish to be jealous of them! But he had brought her here and thrown her in their way, and now he could hardly blame them if they began to appreciate all her good qualities. Nor could he blame her if she were to choose one of them...

Yet the more he thought about it, the more he realised it was true — he wanted her for himself.

He licked his lips nervously, but he had to know. The uncertainty burned within him like fire. "Have you... reached a decision yet? About Brockscombe and Medhurst?"

She pulled a face. "I cannot say that I have, although I managed to extract a kiss from each of them. Their kisses were... not satisfactory."

Bertram laughed, his spirits soaring at her words.

"But I still have another possibility," she said calmly.

"Fielding?" he said tentatively.

"No, silly! He is no lord, nor likely to be, although he is very charming, and looks at me so adoringly. If he were even a baronet, I should be tempted."

"Then you must mean Grayling," Bertram said, alarmed. "Bea, you must not. He is... he *seems* pleasant enough, but he is not in the market for a wife, I assure you. He has said as much."

"Oh, I know he is not on your list, but he is a lord and he seems to like me, so perhaps he will be tempted, who knows? He has until the end of next week to declare himself, if so, and if he does not... well, I shall not break my heart over him, you may be sure."

"Do you have a heart to break, Bea?" he said teasingly, and for some reason, she coloured up a vivid red.

"It must be time for breakfast," she muttered.

A little surprised, Bertram followed her down the stairs, but her response threw him into a fury of wondering. She might not break her heart over Grayling, but her fiery blushes suggested that she might break it over someone else. But who could she mean? Brockscombe and Medhurst offered her unsatisfactory kisses, and Fielding had no title. Was there someone else? Perhaps she was now regretting her precipitate jilting of Walter. He was a handsome fellow, his cousin, with a careless charm that ladies seemed drawn to. It would be easy to throw him over on a whim, and then discover later that she had been more attached to him than she had supposed.

But Walter still had no title, and could never have one, and that would never do for Bea. Her heart, breakable or otherwise, was still firmly set on marrying into the nobility.

And what of Bertram himself? Even if he were to decide that he would like to marry Bea after all, he could not be sure he would inherit the earldom. His uncle was young enough to marry again and sire a whole brood of sons. No, he could not in all honesty pursue Bea, even if he wanted to marry her.

He pulled himself up sharply. Of course he did not want to marry! A wife would distract him from his work, would be constantly interrupting him in the library to ask if he would prefer goose or mutton for dinner or to complain about the scullery maid. There would be children crying at all hours, and no peace to be found for a man of scholarly bent.

But he had a sudden vision of children running across the lawn at Westwick, chasing each other, laughing. Girls perhaps, with black curls spilling down their backs, vivid blue eyes and a forthright way of explaining precisely why they had to have another doll or gown or pony, and not taking no for an answer.

The image made him laugh out loud. Of course he wanted to marry, and have a string of children just like their mama.

Bea turned on the half-landing, her foot still on the last step. "Bertram, whatever has got into you these days? Is the moon full just now? Are you going mad?"

And she laughed up at him, her blue eyes and dancing curls so bewitchingly like the child in his mind that he laughed again, but he could not speak a word, only smile at her. Such enchanting eyes, and those tempting lips… if only he could taste them again…

"Will you ride with me this afternoon?" she went on, one hand resting on his lapel. "I should like you to explain about questions again. Would you mind?"

He shook his head, and laughed a little more. "Bea Franklyn, you are the most astonishing girl I have ever met." Then he leaned forward and kissed her lightly on the lips. "I hope one day you find a man worthy of you."

15: Poetry And A Proposal

Bea blushed again and again, keeping her face averted as they descended the stairs, hoping he would not notice her discomposure. He had caught her completely off her guard with that kiss, not even a proper kiss, no more than a peck on the lips, but she could feel the warmth all the way to her toes. She tingled with it, as if she were standing too close to the fire. It was most unnerving.

He had asked her if she had a heart to break, and oh, how she longed to answer him truthfully! Yet she could hardly tell him that his was the kiss which set her on fire. She had promised, and she would keep to her word, whatever happened. She would *not* pursue Bertram, no matter how tempting. For the moment, her primary target must be the amusing Lord Grayling, and if she could inveigle a kiss from him, then she would be able to make a choice.

And yet... if only it could be Bertram! He was not handsome like Walter, nor was he powerful like Lord Grayling, a man who walked with a sort of swagger that was more than mere aristocratic haughtiness. She had seen enough of that at Marshfields to understand the arrogance of the nobleman. The baron had that, true enough, but he also exuded a physical presence that she could not quite explain, yet it made her a little uneasy. Whereas Bertram was as comfortable as her old walking boots, which were worn and misshapen, but raised her spirits every time she put them on. Which was a very odd comparison, now that she thought about it.

There was no time to consider the matter further, for as soon as they reached the breakfast parlour, she was surrounded by Bertram's friends, all talking to her in Latin, and she had to concentrate to answer them with her limited vocabulary. They professed themselves delighted to hear that she was to join them for the meeting that morning.

"An excellent day to choose," Mr Fielding said. "Embleton's poetry is glorious — you will not find better, even in Horace."

Bertram took exception to this slur on his favourite, and the conversation rapidly became too difficult for Bea to follow. Once breakfast was over, Bertram escorted her courteously to a prime seat in the old chapel, right in the front row. With a grin of triumph, Fielding was quick to take the seat beside her, but since she was positioned on the end of the row, Lord Brockscombe and Lord Thomas were obliged to sit behind her. The rest of the seats filled up, but Bea was the only lady present. One or two of the gentlemen frowned as they saw her, but the marquess smiled and waved as he passed her by.

Bertram began almost at once, standing at the front with an assurance she had seldom seen in him. He was a self-effacing man as a rule, but here he conveyed a quiet authority which commanded respect. The audience fell immediately into silence as he spoke, and listened intently.

She could understand little of it. She caught the marquess's name once or twice, and '*poeta*', which was easy to translate, but after that, it was only an occasional word. It hardly mattered. She had Bertram's warm voice to listen to, and the cadences of the poems themselves, each one different from the one before, the words hovering in the air like the notes of a musical piece, weaving themselves into a magical whole. It was wonderful, and Bertram read with such feeling that she almost felt she could understand the meaning from his voice alone. Sometimes, at the end of one or other piece, she would be moved almost to tears, and a soft sigh ran round the room from the gentlemen. But no one spoke or clapped or made any sort of noise

After a while, Bertram stopped reading and said something directly to the audience, and at once they began talking amongst themselves, but that, too, was in Latin and beyond her comprehension.

Mr Fielding turned to her. "Did you make anything of that, Miss Franklyn? Embleton is an excellent poet but convoluted, sometimes."

"I did not understand any of it, but I very much enjoyed listening to Bertram's reading. What is happening now? What is everyone talking about?"

"We will form small groups and discuss the poems — the metre, the structure, the word choices and so on. It gets rather technical."

"There are no more poems to be read?"

"No, although one or two might be read again at the end. I am afraid this part of the meeting will not greatly interest you. Should you care to return to the other ladies now?"

She pulled a face. "Embroidery is very tame by comparison, but I had better go and find my mama, and see if she has any duties for me this morning."

"Then allow me to escort you."

Mr Fielding offered her his arm, and although she could find her way perfectly well, she had no wish to appear rude, so she smiled and placed her hand on his arm.

"Shall we walk around for a little while?" he said, as soon as they had left the chapel. "It is pleasant to stretch one's legs a little after sitting in one attitude for so long."

Bea never minded a walk in fine weather, for she had always plenty of energy which sitting about with books or embroidery did nothing to dissipate, so they walked out into the colonnade and thence into the summer warmth of the southern garden. She laughed and turned her face to the sun in delight, but her moment of happiness was cut short.

"Miss Franklyn, oh, *dear* Miss Franklyn!" Mr Fielding spun her round, seizing her roughly by her arms so abruptly that she gave a squeak of alarm. "Forgive me, but I must speak or I shall burst! From the moment I first saw you, I have been your devoted slave, and I know I have no great title or fortune, nothing to set my claim above others who might also be drawn to you, nothing but my very great admiration and affection... my undying love and devotion... and a house, as snug a parsonage as you could wish for, and a sufficient income... it is not much, I know, and quite unworthy of you... *I* am unworthy, but your father encouraged me to—"

"My father encouraged you?" she cried, this revelation startling her into utterance. "Why?"

"Why?" He licked his lips, a frown crossing his face. "Well... he said... he said... he wished me well in the endeavour."

"Yes, but *why?* Why would he imagine I would marry *you?*" Anger and surprise made her abrupt. "I was betrothed to Viscount Birtwell, Mr Fielding, when he *was* Viscount Birtwell and heir to the Earl of Rennington, and I broke that engagement when he would no longer inherit. I have no objection to you personally, for you are as agreeable a man as I ever met, but why would I marry a *clergyman*, no matter how snug the parsonage may be? And frankly, I am not accustomed to snug houses, sir. They sound most disagreeable. I am very sorry if you have harboured unrealistic hopes, but I should very much prefer to live in a house with a dozen bedrooms, at least, and a gallery long enough to hold a ball in comfort."

He stared at her, his face drooping with chagrin, and she stepped backwards so that he was forced to release her. Her arms throbbed — she would have hideous bruises there, she knew it! Still, she could not but pity him.

"I am sorry, Mr Fielding, but I cannot possibly marry you." When he still said nothing, she went on, "I shall go to the saloon and find Mama."

She half expected him to come running after her, or to say something, anything, but he stood transfixed as she turned and walked away from him. When she entered the colonnade and looked back, he was still standing there as if rooted to the spot.

Anger sped her steps through the multitude of passageways to the saloon. How dared he offer for her! He was not even on the list. Lord Brockscombe, Lord Thomas Medhurst and Lord Embleton — those were her targets, together with the possible outside bet of Lord Grayling. But definitely *not* Mr Fielding! Her fortune and her stepmother's connections meant that she could at least expect a title. What gave Mr Fielding the right to offer for her, and as for Papa—! What on earth was he thinking, to encourage the pretensions of a man like that?

Had she inadvertently encouraged him? She had certainly been open and friendly with him, just as with Bertram's other friends. It had not occurred to her to do otherwise, but she had never supposed him to be a suitor. Not that there was anything wrong with him beyond the lack of a title, she supposed. And the parsonage... she shuddered. She could not see herself living in a parsonage, and doing good works about the parish as a dutiful vicar's wife.

She was so engrossed in her own thoughts that she failed to see her stepmother at the top of the service stairs.

"Beatrice? Wherever have you been? I have been looking for you."

She jumped, and executed a hasty curtsy. "Oh! I beg your pardon, Mama. I was just coming to find you."

"Have you been out walking? Remember to conserve your strength for the ride this afternoon."

"No, I was attending the gentlemen's meeting."

"The gentlemen's meeting? Whatever are you doing mingling with... with *intellectuals?"*

"Why should I not? I am learning Latin, so—"

"Learning Latin? Beatrice Franklyn, how many times must I tell you that this wild behaviour just will not do. Ladies do not learn Latin. French, perhaps. Italian, certainly — most respectable, although one only needs a very little, to carry off a song, and you have already achieved an adequate degree of accomplishment there. No further book learning is necessary after leaving the schoolroom. You will only addle your brain, and give any rational gentleman a disgust of you. You are to give up all thought of learning Latin, do you hear me?"

"Yes, Mama," she said miserably, dipping a curtsy.

"You will go to the saloon at once, and spend the rest of the morning in useful occupation. I shall expect to see two additional roses on your tapestry before you leave for your ride."

"Yes, Mama." Another curtsy, and she was permitted to creep away to the saloon, find her work basket and take up the hated tapestry.

There was no one else in the saloon, but she dared not abandon her task, in case she should be forbidden from the ride that afternoon. So she stitched diligently until Harper came to fetch her to change into her riding habit. Her spirits lifted at once, for she would have Bertram's company for a few hours, and she could ask him some questions about the ablative, which were puzzling her rather. That would not contravene her stepmother's prohibition, would it? It was not book learning, merely talking, after all.

Such anticipated treats rarely materialise, however, as she should have realised. Time after time her hopes had been raised and then dashed. The glorious success of a season in London, the spectacular marriage into the nobility, even the acceptance into her stepmother's exalted family — none of it had come to pass. The Bucknells had never liked her. They had smiled to her face and sneered at her behind her back. Then there were the trivial mishaps of everyday life — the new bonnet that disintegrated at the first drop of rain, the silk that had looked so fetching in the drapery but made her look bilious, or the planned outings that had to be put off because of inclement weather. Life was one long succession of disappointments.

Here was another such, for instead of Bertram and the pleasures of the subjunctive, she found herself lifted into the saddle by Lord Grayling, who sprang onto his own horse and positioned himself alongside her as their group trotted away from the stables. Well, that was a pleasure of a different sort, and the ablative could wait.

At first, they spoke only of the warmth of the afternoon sun, and the welcome shade of the limes along the drive, as his highly strung horse danced and pranced along, with many a toss of his fine head. Then there was a narrow lane to be negotiated before they came to more open country and could spread out a little. The baron controlled his mount without effort and then adjusted their progress, she noticed, to put a little space between the two of them and the other riders in the group. Bertram was now some way in front with his friends and Miss Grayling. Behind them, the duke and the marquess were escorting Miss Hutchison and the nervous Miss Pikesleys, their pace slow. Mr Fielding had not come out at all.

"It was a pleasure to see you at the meeting this morning, Miss Franklyn," the baron said, with a harder than usual tug on the reins to bring him closer to her. "Is it Embleton's odes or the man himself who interests you most, I wonder? I am mortified that you did not attend my own presentation on Seneca, but then a mere baron such as myself cannot hope to compete with a future duke who also writes amorous poetry."

Amorous poetry? That was an interesting element to the character of a man who seemed uninterested in women.

"I am sure your speech was very interesting, sir, but I could not understand any of it."

"You heard it?" he said, eyebrows raised.

"Very clearly from my position in the chapel gallery, but as I say, I understood none of it, so I did not stay long. Poetry is more interesting to me, with its rhythms. Whatever the subject of Lord Embleton's poems, Bertram read them beautifully."

"Ah yes, the future earl. If it comes to pass, that is."

A strange comment. "Why should it not? Lord Rennington has no legitimate heirs of his own, so his brother will inherit and Bertram after him."

"Perhaps," Lord Grayling said, his eyed hooded. "The earl is still young enough to sire more sons."

"But the countess is not."

"He is not married to the countess, is he? The marriage is invalid, and he has sent her away. If he marries a younger woman, he could easily put his brother's nose out of joint, and your friend Atherton's nose, too. That would be amusing, would it not?"

Bea was struck dumb. It was an idea which had not for one moment occurred to her, but now that it did, she saw all too clearly the plausibility of it. Her stepmother had wondered many times why the Countess of Rennington had left Corland Castle at just the moment when it might be supposed that her presence would be of most benefit to her family. Bea had not been very interested in such speculation — once she had jilted Walter, his family was of no consequence to her. Now she understood the reason for her stepmother's concern.

Lord Grayling's attitude struck her as odd, however. "Amusing? How would that be amusing?"

"Why, it would mean that any lady who set her cap at Atherton, thinking to become a countess one day, would be sadly disappointed."

Bea bristled at his supercilious smirk. "I hardly think any lady so fortunate as to marry Bertram would be disappointed in her situation, title or no."

She spoke louder than she intended, perhaps, for several of the riders ahead of them turned round with curious expressions, but Lord Grayling only laughed. However, when he spoke, his tone was thoughtful. "Indeed she would. Atherton is a fine young man, in many ways, and his wife will be blessed indeed." Then he spoilt the effect by adding mischievously, "I wonder who she will be? Can you think who it might be, Miss Franklyn? You are deep in the gentleman's confidence, so I am sure you have some inkling of where his thoughts lie."

"His thoughts lie mostly with Horace," she said, chuckling.

The baron laughed again, louder this time, so that Bertram again turned round to frown at them. "That is true of most of the gentlemen here," Lord Grayling said, his eyes twinkling merrily. "They may fawn over the ladies in the evening, but it is an absent-minded sort of attention, for their minds race ahead of them to the next talk."

"And yours does not?" she said archly.

"Not even Horace has any power over me when there is a beautiful young lady present."

"So that is why you take your sister about with you, I suppose, to protect you from thoughts of Horace."

"She is lovely, is she not?" he said, smiling fondly at Miss Grayling ahead of them, the delicate feathers of her hat waving as she cantered along. She rode as well as she did everything else, and how unfair to lesser beings that any girl should be so beautiful and so accomplished, too. Lord Grayling leaned across to whisper in her ear, "But it is not she who distracts me from the Latin poets." Before Bea could reply, he had straightened himself and went on in a more normal tone, "Miss Franklyn, my horse is restless, I would stretch his legs a little and there is a very tempting hedge over there. If you permit, the challenge would be amusing to me. You may follow the others through the gate and I will meet you again in the next field."

Without waiting for her reply, he urged his horse into a gallop and tore away across the field to leap the hedge at a low point near the furthest corner. It was bravely done, and Bea could only watch and admire. By the time she reached the gate, which Bertram was holding open, Lord Grayling had already slowed his mount and was coming round to meet her again.

"Showing off in front of the ladies," Bertram muttered as she passed through the gate. "Why can he not go through the gate like everyone else? What were you talking about, the two of you, that so amused him?"

"Everything amuses him," she said. "He is a light-hearted man. Thank you for holding the gate, Bertram."

She urged her horse forward with a smile to meet Lord Grayling, for at that moment his twinkling eyes were far more enticing than whatever crotchets were producing the ferocious scowl on Bertram's face. Besides, the baron had paid her a very pretty compliment, had he not? *'But it is not she who distracts me from the Latin poets.'* Who else could he mean, when he looked at her in that meaningful way?

As she complimented him on his horsemanship, noticing the strength in his thighs and the masterful control he exerted over his spirited mount, she exulted in her success. Now this was more like it! A handsome and charming man, a baron, no less, and giving her clear signs that he preferred her company above others. It was all very promising… very promising indeed. All she had to do was to push him a little into making his offer.

Only the shortness of time gave her any concern. A week, that was all she had left. Would it be enough?

16: Letters

Bertram seethed quietly over Grayling's behaviour. He could not be sure whether his annoyance was jealousy at the fellow's monopoly of Bea, or whether it was masculine disapproval of such a vainglorious display. Or perhaps it was pure envy, he thought gloomily. Bertram had not the skills to manage anything more than the smallest jumps. A fallen tree trunk was just about within his capabilities, but he would never attempt a solid hedge, even one recently trimmed, as this one had been. Yet Grayling had sailed over it and, even Bertram could admit, he cut a fine figure. He had the sort of muscular body that was precisely designed for such an exercise — powerful and masculine. As unlike Bertram's slender form as it was possible to be.

And now Grayling was riding beside Bea again, smiling at her and leaning nearer to say something that made her laugh. How did he do that? It was flirtation, Bertram supposed, as he closed the gate after the last riders and followed them across the field, but he himself had never had the way of it, that light tone that amused and beguiled and... something else. Some hint of admiration that ladies responded to like flowers unfurling their petals in the sun. Even so straightforward a girl as Bea Franklyn could not help responding to Grayling's charm.

For the rest of the ride, Bertram followed the two of them, returning to Landerby Manor in a very disgruntled frame of mind, but quite unable to think of any way of distracting Bea away from the enticing charms of the baron.

The mail had arrived during the afternoon, and as the company gathered around the table in the entrance hall where the letters were laid out, the butler approached Bertram.

"Begging your pardon, sir, but this came today. I thought it might be best for you to give it to him yourself."

He handed over a letter addressed to *'John Whyte, groom to Mr B Atherton'*.

"A letter for Whyte? Oh, Lord. It must be bad news from home, I imagine."

"That is what I suspected, sir."

"Thank you, Graves. I will take care of it."

He went straight back to the stables, where Whyte was still rubbing down Catullus.

"There is a letter for you, Whyte."

"For me? Who'd write to me? I don't recognise the writing... oh, I do, it's Mr Dewar's, the parson. It must be from my grandda. He can write well enough for his own needs, but not a letter. Dear Lord, what does he want, I wonder?" He turned the letter over and over in his hands, frowning at it.

"You will not know until you open it."

"Aye, true enough." Even then, he hesitated for a long moment before tearing at the wafer and unfolding the paper. "Oh. Well. That's... odd.

Captain Edgerton wants to see me... that fella who's looking into poor Mr Nicholson's death. You read it, sir, for I'm sure I don't know what it's a bout."

Bertram took the letter from him.

'John, Mr Dewar is so kind as to write this for me else it would not make a word of sense for my hands shake too much to write. That man from the castle has been here wanting to talk to you about your family connections, the one who is looking into the chaplain's death. He knows a great deal and suspects a lot more and I could barely speak civilly to the man. Mr Dewar will not let me write down what I would like to do to that man. Captain Edgerton, that is his name, although what he is a captain of, I'm sure I don't know. I sent him away with a flea in his ear, you may be sure. I hope you're well and giving satisfaction and taking good care of Mr Bertram's fine horse. Your loving grandpa, Joe Whyte.'

"Family connections?" Bertram said, puzzled, then remembered that Whyte was the illegitimate child of Joe Whyte's daughter. "Oh... Nicholson?"

Whyte nodded. "Aye, he's me da, seemingly, though not a bit of notice have I ever had from him. That's why Grandda's so upset about it. These things happen, but a man should take care of his children. So Grandda says."

"And what do *you* say?" Bertram said.

"That I never wanted nor needed him, sir. I grew up in the smithy with me cousins, learnt me letters at me mam's knee, like them, learnt about horses from me grandda and me uncles, got meself a fine job at Westwick Heights, sir, and I don't want to do nothing to muck that up. What good would a gentleman like Mr Nicholson ever have done me?"

Bertram smiled wryly. "He could have given you a proper education, like a gentleman."

"Which would have fitted me for nothing at all," Whyte said hotly. "Me ma's a smith's daughter, sir, and that's me proper place in the world, working for a living and not swaggering round like a lord, expecting the world to fall at me feet. No offence, sir."

"None taken. But this is nothing to worry about. Captain Edgerton seems to be a very thorough man who wants to find out every little detail of Mr Nicholson's life. He has heard of your connection and wants to talk to you about it, that is all."

"He won't arrest me nor nothing, will he?"

"No, no. You need only tell him what you have told me, Whyte. He is a reasonable man, and will not suspect you of anything. Besides, you were at Westwick on the night Nicholson was murdered, were you not?"

"Aye, and never knew nothing of it til late in the morning when Mr Halliwell's boy came by with the meat for the kitchen and told us."

"Then you may tell the captain that, and he will go away and leave you in peace."

Whyte nodded, but he still looked troubled. "You'll speak for me, sir, won't you? Tell him I've done nothing wrong."

"Of course I will, but you will have to speak for yourself, too. Nothing will happen just yet, I am sure. I doubt the captain will come all the way out here. It is a two day journey, after all, and he must have more important matters to deal with. I will send word to him when we return to Westwick, so you may put it out of your head until then."

***

Bea retired to bed that evening with very confused feelings. Lord Grayling's attentions were very pleasing, boosting her spirits wonderfully. He had ridden by her side for the whole of the afternoon, apart from those times when he dashed off to display his superior skills on horseback. She could see Bertram looking daggers at him, for Bertram was the type of rider who cautiously crept through the gates even in the hunt, and was usually far behind with the old men and the few ladies who took to the field. She liked Bertram, of course, and he was a true friend to her, and she would always cherish the memory of that wonderful kiss, but there was no doubt that Lord Grayling was a great deal more dashing.

As if the ride had not been encouraging enough, for once he had not played cards with his own friends after dinner, but had drawn her aside to play backgammon with him. Bertram and his friends turned round to glare at them whenever there was a burst of laughter from their table, which happened often, for Lord Grayling was a most amusing man and he seemed to find Bea's little jests funny, too. Really, they got along remarkably well.

Mama had thought so too, for she had smiled and nodded encouragingly whenever Bea caught her eye, and when they retired to bed, she followed Bea to her room to gloat over the baron.

"Upon reflection, Beatrice, I do not think you could do better than Lord Grayling," she said, pacing back and forth in the tiny room, making Bea feel quite crowded. "Bertram is all very well, and a much better title, but when will he have it, that is the question? At least with Walter you would have been a viscountess while you waited for him to inherit, but with Bertram you could be Mrs Bertram Atherton for thirty years or more, and who wants to be Mrs anything? There are few other possibilities here. I cannot see the marquess coming up to scratch, and Lord Thomas Medhurst is only a younger son, with no money or estate of his own. You would be bringing everything to the marriage, and that is no good. Lord Brockscombe… he is possible, I suppose, but is he serious? It is very difficult to tell. So Lord Grayling will do very well, if he makes an offer. Only a baron, but that is better than nothing… a great deal better than nothing."

Bea could not tell her mother that she had already found Lord Brockscombe and Lord Thomas wanting, nor that Bertram was not an option at all. But since Lord Grayling was now the only possibility, it was only proper to have her mother's approval.

"So you do not mind if I encourage him a little?" she said cautiously.

"Encourage him all you like. You are very good at that, after all. Yes, it would be most agreeable to have you settled before the autumn sets in, and this time you should not stand for a long engagement. Get him to the altar as soon as may be. It will be for the best, you may be sure."

Bea knew how to interpret that — even her stepmother was tiring of Bea's endless dallying, and wanted her married off and out of the way. She wanted it herself, but she felt instinctively that Lord Grayling was not a man to be pushed into anything. Her simple strategy with Walter of asking if he were ever going to propose would not work with a man like Lord Grayling. Nor could she leave matters to develop in their own time. He was an accomplished flirt, and who knew how many women he had toyed with over the years, yet he was unmarried still.

It was a conundrum. If only she had not been persuaded by Bertram into this agreement. She would have worn down his resistance in the end, she was sure, and then she would have had a husband whose kisses warmed her in some inexplicable but quite delightful way.

But perhaps Lord Grayling's kisses would warm her, too? And with that thought, she climbed into bed and, buoyed by optimism, fell asleep.

She woke fretfully in the dark. Even though she had left her bed curtains open, no light filtered through the shuttered windows yet. Turning over, her eyes resolutely closed, she waited for sleep to return, but her mind was no longer amenable to the idea. Lord Grayling had been pushed aside and in his place, she saw Bertram's smiling face, and felt his lips burning into hers. Not the proper kiss, which had quite understandably set her on fire, but that affectionate little peck — brisk and not romantic in the slightest, but she would have traded almost anything at that moment for another one... or two. Or as many as she could get. If only his friends could kiss so bewitchingly—

She sat bolt upright. *Mr Fielding!* As soon as she thought of Bertram's friends, her mind's eye summoned the image of them and there was Mr Fielding, laughing and joking with the others, smiling fondly at her... and then, unbearably, as she had seen him last, miserable and immobile in the garden. Her spurned suitor, whom she had made no effort to listen to with civility. *'Why would I want to marry you?'* So she had said — such cruel words! And he had not joined them on the ride, he had not even appeared for dinner.

He had taken her by surprise, that was the trouble, and then she had blurted out all manner of infelicitous things. If only she could curb her instinct to say the first thing that came into her head! If only she were more ladylike, more like Mama...

Poor Mr Fielding! What had happened to him since their last encounter? Was he quite well? Or worse, had he decided he could not face her at all, and quit Landerby altogether? But no, she would certainly have heard if he had left. What could she do? She would not be easy about him until she had seen him again, and heard that merry laugh of his. Most of all, she wanted to know that he had forgiven her.

A letter! That was it… she would write to him. That way, she could choose her words carefully and not burst out with one of her honest but not very polite remarks. And although it was not entirely proper to write to an unattached man, surely she could be permitted to write a note apologising for her dreadful behaviour?

Scrambling down from the high bed and hastily lighting a candle, she crossed to the window where a small table was laden with writing equipment. Sitting down, she pulled paper, ink and quill towards her and began to write. As soon as she began, the pen broke. When she had mended it and begun again, she discovered the ink was lumpy. With a sigh, she retrieved her own travelling writing box from a drawer, and began again.

'Mr Fielding, I am consumed with guilt for the discourteous way in which I responded to your very generous sentiments yesterday. It was unpardonably rude of me, and I would like to express my sincere regret. I do not expect to be forgiven, but I know your kind and open-hearted nature will permit me to say now all that I should more properly have said to you at the time. Firstly, may I thank you with all my heart for the compliment you paid me in wishing me to be your wife. I am deeply sensible of the honour you do me, and could only wish that my answer might today be different. But it cannot. I am very, very sorry, but I cannot marry you, not because of any defect in you or your character, for you are all that a man ought to be, and more, and your circumstances are respectable, and despite my adverse comments regarding your parsonage, upon reflection I believe it was quite wrong to dismiss it so forcefully. I am sure it is a very pleasant parsonage, and one may always hire an assembly room if one is in need of a ballroom. Nevertheless, I cannot marry you because—'

Here she stopped and laid down her pen. Why could she not marry Mr Fielding? She needed to give some explanation for her refusal, and not a frivolous or selfish reason, like the lack of a title or his snug parsonage, but an honest and respectable reason. What had her stepmother told her to say? That she was much obliged but she did not think they would suit.

But in many ways, Mr Fielding would suit her perfectly. He was respectable, he had his living and parsonage, and enough money to defend himself from the charge of fortune hunting. And she liked him very well, if she were to be completely honest. He was, until her careless rejection of him, always cheerful, he admired her and they even had a mutual interest in Latin. *He* would not forbid her from learning the language!

Yet she knew beyond question that she could not marry him. He was like Lord Brockscombe and Lord Thomas — he sparked no flames within her, and that settled the matter beyond question. She took up her pen again.

'I cannot marry you because I do not feel for you that deep regard that a woman should feel for a man who is to be her husband, nor do I believe I could ever come to feel such a regard. I shall always consider you as my very good friend, and I hope you would see me in the same light, but we can never be more to each other. I am very sorry. With every good wish for your future, and the hope that you will in time find a woman worthy of you, yours in friendship, Beatrice Franklyn.'

She folded it and sealed it with a wafer, then tucked it safely in a drawer. As soon as she dared, she summoned Harper to dress her. Then, when the lady's maid had withdrawn, sniffing at such an early start, Bea retrieved the letter, crept from her room and through the dusty passageways, still in the gloom of early dawn, until she reached the room where Bertram and his friends slept. Outside was a bench where their valets would wait at certain times to be summoned, since there were no bells connected to the kitchens two floors below.

Here she sat and waited patiently, amusing herself by listening to the distant snores, until one of the valets — it was Bayley, Bertram's man — appeared bearing a ewer of steaming water.

"Good morning, Bayley. I have a commission for you, if you would be so good. Will you see that Mr Fielding gets this letter?"

"Of course, madam. Is it urgent? Do you want me to wake him specially?"

"No, not urgent. It is only an apology. But if you have to go off and do other things, you can leave it with Mr Atherton."

"Very well, madam."

He was too well-trained to do more than raise his eyebrows very slightly, for a lady writing to a gentleman was not at all proper unless an engagement was in effect, but Bea hoped she had forestalled him by talking of an apology. That could be taken as nothing but the polite response to an invitation, perhaps, and would attract no opprobrium, and it was true, as far as it went.

He bowed, and Bea walked away, feeling that she had assuaged the worst of her own guilt and, she hoped, made Mr Fielding feel a little better, too.

Then she went to the old schoolroom, which had become her retreat in times of worry, where she could consider her options and decide what to do next. For now she knew what she wanted in a husband, above even a noble title — she wanted a man who sparked flames inside her, and in her entire life, only one man had ever done so, and that was Bertram Atherton.

But there was still Lord Grayling, who drew her to him in a multitude of ways. And he was *exciting*, as Bertram was not, for there was an edge to him that challenged her, as if he were saying, *'I am dangerous... do you dare tangle with me?'*

Dangerous… an odd word to attach to a gentleman and a baron, no less. Certainly there was risk in pursuing him, for if, as Bertram said, Lord Grayling is not looking for a wife, then she would have wasted her time at Landerby and would have to begin again. On the other hand, the triumph if she could manage to attach him, if so accomplished a flirt could be caught by Miss Beatrice Franklyn, the daughter of an attorney. That would be something!

But dangerous? She frowned. What danger could she possibly be in, except to her heart? Not even that, for perhaps Bertram was right, and she did not have a heart at all. What a lowering thought.

17: Defiance And Obedience

Bertram was barely awake when Bayley shook him.

"Good morning, sir. Your hot water, sir." He spoke in a low whisper, so as not to wake the others.

Bertram groaned. "Is it morning already, Bayley?"

"I'm afraid it is, sir. Your big day. Shall I lay out the burgundy today?"

"Whatever you like, Bayley. No one will care what coat I wear."

"Of course, sir." He coughed discreetly. "I have been given a letter to deliver, sir."

"A letter? Have you? Then you had better hand it over, Bayley."

"It is not for you, sir. It is for Mr Fielding, from Miss Franklyn."

Bertram shot upright in his bed. "Miss *Franklyn?*"

"Ssh, sir, if you please. The other gentlemen are still fast asleep. Yes, from Miss Franklyn. She said it is an apology, and I am not to wake Mr Fielding specially but—"

"But he will want it at once!" Bertram cried, so loud that some of the others stirred, even as Bayley flapped his hands at him in distress. "Give it to me, Bayley."

The valet produced the missive, and Bertram slid out of the big bed he shared with Medhurst, and rushed across the room to the low cot where Fielding slept.

"Fielding? *Fielding!* Wake up, man. She is writing to you — Bea has sent you a letter."

To his credit, Fielding was almost instantly alert, his excitement palpable. "A letter? From Miss Franklyn? Give it to me — at once!"

"It is an apology, sir," Bayley said.

Fielding almost visibly deflated. "An apology. Ah." He turned the letter over and over in his hands before abruptly ripping it open.

Bertram watched his face as he read it, the eagerness giving way to a calmer expression, then a smile and a burst of quiet laughter. At the end, he was still smiling, although a little sadly.

"She is very kind," he said, with sorrow in his voice.

Bertram dismissed Bayley with a flick of his head, then said, "What happened? Something must have happened for her to apologise to you."

"I offered for her," Fielding said, with a heavy sigh. "It was madness, of course... so presumptuous of me, and she quite rightly rang a peal over me. No, that is not true, but she showed me just how impertinent I had been. I have been thoroughly ashamed of myself for having the temerity to raise my eyes to such a person, so far above me in every way. And now she has written to me with such kindness... she hopes we shall always be friends, she says.

'You are all that a man ought to be'... is that not a magnificent compliment? Here, read it and see for yourself. Such a gracious letter!"

"You do not mind? It is not... private?"

"I have no secrets from my good friends," Fielding said.

Bertram read it in haste, looking for... he knew not what. But it was just as Fielding said, a gracious apology and a very firm rejection. Nothing about his lack of a title, only that she did not love him. As gentle a way to be refused as any man could expect. He wondered then what she had said to Walter, when she jilted him. She could hardly have dressed that up in any language that would have spared him pain. She had accepted him because he would be an earl one day, and rejected him the instant he lost that possibility. No, that could not have been gracious at all. Poor Walter!

And here she was, still in pursuit of a title, and nothing else would do. Despite that glorious kiss and the way the memory of it haunted his dreams, at that moment Bertram was not sure he liked Bea very much.

The others had woken by this time, and huddled round Fielding to discuss the letter and his failed offer and what it all meant. Bertram called Bayley back in to dress him, and then took himself to the schoolroom.

She was there, sitting forlornly at her table, her head down, her Latin book closed. Instantly, all his antagonism crumbled into dust. If only there were some way he could comfort her!

"Bea? *Quid agitis?*"

She looked up and he clearly saw tears on her cheeks. "*Valeo,*" she whispered.

But she was not well at all. *"Non ita. Non vales, amica mea."* Such inadequate words. Her friend... if only he could be more than her friend.

He passed her his handkerchief, and she murmured, *"Gratias."*

"Bea, is this about Fielding? Because—"

"Oh, no... not at all. I am very sorry I have made him unhappy, but I could not marry him just because he wants me to."

"No, that would be absurd," Bertram said, smiling. "Your letter was kindly done, and thoughtful of you, especially the part where you said you did not have the proper regard a woman should have for her husband. And nothing about his lack of a title."

She looked up then, her expression serious. "I am beginning to realise — rather belatedly, I am sure you will agree — that a title is not the only measure of worth in a man. There has to be something more... *I* have to have something more. I have to *feel* something for a man with whom I plan to spend the rest of my life."

"Such as? Are you talking about love, Bea?" His stomach was surprisingly lively, swirling in the most alarming way at the intimacy of this conversation. Breath was hard to come by.

"I cannot tell you — only that there ought to be *something.* But that is not why I am miserable this morning."

"Oh." He could not be sure whether relief or disappointment was uppermost in his mind at that moment. More than anything, he wanted to know what was in her mind... in her *heart.* He had teased her about not having a heart, and she gave a very good impression of a girl who cared for nothing but a title, but if she had feelings, then he would be in an agony of suspense until he knew the direction where those feelings lay. Could it be him, his own heart whispered? But he dared not hope for that.

She was not going to tell him. But if she were not upset about Fielding, what was it that reduced her to tears?

"Mama has forbidden me from learning Latin," she said dolefully. "I am not to addle my brain with book learning, she says."

"Then what are you supposed to do with your time, hem handkerchiefs?"

"Embroidery, tapestry, painting with water colours, netting purses..."

"That sort of thing will addle your brain far more than a bit of Latin. Besides, if you can read Latin, you have the most amazing body of literature at your disposal, and no one could possibly object to that."

"I can read the translations, as I was doing with Horace."

"There are a thousand translations of Horace, all of them inferior to the original. Life would be insupportable without Latin, and the ability to reread the Odes on a regular basis — at least once a year."

"Or to hear them spoken, as you do so well. That first meeting I overheard, when you read out that splendid poem. *'Donec gratus eram tibi nec quisquam potior bracchia candidae cervici iuvenis dabat.'* That one. How does it go on?"

"*'Persarum vigui rege beatior.'* Should you like to learn it by heart? I can teach you."

"I am not allowed to open a book."

"No, but I am, and if I were to write it out for you on a piece of paper, you would not need to open a book at all. And I should be very happy to help you with the metre and pronunciation."

"Do you think...? But Mama would not be happy about it."

"Bea, learning poems by heart is something that everyone does... or pieces from Shakespeare or the Bible. Besides, this is only a temporary prohibition. Once you are married, you will be able to spend all day buried in your books, if you want to."

"As you do."

He laughed. "As I do. Just make sure to marry a Latin scholar, who will help you with your deponent verbs and eccentric metres. Now, let me recite the first few lines for you to learn."

Her smile of pleasure should have been its own reward, of course, but his treacherous insides jolted with excitement — he had convinced her to continue their morning lessons, and he had planted the idea that she might take a Latin scholar as her husband. And who better to fill that rôle than Bertram himself?

***

Bea buzzed with excitement, but she was nervous, too. She was not a naturally rebellious person. Thoughtless, sometimes, yes, but she had never deliberately defied her stepmother's orders, and she was very much afraid that learning a Latin poem by heart came perilously close to defiance. But Bertram was not explaining the meaning of the words, only helping her remember them, so it was not precisely learning the language, was it? And recitation was one of a lady's approved accomplishments. She had memorised many poems over the years, some of them in French or Italian, without having the least idea what she was saying, and this was no different. Or so she told herself.

After breakfast, her stepmother planned to keep her out of trouble by making her accompany the duchess on her domestic rounds.

"That way, you will have some idea of all that is involved in the running of a great house such as this, and Landerby is but one of the duke's many estates. Since you will marry into such circles yourself one day, you should be prepared for the responsibilities which will be your lot."

"Very well, Mama, although I believe you have already trained me well in household management."

"Oh, at Highwood we have no more than twenty servants, and not even an under butler. That is nothing at all. At Marshfields, there are more than thirty indoor servants, let alone the gardeners, gamekeepers, dairymaids and so forth. Six just in the kitchens... no, seven. I forgot the pastry cook. I was remiss not to show you the scale of the operation there, to give you an idea. Never mind, we shall begin today, and if we are invited to Marshfields this autumn, we may take advantage of the visit to teach you a little more."

"Yes, Mama," Bea said dispiritedly.

All day she trudged along behind her stepmother and the duchess. They made a strange pair. Lady Esther fizzed with energy, clearly happy to be in her rightful place in society, issuing orders with authority and finding fault with everybody. The servants eyed her warily as she approached, took their reprimands stoically, and glowered after her as she left. The duchess, by contrast, skipped from room to room with a smile and a compliment and a casual, "You will know how best to do it, I am sure." The result was that everyone smiled at her, and she left them all cheerful and willing. It was fortunate, perhaps, that Lady Esther swept into a room first, and the duchess followed in her wake, to smooth over the ruffled feathers. She never countermanded Lady Esther's orders, merely modified them slightly. "Perhaps not quite so much syllabub," she would say. Or, "Only if you have the supplies... or the time... or can spare someone to do it."

At the end of the day, Lady Esther turned to Bea with a smile of triumph. "There now, I hope you have a better idea how to go on."

"Indeed I have, Mama. I have learnt a great deal today. Thank you for allowing me to see you at work."

And her stepmother basked in the supposed compliment, and, fortunately for Bea, never thought to ask precisely what it was that she had learnt. Such a question would have tested Bea's powers of invention to their limit.

The only drawback to spending her day thus engaged was that Bea missed Bertram's presentation to his fellow Latin scholars. She had been looking forward to hearing his lovely voice again, and seeing him striding up and down, the words of men dead for millennia echoing around the room. However, he was one of the first in the saloon before dinner, and she was able to ask him how it had been received.

"Very well, I think," he said, settling on the sofa beside her. "Medhurst was a bit scathing, but then he always is."

"But he is your friend!" she cried, appalled by this seeming betrayal.

Bertram only laughed. "Indeed, we are the best of friends, but that does not mean he will concede to the rightness of my arguments. Nor I to his," he added, eyes twinkling merrily. "Where the Latin poets are concerned, it is hard to find a single point of agreement between us, but that is the fun of such meetings."

"Fun? It is fun to argue?"

"It is the greatest amusement in the world to quarrel gently over the meaning of a single word in a poem written two thousand years ago. There are any number of other matters we could dispute, but we do not. Medhurst thinks riding to hounds is a splendid way to pass a wet day in December. I beg to differ. I believe that the North Riding is the finest place in the world."

"And so it is!"

"Medhurst would take issue with us both, then. He likes the softer, less challenging terrain of the south. And so it goes, but we do not fall out over such matters. We simply shrug and wonder why the other, who seems a reasonable fellow in other ways, could be so bone-headedly wrong."

She laughed, but said wistfully, "I wish I had a friend like that. Or three friends, as you do. Friends who would chaff me gently but not quarrel with me — except over a Latin poem."

"But you do," he said surprised. "You have all four of us as friends."

She sighed. "Yes, but it is not a friend I need, Bertram, it is a husband. Oh, to be mistress of my own establishment, and order my time as I please! I have spent the entire day in the basement with Mama and the duchess.... No, that is not quite true. There was an hour in the attics, too, and I do believe there was an interlude in the linen cupboard. But I must refrain from speaking of that, lest the excitement overwhelm me."

He chuckled. "Dearest Bea, you were not made for domesticity, were you? Let me tell you a secret — servants can manage a house perfectly well, if left to their own devices. My mother does nothing more than order the meals each morning, and look over the accounts now and then, to be sure no one is cheating us. Otherwise, she leaves well alone. If there is anything amiss with the linen cupboard, Mrs Lynch will tell her of it. As for Lady Strong, I am not sure she knows where her linen cupboard is, for she spends every waking hour in her garden."

"Which is much better than terrorising the servants. What does your mama do for a hobby? Her health, of course. She must spend half her days in the still room concocting remedies for every little cough or itch."

"She is not very good at concocting, so she keeps on very good terms with the apothecary," he said in a conspiratorial whisper. "But do not let her know that I have told you that."

"My lips are sealed," she whispered back.

The room had filled up as they talked, and even Mr Fielding was there, with a hesitant little smile for her. The duke's extremely grand butler announced dinner, Bertram offered her his arm, and, with a little burst of pleasure, she allowed him to lead her into dinner and then to sit beside her.

It was an odd thing, but no matter how despondent she became, Bertram always made her feel better. He was such a good friend to her. If only he could be more than a friend, but she had given her word.

18: Sunday

Bea enjoyed Sundays, for it was the one day of the week when she could be sure of having her father to herself for a little while. Mama always took the carriage, but Bea and her father chose to walk to church. It was a bone of contention between them.

"Persons of quality do not walk with the servants, Mr Franklyn," Mama said disdainfully.

"We are all equal in the sight of God," he replied. "On the Sabbath, I like to walk to church in humility and penitence, like the sinner I am."

But Mama did not see herself as a sinner, and saw nothing wrong with putting the horses to on a Sunday, even for the short journey to church. Bea did not mind, for she could walk with her father and it was, for a little while, as if Mama had never come into their lives.

She had no objection to Mama in principle, for she had seen for herself how the little worry lines that had begun to cloud Papa's forehead vanished after his marriage, and he smiled a great deal and seemed very happy. No loving daughter could object to that. But for herself, she found Mama oppressive and restrictive, and was therefore disproportionately pleased when she could enjoy her papa's company alone.

Today she tucked her arm into his as they set out. "This is pleasant, is it not? No rain, and it is not uncomfortably hot. But sadly our last Sunday at Landerby. How we shall miss our new friends!"

"You have enjoyed yourself, I think, mingling with all these great ones. More than at Marshfields, or am I wrong about that?"

"Not wrong, no. The Marshfields people always seemed to look down on me, so I could never be quite comfortable there, but here... would it be improper of me to say that there is more generosity of spirit?"

He nodded slowly. "My inclination is to agree with you. Shall I tell you a secret? I never feel comfortable at Marshfields, either, for all that they are my wife's relations. They look down on me, too, and, which is worse, they look down on your stepmother, because she married a man like me."

"Why do we keep going there, if neither of us enjoys it?"

"Because it is your stepmother's home, and it gives her great pleasure to stay there. And I confess, it is amusing to write to one's acquaintances and mention that one happens to be staying at the Duke of Camberley's seat. Or here, as guests of the Duke and Duchess of Wedhampton."

"Have you written to *all* your acquaintances while we have been here?"

"Hmmm... yes, I believe I have. Some of them twice. We have come a long way, you and I, from that little house in Newcastle."

"I liked that little house," she said.

"Oh, so did I, and we were very happy there, but I like Highwood Place a great deal more. My inheritance was most unexpected, but our lives have improved immeasurably because of it. We live more comfortably, and have been given the opportunity to raise ourselves in society. As a result, I have a most excellent wife, and you will soon have a husband worthy of you."

A husband worthy of you. Those were Bertram's words, too. "Who is a husband worthy of me?"

"Why, a nobleman, of course, who will make you noble, too. Is that not your aim?"

"Then why did you encourage Mr Fielding to propose to me?"

He laughed. "Should I not have done so? I imagine you gave him short shrift. I cannot see you in a parsonage, somehow."

She was uncomfortably silent for a moment. "I was rather rude to him, I confess. But if you think I should marry into the nobility, why encourage him at all? You could have sent him packing, as you have done with plenty of others you deemed to be fortune hunters."

"I take my lead from your stepmother in such matters, Bea. We are moving in her world now, and she knows how to judge these people better than I do. My duty is only to determine a man's financial position, but she decides who is suitable to encourage and who is not. Who is *eligible.*"

"But Mr Fielding?"

"I know. He was a sizar at Cambridge. Do you know what that means? He worked his way through university. His lordly friends merely paid to attend, and did not even have to take any examinations to achieve their degrees, whereas he paid a lesser amount and acted as a servant while studying hard for his degree. I admire such perseverance, but your stepmother would not normally approve of such a suitor for you. However, here she tells me that everyone is acceptable since everyone is a friend of the Duke of Wedhampton. So, I felt safe in allowing him to approach you."

"Even though you knew I would turn him down?"

"You might have been harbouring a *tendre* for the man, Bea. I live in hope that one day you will discover the joy of falling head over heels in love."

"Now that would be unforgivably foolish of me," she said, although it was odd how her thoughts flew instantly to Bertram, and those fiery kisses. "Unless I should happen to fall in love with a man of noble birth."

But her father did not laugh. "I am serious, Bea. No title, no grand estate, no amount of money will ever outweigh the pleasure of a smile from the person you love most in all the world, or the warmth in your heart as you return it."

"Mama?" Bea said wonderingly.

"Not this mama, no, although I am very fond of her. It is your true mother of whom I speak. My dear Eloise." His face softened into a smile, perhaps drawn by some happy memory. "I was very fortunate to have her for a little while, and I do not expect ever to receive such a blessing a second time. I married your stepmother for other reasons, and she too has brought me happiness... of a different kind. Every marriage is unique, unlike any ot her."

"But love is not necessary for happiness," Bea said firmly. "Mama says that love is an illness, and if one catches it, one must endeavour to recover as quickly as possible."

Her father laughed, but shook his head. "With weak beef tea and regular bleeding, I suppose? Your stepmother is an admirable woman in a multitude of ways, but she does not know everything."

They were joining the throng approaching the church by this time, so the conversation lapsed, but as they waited for Mama's carriage to arrive, Bea pondered her father's words. She had never heard him speak so openly about his two marriages before, although there was nothing that surprised her. She remembered very well his grief after her own mama had died, and her baby brother with her, and she knew precisely why he had married her stepmother — to secure his new position in society as a gentleman, and to provide a chaperon for Bea, so that she could make a good match. *A husband worthy of you*. But who? If only Bertram—

But such thoughts were fruitless. She had given up Bertram, and must find a different husband. There must be another man in the world who set her afire. Just a few days ago, she would have said that all she looked for in her husband was a title and an income commensurate with his rank, but now, she knew there must be something more.

After the service, the congregation milled about outside the church for some little time, and a great crowd set off for the walk back to Landerby. Bea found Mr Fielding beside her.

"Miss Franklyn," he began in a low voice, and for an instant she was terrified that he would renew his addresses. But he went on in a humble tone, "You must allow me to thank you for your most gracious letter. Despite my despicable presumption in approaching you—"

"No, no! You must not say such things."

"Indeed I must, for is it not true? It was insufferably arrogant of me, and I know now that I am not worthy of you... could *never* be worthy of you, and therefore I cede the field to those better qualified than I. But these few weeks have been the happiest of my life. You have given me an ideal of womanhood, and I shall never forget you. Thank you!"

Before she could reply he melted back into the crowd and was instantly lost to view, while Bertram and his other friends drew forward to her side, as if by prearrangement. They immediately began to rattle away light-heartedly, but she was not in the mood for frivolity. Her thoughts were filled with poor Mr Fielding, who was so besotted with her that he regarded her as an ideal of womanhood! Was ever a man so deluded?

Oh, but to be loved so well! It was gratifying. It was humbling. She recalled her father's words… something about a smile, and how it warmed the heart, and she wished — oh, how she wished! — that she could love that way and be loved in return. Perhaps her father was right, and a title would mean nothing beside such happiness.

***

Sunday evenings were normally dreary. No music or dancing, no cards, no reading beyond religious tracts and nothing to do beyond desultory conversation, for no one was very lively. The only blessing Bea could see was that she could put aside the hated needlework for one day.

This evening, however, the duchess had a plan for their amusement. Chairs were arranged in the saloon, and when all had taken their places, she stood at the front, beaming at them.

"We will all recite from memory," she announced. "It does not have to be strictly religious, although passages from the Bible must always be acceptable, but quotations from great literature would be welcome, too. Shakespeare… and similar writers of great merit. The duke will begin… you have a patriotic piece, I believe?"

"It is *'We few, we happy few'*. I am sure everyone knows it. From Henry the Fifth." He struck an attitude, as if he were on a stage, and began his recitation, and if occasionally he muddled the words or needed a prompt from the audience, no one minded, for it was better than sitting about being bored.

Then the duchess recited a pretty little poem, and one by one the company rose to take a turn, in rank order. Only the marquess, whose difficulties with speech rendered him ineligible to participate, was exempt.

As she waited for her turn, Bea pondered what she should recite. She had a number of poems at her disposal, but it was a question of what would best please the company. But then Bertram whispered in her ear.

"Horace."

She turned to him, eyes wide. "No! I cannot... can I?"

He grinned at her. "Why not? Is it not perfect for a gathering such as this?"

Did she dare? She was breathless with excitement — to speak in Latin, publicly! She glanced at Mama, smiling benignly, her own performance completed satisfactorily. She would not smile if Bea were to use her Latin! But a learned poem was not the same as knowing the language, and she barely understood a quarter of Bertram's ode. Surely she had the courage to do it?

When her turn came, she rose and walked slowly to stand before the audience. Even then, there was time to draw back, to stay with the safety of Shakespeare or Wordsworth or Scott. *The Lady of the Lake* — she knew a good piece from that, and Mama would smile and be pleased with her. But she caught Bertram's eye, nodding encouragingly to her and the die was cast.

She set her feet at the proper angle, arranged her arms and straightened her spine. "*Carmina liber tertius, carmen novem.*"

A murmur passed through the room, as soft as a summer breeze. She saw surprised looks exchanged, expressions become more alert, as anticipation filled the air.

"*'Donec gratus eram tibi nec quisquam potior bracchia candidae cervici iuvenis dabat, Persarum vigui rege beatior'*," she began, the words of the long-dead Quintus Horatius Flaccus ringing out, tentatively at first and then with growing confidence. She tried to capture Bertram's intonation as best she could, but in the end, the magic of the words caught her in its thrall and she forgot the watching company, forgot everything but the beauty of the ancient words.

She came to the end, and silence fell. Then the room erupted in cheers and applause and cries of *'Splendida!'* and *'Magnifica!'*. She curtsied to them, laughing, and as she made her way back to her seat. The marquess murmured, "Wonderful, M-M-Miss F-F-Franklyn," as she passed, beaming at her. She caught Bertram's eye again, and saw him smiling... smiling so widely that her heart lurched in delight. She must have done it well, for he was pleased with her!

She took her seat and someone else stood up to perform, but she heard none of it. Her heart still raced with excitement. She had done it! There were one or two words she was sure she had mispronounced, and one line in particular where she had muddled the metre, but on the whole it had gone off tolerably well. The gentlemen were pleased, anyway... Bertram was pleased, and that made her glow inside. It was odd how she valued his approbation above that of anyone. No doubt that was because he had been at such pains to help her learn. It was gratitude she felt for him, nothing mo re.

Eventually, she dared to look at her stepmother, but she was gravely attending to Miss Pikesley's stuttering performance, so there was no hint there of her reaction, but her father smiled benignly at her. *He* was pleased, at least, and that must also be an object with her.

By the time all had performed, the room felt horridly warm, the air close, all the ladies plying their fans vigorously. Someone threw open the doors to the terrace and there was a general movement outside. Bea heard Lord Grayling's voice in her ear.

"Shall we walk, Miss Franklyn?" he murmured.

At last, an opportunity to see if the baron's kiss could set her on fire. "That would be delightful."

He offered his arm and they strolled along the terrace and then onto the narrow strip of lawn beside it. Without a word being spoken, he steered her onto the nearest path and then outwards, into the garden. It was full dark by now, and no light from the saloon penetrated so far, but she was not afraid. Lord Grayling was with her, and no harm could come to her in his company. They walked slowly, and before long her eyes adjusted to the gloom well enough to make out the dark shapes of the overgrown shrubs and the pale line of the gravel path unfurling before their feet. She knew where she was — just around the next corner was the marble seat by the old fountain. They reached it, and with one accord, stopped. She turned expectantly to face him, he lowered his head, she closed her eyes...

"Miss Franklyn! Miss Franklyn!"

Distantly, from nearer the house, several voices called out. Bea heaved a sigh, but Lord Grayling chuckled. "We are not to be permitted a moment alone, it seems. Is that Atherton's voice? And Fielding, I fancy."

"Whatever can be the matter? Why are they looking for me?"

"Let us find out." Raising his voice, he called out, "Miss Franklyn is here."

"Where are you?"

"The Minerva fountain," he called back.

Footsteps on the path gradually became louder, until Bertram and Mr Fielding appeared at a rush. Bea heaved a sigh of pure annoyance.

"There you are, Miss Franklyn," Bertram said, waving a shawl at her. "Do, pray, wrap yourself up and come back to the house. The night air... my mother would never forgive me if you were to catch a chill."

"I am not cold," Bea snapped. "I can hardly catch a chill on such a balmy night. What is the matter with you, Bertram? You have windmills in your head if you think I would— Wait a moment. That is not even my shawl."

"Never mind," he said, wrapping it around her shoulders. "You should not go directly outside from an overheated room into the night air without a shawl. Do come back to the house."

"Miss Franklyn is well protected now, and I shall not keep her out long," Lord Grayling drawled. "I thank you both for your solicitude, but you may leave Miss Franklyn to my care."

"Absolutely not!" Mr Fielding said hotly.

"She will be better protected inside the house," Bertram said, glaring at his friend. "Come, Bea. I will not have you risk your health like this."

"I am not some weakling who—" she began, but there was yet another interruption in the form of an irate Miss Grayling.

"That is *my* shawl, Miss Franklyn, and I will thank you to hand it over at once. And Mr Atherton, I would remind you that taking another person's property is theft. Whatever were you thinking?"

"I beg your pardon, but I was so concerned for Miss Franklyn's health that I picked up the nearest one to hand."

"If you had asked, I could have told you that the green cashmere was hers, which at least matches her gown."

"Here, take it," Bea said, ripping the shawl from her shoulders and thrusting it into Miss Grayling's hands. "I neither want nor need it. Mine is much finer, anyway."

"Certainly, if one has more money than taste. I shall leave you to your tryst with my brother."

Head high, she stalked away.

Lord Grayling chuckled. "Miss Franklyn, unlike my sister, I suspect these two gentlemen are not intending to leave us to our tryst. Shall we relieve them of their anxiety on your behalf and return to the house? After all, Mrs Atherton would never forgive her son if you were to take a chill, and we would not wish to cause a family rift, would we?"

"Well..."

He leaned close to whisper in her ear. "There will be other evenings, and other trysts, I sincerely hope."

In the still night air, his words carried and Bertram glowered at him. Now, why was he so anxious to interfere? It was too bad of him to prevent her from testing Lord Grayling. There was so little time left! Only three more evenings at Landerby, that was all. Three more opportunities for a tryst, whatever that was. Surely Bertram understood the urgency? But there was nothing to be done about it tonight. Silently, the group made its way back to the house.

19: Prospects

Bertram followed Bea and Lord Grayling seething with rage. Even now, Grayling was flirting with her, and she, silly girl, was drinking it all in. Perhaps she was already halfway to being in love with him, and who could blame her? He was everything that a girl could want in a man — except steady of character, of course. Grayling was a hardened libertine who had no intention of marrying her. She had to be protected from him, and if her parents would not do it, then Bertram and his friends must step into the breach.

How fortunate that Fielding had been watching Bea, and saw her disappear with Grayling. He had summoned Bertram to his aid, and Bertram had snatched at the only excuse he could think of. His mother's ploy had worked once before, and happily it had worked again. Bea was safe for the moment, but how to keep her safe in the future? How was she to be kept away from Grayling? He shied away from the prospect of explaining his true nature to her. For one thing, she would not believe him, and he hated to destroy her innocence. An unmarried woman should be pure and trusting, and he could not bear to tell her of the wickedness of the world.

But she had to be protected somehow, so as soon as he returned to the saloon, Bertram sought out Lady Esther.

"I wonder if I might have a word with you, ma'am — privately?"

She was too well-bred to show any sign of surprise, merely inclining her head in acquiescence and leading him out of the saloon into an ante-chamber. It was one of the unused rooms, so their feet threw up clouds of dust, and the flames on the candelabrum he carried flickered in the draught from a broken window pane.

"We are quite private here, Mr Atherton. What is it you wish to say to me?"

"Were you aware that Miss Franklyn was out in the garden with Lord Grayling just a few minutes ago?"

"And what of it?"

Such a response threw Bertram entirely off his stride. "You knew? But... it was dark... they were very secluded."

She laughed easily. "Mr Atherton, the young must have time alone to discover whether they are suited or not. A man may be brought to the point of a proposal the more readily by a closer degree of intimacy than is afforded by a crowded saloon."

"A proposal! I do not think he has a proposal of marriage in mind, Lady Esther. I have heard him say so, just a few days ago."

"So say all men, until it happens. Believe me, Mr Atherton, your concern for Beatrice does you the greatest credit, and even though I cannot approve of your encouragement of her inclination for book learning, I am deeply grateful to you for obtaining this invitation for us. It is such an excellent opportunity for Beatrice, and there is Lord Grayling, so attentive and such an *eligible* match. A baron, and with a good income! *Most* eligible. If he has an eye for her, then I shall not be the one to throw a rub in his way, of that you may be sure, and I shall thank you not to interfere. You take a great interest in her affairs. I cannot help thinking that, despite your protestations to the contrary, you want her for yourself."

Bertram could not in honesty deny it. But even if it were true that he wanted to marry Bea, and at that moment he wanted it very much, if only to save her from Grayling's clutches, he could not be sure that he would ever be able to provide Bea with the noble title she wanted and deserved.

If only he could convince her that Grayling was a libertine who had no intention of marrying Bea... but there was no hope of that. Lady Esther had set her mind too firmly on the prospect of marriage. She saw only a man of charm and great address, well-mannered and unfailingly courteous. With the title and all that went with it, nothing could make her believe him unworthy of Bea's affections.

So he bowed and said no more. Lady Esther smiled and swept majestically from the room.

When he returned to the saloon, the first sight to greet his eyes was Bea and Grayling sitting side by side on a sofa, closer than propriety dictated, their heads together in intimate conversation. Bertram almost groaned aloud in despair. Something must be done, and at once! There was not a moment to lose, for tomorrow he might find a way to get her alone. But what could he do? He had no right to interfere directly. Only one man could do that...

Mr Franklyn was in a gaggle of other men talking heatedly of the political situation. Bertram went to him at once, managed to extricate him and drew him agitatedly into the same ante-chamber he had used when speaking to Lady Esther.

"I beg your pardon for drawing you from your discussion, but something must be done to protect Bea. What he proposes… it is unthinkable! She must be got away from him at once! Lady Esther will do nothing. You must rescue Bea before she is irrevocably entangled with him."

Franklyn raised a delicate eyebrow. "We are speaking of Grayling?"

"Yes, yes, of course Grayling! He is trying to ensnare her… she was out in the garden with him just a few minutes ago, but Fielding and I got her back inside before he could do anything to her. I have talked to Lady Esther but she sees nothing wrong in him… she does not understand… thinks him a pattern card of upright behaviour, no doubt."

"He is a baron, and that will weigh with her," Franklyn said. "It does not weigh with me, however. What do you know of him?"

His calm tone soothed the worst of Bertram's agitation. "He is a libertine, sir. He has kept a succession of mistresses since he came into his inheritance, discarding them as soon as he is bored with them… six months is about the usual length of time. This I have had from Brockscombe and Medhurst, who know him well — better than I do, for I never go to town."

"And you believe that Bea is his next target? Why?"

"He has said very clearly that his intentions towards her do not include marriage."

The eyebrows lifted even more. "He has said so explicitly?"

"Yes, sir. I heard him myself, and so did my friends. You may ask them, if you wish. With his reputation, we fear the worst, and Bea — sweet, innocent Bea who hurls herself into life with such delightful enthusiasm, must seem like an easy target to as experienced a man as Grayling."

Franklyn nodded. "I understand your concerns, but I wonder if you do not refine too much upon his history. To me, he seems like a practised flirt, and if I had to guess, I would imagine there to be a ladybird in his keeping somewhere, but I find it hard to believe that he would seduce her here under the duke's roof, where she is a guest. I would think he is merely amusing himself for a while, trying to see how far she will surrender to his charms."

"And if she should surrender?"

"She cannot be permitted to do so, of course. You say she was out in the garden with him — alone?"

"Quite alone, and some distance from the house, a very secluded spot. Fortunately, Fielding saw them go, and we went after them and persuaded them back to the house."

"Then I thank you for that. Was she cross with you?" he said, eyes twinkling.

"She was rather," he admitted sheepishly. "It is not my place to interfere, but I could not stand by and do nothing, and it would have taken too long to find you or Lady Esther and explain the situation."

"Yes, and it would have created a great to-do and everyone would have known what was going forward. Your way was far more discreet. However, you have now quite correctly informed me of the matter, and may safely leave it to me."

"You are not going to sit on your hands and do nothing, I hope," Bertram said suspiciously.

Franklyn smiled. "No, I am not going to do that."

"Then… are you going to take her away?"

"I am not going to do that either, for it would draw unwanted attention to the matter."

"So will you—?"

"No more questions, I beg of you," Franklyn said, laughing and raising his hands defensively. "I shall deal with it in my own way, and, I sincerely hope, in a manner which will not raise awkward questions. Do you think it will rain tomorrow? I believe it will."

And not another word would he say on the subject, and Bertram could only retreat to his own room and lie awake for half the night fretting about Bea.

***

Bea retired to bed in a dispirited mood. After her triumph in the recitals, the rest of her evening had turned into a disaster. Bertram, of all people, had spoilt her attempt to put Lord Grayling's kissing to the test, and then Papa had drawn her away from Lord Grayling altogether, and into a discussion with the marquess, who was a charming man, of course, but difficult to talk to, it had to be said, although she had done her best.

The evening became immeasurably worse, however, when Mama sailed into her room, looming over the bed with a candelabrum in her hand, so that Bea squinted into the sudden brightness.

"So you are awake. Good." Setting the candelabrum down on the table beside the bed, she pulled a chair near to the bed and sat down with a grim expression on her face.

Suppressing a sigh, Bea hauled herself upright, and prepared to be harangued.

"You think you are very clever, no doubt, Beatrice, with your Latin poetry, and I will admit that it went down very well with some of the gentlemen. It makes no difference, however. That sort of learning, and by a female long out of the schoolroom, is most unbecoming, and you will not repeat it, nor pursue any further study of Latin... or Greek or Hebrew or any other long-dead language. You will restrict yourself to suitable employment for a lady, such as I have always taught you, and not let this friendship with intellectuals go to your head. Is that clear?"

"Yes, Mama," she said dolefully.

"I am sorry Bertram interfered between you and Lord Grayling, for time is running out, I very much fear."

"Only three more days before we leave," Bea had said.

"I am thinking more broadly than that. You are one and twenty, Beatrice, and you should have been settled long before this. I have done my best, heaven knows, to instil the principles of demure behaviour into you, such as a man of rank looks for in his wife, but I fear it has not answered. There is just enough of the unseemly in your manner to deter the most particular. I always knew it would be difficult with your background, but I thought, with some effort on your part, and the size of your fortune, and... well, you are not unattractive, when your forehead is not creased up from studying too much, but here we are. I was insistent that you should not have to compromise, as I did."

"Compromise?" Bea said, puzzled.

"By marrying your father. As a duke's daughter, I should have married into the nobility. A younger son, perhaps, but at least an Honourable." She sighed. "But year after year I went up to town and dutifully danced at every ball. I was accomplished, I was ladylike and I had admirers, certainly, but none worthy of my rank. My sisters came out one by one, and all married well. Two earls and a baron. The younger son of a marquess. And still I waited. But then came the year I was twenty-six, still unwed and Grace waiting in the wings. Grace. My youngest sister. Sixteen, as lovely as an angel and she had *thirty thousand pounds.* So unfair! What could I not have done with thirty thousand pounds? An earl, at least. Or Lord Henry, who was only a younger son, but such a darling. However, with so many daughters, Papa could not give any of us more than ten thousand. Then Grace's godmother gave her thirty thousand. *Thirty thousand pounds!* My godmother gave me a silver cross when I was confirmed. Oh, and a prayer book bound in ivory. So you will understand why I had to act, before Grace swept in and took all London by storm and married a duke, and cast me entirely into the shade."

"But... this is the Lady Grace Skelton?" Bea said wonderingly.

"*Skelton!*" Lady Esther spat, her lip curling. "With all those advantages, she had to throw herself away on a nobody. Although, to be fair, he was the heir to an earldom until his uncle married the governess and started breeding sons. The governess! What a family!"

"I like Mr Skelton," Bea said.

"Everybody likes George Skelton, but one does not marry a man just because one likes him. He has to bring more to the marriage than a handsome face and charming manners. So I went to stay with my friend in Newcastle, and there I met your father who saved me from being an old maid."

"Even though he is a mere mister?" Bea said mischievously.

"He is an extremely wealthy mister," she said seriously. "Money is important, too. Perhaps even more important than rank. And he is undeniably handsome, and in very good condition for his age. *Extremely* good condition." Her expression softened momentarily. "That is important, too. Lord Brockscombe, for example, is well enough now, but one can tell at a glance that he will be stout before he is forty. I do not like stout men."

Her stepmother fell silent for a while, lost in some thoughts that were clearly pleasant for her lips curled up into something resembling a smile.

Eventually she sighed, and rose to her feet. "It is late, and you should be asleep. Time is short, Beatrice, but I do not yet despair of your prospects, nor fear that you will be unwed at twenty-six. There is still a possibility of Lord Grayling, but if that fails, you must keep going with Bertram. Persevere, Beatrice, persevere. You are very good at perseverance."

"Bertram does not want to marry, Mama."

"Nonsense! Look how attentive he has been these last few weeks. It will not take long to bring him to the point of a proposal, and you know well enough how to do that. I have given you enough hints. You will have your title yet, my dear."

"I am not sure I want a reluctant husband, Mama."

"No, indeed! Who would? It is up to you to ensure that he is not reluctant. But if Bertram cannot be brought round, then we shall go to Marshfields in the autumn... or Brandlebury... or Bath! There is an idea! All manner of men go to Bath over the winter. Yes, that might answer. But no more Latin, understood?"

"Yes, Mama."

"No more book learning of any sort. Remember always that you are a lady."

"Yes, Mama."

"Good. I am glad we understand each other. Now sleep, for tomorrow is another day, and another chance to secure a husband. And not a Sunday, thank heavens, so we will have some more interesting activities to amuse us than recitations from Shakespeare. Your father says that it will rain tomorrow, which seems to please him, but we must hope he is wrong about that. Good night, Beatrice."

"Good night, Mama."

Lady Esther picked up the candelabrum and left, plunging the room back into darkness. For a long time Bea sat unmoving, not even bothering to lie down again, mulling over her stepmother's words.

Lady Esther might be confident that Bertram could be brought round, and perhaps she was right. Bea had always been good at getting what she wanted, by the simple expedient of never giving up. Her indulgent father had always been an easy mark. Aunt Betty, who had looked after her when Mama had died, was just as unresisting. Walter had drifted into her net almost without realising it.

But there were some people who were immovable. Her stepmother was one such, and Bea had long since given up trying to convince her of any point she refused to concede. Bea had an uncomfortable feeling that Bertram was cut from the same cloth. Yet she could not pursue Bertram at all, for she had given her word and that was binding. She might not always behave in a ladylike manner, but she knew that a promise was sacrosanct, and must never be broken.

Yet if not Bertram, who else was there? Lord Grayling, who may be merely flirting with her? Mr Fielding, who loved her but was a mere clergyman? Lord Brockscombe, who kissed her only to steal a hairpin? Or Lord Thomas Medhurst, who forced a kiss upon her without so much as asking?

None of them set her heart racing, or warmed her inside, but at least if she married a man with a title she would have some standing in society. She would be Lady Grayling... or Lady Brockscombe... or Lady Thomas Medhurst. She would have a place in the nobility, and even the haughty Bucknells of Marshfields would have to acknowledge her as one of them. They would not be able to sneer at her as they now did... as they did even to Mama, for marrying a man without a title.

And that would be something, even if her marriage was not perfect. Surely that would be enough? She supposed glumly that it would have to be.

But as she lay down and closed her eyes ready for sleep, the image filling her inner eye was of Bertram, his sweet face and his smile of approbation as she recited Horace. And his kiss! Her whole body wriggled with pleasure as she recalled that glorious kiss.

If only she could marry Bertram! Then she would have a husband who lit fires inside her, and she could learn Latin too, and what could be more perfect?

If only.

20: A Wet Monday

Monday morning was grey and damp, the sky heavy with the promise of more rain to come. It was all in perfect accordance with Bea's mood. Once she had skipped along the echoing passageways to the old schoolroom each morning, but now her steps dragged. She hardly knew why she went there, for the Latin primer sat balefully on the table, willing her to open it. But she was forbidden, so she simply sat, arms folded, head lowered, deep in misery. She was so lost in her own depressing thoughts that she did not hear Bertram enter the room.

"Bea? Oh, Bea, whatever is the matter? You have not even opened your primer this morning."

"I am still forbidden from any sort of book learning, Bertram. Mama came to my room last night especially to tell me so, and to point out that my time is running out to find a husband."

"It is true that you will soon be leaving Landerby Manor, but that does not mean all is lost," he said.

"No, but I am one and twenty, and Mama believes I am quite on the shelf. She is thinking of taking me to Bath for the winter, but Bath is full of gouty old men and I do *not* want to marry a gouty old man."

"Not even for a title?" Bertram said teasingly, tipping his head to one side in a manner that reminded her of a bird. A robin, perhaps, for he wore a burgundy waistcoat this morning.

"Not even if he is a duke," she said despondently. "There has to be more to a man than his title. Oh, Bertram, it is so difficult! I want to marry, and to marry well, so that Mama and Papa will be proud of me, and the Bucknells will not sneer at me, but I also want a man who—" She had been about to say *'whose kisses set me on fire'*, but stopped herself in time. That would lead to awkward questions that she could not answer — at least, not to Bertram. He must never suspect how he had made her feel, for that brief, glorious moment.

"Who is congenial?" Bertram suggested gently. "Someone, perhaps, who is a friend as well as a husband?"

"Yes," she said, for it was as good a description as any. "Someone I like to be with. And someone who permits me to learn Latin," she added, with some heat. "I am not cut out for tapestry work."

"I cannot imagine anything more tedious," he said, laughing. "It is so disappointing that Lady Esther is still of the same mind. I was so sure her opinion would soften once she saw how well your recitation was received. It was my idea, you know, to show you off to everyone, and you did it admirably, Bea. I was enormously proud of you."

"Were you?" she said shyly. "Then it was worth it, even though Mama disliked it. I enjoyed it, too. The words roll around in my head in such a majestic way. Will you let me listen to you, sometimes? Will you read

Horace to me... or any of the poets? And pity me whenever you see me with my tapestry."

He reached across the table and took her hand in his. She almost gasped at the sudden contact. His hand was warm, sending energy pulsing through her. Such lovely hands he had, with long, sensitive fingers that she longed to stroke. Her heart took off at speed, and when she dared to look into his eyes, she was mesmerised, held fast in his gaze. Brown, but such a light, vivid brown, so alive with... affection? The affection of friendship, perhaps. But how odd, because Walter had never looked at her that way, even when they were betrothed. He had never made her heart race, either, or made it hard to breathe, or kissed her in a way that made her melt into an unfathomable swirl of emotion. He had never kissed her at all. Not like Bertr am...

His voice swirled around her, warm and intoxicating.

"You must not worry about it. I promise you will find a husband, and a congenial one, too, and you will be able to drown in Latin, if you want. I promise, Bea."

And that just made her angry. Snatching her hand from his, she jumped up and away from him. "Don't make promises you can't keep!" she spat at him, her old Newcastle accent rising up to overcome years of Mama's careful training. "You can't promise anything!"

"But I can. I mean it, Bea." He followed her, reaching out to cup her face.

At the first touch she stilled, her anger replaced with... what? Some whirlpool of emotions she could not even identify. Fear was in there somewhere, and confusion, and wariness, and agitation, and uncertainty, for what could he possibly mean? But she stood, her breathing uneven, waiting... waiting...

Out of that raging torrent of feelings, it was hope that bubbled to the surface. Hope, because he was so close, so unbearably close, holding her face in his hands and surely he would kiss her again? How could he not? She wanted it so badly she ached inside, longed for him to hold her against him, to put his mouth on hers.

He would, he *must*...

A brisk rat-a-tat-tat on the door sent them spinning apart. Of all people, it was her father.

"So this is where you hide yourself away, Bea. Good morning, Atherton."

"Sir."

"Oh, is this your Latin book, daughter? *'A Schoolboy's First Latin Primer'.* So this is what the sons of gentlemen learn."

He was so cheerfully normal, as if he had not just burst in upon them on the brink of kissing. Bea could not look him in the eye, and was utterly incapable of speech. Fortunately, Bertram contrived some degree of composure and the two men talked of Latin lessons and tutors and school lessons, with only the slightest stumbling now and then on Bertram's side to suggest his own agitation. Was that merely embarrassment at being so nearly caught out, or was there more to it?

Eventually, her father said, "I was not looking for you in particular, Bea, but now that I have found you, perhaps you can help me. Is there such a thing as a large blackboard in here?"

"Oh... um... yes, I believe so. In the big cupboard over there, I think."

He rummaged around until he found what he was looking for, then called on Bertram to help him retrieve it. It was certainly large, and it was also filthy, coated in decades of grime and cobwebs.

"That will need a good scrub," Bea said.

"So it will. I shall send some footmen to take it down to the nether regions for the attention of the maids."

"What are you up to, Papa?"

He grinned boyishly. "The board is to keep the scores for a fencing tournament. Since the rain is likely to keep us indoors all day, the gentlemen will need some way to expend their energy. I have already recruited the duke and the marquess to the enterprise, and I believe Grayling is an exponent of the art, too. What about you, Atherton?"

"I am not very skilled with a blade," Bertram said dubiously.

"Your books are more enticing, no doubt. But this is only for fun. If you will be willing to make up the numbers, I shall allow you to be honourably defeated in the first round and retire to the library."

Bertram laughed. "Very well, sir, but I shall hold you to that. I will engage for no more than a brief appearance on the field of battle."

Breakfast was spent recruiting more competitors for the tournament. Then, when the gentlemen went off to their meeting, Bea and her father arranged the great hall in preparation, setting up the board with all the names, instructing the footmen to push all the furniture away to the sides of the room, and examining the available fencing swords for suitability.

Her father almost purred with satisfaction as they worked.

"You are looking forward to this," Bea said, amused. "Have you been horribly bored these past weeks?"

He paused from chalking names onto the blackboard. "I would not put it like that. I have felt a little *spare*, to be honest. My Latin is too poor for the scholars' meetings, and a man cannot be out riding all day every day. You and your stepmother are busy, so I am alone for most of the morning."

"You could have stayed at home."

"By myself? No one to talk to? That does not appeal! One cannot always be at home, and there is a deal of pleasure to be had in seeing my two ladies enjoying themselves. Still, I confess I shall be glad to return to my own house... my own bed. I miss the boys, too. Charles is at such an interesting age, and Henry is becoming quite a little man, learning to ride and to shoot."

"Is it my imagination, or might there be another one arriving before too long? Mama is looking very peaky in the mornings."

He laughed. "So it would seem, but for myself, I should like a daughter this time — a little girl just like you."

"Heaven forbid!" Bea said, eyebrows raised. "Another trouble-maker?"

"You have never been the least trouble, Bea," he said with a smile. "Your manners appal me sometimes, such as when you jilted Walter Atherton without a single kind word, but even if you are occasionally thoughtless, you are never malicious. You have a good heart, you just have to learn to consider the feelings of others a little more."

That stung! But she could not deny the truth of it, and poor Mr Fieldings' woebegone face rose up in her mind to chastise her even more. "I was very rude to Walter," she said miserably. "Do you think he was very upset? I never thought he cared much whether he married me or not."

"Nor did I," her father said. "He is lazy, like his father, and he took you because it spared him the bother of exerting himself. It will be good for him to have to earn his living. Sir Hubert tells me that he has done well in London, so there is hope for him yet."

"You have heard from Sir Hubert, have you? Did he mention Winnie? Is it official yet?"

"No, it is all off, seemingly. Her mysterious suitor has vanished just as suddenly as he appeared."

"Poor Winnie!" Bea said. "To be jilted at twenty-four — how humiliating!"

"There are worse fates in life," he said lightly.

"Such as what?"

"Better to be jilted than to become entangled with the wrong man," he said in surprisingly serious tones. He stepped back to scrutinise the blackboard. "There! I have arranged it so that the strongest fencers will not meet too soon, and I still have one spot left, in case Mr Fielding should change his mind."

Bea enjoyed the tournament enormously. There was a great deal of pleasure to be had in seeing men who were usually so formally attired, with starched cravats and fitted coats to give them dignity, stripped to their shirts and engaged in physical combat. Nor was it a game to them. It was thrilling to see the intensity with which they approached each match. Every point was a duel to the death, in their minds.

Mr Fielding, who was not participating, sat beside her, not saying much except the occasional comment on the current match, but his quiet company was pleasant. She was glad that he was no longer avoiding her company, although once or twice she caught a certain look in his eye as he looked at her, a wistfulness, perhaps, that made her feel guilty all over again.

Once he had been defeated, Bertram attired himself properly again and he too came to sit with her as she watched, and gradually his friends, too, as they were removed from the competition. There were few other ladies there. The duchess and her sisters watched for a while, and Miss Grayling hovered around the marquess as much as she could, but Bea's stepmother had shuddered at the very suggestion that she might attend.

"I cannot prevent you from being there, since your father has always indulged your interest in the sport, and perhaps it is no bad thing to see how gentlemen display their prowess with a blade, but I cannot bear to watch myself. Such primitive violence!"

Bea did not think it primitive at all. She had seen a bare-knuckle fight once at a fair, and that was a display of primitive violence, beyond question. So much blood! And one of the fighters had been knocked out cold on the ground and carried off by his friends, which quite spoilt her enjoyment of the day until she saw him walking around later with a tankard of ale in his hand, and laughing as if nothing had happened. But fencing — there was an art to that, and she loved to watch it.

Once again, the quiet marquess, so self-effacing in company, demonstrated remarkable ability. His light-footed grace in the dance was also an advantage when fencing, and he defeated his first opponent without effort. Lord Grayling had a different kind of talent, more powerful and inclined to overwhelm a more timid opponent. He made short work of Lord Brockscombe in the first round. Bertram had not overstated his ability, accepting his defeat at Lord Thomas's hands with grace.

One by one, the less adept fell by the wayside. The longest bout was between Lord Embleton and Lord Grayling, but in the end the baron's superior strength had the advantage. Which left a final round between Lord Grayling and Bea's father.

"You have had an easy run so far, Franklyn," Lord Grayling said, as they rested before the start of their match.

"One of the benefits of arranging the tournament is to choose my own place in the lists," her father said. "I imagine I am about to be tested to my limits now, however."

"Or beyond them, I sincerely trust," the baron said, grinning wolfishly.

Bea's father only smiled.

As soon as the match began, it became clear that the baron had underestimated his opponent. He lost two points very quickly, and his posture changed subtly. Bea guessed that he had judged her father, a man beyond forty, to be no more than a casual amateur, and it was true that his early rounds had not stretched him at all. Now the baron was forced to reconsider, and change his strategy.

For a little while they were more evenly matched, and Lord Grayling even managed to gain a point. But then, as if he tired of playing with his opponent, her father drew on his long experience and dispatched his opponent in a few swift bouts.

"Thank you, my lord, a most enjoyable match," Mr Franklyn said, as they shook hands.

Lord Grayling was too well-bred to show his displeasure openly, for he laughed a little and answered easily, "More so for you than for me, I imagine. I am not accustomed to be defeated quite so comprehensively. You keep yourself remarkably fit for a man of your age, Franklyn."

"Ah, but it is necessary, for I am the father of a daughter, and one never knows when one may have to deal with a presumptuous fellow. I like to be prepared."

"How very commendable," Lord Grayling drawled. "I do not think you will be much troubled by men of that sort."

"I certainly hope not."

Her father found a notebook, and began to record all the scores from the blackboard. At first the men stood around discussing the various matches and the skills on display, but gradually they wandered off to bathe and change, and the great hall emptied.

"You are going to send a report to the club," Bea said, as she watched her father busily writing.

Her father turned to her with a grin. "Certainly I am. They will love to hear about all these fine lords, and how they performed. I shall write it up in some detail and send it to Mr Potter to read out at the next meeting."

"You are enjoying this far too much, Papa, you sneaky thing. You did not tell them you were a champion in Newcastle."

"Well, I may have forgotten to mention it, but even if I had, they would not have believed I still have the skill. They look at me and see a few grey hairs, and think I am past it."

"And you carefully arranged to take on only the dawdlers before the final. Did you know that you would be facing Lord Grayling?"

"One can never know for sure, but if not him, then it would have been the marquess. Either would have served my purpose. Do you know why I arranged this tournament, Bea?"

"You just like showing off your skill."

He gave a bark of laughter. "That is certainly a part of it, and I have few enough skills, heaven knows, so I must make the most of those I have. Besides, all that practising in the attics should not go to waste, should it?"

"Papa," she said hesitantly. "You mentioned me... or at least, you mentioned having a daughter, and I can guess what you mean. Would you truly fight a duel?"

He folded his notebook, and tucked it into his coat pocket. "If I had to, yes. I would hope it would never be necessary."

"To deal with presumptuous men, yes," she said thoughtfully. "Are there any such here? Was all this a warning for someone in particular? Lord Grayling, perhaps?"

"He has a certain reputation, it is true," he said slowly. "I cannot be sure of what he might do if he finds himself alone with you. Who can see into a man's heart? If a man pays you marked attentions, that may be mere chivalry, or it may be mischievous, an idle flirtation. Or, if his intentions are honourable, he will eventually present himself to me for approval, as honest Mr Fielding did. But until that happens, one does not know what a man has in mind, and I would not like any man to think that you are unprotected. That is all."

"No one could imagine I am unprotected, Papa. You and Mama are here with me, after all."

"But your stepmother is not always with you. She thinks the duke's protection is enough, and perhaps it is, but I should not want there to be the slightest misunderstanding. Bea, I shall be honest with you. I have always given you enough room to be yourself, to make your own mistakes, but some men will take advantage of that. I do not want you to be subjected to any... unpleasantness, that is all. So I have had an afternoon's fun and, I sincerely trust, you will not be importuned by any unwanted attentions. But tell me, Bea, since we are being so open, what is this business with Latin? Is that simply a fine excuse to mingle with the gentlemen?"

"No, no! I enjoy the language, that is the only reason. I should love to become fluent so that I can understand everything, and not just learn poems by rote. The Latin poets have been dead for thousands of years, but their words bring them to life. They are immortal, Papa! Is that not amazing? I can read their words and imagine them walking about the streets, meeting their friends, gazing at a lover and admiring her white neck. I want to get to know them, to understand them. It is a great disappointment to me that I cannot learn more, although..." She giggled, hand to mouth.

"Bertram says I shall be able to do whatever I want when I am married, even learn Latin."

Her father smiled, but said, "That is a bad reason to marry. You should marry a man who will take care of you and cherish you, Bea."

"Someone like Mr Fielding, you mean?" she said archly.

"Well, yes," he said laughing. "He is truly in love with you, although he seems to think you need to be sheltered from every wind that blows, which is not how I see you at all. Nor can I see you living in a parsonage, either."

"Oh, but it is a very snug parsonage, Papa. He told me so himself."

"What a dolt! He should have told you he would put a curate in the snug parsonage, and set you up in a fine estate — using your own fortune, naturally. But no, he would not suit you, I can quite see that."

"No, indeed, for I should not like to be plain Mrs Fielding."

He folded his arms and looked askance at her. "Are you so set on a title? Is it really so important?"

"It is. I want to be respected, Papa. I want all those superior folk at Marshfields to acknowledge that I am every bit as good as they are."

He was silent for a long time, then he said slowly, "But you are not, Bea."

It was as if her heart had stopped beating. "What do you mean?" she whispered. "I know you were an attorney once but—"

He waved her to silence. "It is not that. Not entirely that, anyway. Bea, your mother was already with child when I married her. She had... there was a man, he left her in difficulties, she told her father, and he asked me to marry her. I was only two and twenty, and still learning my trade under her father, but I had been in love with Eloise since the day I met her. I had always hoped one day to be made a partner in the business and marry her, but there it was, offered to me at once. We were married within days."

"But who is my father?"

"*I* am your father!" he said with fierce intensity. "In every way that matters, I am your father. I held you in my arms the day you were born, and I have loved you unreservedly ever since. I will always love you unreservedly, because that is what fathers do."

She was shaking, she realised. Why had she never been told this before? "Who knows about this?"

"Everyone in Newcastle, of course, for they can all count and you were born seven months after we married, and since your mother was staying with her cousin in Hartlepool, you are clearly not of my blood. But no one there treated you in any way disrespectfully, or Eloise, either. In an attorney's family, no one cares. It was only when I came into my fortune and we moved up in the world that it seemed to matter, so I told your stepmother of it. Unfortunately, her relations found out about it, too, probably from connections at Newcastle, and now they hold us in contempt — you for tainted blood, as they see it, me for accepting another man's child, and your stepmother for marrying into such a disreputable family."

"I do not see why anyone needs to know," Bea said with sudden heat. "It is what I am that matters, surely, not who my father was."

"For my part, I agree entirely, but these aristocratic families are obsessive about blood lines. There is also your mother's behaviour — getting herself with child before marriage. That shows a certain wildness, which might also show itself in you. When you come to marry, your husband will have to know, naturally, but if there had been any defects in your ancestry, they would surely have manifested themselves by now. So now you know why some of the Marshfields family look down on us, and many of their acquaintances in town, although not all, happily. The Athertons never minded about it. And I suspect that no one here knows of it, for you have been treated with every courtesy, have you not?"

She nodded, not sure she could trust herself to speak. She was as good as illegitimate! Her mother had been... she did not even know the word for it, except the Biblical ones that even Mr Dewar would not speak out loud.

"What can I do?" she whispered.

"You can forget all about it and be your own natural self," he said promptly. "I once thought... well, part of the reason for marrying your stepmother was the idea that she could teach you to be demure and ladylike, but I have come to realise that I like you much better the way you are, bumptious and unladylike as you sometimes are." He grinned. "And so will your husband, when you find the right man. So do not focus your search too narrowly on noblemen. A title is no guarantee that a man is of good character. Let your heart be the judge, Bea. Find a man who loves you for yourself, just as you are."

"Unreservedly?"

"Unreservedly," he said, smiling at her. "That is a love that will last for your whole life, and is a thousand times better than a peer's coronet, believe me."

21: A Lady In Distress

Bea was stunned. She felt just the way she had when she had fallen out of the old apple tree at the age of six or seven, all the breath knocked out of her and her lungs incapable of bringing in more. Everything she knew about herself was wrong. Even Aunt Betty, her father's oldest sister, who had looked after her for years, was not her aunt at all.

After her father had gone to change, she walked blindly out into the garden, finding even the high ceilings of Landerby too oppressive in her current mood. She needed air, cool air and a fresh breeze. What she found was air that was still damp from the rain, but at least it was pleasantly cool, and there was a slight breeze to fan her.

She walked here and there, although she hardly knew where, but only one thought was uppermost in her mind — how arrogant she had been, to think herself just as good as these people! To aspire to marry into the nobility! And all the time, she was no one at all, the child of an unknown father and a mother who was what Mrs Dewar described with a sniff of disapproval as a *'fallen woman'.* Someone who conceives a child without a husband, although Bea was hazy about quite how that could happen. Nobody took much notice if it was Maisie Whyte, the smith's daughter, but if it happened to a gentleman's daughter she was described as *'ruined'* and obliged to marry in haste to the nearest man who would have her. It was the same with an attorney's daughter, apparently, for her mama had been swiftly married to her father.

And if she had not, Bea would have been a bastard and not a respectable, or at least a *relatively* respectable daughter of a gentleman.

She found herself beside the nymph fountain, without the least idea how she had got there. It seemed a suitable place to stop her agitated perambulations, however, since the marble bench had been sheltered from the rain by the shrubs towering over it, and so was merely a trifle damp.

It was there, as she sat contemplating the poor, neglected statue, that she reached a resolution. She must stop chasing after the mirage of a titled husband, now that she knew her true origins. In fact, she was not at all certain that she was a fit wife for anyone. She would go home and be good and work at her tapestry, and try to be worthy of whatever man deigned to offer for her. Perhaps she should accept Mr Fielding after all, and live in the snug parsonage...? No, she was not quite that desperate.

She was so lost in her thoughts that she almost jumped in shock when a tall figure loomed over her. But it was only the marquess, his face creased in worry.

"You are s-s-s... unhappy, Miss F-F-Franklyn."

"Oh... not really... it is nothing that need alarm you, Lord Embleton. I have just received a shock, that is all."

At once, the worry lines deepened. "Not a death in the family? Not a t-t-tragedy?"

He sat down beside her, taking her hand in his. Without gloves, it felt scandalously intimate to hold hands in that way, but she did not want to insult him by snatching her hand away. He had attractive hands, she decided, soft and white and cool. Not as shapely as Bertram's, which were long and slender, but very pleasant to hold.

"No, no, nothing tragic. Nothing recent, in fact. Some family history of which I was unaware, that is all. Something a little surprising... about myself, so I have come to realise that I have been very foolish, and setting myself up for failure. I came to Landerby to find—"

She stopped, aware of the impropriety of spilling all her secrets to this man she scarcely knew.

"A husband?" he said gently.

She nodded. "And now I realise how presumptuous of me that was. I do not think I even have the proper character to be the wife of any man, let alone a lord. I am too selfish... too brazen. Even my own father calls me bumptious."

The marquess laughed. "But you are also k-k-k—" He stopped, sighed, tried again. "K-K-K—" Again he stopped, then almost shouted, "*Kind!* Very."

"But I am not," she said sadly. "I am rude and thoughtless and say whatever comes into my head, without considering how it may upset the other person. It is only afterwards that it occurs to me that I should have been more subtle, and dressed things up a little to avoid giving offence."

He shook his head violently. "Not s-s-subtle. I *hate* subtle. People s-s-say things, b-b-b—" He gave an exclamation of annoyance, and released her hand to reach into a pocket and produce a small notebook and pencil.

He scribbled away furiously, tearing off each page as it was filled, and passing it to her to read.

'Miss Franklyn, I am surrounded by sycophants who smile and tell me lies. They may be subtle but they are also hypocritical and I wish I could escape them once and for all. You have never been like that. You never get impatient with my speech and try to guess what I am trying to say. You have no idea how much I hate it when people do that! Also, when we first sat on this bench, you chattered away to keep me company without needing me to say a word, which was delightful. And yes, you are kind. You may speak before considering the consequences sometimes, but you are willing to admit to that fault and correct it as far as possible. Look how considerately you dealt with Mr Fielding in the letter you wrote to him, which he has proudly shown to his particular friends as an example of your generous heart. It is the gentlest rejection a man could ever hope to receive. So never say of yourself that you are unkind, for it is untrue. You may be selfish to a degree, for which of us is not? Only a saint, and who wants to be a saint? An entirely good person would be tedious company, I think. Miss Franklyn, you have one quality that I, and many others, value above all others, and that is honesty. I despise all those who say one thing to my face and another behind my back. How can one ever trust such a person? You are worth a thousand of such miserable snakes. I hope you will never change. Please, do not be sad any longer.'

Impossible not to smile at such words! "Thank you," she whispered. "I feel much better now, but I must go and dress for dinner."

He nodded, smiling, then reached for her hand again and raised it to his lips.

Impulsively she leaned towards him and kissed him full on the mouth. "You are a dear, sweet man, and I hope you find a wife who values you as you deserve."

Then, giggling slightly at the stunned expression on his face, she skipped away down the path.

***

After that strange moment in the old schoolroom, when he had as good as declared himself to Bea and then almost kissed her, Bertram stumbled through the day in a daze. He was silent at breakfast, silent through an interminable and dull lecture on Tacitus, silent during most of the fencing tournament. He was still silent as Bayley dressed him for the evening.

"Have you had a good day, sir?" Bayley said politely, as he fitted Bertram's shoes onto his feet.

"Yes, thank you, Bayley."

"Did you enjoy the tournament, sir? Mr Franklyn won, I gather."

"Yes. Franklyn won."

"Against Lord Grayling."

"Yes."

Bayley gave it up, and uttered not another word. Bertram barely noticed, so lost in his own thoughts was he. His mind was in such turmoil that he felt himself unfit for company, so when his friends arrived to dress for dinner, he slipped out of the room and made his way to the chapel gallery. Below him, the low sun cast long shadows across the floor, but up in the gallery where no rays could reach it was almost dark, and blessedly quiet.

There he gave himself up to the tumultuous thoughts spinning through his head. Joy and astonishment and exaltation and hope and exhilaration and terror chased each other like hounds let off the leash, wild with excitement. He wanted to race around like that himself, running and leaping and howling with the bliss of his first love. What was Horace to this delirium? How had the poets ever had the power to move him, when set beside the delicious sight of a tremulous smile or a scorching glance or a pair of soft... oh, so soft lips? She burned into him and yet he yearned with all his being for her touch. How many times had he read of such feelings? The reality was a thousand times better.

Yet there was also remorse. What a fool he had been, to say such things to Bea, to make promises he could not keep and even to be on the brink of kissing her again. It was only an inch away from a proper declaration, yet he could not, *must* not tell her all that was in his heart.

If only he could be sure of inheriting the earldom! With that prospect before him, even if many years away, he could go to Bea with a light heart and speak of love and marriage and how much he wanted to hear her talking in Latin for the rest of their lives. Or English, if ever she tired of Latin, it mattered not, so long as she were his wife.

But Lord Rennington might yet marry again and sire an heir, and then Bertram would be merely Mr Atherton forever more, and could not offer Bea the title she wanted and so richly deserved. He was in no position to make promises to her, and yet he so badly wanted to tell her everything. He quite understood Fielding's precipitate proposal. When he was with Bea, he could think of nothing else, with his senses overwhelmed by her closeness — her smooth skin that made him want to touch her, the blue eyes gazing at him so clear-sightedly, the hearty way she laughed, not a mild titter like most women. There was such life in her, and she filled him with life, too. She was like a fountain spilling energising water into a pool, and he was suddenly parched with thirst. Never before had he needed anything but his books and his family, but now he needed Bea with an aching that tormented him day and night.

But for all the anguish of unrequited love, he could not help laughing out loud for the sheer joy of it. He was in love, so deep in love that he might never find his way back to reality, but he did not care. It was enough to *feel* as he had never felt before. What a strange half-life he had been living, trapped in the world of two thousand years ago and not seeing the world around him in the present day.

Now that his eyes had been opened, he knew precisely what he would do. He could not speak yet, not until he knew for certain of his uncle's intentions, but once that question was settled, then he would open his heart to Bea. Perhaps she would reject him at first if the title was unlikely to come his way, but he was sure he could win her over, in time.

He was no longer concerned that she would marry one of his friends. She had rejected Fielding, Brockscombe seemed to be satisfied with a kiss and a hairpin, and Medhurst was still mooning after the lovely but vapid Miss Grayling. As for Miss Grayling's brother, Franklyn had seen him off comprehensively. That was an elegant way to deal with a man with questionable intentions! Now Grayling knew that if he dishonoured Bea in any way, Franklyn would call him out and would very much have the upper hand. Grayling was no fool, and would not risk that sort of scandal.

Dinner that evening was dominated by a point by point discussion of the fencing tournament, every move analysed to within an inch of its life. Bertram was amused to see Franklyn accorded an unaccustomed degree of deference. Franklyn was self-effacing, and pointed out that he himself had enjoyed a very easy run, while Grayling had suffered a long and strenuous match against the marquess, but he seemed to be flattered by the attention, nevertheless.

As for Bea... Bertram's heart ached for her, for it was clear she was miserable. She was situated beside the marquess, but he had Miss Grayling on his other side who monopolised his attention. Medhurst was on Bea's other side, having failed to find a place beside Miss Grayling, but passed the entire meal trying to overhear her conversation with Lord Embleton. No one seemed entirely happy with their situation. If only Bertram had been quicker, perhaps he could have secured Bea's company for the meal. Surely he would have done a better job of making her smile than Medhurst.

After dinner, there was dancing again, and at least Bertram managed to stand up with Bea once, but only for a reel which was too energetic for conversation. By the time Lady Esther rose to retire, taking Bea with her, he could not claim to have exchanged more than a dozen words with her all evening. It was maddening.

Once the ladies had withdrawn and the serious card players had settled down with brandy to hand and steely determination in their eyes, Bertram and his friends drifted away, first to the courtyard to get some air and then to their room for a final brandy before bed.

Fielding turned on Medhurst almost before they were through the door. "What was amiss with Miss Franklyn, Medhurst? She looked so down-pin tonight, I could hardly bear it. No bad news from home, I trust?"

"Nothing like that," Medhurst said, ripping off his cravat with a sigh of relief and accepting a glass from Bertram. "Lady Esther forbids her from learning Latin, that is all."

"That is all? *That is all?* The heroine of Sunday night, who recited Horace as well as anyone could... well, almost... only one or two minor mistakes... but that she should be *forbidden* from progressing with the language! Why? What is so bad about Latin, which every schoolboy learns?"

"It is not ladylike," Bertram said, with a wry smile. "A lady is supposed to sit about with her needlework, apparently."

The others burst into laughter. "I cannot see her being happy with *that,"* Medhurst said. "It seems an unwarranted interference. Who is Lady Esther to be so high-handed?"

"She is Bea's mama," Bertram said testily. "Until she marries, a girl must do as her mother bids her."

"Then she must marry at once," Fielding said, "if only to save her from the wretchedness of a future without Latin. Such a waste! Oh, the delight of finding a woman who can understand one's interests, and discuss them rationally. So many husbands and wives might as well be in different countries for all the commonality they share. I shall approach her again and assure her of my unchanged regard, while pointing out the advantage to her of marrying a man already fluent in Latin. Who better to teach her than a devoted husband?"

"You have already had your chance with her," Bertram said, seriously alarmed by this sudden turn, for Bea might be sufficiently cast down to accept Fielding this time. "She refused you, remember?"

"I took her by surprise," Fielding said. "I was too precipitate, perhaps... forgot to prepare the ground in advance. Now that she has had time to consider the matter, she might feel differently."

"She will never marry a clergyman," Bertram said hotly.

"Has she told you that?"

"Yes. She wants a title. That was why she jilted my cousin, because he is no longer the heir."

"Truly?" Fielding said, deflating at once. "Oh. Of course, she deserves it."

Brockscombe glowered at Bertram. "Is this true? She threw him over because of a title?"

"And an income of eight thousand or more, Corland Castle, a house in London and half a dozen other properties," Bertram said. "Walter is merely the illegitimate son of an earl now, with no expectations at all. Everything is entailed."

There was a sigh as they grasped the implications. "Eight thousand a year!" Medhurst said, shaking his head sorrowfully. "And the castle, of course, and a multitude of other properties. The world is very unfair sometimes. And he would have had Miss Franklyn's forty thousand, on top of all that," he added meditatively. "Another two thousand a year."

"I quite see why she dropped him," Brockscombe said, "but I would have thought you were the natural successor to your cousin, Atherton. You are the heir now, after your father."

Bertram hardly knew how to answer him. He had backed himself into a corner, for if he admitted that Bea had indeed set her sights on him but he had turned her away, he could hardly admit that marrying her was now exactly what he wished to do.

It was Fielding who intervened. "Oh, I see it now! That is why you brought her here and sang her praises up and down, so that Brockscombe or Medhurst would take her up." He laughed. "So that was why you sounded as if you liked her yourself."

"I *do* like her!" Bertram cried, stung. "She is a darling, and she did think about me, it is true, but... but I thought she ought to have a wider field," he went on, improvising hastily.

"No, you said you did not want her," Brockscombe said. "You did not want anyone, in point of fact. I remember it distinctly. *'Take my advice and steer clear of the wedded state.'* Those were your words."

Bertram cursed Brockscombe's excellent memory. "Well, perhaps I have changed my mind. Better she should marry me and learn Horace and

Virgil than end up in a parsonage with Fielding, who would have her head filled with battles and troop movements and all sorts of nonsense."

"There is nothing wrong with the Caesars in general, and Julius in particular," Fielding said at once, "and I think it most unfair of you, Atherton, to try to cut me out at this point."

"It is Miss Franklyn who has cut you out," Brockscombe said, "but I agree that Atherton should stay out of this. He has renounced all claim to her hand, so—"

"I have done nothing of the sort!" Bertram said hotly. "I stood aside to give you two a chance — *not* Fielding, since she wants a title — but neither of you has offered for her."

"It is a momentous decision to make," Brockscombe said. "It requires a lot of thought."

"I cannot see that you have thought about it at all," Bertram said. "All *you* have done, Brockscombe, is steal a kiss and a hairpin, so be satisfied with your trophies and leave her alone."

"I shall not!" Brockscombe began.

"Now see here," Medhurst said. "*I* am the one most in need of her forty thousand pounds."

"But I laid claim to her before any of you," Brockscombe said. "She is mine."

"Stop it!" Bertram yelled. "Stop talking about her as if she is an apple to be picked from the tree whenever you want. She is a person, for heaven's sake!"

"What has got into you, Atherton?" Brockscombe snapped. "You are impossible these days. *I* am going to offer for her, and if she turns me down... but why would she? A viscountcy, five thousand a year and as pretty an estate as you would see anywhere. No, she will not turn me down, but if she does, then you may try your luck, Medhurst."

"Why should *you* have the first turn?" Medhurst said, poking Brockscombe in the chest.

"Why should he have *any* turn?" Bertram cried, throwing caution to the wind. "Why can you not leave her alone, both of you?" Seeing Fielding about to speak, he added, "*All* of you. Let her go home, recover from the annoyance of you three and then, in a few months—"

"A few months!" Fielding wailed.

"I see no reason why we should wait," Medhurst said. "Despite your carping, Atherton, I *have* been thinking about it, for I need to marry, and soon, since my poor brother is woefully short of heirs. I should not have rushed into it quite so quickly, but here is a lady in distress, deprived of the joy of Latin, and I have the ability to make her happy again. *And* raise her up in the world. Lady Thomas Medhurst — it sounds well, do you not think?"

"Lady Brockscombe sounds better."

"And Lady Rennington sounds best of all," Bertram said recklessly.

"And how long would it be before she could call herself that?" Brockscombe said. "Many decades, we must all hope. You have no title yet, Atherton, not even a courtesy affair, so you are out of the reckoning. I shall go first and—"

"She should have a proper choice," Bertram said. "If we all want to save her from the desert of a life without Latin, then we should all go to her at once and lay this question before her. Then she can decide for herself."

It was a gamble. Surely they would not take him up on it?

But they did.

"Very well," Brockscombe said.

"All of us at once," Medhurst said. "Even Fielding. And you, Atherton, I suppose. Then she can see what is on offer, and pick the best."

"When?" Fielding said.

"She will be in the old schoolroom before breakfast," Bertram said. "Eight o'clock."

"Eight o'clock?" Brockscombe said, horrified. "That is the middle of the night!"

"You need not come if it is too early for you," Bertram said.

"No, no. I shall be there." He exhaled sharply. "Lord, eight o'clock! In the *morning!* I shall never hear the end of it."

22: The Delights Of Bath

It was habit that took Bea to the schoolroom that morning. Her Latin primer would still be there, sitting unopened on the table, calling to her but untouchable. If only she dared... but she could not disobey Mama. It was almost the first lesson her stepmother had taught her, all those years ago, even before the struggle with the accent, the deportment lessons, the expensive masters to teach her music, singing, dancing, painting.

"Whatever else you do, Beatrice," she had said, "if you always do as you are told — *precisely* as I tell you — then you cannot go wrong. Obedience is the golden rule, do you understand?"

"Yes, Mama."

"Good girl. We shall make a lady of you yet, and then you will be able to marry a man of high rank and the world will be at your feet. But it will only happen if you do as you are told. Disobedience is the greatest sin there i s."

And Bea had been very obedient and done as she was told, and Walter had dropped into her lap like a ripe plum, just as Mama had predicted. But now there was no plum and no replacement on the horizon, either, and not even obedience could wash away the stain of her unknown father. Obedience had failed her, ultimately, but still she could not break the golden rule. The Latin primer would sit, unopened, in front of her, although she could not quite bring herself to put it back on the shelf.

She would write to Aunt Betty, she decided, and tell her all about the tournament and the gentlemen she had danced with last night. Her aunt would enjoy that, and the letter would be passed around all their former friends and neighbours, so that they could read, wide-eyed, about the duke and duchess, the marquess who would be a duke one day, and all the other lords. Just as Papa's friends at the fencing club would enjoy hearing about so many great men, so would Aunt Betty and her friends.

Perhaps she would write to Winnie Strong, too, who had returned from London without her suitor and was firmly back on the shelf again. A letter might cheer her up.

With her writing case in hand, she entered the schoolroom, to find it filled with gentlemen, shuffling their feet awkwardly and greeting her with diffidence, instead of their usual casual friendliness.

"This is... a surprise," she said, with some feeling. "What brings you all here at this hour? It is usually only Bertram."

More foot shuffling. Even Bertram could not quite look her in the eye.

"Whatever is the matter?" she said.

Lord Brockscombe tugged at his neck cloth. "We... wanted to talk to you," he muttered. "Atherton?"

"You will explain it better," Bertram said. "Or Medhurst."

But it was Mr Fielding who stepped forward and said impatiently, "Oh, for heaven's sake! Miss Franklyn, we are here because we are all concerned for your happiness. You looked so miserable last night, and knowing that it arises from Lady Esther's prohibition on the learning of Latin, we are here to propose a solution."

Bea brightened. "You know of some way to convince Mama? I should be very happy to hear of it."

"Not... not that," Mr Fielding said, licking his lips. He looked at the others, but none of them seemed inclined to speak, so he went on, "The solution, it seems to us, is for you to marry... and marry someone who will not mind... will encourage you to learn."

"You, Mr Fielding?" she said gently.

He gave a nervous smile. "There is nothing I should like better, as you know, but... not necessarily me. One of us... any one of us. We would all... be happy to... to..."

"To marry you," Bertram put in, rather loudly. "You can choose, Bea."

She gazed round at them, puzzled. What were they saying? What did it mean? Could they really *all* want to marry her? Even Bertram? No, it was impossible.

"All of you?" she said, her voice rising.

"All of us," Bertram said.

"Even you, Bertram?"

He flushed, but looked her straight in the eye and nodded.

"Marry any one of us you like," Lord Thomas said.

"The title of your choice," Lord Brockscombe said.

"But...?" she floundered. "Are you proposing to me... are *all* of you proposing because you are sorry that I am not allowed to learn Latin?"

"Not me," Mr Fielding put in quickly. "I have other reasons. As you know."

"We have other reasons, too," Lord Thomas said. "It is not *just* the Latin."

"Yes, you want the dowry, too," Mr Fielding said. "You all want the dowry."

"It is not about *money*," Lord Brockscombe said testily. "Honestly, Fielding, you make it sound so sordid, as if we were nothing but fortune hunters."

"Well, why do else you want to marry her, if not for that?" Mr Fielding said hotly. "It is not as if you *love* her, is it?"

There was a long silence, heavy with tension, as three of the men glared at each other. Lord Thomas's hands clenched into fists, as if he wanted to hit one or other of his friends. Bertram simply stared at his feet, red faced.

Bea was almost too angry to speak, but then she saw the funny side of the situation, and started to laugh. At once, the tension dissipated, like the popping of a soap bubble, and the men smiled, too.

"You must not fall out over me," she said. "Or for any reason. You are all very kind but..."

But...? Was she truly going to turn them down... *all* of them? It was madness. Here was everything she had always wanted, offered to her freely. A respectable marriage, even a title, the summit of her ambition for much of her life, and she could even have Bertram, and those kisses that tormented her dreams. She could be the Countess of Rennington, just as she had always intended. The plum was hers again, and all she had to do was to reach out for it.

No. She could not do it. She knew that Bertram did not wish to marry — not her, not anyone. He had told her so a score of times. He was offering, and his friends were offering too, because of pity, not love, and that was a bad foundation for marriage. There must be love, or at least affection and respect, on both sides.

For once, her head and her heart were in agreement. It would not do.

"I am very sorry, gentlemen, and I thank you most sincerely for the honour you do me, but I cannot marry any of you."

Lord Thomas frowned. "Are you sure? Why not think about it?"

But Bertram said, "Miss Franklyn has spoken, Medhurst. Pray respect her decision."

"Indeed, that was a very settled no," Lord Brockscombe said, but he smiled at her, as if he were relieved.

Bertram gave her a watery smile, too, and heaved a deep sigh, as though he had completed a difficult assignment and was now free of duties for the rest of the day. Yes, she had done right to refuse them. Never had she encountered such reluctant suitors! They filed out silently, and, shaking her head in bemusement, she sat down at the table and opened her writing box.

But for a long time she sat and stared into space. This was what they thought of her — what even Bertram thought of her, as an object of pity. She was so pathetic a creature in his eyes that he would even overcome all his own scruples and offer to marry her. It was humiliating.

Hot tears dropped unheeded onto the paper in front of her. It was too much to bear. How could she hold her head up in public anymore? She was nothing... nobody. Not her father's daughter, and not even worthy of respect from an honest man, never mind a lord. No wonder she had never found a husband in town. Only fortune hunters, or Walter, too lazy to object, or Latin scholars who pitied her.

How had she come to this position? And what on earth was she to do with her life now?

***

Bertram was elated. He had declared himself, after a fashion, and Bea could be in no doubt that he was willing to marry her. She had not accepted him, but at least she had not accepted any of the others, either, which would have been a severe blow. He could not quite say how it had happened, but by degrees he had come to think of her as his own, and would have taken her loss badly.

With their time at Landerby almost over, there was very little time left for anyone to sweep in and scoop her up. Grayling had taken Franklyn's covert warning to heart and had avoided Bea ever since the tournament, and there were no other rivals. Bertram and the Franklyns would return to the North Riding, and he then had all the time in the world to court Bea properly and win her hand.

This plan received an unexpected boost at breakfast, when Franklyn came to sit beside him. "What are your plans for the homeward journey, Atherton? You have no carriage here, I notice."

"I have a post-chaise ordered for Thursday, sir."

"We travel on Thursday, too. Would you care to take up the last seat in our carriage? There will be room for your man in the luggage coach."

Two whole days in Bea's company! What better start to his campaign for her heart and hand could there be? But perhaps this was an impulsive offer that would be squashed by Lady Esther.

"How very kind you are, sir, but I should not wish to inconvenience the ladies at all. If the Lady Esther should dislike the plan—"

"Not the least inconvenience in the world. It was my wife's idea, and your company will be most welcome."

"In that case, I gladly accept. I will send word to cancel the post-chaise. My groom can ride ahead to ensure our accommodation is ready."

Two days later, after an early breakfast, Bertram found himself seated in the Franklyns' palatial carriage, directly opposite Bea. He had armed himself with a book to read so that he would not be tempted to look at her continuously, but it was not easy to read when she was so close to him. It was fortunate that he was not especially tall, or their knees would have bumped together with every lurch of the carriage, but every time he raised his eyes from the page, there she was.

He tried to recall a time when he had not noticed her at all, but he could not. His earliest impressions of her when she had first moved to Birchall as a girl of sixteen had not been favourable, but he could not now understand why. He had thought her liveliness too forward, perhaps. The mass of lovely curls that surrounded her face distracted from her delicate beauty. One noticed the richness of her clothes rather than the elegance of her dress or her well-formed figure.

And then she had quickly attached herself to Walter and had hardly been seen at Westwick after that, apart from the minimum that politeness dictated. Lucas had called her a leech, and Bertram could understand that, for her pursuit of Walter had been relentless. Bertram had seen little of her, and had scarcely thought of her from one month to the next. Now he thought of little else. He looked up from his book surreptitiously now and then, just to see the curve of her cheek, or those luscious curls bouncing with the movement of the carriage. He could not see her eyes, for mostly her head was turned away from him, gazing out of the window at the passing scenery, and the sides of her bonnet hid much of her face. But every time she spoke, she turned back a little, and then he could see the whole of her lovely face, if he dared to look.

Not that she spoke often. Nor did her father speak, for no sooner had the carriage rolled away down the overgrown drive of Landerby Manor than he removed his hat, leaned back against the squabs and closed his eyes. It was Lady Esther who carried the conversation, more or less single-handedly, starting with a summary of all that had happened at Landerby, as if they had not all been there and experienced these events for themselves. The monologue then moved forward to encompass the journey home, mentioning, with wearying detail, every single inn, village, town and way point of interest.

None of this required much participation from her captive audience, but Bea threw in a *'Yes, Mama'* or a *'No, Mama'* from time to time. Lady Esther came eventually to their return to Highwood Place, and the letters she expected to be awaiting her there, and here she turned more directly to Bea.

"I have written to Charity Ramsey to press her on the matter of our visit there this autumn, for she did promise... well, perhaps it was not quite a promise. Something about expecting us there. Do you remember her exact words, Beatrice?"

"I believe she said that she expected to be entertaining at Brandlebury this autumn, so that Marshfields would be quieter for his grace."

"Ah yes, although Papa may be quiet enough if he stays in his own apartments. One does not have to clear the whole house just because one member of it may be indisposed."

"But the music... the constant noise," Bea said. "You said that you all had to creep about, for fear of disturbing him."

"Of course, but that was some weeks ago, and he is much better now. Besides, the ballroom is a great distance from the Old Tower. Still, one must humour a duke, so I do not blame Charity for that, although Brandlebury is considerably smaller. I do not know how she will fit us all in, but I have written to remind her that she invited us... or at least, that she *ought* to invite us. I do not care for myself, but time is marching on for you, Beatrice. I should like to get you settled before the spring. So if Charity fails us, we shall go to Bath."

"Must we, Mama?" Bea said. "Is it not very unfashionable to be seen there now?"

Lady Esther hesitated, then went on smoothly, "It has not the superior society to be found in London, certainly, but it is very elegant, and so much smaller that one may make a splash more readily."

"Is it essential that we make a splash? Perhaps we could have a quiet time at home, for a change."

Lady Esther gave a dainty laugh. "One must be *seen*, Beatrice. Only country squires spend their lives quietly at home. Persons of quality must be visible in society. You wish to be a credit to your father and to me, I am sure."

"Of course, Mama," Bea said quietly.

Bertram had been watching the colour come and go in Bea's cheeks, and trying to divine what it might signify. Now she looked rather glum, so he said, "Bath is a very gay place, with assemblies, musical evenings, galas and all manner of excitements. And the shops are excellent, and very conveniently gathered in one small area, rather than being scattered here, there and everywhere. There will be plenty to amuse you."

Bea frowned at him, which was puzzling, but Lady Esther said, "And plenty of eligible gentlemen, one hopes. Have you been there, Mr Atherton? I suppose your mother takes the waters there, or does she confine herself to Harrogate?"

"Oh... yes, Mother has been there several times. She has tried most of the well-known spas, I believe. I went along on one or two trips, when I happened to be down from Eton. It seemed a very lively place to me, with entertainments every evening, although I was too young to participate, and I doubt it has changed much in ten years. It is old-fashioned, though, so you will have to learn to dance the minuet, Miss Franklyn."

"That is an excellent point," Lady Esther said. "Beatrice knows the movements, of course, for she has been well taught, but we must practise a little. And the costume, too! I believe Bath still requires the full costume, with lappets. So quaint, but such an elegant dance. Ten years... Mrs Atherton has not been there lately? And yet her health still so indifferent."

"Nowadays she seldom ventures further afield than Harrogate."

"Yet nothing seems to mend what ails her, does it?" Lady Esther said. "I do wonder if she might go on better if she thought less about her health. It sometimes happens that a female who dwells upon every little ache and twinge may cause the very affliction she fears. I knew a lady who was a great sufferer, but once she married and had children she had no time to spare for maladies."

Bertram laughed. "I wish it were so with Mother, but when she leaves Westwick she is always ill, and genuinely so. Her life was despaired of when she was no more than Miss Franklyn's age. But the good, clean air and water of the North Riding cured her of her ailments, if not of the worry of them. She will be very happy to let you know of the best baths and physicians in Bath, and to inform her friends there of your visit."

"Oh, I have my own acquaintances there," Lady Esther said, her well-bred voice displaying only the faintest hint of surprise that anyone would consider her to need introductions to any society. "The Lady Louisa Horsfell, Lady Mellish, General Sir Marmaduke Grimsby, Lady Watson… I shall write to some of them. The York Hotel is the most superior establishment, I believe. We shall stay there."

She continued to talk of Bath for some time, but since she required little response apart from Bea's occasional murmurings, Bertram felt safe to return to his book, or to pretend to, at least. There was a certain set to Bea's mouth when she looked his way that worried him. Had he offended her in some manner? Yet when he reflected on his contribution to the conversation, he could find no cause for offence. It was puzzling. But she had been out of sorts in some way ever since he had rushed out into the garden to save her from Grayling. It was beyond his understanding.

They reached the Crown at Bawtry, their overnight stop, in good time for dinner.

"This looks a pleasant place," Franklyn said, as ostlers rushed forward to attend to them, and a respectable innkeeper and his wife appeared, holding umbrellas to shield them from the rain.

"I shall need to inspect the bedrooms," Lady Esther said.

"Mr Atherton has stayed here many times, and recommends it," Franklyn said. "Besides, we have our own sheets."

"That does not help if there is the slightest dampness in the bed itself," she said. "I always inspect the rooms in a new place, Mr Franklyn, as you know very well." So saying, she accepted the innkeeper's arm to alight and swept into the inn.

"So be it," Franklyn said, without rancour. He turned to Bea and Bertram. "You two had better wait in the carriage until we are settled. The rain is fierce, and there is no point getting wet unless you have to. This will not take long, I hope."

He followed his wife, and for a moment silence fell. Bea still had that odd look about the mouth, so Bertram hurried to fill the silence.

"This is an excellent place. I am sure Lady Esther will find no fault."

"Of course she will. She always finds something amiss. Except at Marshfields. Nothing is ever wrong at Marshfields."

Bertram raised his eyebrows at the unusually sharp tone in her voice. "Ah well, there is nowhere so perfect as home, is there?"

But she glared at him. "Why do you always take her side? Papa I can understand, since he chose to marry her, but *you* have no reason to support her rather than me. I thought you were my friend, Bertram."

Bertram floundered against this unexpected attack. "I am only being polite, Bea."

"You could be polite to *me* for a change."

"When have I not been polite? I am not aware—"

"No, of course you are not aware! You never are. Quite oblivious to what *I* might be feeling, so when I tried to deter her from this wretched Bath scheme, you had to jump in feet first and make it sound oh, so wonderful! Assemblies! Musical evenings! Galas! And shops! As if I cared about galas or shops. What is the matter with you? Why are you so contrary? I thought you were a straightforward sort of man, and now I find you to be just as twisty and devious as the worst of them."

Bertram's mouth opened and closed ineffectually in astonishment. Twisty? Devious? Was that truly how she saw him?

"Bea, I am sorry if I said the wrong thing. I was only trying to help, and clearly I should never have intervened. But if you truly hate the idea of Bath, then tell Lady Esther so."

"She would not listen!"

"But your father would. You are not a child any more — you are one and twenty, a grown woman and fully entitled to your own opinions. Tell her—"

Franklyn's head appeared at the open carriage door, a wry smile on his lips. "The Lady Esther is pleased to approve the accommodations. We may enter. Take care across the yard. The rain has made it slippery."

He offered his hand to Bea as she descended, and Bertram was left to follow them into the inn in such a disordered state of mind that he hardly knew what he was about.

23: An Explosion

Bea felt like a kettle that was just about to come to the boil. She had spent hours cooped up in the carriage listening to endless plans for Bath, and Bertram could not even stand up for her, but had to point out what a wonderful place it was. Bath! Which was full of dowagers and retired generals and no one below the age of sixty to talk to. And no Bertram, she thought miserably. No Latin. No long walks on the moors to work out the fidgets. Nothing but confinement and polite smiles and banal conversation. Just like London, only with the minuet, danced with a hooped skirt and lappets.

She could scream!

Ripping off her bonnet, gloves and pelisse, she splashed her face with the warm water already waiting in her room, and then whisked downstairs, meeting Harper on the way up.

"Don't you want to change your gown, Miss Franklyn? And maybe tidy your hair a little?"

"How could it have become *un*tidy? I have done nothing but sit in the carriage for hours. My gown will do well enough for an inn dinner."

"Very well, miss." Harper's mouth set in a disapproving line, but Bea did not care.

In their private parlour, the table was still being laid for dinner, and various bottles and glasses set out on a sideboard. Bea poured herself a glass of wine, and prowled about the room until the servants left and she was alone. Then she hurled herself into a chair beside the empty hearth, and pondered her position.

On one point she was quite decided — there was to be no more chasing after lords. Or anyone, come to that. She was finished with all of that nonsense. If only she could go back to Newcastle and start again! To be back with Aunt Betty and Papa in the old house, where she had been happy. Before the fortune had dropped into Papa's lap. Before the big, new house. Before Lady Esther Bucknell.

And there she stopped. All of this, all her ambition had been driven by Mama. It was Mama who had tried to turn Bea into a lady. It was Mama who had convinced her to aim for the peerage. All of her present woes stemmed from Mama.

Yet she had rung a peal over Bertram, as if it were his fault! That was unfair of her, when he had been so kind to her.

So when he came into the parlour a few minutes later, armed with a book to read, she said, "I am very sorry I was so cross with you just now, Bertram. I did not mean it."

"Oh... it is of no consequence," he said absently, tossing his book from hand to hand.

"May I pour you a glass of wine?"

"Thank you. Yes... thank you." He took it from her hand without looking at her, and went to sit by the window, where raindrops chased each other down the uneven panes of the window.

She understood him. Now that she had rejected him, he had withdrawn again, and the easy terms on which they had existed for the past few weeks, which had given her such irrational hope, were gone. She sank even further into gloom.

Her father came in with the news that dinner was delayed. "Lady Esther is resting after the privations of the journey, so we shall not eat for another two hours. Atherton, feel free to order something if you are hungry."

"No, no, sir. I am perfectly ready to await Lady Esther's convenience."

"Has your groom arrived safely?"

"No, not yet." Bertram frowned a little. "I had expected him to be here well before this, for he left before us and we have been proceeding at an easy pace. Not much above forty miles!"

"He is taking very good care of your horse, I expect. A fine beast like that — he will not want to push him at all."

"True, and Whyte is an excellent groom. He will not risk Catullus."

"Then I expect he has merely taken a wrong turn somewhere. It is easily done."

"Yes, most likely that is all it is," Bertram said, with a quick laugh. "I told him to rest when he thinks it necessary, and stop for the night wherever convenient if he cannot reach Bawtry. He has money, and a letter of authority from me. I just wonder if he has encountered trouble — footpads, or some such. Horse thieves, perhaps."

"Then he will find the nearest parsonage and ask for help," Mr Franklyn said easily. "He seems a sensible lad."

Bertram gave a wry laugh. “I am worrying unnecessarily, I am sure. Next time, I shall do as you did and send my horse home a day or two earlier, to avoid all this.” He returned to staring gloomily out of the window.

Bea’s father smiled at her. “We have time for a walk before dinner, if you would like to stretch your legs, Bea.”

She gazed at him in astonishment. “It is *raining*, Papa!”

He laughed. “Very well, then. How about a game of backgammon instead?”

“If you wish.”

They played for a little while, but when Bea had lost three games in succession, her father put the set away. “We are all too tired and hungry to concentrate. Perhaps Mr Atherton would be so good as to read to us.”

Bertram picked up his book with a rueful smile. “It is in Latin, sir. *The Aeneid*.”

“I feel confident that a little Virgil will not corrupt my daughter beyond hope of redemption.”

Bertram smiled, opened the book and began reading. It was a strange thing, Bea pondered, as the majestic words wove their magic around her, that Bertram was such a quietly-spoken man as a rule, not timid but never putting himself forward. Yet when he read aloud, his voice became that of an orator. It was as if the power of the man who wrote those words, so great that they survived to be reverenced in the modern age, transmitted itself to the man who merely read those same words. For a few minutes Bertram in a sense became Virgil, or Horace, or whoever he happened to be reading.

For a little while, all Bea’s troubles drifted away in a cloud of Latin poetry. Her pleasure lasted precisely until her stepmother reappeared.

“Latin, Mr Atherton?” she said in her well-modulated voice. Did Mama ever raise her voice? Bea could not remember such an occasion.

"At Mr Franklyn's request, ma'am," Bertram said stiffly. "Poetry is very soothing at the end of a tiring day, do you not agree?"

She looked at him with slightly elevated eyebrows, as if astonished at such an outrageous suggestion, but turned smoothly to her husband. "At what hour have you ordered dinner to be served, Mr Franklyn?"

"In about an hour's time. No..." He checked his pocket watch. "A little under an hour, now. Should you like something at once? Some ham, perhaps, or—"

"No, thank you. My insides have been so jounced about I am not sure I could eat just yet."

"A glass of wine, then? That would settle your insides a little, I am sure."

"Well... perhaps."

Bertram closed his book with a snap. "I shall go and see if Whyte has arrived yet."

"Whyte?" Bea's stepmother said after Bertram had left, as she accepted the wine from her husband.

"His groom. He should have been here by now."

"Mr Atherton is concerned for his horse, I dare say."

"And for his groom," Mr Franklyn said sharply. "A boy of only sixteen years, who is not well versed in the ways of the world."

For a while, as Lady Esther sipped her wine, there was silence in the room, but it was not a comfortable silence, as between relaxed travelling companions. For Bea, her nerves already stretched to breaking point, it felt more like the charged atmosphere before a storm. She was not sure how much of it she could take and remain calm. So long as Mama said nothing more about Bath!

She could not be still, but her restless pacing drew immediate censure.

"Do sit down, Beatrice," her stepmother said. "You are making me dizzy with all this prowling about."

"She has been confined to the carriage for hours and it has been too wet to go out," her father said, in his mild way. "Let her walk about for a while if she wishes."

Lady Esther did not deign to acknowledge this comment. Instead she said, "Beatrice, I hope you will take advantage of this opportunity to enhance your friendship with Bertram Atherton. I have not yet given up hope of a match there, despite the lack of progress while we were under the duke's roof. He is attentive to you, certainly, but one would hope for something more by now."

Bea had nothing to say on the subject of Bertram. Let Mama harbour hopes in that direction if she chose, but Bea knew that they would come to nothing.

"Nor does it seem as if any of the other gentlemen present were swept off their feet by your attractions, either. Well, apart from Mr Fielding, and I trust we can do a little better than *that.*"

Her father had found a local newspaper to hide behind, but Bea had no such shield and felt horridly exposed. Had Mama always been so... so *cold?* Poor, gentle Mr Fielding, to be so disdainfully dismissed! And Bea herself had been just the same until Bertram had kissed her and awoken her to the possibilities of a different approach to matrimony, one involving the heart as well as the head. And now that she was thoroughly awake, she was shocked by her old self. How avaricious she had been... how heartless!

Her stepmother ploughed on relentlessly. "When we are at home again, you will have a better opportunity to secure Bertram once and for all, but we cannot delay too long, nor can we depend upon Marshfields or Charity Ramsey. So I shall begin planning for Bath—"

"For pity's sake, no more about Bath!" Bea cried.

"But we have to begin making arrangements," her stepmother said.

"No. No arrangements. No plans. No Bath. I am not going to Bath." Her tone was forceful, but she was insistent on being heard this time. Surely Mama would listen to her — she must!

Her father lowered his newspaper and looked at her in surprise.

Lady Esther merely raised her eyebrows a delicate fraction. "Are you confident then that you can secure Bertram?"

"I am not even going to try."

Her father folded the newspaper and put it down.

"But Beatrice," her stepmother said, "what then will you do? Do you have someone else in mind? One of the Landerby gentlemen? Lord Grayling, perhaps?"

"Not Lord Grayling. Not anyone." Her voice rose even higher, and the Newcastle accent broke through, but Bea no longer cared. "I'm not going to marry anyone. Who am I to marry a lord, anyway? I'm not you, Mama! You've spent *eight years* trying to make me a lady and it hasn't worked. I'll never be a lady like you, never, because it's bred into the bones from birth. I'm nobody, nobody at all, and I'll never be fit to marry even someone like poor Mr Fielding. I can't do it, and you can't make me, not any more. I'd rather go and live with Aunt Betty than go on trying and trying and failing over and over again, like you did. Because that's all this is, isn't it? You want to succeed with me where you failed yourself. I have to marry a lord because you didn't and had to settle for Papa, instead. And I don't want to! Do you hear me? *I don't want to!* I've had enough! I'm sick and tired of being paraded about like a prize cow, so leave me alone and let me be an old maid if I want to. There's nothing wrong with being an old maid, because then I could do as I please and learn Latin and not try to be something I'm not, and that has to be better than settling for someone — *anyone* — just to get a ring on my finger and say I'm married."

So saying, she stormed from the room, slamming the door behind her for good measure.

Harper was in her room, laying out her nightgown, but a peremptory "Out!" sent her scurrying away. Then Bea hurled herself onto the bed and sobbed for a full ten minutes.

She never cried for long, however, and so it was on this occasion. She sat up, dried her eyes on her sleeve and washed her face. Then she was left with a dilemma. She would have to return to the parlour to apologise. Not to take back the substance of her tirade — certainly not that! But to apologise for the manner of it, that would have to be done. But if she went down too soon, she would have to sit and be chastised by Mama until dinner arrived, and that could not be borne. And if she went down too late, she would miss dinner and that was not to be borne, either.

As she puzzled over the problem, however, there came a tap at the door and her father's head appeared. "May I come in?"

"Only if you are *not* going to tell me I have behaved very badly, for I know it perfectly well."

He laughed, and came in, closing the door behind him. "I came to see if there is anything you need. A glass of wine? Shall I have your dinner sent up to you? There is no need to come downstairs if you prefer to be alone."

"Is Mama dreadfully cross with me?"

"Cross? No. Upset, yes. And very, very shocked." He gave a little chuckle. "I should not say this to you, Bea, and you must never tell a soul, but I enjoyed your little rant very much, if only to see the expression on your stepmother's face. Very few people dent her composure, but you managed it tonight."

"Oh! You certainly shouldn't tell me that, or I'll be tempted to do it again."

He laughed outright at that. "Do you truly want to go to your Aunt Betty? I should be extremely sorry for it if you do."

"Would you let me?"

The bed strings stretched and the mattress wallowed as he sat down beside her. "Of course, if it is what you truly want, even though I should miss you abominably. And you need not go to Bath or do the season or even go to Marshfields again, if you dislike the idea. You are of age now, and so long as you are suitably chaperoned, your life is yours to order as you please. You need not go anywhere or do anything against your will."

"Oh! I wish I had known this sooner."

"And for my part, I wish I had known sooner that you were unhappy under your stepmother's regime."

"Not so much unhappy... mostly bored, I think. Then may I learn Latin?"

"Of course. I am sure that Bertram would be delighted to assist your studies. I had planned to arrange it all once we got home, but you have pre-empted me. I think perhaps I have left you too much in your stepmother's care. I thought she knew what was best for you, but perhaps I should have intervened more to be sure you were being brought up to be yourself, and not moulded into something you are not. If learning Latin would give you pleasure, then by all means go ahead. I want you to be happy, Bea, and to be your true self. I was not comfortable with some of the ideas your stepmother put into your head. I only wish that you had exploded a little sooner, so that we could have spared you some, at least, of the misery you have clearly been suffering under for some years."

"It has not been so bad as that, Papa. I was content to follow Mama's advice, on the whole. For a long time I did as I was bid, because I believed it was what I wanted. It was only recently that I began to wonder at it."

"Because I told you that you are not of my blood?"

She hesitated. "That is part of it. Papa... do you know who he is, my *other* father?"

"No. I never asked and your mother never told me. Nor was there any clue amongst her private papers. The secret died with her."

"Did she have hair like mine? Because no one else in her family does."

"That came from your father, presumably."

She was pensive for a moment. "He could not have been a good man, could he? He should have married her. He should at least have looked after her."

"Without knowing all the circumstances, it is hard to say," he said slowly. "I do not like to condemn a man out of hand. Sometimes between men and women... things happen, Bea. It is not always easy to be sensible when one is young. I wonder sometimes if he ever thinks of your mother now, all these years later, and wonders what happened to her, and whether there was a child, and if so, what happened to *her*."

Bea was assailed by a sudden terror. "Could he... if he ever found me, could he... take me away?"

"No, absolutely not. There is no way in law for him ever to do so. You were born into my marriage to your mother, so I am your legal father and nothing can change that."

"Thank goodness!" She tucked her arm into his. "You are very good to me, Papa. When Nellie Blenkinsop shouted at her mother, she was confined to her room with nothing but bread and water for a week."

"What an excellent idea!" he said gleefully. "Or shall I just beat you until you submit?"

"And if I never submit?"

His laughing face took on a more intense expression. "I sincerely hope you never will, daughter. Always stand up for yourself and what you believe in. To be honest, I am astonished it took you as long as this to do so."

"Well, I have tried to hint to Mama that perhaps I am not suited to a life of embroidery and ladylike pursuits, but she is impervious to hints."

He laughed at that. "Your stepmother is an admirable woman, Bea, but her tenacity is almost the equal of yours. I set her the task of turning you into a proper lady, as she is, and she has worked diligently to achieve that aim. You have both worked diligently."

Bea sighed. "She had poor material to work with, I fear."

Her father shook his head at her. "Never say such things. The two of you are... different, that is all, but I love you both just the way you are."

"Unreservedly?"

"Of course. I was very proud of you when you recited your Latin poem at Landerby. In such company, that took inordinate courage, but then you have never lacked courage. Do you want some dinner now, or shall I order some bread and water sent up to you?"

"I will come downstairs, Papa."

Bea could scarcely believe how quickly the storm blew over. Papa was mildly amused by her outburst, and even Mama, who accepted Bea's heartfelt apology with her usual grace, had a twinkle in her eyes when she murmured, "You were wrong about one matter, Beatrice. I did not *'settle for'* your Papa, as you put it."

Beatrice, kneeling penitently before her, rocked back on her heels. "But it was a compromise — you said so!"

"Oh yes, because one is fearfully unrealistic when one is young. Especially so in a family of high rank, like mine, so that one grows up expecting one's husband to be perfect. For me, the perfect match encompassed three elements. Firstly, he should be noble, naturally, for I was noble myself. Secondly, he must be wealthy. And thirdly, he should be handsome and manly and... desirable. Well, when I married your Papa, I got two out of the three, and I discovered after I was married that there were other qualities in a husband just as important. Kindness, for instance, and generosity, and unstinting affection. And I still believe, Beatrice, that you could have all three, as well as the other important qualities, if you marry Bertram."

"But he does not want to marry me!" Bea cried. "He does not want to marry at all."

"Are you quite sure about that, Bea?" her father said.

"Oh, yes! He has told me so many times, and even if sometimes he may act as if... as if he holds me in some affection, that is just his kindness. Truly, he does not want to marry."

Their dinner arrived at that point, and then Bertram in a cloud of anxiety.

"Whyte is still not here?" Mr Franklyn said.

"No, and I begin to feel he will not arrive tonight at all. I wonder what on earth can have become of him?"

"It may be no more than a cast shoe," Mr Franklyn said. "There is nothing we can do about him tonight, so eat your dinner and put the boy out of your head for the moment. It will be time enough to worry if he does not arrive back at Westwick Heights."

Bertram nodded and said no more about it, but Bea thought he was unusually subdued for the rest of the evening.

24: Lessons In Latin

Bertram woke in better heart. Mr Franklyn's calm good sense soothed the worst of his fears for John Whyte. His disappearance would prove to be some trivial mishap — a wrong turn somewhere, a miscalculation on distance, or a lost shoe necessitating the finding of a smith or farrier. There was no need to imagine anything more serious.

Breakfast proved to be a pleasant meal, with only Bea and her father present. Bertram did not dislike Lady Esther, but her regal manner and unbending dignity were not conducive to a relaxed atmosphere. He could not imagine telling jokes in her presence, or speaking disparagingly of the government, as Franklyn did that morning. She often had a suffocating effect on her stepdaughter, as well, and Bertram far preferred Bea lively and bouncy.

That day she was full of the joys of spring, and when Bertram enquired why, she lowered her voice melodramatically and said, "What do you think? I am to be allowed to learn Latin after all!" Gurgling with merriment, she went on in her normal voice, "Papa has decreed it, and Mama has graciously agreed that it is of no consequence what I do, since I am clearly destined to be an old maid. No more netting purses, Bertram! No more trying to paint flowers that end up looking like some strange kind of fruit. No more aching fingers from practising scales on the pianoforte. It is glorious. Do you want some coffee? It is not very good."

"You are not going to be an old maid, Bea," he said confidently, reaching for the jug of ale.

"Oh, you need not pity me. I shall go on admirably, I assure you, but I have given up trying to find a husband. I have reached the conclusion, which I ought to have seen years ago, that I am very bad at it and would only make a terrible mistake. Take Lord Grayling, for instance. You tried to warn me against him, but I would not listen."

"He has a great deal of charm," Bertram said. "It is very easy to be drawn in by such a man."

"Is he *very* wicked?" she said, turning innocent eyes on him.

A difficult question to answer without delving into the matter of seductions and mistresses. "Well... he does not always behave as he ought."

"And I foolishly went into the garden alone with him, but you and Mr Fielding heroically came to my rescue."

That made Bertram laugh. "There was nothing heroic about it."

Franklyn, who had been listening intently while steadily working his way through a plate of ham and cold beef, laid down his knife and fork at this point. "I think it was in fact rather heroic, Atherton. You were looking after my daughter better than my wife or me. We are both grateful to you."

"And so am I," Bea said, smiling at him so warmly that he felt himself flushing. "I was very cross at the time, but I understand now that you were protecting me from... Lord Grayling's wickedness. His misbehaviour, as you put it, which I was too stupid to consider. No, no, do not protest. I *was* stupid, but no more. I am leaving off all thought of a husband, and will devote my life to ablatives and vocatives and gerunds and deponent verbs and the subjunctive — whatever that is. I shall need to obtain a new primer, but that should not be difficult. Will you help me, Bertram? Answer my beginner's questions and correct my pronunciation, that sort of thing?"

"Of course! I should be delighted... if Mr Franklyn permits?"

"I have no objection. We will consult with Lady Esther as we wend our way home to devise a suitable schedule."

"May I not devise my own schedule, Papa?"

"No, because your stepmother will still expect you to receive guests and pay morning calls with her, and there will be domestic duties to attend to. Latin merely replaces the netting of purses, Bea, it should not consume every waking hour. And it would not surprise me if her ladyship still harbours other plans for you, in the matter of the acquisition of a husband."

"I have given up all of that, Papa."

"But your stepmother has not. You may have evaded the dire prospect of Bath, but if you will not seek out a husband yourself, he must seek you. You may be thinking that your stepmother is taking an unusually long time to dress this morning. You are mistaken, however. She is already dressed, and fully engaged in making lists of suitable young men to invite to Highwood Place this autumn. The house will be full to the rafters of eligible suitors, if she has her way."

Bea's face fell so dramatically that Bertram's heart twisted in the most painful way. He had managed to protect her from Grayling, but he could do nothing to protect her from her own stepmother.

But Franklyn only laughed at her chagrin. "Not to worry, I give you my hearty support to reject them all. In fact, you may greet every one as he arrives with the words, *'Welcome to Highwood Place, and no, I shall not marry you.'* Or perhaps that should be, *'I shall not even consider a proposal unless spoken in Latin.'* And you should say all that in Latin, too. That should deter all but the hardiest souls."

"All gentlemen learn Latin at school, Papa."

"So they do. Not being educated as a gentleman myself, I had forgotten that."

Bertram chuckled. "I have a better test. No suitor will be considered unless he can propose in the form of an original poem in Latin, using dactylic, iambic, Aeolic, and anapestic metres, one verse for each."

"Oh, excellent!" Franklyn said. "That sounds sufficiently formidable an obstacle. Could you do that?"

"I could scrape something together, but it would not be very good. The only person I know who can produce high quality Latin poetry of any form is the Marquess of Embleton."

"Then I am perfectly safe," Bea said happily.

Bertram instantly resolved to begin work on a suitable poem. Surely that would convince her to change her mind about marriage?

***

Bertram was relieved to be at home again, a place where he could hide in his library and consider his future. For once, he had no urge to retreat into the past, for the present was heavy with delicious possibilities. He had never before understood the wonder of being in love. He must have read about it and heard a thousand different interpretations of it, yet the nature of the experience had been beyond his comprehension. But now, all he could think about was Bea. Even as the carriage drew up at Westwick

Heights, as the steps were let down, as he stepped onto the drive, his eyes turned to her, unwilling to lose even one second of that precious sight.

His whole family came out onto the steps to greet the Franklyns and thank them for conveying Bertram home. The Franklyns would not stay, however, being keen to reach their own home. As soon as Bertram's boxes were unloaded, the steps were folded away, the door was shut and the coachman urged his team into motion.

"Goodbye for now, Bertram," Bea said with a cheerful smile and a wave, her curls bouncing as she leaned out of the lowered carriage window. "I shall see you tomorrow at noon. Don't be late!"

"I will be there," he said, laughing. The carriage rolled away down the drive, Bea waving energetically until a turn of the drive hid her from view.

"Come inside, dear," his mother said. "Goodness, you look pale! Have you been at your books for the whole month? A little fresh air every day, if there is no dampness about, is not at all harmful. I expect you have been eating too much rich food, so I have asked Mrs Place to boil some chickens for you, and prepare some clear soup. That will do you all the good in the world."

"Excellent. I am very tired of turtle and lobster."

"Turtle! Lobster! Bertram, how many times must I tell you that any kind of shellfish is injurious to the health? Oysters, perhaps — I might allow that oysters are harmless, but turtle! Lobster!"

Julia and Penelope took one of his arms apiece and towed him up the steps and into the house, with the beaming Emily in their wake. "Never mind the lobster, Mama. He is only teasing you. What *we* want to know is whether he is betrothed to Bea Franklyn yet."

"Of course not," Bertram said, with an uneasy laugh. After all, he had in fact proposed to Bea just three days earlier. If she had accepted him... His heart lurched in sudden delight at the thought. But it would have been so awkward! After all he had said, and all the jokes about Bea's forwardness, to have come home and confessed that she had caught him in her web after all, and he had walked into it willingly... joyfully... No, it would have been too difficult. It was better this way, for now he had all the time in the world to change her mind about marriage.

"Then why are you going to see her tomorrow morning?" Julia said. "You have seen her every day for a month, you travelled home with her and now you are rushing off to see her the very next day. That sounds very close to a betrothal to me."

In the entrance hall, with the servants hovering nearby, Bertram was silent, but when they entered the drawing room, he said, "Miss Franklyn is learning Latin, and I am helping with the irregular verbs."

"Bertram is too clever to be ensnared by Bea Franklyn," said his father. "But where is Catullus? I thought Whyte was to be travelling with you."

"He took a different route, and failed to meet up with us at Bawtry, so I suppose he encountered some minor mishap."

"That is a valuable horse he has in his charge," he said, frowning.

"He knows that well enough, Father," Bertram said. "He has met with some delay along the way, undoubtedly, but he cannot be far behind us. It is no great distance from Landerby, after all. Mr Franklyn thinks there is no cause for alarm just yet."

"Still, if Whyte is not here by Monday, I shall send Morton out to make enquiries at the turnpikes and staging inns."

And that was all the allowance the ladies would make for horses, for they had news of far greater import to deliver — Winnie Strong's mysterious suitor had arrived from London, had proposed and been accepted.

"Such a fine man!" Penelope said, almost bouncing with excitement. "Handsome and tremendously fashionable, and he has four thousand a year, and an estate in Oxfordshire. And Winnie all but an old maid, too. Is it not wonderful?"

"It is," Bertram said. "I am very happy for her, for no one deserves a good match better than Winnie."

There were visitors in the house, Bertram discovered. A widowed friend of his mother's, a Mrs Vaughn, an insipid woman with nothing to say for herself, and two friends of Julia's, the Miss Pailthorpes, who had all too much to say for themselves, and very loudly. With so much news to exchange, the evening passed in animated discussion of all the doings of the North Riding, or the small part of it that surrounded Westwick Heights, and questions about the distinguished occupants at Landerby Manor, and not another word was said about Bea Franklyn.

***

Bea was happy. In fact, she could not recall a happier time since they had left the old house and set out to become gentry. Even her betrothal to Walter had been more a matter of relief, that after all her efforts he had finally succumbed to the inevitable, and she was not, after all, to suffer the ignominy of a rebuff.

Now there was no more worrying whether she was to be nothing but a dried-up spinster. Who cared whether she ever married or not, for she was going to be a Latin scholar like Bertram and his friends, and read Virgil and Horace and the war-minded Julius Caesar instead of sewing stupid roses onto handkerchiefs.

Papa threw himself with enthusiasm into the project. The library was reorganised to accommodate two desks, one in front of each window, so that Papa could act as chaperon while Bertram was present. He usually spent the morning hours in his more modest study in the old part of the house, but he would watch over the lessons in the library.

"I might even learn something myself," he said, winking at her.

A shelf was cleared for Latin books, although it was depressingly empty.

"I am only sorry that I have no books of my own to contribute," Papa said, "but I never learnt more Latin than was necessary for my work, and not from books. I shall write to the booksellers in York and see what they can suggest, Bertram will bring you some of his books, and Mr Dewar may have some suitable works."

"Oh, I forgot about him," Bea said excitedly. "A clergyman is bound to have lots of Latin books."

"Perhaps, but he is not wealthy enough to have many."

Bea sighed. "Such a pity I could not keep the duke's primer! That was lovely to work with."

"We shall obtain another primer for you," her father said. "I like this new enthusiasm, Bea. Will it last, do you think?"

"Oh, yes! When I set my mind to something, I keep going."

He laughed. "That is true enough. Ah, is that a rider approaching? Your tutor, perhaps, arriving exactly to time."

Bea bounced from her chair and rushed to the window, waving vigorously. "It is Bertram! He is going straight round to the stables. He has a bag over his shoulder, so he's brought me something to read. I can't wait to get started. May I go and meet him?"

"No, you will wait for him here like the lady you are," her father said, but his smile took the sting from his words. "Hobbs will show him in here. And slow down your speech a little. You are slipping into Newcastle again."

"May I go to the stairs to—?"

"No. Sit, wait, be patient."

Being patient was not Bea's strongest suit, but she managed it until she heard footsteps outside the door and then the door being opened. She shot across to intercept Hobbs and Bertram before they had even crossed the threshold.

"There you are, Bertram! I thought you were never coming!"

He looked startled. "But I am not late... am I?"

"No, not at all, but the morning has been interminable. I cannot wait to get started. Come and see what Papa has done. He has arranged everything so neatly. I have my own desk, look!"

She towed Bertram across the room. He laughed, and said to Papa, "Good morning, sir. Pray forgive me for not bowing but you see how it is."

"I do indeed. Your pupil is keen to begin, and let us not hinder her learning by such trivial matters as the conventions of polite society."

"Oh, Papa! Must I pretend not to be excited?"

But it was Bertram who said, "Miss Franklyn, you and pretence are strangers, and long may it remain so. If I may disengage my arm for a moment, I have something for you."

"Books? Have you brought me some books?"

"I have and one in particular. May it bring you great pleasure."

Released from her grip, he opened his bag and pulled out a small parcel, neatly bound up in ribbon-tied cloth, and handed it over with a little bow.

Unwrapping it, she exclaimed in wonder. "My primer! You have brought my primer from Landerby."

"I should have given it to you the instant you were permitted to take up your lessons again, but it was at the very bottom of my box. I did not expect to be able to present it to you quite so soon."

"But it is the duke's. I cannot keep it."

"Read the inscription."

Opening the cover, she read the words, '*To Miss Beatrice Franklyn. May this volume bring her great pleasure, so that in the future she may regale her friends at Landerby with many more magnificent recitals and join in the learned discussions. Wedhampton.*'

"How kind," she breathed, trying very hard to banish the tears that lurked close to the surface. "How very, very kind of his grace. And how kind of *you*, Bertram, to think of it."

"Well now, we cannot have you separated from your primer, can we? I thought we might continue where we left off, with pronouns and questions, and then I have a piece to dictate to you, so that you may practise writing in Latin, and another piece for you to read for discussion purposes. If Mr Franklyn permits?"

"You are her tutor, Atherton," Papa said. "I am going to work on my accounts over here, and you may sit opposite Bea. You have precisely one hour, and if I see or hear or even suspect the least impropriety between the two of you, these lessons terminate immediately. Is that clear?"

"Yes, sir."

"Yes, Papa."

Bea sat down, opened her primer and the lesson began.

25: News From Corland

Bertram wandered into his father's study one morning. His father was writing a letter, but he willingly broke off from the task.

"You are sending Morton off to find Whyte, I hear," Bertram said.

"Yes. I am just writing to this Edgerton fellow to let him know the boy is missing."

"But you cannot think that Whyte is involved in Nicholson's murder?" Bertram said. "We know he was here on the night it happened."

"Do we? And even if Whyte himself were innocently tucked up in his bed, he has brothers and cousins and friends enough who could have acted on his behalf. Running away, if that is what he has done, proclaims his guilt loudly enough. Edgerton will want to know, and he can decide what to do about it."

Bertram said no more, ambling about the room and idly polishing his spectacles as his father returned to his letter. When it was sanded and folded and sealed, however, he turned to look at Bertram curiously.

"Was there something else?"

"Father, I am thinking of getting married."

"Good. You are five and twenty now, which is a proper age to begin looking about for a wife. Unless... perhaps you have someone in mind already?"

"I do, in fact."

"I trust she is not one of these two friends of Julia's who arrived on our doorstep the day you were expected home, and not by accident, I suspect. As the possible heir to an earldom, you are a person of the greatest interest to young ladies of a certain type."

"I am happy to reassure you that young ladies of a certain type are of no interest to me. I would like the Miss Pailthorpes better if someone could convince either of them that their singing is not fit for public performance."

His father winced. "Oh, Lord, yes! They are terrible! Miss Parish is the only girl in these parts with any aptitude for music, since Izzy moved away. Lily Strong, I suppose, and at least the harp is a peaceful instrument. One can sleep through it very well, I find, which one cannot do with the Miss Pailthorpes. But if not one of those two, then it must be someone you met at Landerby."

"Not exactly. Someone I already knew. Bea Franklyn."

His father's eyebrows shot up. "Bea Franklyn? This would be the Bea Franklyn that Lucas describes, not without some justification, as a leech?"

Bertram laughed. "Yes, *that* Bea Franklyn."

"The one you swore never to marry? The one whose own father suggested you leave the country to avoid?"

"The very same. I have got to know her a little better these past weeks."

"Bertram, are you in difficulties with the girl? Have you done anything you should not have done?"

"Done anything—? Oh! No, no, no, nothing of that sort. She has not been compromised, if that is what you mean. Father, you must know that I would never—"

"Yes, of course, but she is a conniving minx, and I would not put it past her to try a trick like that."

"She would not stoop to such stratagems," Bertram said huffily. "She is open and straightforward in all her dealings, you must know that of her."

His father gave a grunt that might have been laughter. "There is something in what you say. After all, she said openly that she intended to marry you, but you were steady in your resolve not to be drawn in, as I recall. What happened to change your mind... if you can tell me, that is?"

"I kissed her," Bertram said, smiling at the memory. "Or rather, she kissed me and... and I suppose I realised there was more to life than Roman poets."

"There is more to life than Bea Franklyn, too," his father said sharply. "But... have you spoken to her already?"

"No... at least, not precisely."

"What does that mean?"

Bertram sighed heavily. "She was so miserable at Landerby, Father. She had begun learning Latin, and recited a Horace ode so splendidly, but then Lady Esther would not permit it, and Bea was quite cast down. So I... several of us, in fact... went to her and... and offered to marry her. She turned us down... all of us, but at least she knows now that I am willing. It was too precipitate, of course, I realise that now. I cannot in all conscience offer for Bea... for *anyone* until I know whether I am to inherit the title or not, so until Uncle Charles decides, I can do nothing."

"Even then, you might not know," his father said. "If he remarries your aunt, then that settles the matter, but suppose he decides to marry someone younger. The marriage might not be fruitful at all. Or it might produce only girls. Or, even if a son is born, he might not survive infancy. Life is uncertain, Bertram. You and I might both be carried off with putrid fevers and Lucas would inherit. None of us can foretell the future, so we can never be guided by it. That does *not* mean that you should rush out and offer for Bea Franklyn immediately, however. I can see that you have developed an attachment to her, but I am by no means convinced that she is the right wife for you. If you are minded to marry, I am very happy to hear it, but I would prefer you to fish from a larger pool than this one small corner of Yorkshire. Let me take you to town and—"

Bertram shuddered.

"Well, perhaps not. But York, perhaps, in the autumn. You would meet a much wider range of potential brides at the assemblies and entertainments there, and the Franklyns might be inclined to spend a few weeks there, as well. Then you can make a rational comparison. Will you consider it? Or at least reassure me that you will not rush into anything."

"I have no intention of rushing into it. I should like you and Mother to get to know Bea a little better, Father. Indeed, I should like to get to know her better myself. These Latin lessons are the ideal means to allow us both to discover what we want. At the moment, she says that she does not wish to marry at all, and Latin consumes her every thought, so there is no question of anything more between us. Franklyn chaperons us ferociously, you know. His presence not ten feet away is a great deterrent against any impropriety."

His father chuckled. "Franklyn is a sensible man. So you will do nothing to further your cause with Miss Franklyn?"

"Not yet. I think we both need a time of reflection."

"Good. And we might discuss the issue of York with your mother. She will be taking Emily there this year, so your presence will attract no comment, and I confess I should be very glad to see you taking your proper place in society, instead of burying yourself in your books all the time."

"You have never mentioned it before, Father."

"I always hoped that one day you would wake up and notice there were attractive females in the world, and be driven to acquire one for yourself. I just never expected it would be Bea Franklyn who woke you. Yes, Carter, what is it?"

The butler bowed. "A letter from his lordship at the castle, sir. A groom brought it just now."

"Is a reply expected?"

"No, sir." He stepped forward and proffered a silver salver, on which lay a sealed note.

"I hope he is not in another pother about the Northumberland estate," Bertram's father said with a smile, as he broke the seal. "Clarke knows what he is doing, and— Good God!"

"Not bad news, I hope?" Bertram said, alarmed.

"I— No, it is good news... or so we must take it. Tom Shapman has confessed to killing Nicholson."

"*Tom Shapman?* The woodworker? But why?"

"Something to do with Tess Nicholson... wait, here it is. *'He wished to marry Tess, but Nicholson refused to consent.'* That is hardly a reason to kill the man. Tess will be of age in a few months and free to marry where she pleases, even a woodworker. That makes no sense to me, and Shapman always struck me as a sensible fellow."

"Still, if Shapman is the murderer, then it cannot be Whyte, can it? But then why has he vanished?" Bertram said.

"Good point. I shall send this letter to Edgerton anyway, and Morton can see what news he can find of Whyte. Well! Tom Shapman! I never would have guessed *that.*"

***

Bea was drawn out of the library one day by her stepmother's insistence that they sit on the terrace awaiting callers.

"Must I, Mama? I have a long passage to translate before Bertram comes tomorrow, and Hobbs can tell me if anyone calls."

Lady Esther was too refined to raise her eyes heavenwards, as Aunt Betty would have done, but she gave a very slight sigh and said, "Bring it outside with you if you must, but tuck it away in your work basket the instant anyone calls."

That was an acceptable compromise to Bea, and since no one at all came to call, she was able to work undisturbed.

"I suppose no one yet knows we are home," Lady Esther said, after she had been forced to move into the shade no fewer than three times as the sun sank majestically in the sky. "I suppose no one will come now."

But even as she spoke, the sound of hooves on the drive brightened her eye a little. "Books away, Beatrice."

"Yes, Mama."

When Hobbs brought the visitor onto the terrace, however, both ladies were surprised to see Walter Atherton.

"Mr Atherton! How charming of you to call," Lady Esther said.

Bea jumped up and rushed across to greet him. "Walter! Whatever are you doing here?" She tucked one arm into his, and towed him towards her stepmother.

He detached himself to make his bow to her stepmother. "Good day, Lady Esther, Bea. I am glad to find you on your own for I have news to impart."

"How intriguing. Pray sit, Mr Atherton. Will you take some wine? Or lemonade is most refreshing in this hot weather."

"Is it?" he said. "I should prefer wine, thank you."

Once Hobbs had been dispatched to bring the refreshments, Walter turned to the ladies and said, "I came at once to tell you, for I should not wish you to hear it from anyone else."

"How very alarming," Lady Esther said.

"Oh... no, nothing to be alarmed about. It is good news... at least, *I* think it is."

His eyes rested on Bea as he spoke, and she was filled with foreboding. It was Bertram — it must be! Some accident, or—

"I am engaged to be married... to Winnie Strong."

Whatever Bea had expected, that was not it. She was conscious of a whoosh of relief... nothing to do with Bertram then.

"I thought there was some man from London," Bea said. "A man with a fine estate and four thousand a year."

"That came to nothing," Walter said. "He was never right for Winnie, and she gave him his marching orders in the end. Which was a piece of luck for me."

"Oh, yes. I congratulate you, Mr Atherton," Lady Esther said smoothly. "Such a sensible match for you in your present circumstances. Miss Strong is an eminently practical girl, she will be able to manage very well on your reduced income."

Walter looked bewildered. "I hardly chose her for her ability to make gooseberry pie!"

"Why did you choose her?" Bea said. "She has no dowry to speak of."

Walter smiled with such warmth that Bea was startled. He had never smiled that way at her! But then she had a revelation.

"Oh! You are in *love* with her! Why did you never say?"

"Beatrice, a lady does not enquire into a gentleman's affections," Lady Esther said gently.

"We established a long time ago that I am no lady, nor ever likely to be," Bea said robustly.

Before her stepmother could reply, Walter laughed. "Bea, I am delighted to see that you are as open and forthright as ever. Lady Esther, I have long been wishing to examine the new parterre below, which reminds me very much of the one at Valmont. I know you will not wish to stroll about in this hot weather, but perhaps Bea may be permitted to show me the improvements?"

Lady Esther laughed. "And you, sir, are as charming a rogue as ever. I doubt you were ever within a hundred miles of Valmont."

"Oh, I am sure I must have been in the same county, at least. It is in Kent, is it not? Or Surrey? Berkshire?"

"It is in Hampshire, Walter," Bea said, laughing. "Home to the Duke of Falconbury. Family name, Litherholm. Mama made me learn all the dukes and marquesses."

"Well remembered, Beatrice," her stepmother said. "The parterre at Valmont is certainly very fine, or it was the last time I visited. A lucky guess on your part, Mr Atherton."

Walter chuckled. "These great houses always have a parterre, and that being so, I have surely seen an engraving of it in a book somewhere. Grandmother was forever showing me such things. You will not mind if I stroll about with Bea?"

She graciously assented, and they descended the steps to the newly planted parterre and walked sedately round the perimeter.

"So tell me about Winnie," Bea said. "How did you come to fall in love with her?"

"I think I must have been in love with her for years," he said, and again his face softened into a glowing smile. "She was always my very good friend, but I never understood how much she meant to me until this fellow started paying court to her."

"And has she conveniently fallen in love with you, too?"

"That is the amazing part of it, Bea. Winnie has been in love with me for years — *ten* years, if you can believe it, and never said a word or showed it in the slightest. I had not the least idea. Did you? Perhaps you suspected something? Did she ever say anything when I was engaged to you?"

"No, not a word. *Ten years?* And you had no idea? I could not do that! If I loved a man so well as that, I should have told him so."

Walter chuckled. "So you should. After all, you told me you were going to marry me and you were not in love with me... were you?" he added, an anxious tone in his voice. "I should not wish you to be unhappy on my account, Bea."

"No, no, no, nothing like that. It was a practical matter for both of us. A suitable match, as Mama would say."

"Bea..." he began, with a sideways glance. "I should not wish you to think... that I was discontented with our arrangement. I went into it willingly, and I think... I truly believe we would have rubbed along together pretty well."

"I think so too," she said slowly. "But... there would have been something missing."

"Exactly!" he said eagerly. "With Winnie, it is so different. I feel so... so *alive*, if that makes sense. As if it is summer every day."

"It *is* summer, Walter."

"Ha! So it is. But it feels like... so much more. Oh, I am no good with words, so I cannot describe it to you properly, but with Winnie I feel as if we complement each other perfectly, as if we are meant to be together, and I am so happy I could burst. I hope... truly I hope you find your perfect match, too, Bea." A pause, and then he went on gently, "How are you getting on with Bertram? Any luck yet?"

"No, I have abandoned my plan to marry him." She tried very hard not to sound subdued, but was not entirely successful. "Unlike you, he has told me very steadfastly that he has no intention of marrying at all, and I have given up all thought of it. In fact, I am not sure I want to marry myself. I am learning Latin and—"

"Latin! Whatever for?"

"It is fascinating, Walter. Bertram is teaching me about future tenses at the moment."

"Oh, *Bertram* is teaching you, is he? So this is just a clever way to win the heart of a bookish man like Bertram."

"You malign me, Walter Atherton. I have no such plan. I simply like learning Latin, that is all."

"What a strange, unaccountable girl you are, Bea." He shook his head sorrowfully. "Latin! Whatever next?"

heart gave a little jump of pleasure at the thought, but she squashed it at once. Bertram would not be here to offer for her, she knew that perfectly well. That strange visit from him and his friends at Landerby was not a serious proposal, and now that he had escaped, he would never repeat it. Had he not told her over and over that he had no intention of marrying? Sometimes she thought she saw a certain light in his eyes which would have given her hope if she had let it, but she dared not. Bertram would never offer for her and she had promised not to pursue him, so that was the end of tha t.

Yet if not Bertram, the visit was a mystery. "Who is it?" she whispered.

Mama whispered back, "The Marquess of Embleton. Oh, Beatrice! You are going to be a duchess!"

Bea was too shocked to speak. A marquess! A future duke! Of course it was gratifying, but— Oh, dear heaven, how could she possibly refuse a future duke?

Common sense intervened. He could not conceivably be here to offer for her. She had hardly spent any time with him at Landerby, and he had given no indication that he was interested in her, or in marriage at all. He had hidden himself away in the garden to avoid the purposeful pursuit of Miss Grayling and her friends. No, his presence here must be for entirely different reasons that had nothing to do with her. Mama had misunderstood, that was all.

At these reassuring thoughts, her racing heart calmed a little. She opened her work basket, retrieved a crumpled piece of embroidery and settled down to pretend to sew. Only the little current of disquiet inside her refused to subside — what if Mama was right? What on earth was she to do if a future duke were to offer for her?

It was only twenty minutes by the clock, but to Bea the waiting was endless. Then, carriage wheels were heard on the drive outside. Mama was up in a moment, rushing to the window in a manner which would have earned Bea a stinging rebuke.

"He is leaving!" Mama said, breathing heavily. "How can he leave without even speaking to you? It is unconscionable! Whatever has John said to turn him away like that?"

Bea had never heard Mama refer to her husband as anything other than *'Mr Franklyn'* or *'your father'*, so to hear his Christian name used told her more clearly than anything else how agitated Mama was. But to Bea, there was nothing but relief. He was not going to offer for her! Either he was here on other business altogether, or Papa had deterred him. Perhaps he had told Lord Embleton the story of her birth, and he wanted nothing more to do with her. That would be an unexpected benefit to her origins!

Voices in the hall, then on the steps outside. The sound of a carriage door closing, a cry of *'Away!'* and the carriage set off down the drive. Moments later, her father came into the saloon.

"What have you *done?"* Mama cried. "Why did you let him go?"

"He returns tomorrow," Papa said. "There is no cause for alarm, my dear. All is well."

"But what did he *say?"*

"Very little, for he is not a man who finds talking easy. However, he has given me a letter for Bea. He does not feel himself capable of finding sufficient words in speech, but he is very fluent in the written form. So sit, both of you, and I will read it to you."

"It is not private, then?" Bea said in a small voice.

"It is addressed to you, but there is nothing of an intimate nature in it. He wishes it to be read aloud."

They all sat and the letter was produced.

'My dear Miss Franklyn, Pray forgive me for writing thus to you words which should more properly be spoken, but you will understand the reason for it, and your generous nature will forgive me, I am sure. When I went to Landerby Manor, I had no thought beyond the call of Latin, and the fellowship of men of like mind. My anticipation was keen for our daily discussions, but I dreaded the evenings, when I would be obliged to join a different kind of company. I have never been easy amongst ladies, especially as the circumstance of my birth and destined high rank makes me a target for the ambitions of a certain type of young lady. On this occasion, I was surprised to find one young lady in the company who displayed no such ambition, who treated me only with kindness, and an open-hearted generosity of spirit that I found utterly beguiling. Such beauty and liveliness, such goodness and tenderness in one person inspires me to the greatest heights. I have not the words in English, but in Latin, oh my dear Miss Franklyn, believe me when I say that the words have flowed from my pen unceasingly. I enclose a sample, with translation." Papa waved a second paper. "*Even then, I might have gone away, a little regretful perhaps, but otherwise heart-whole, had you not bestowed upon me that gentle sign of your affection. When you kissed me, my very dear Beatrice, how could I refuse the sentiments you so freely offered me? I knew then I could not contemplate life without you. I have talked to my father, who is perfectly content to leave my choice of bride to me. I come therefore, most humbly to beg you to consent to be my wife. I shall return tomorrow to hear your answer. Yours in deepest affection, Ralph Embleton.'*

Silence fell. Bea was too horrified to speak, too agitated to sit still. She jumped up, striding across to the window. She was tempted to cry, but it was too serious for that.

"You kissed him?" Mama said faintly.

"Only a... a sisterly sort of kiss," Bea said, whirling round. "I never imagined... how could I guess...?"

"A kiss is a kiss," Mama said firmly. "There is no such thing as a *sisterly* kiss, not with a marquess. You have led him to believe you have an attachment to him, and now he very nobly offers you his name. How wonderful, Beatrice! What a clever girl you are. This is so much better than the Athertons and their mere earldom. May I be the very first to wish you joy ."

Bea was thrown into total confusion. Lord Embleton wanting to marry her! She left her parents to gloat and retreated to the library, the marquess's letter in one hand and his poem in the other, and tried very hard not to cry.

What had she done? She could see her own foolishness all too clearly, in bestowing kisses, even sisterly ones, on men who turned out to be rather susceptible to such behaviour. Even Bertram and his friends had, albeit half-heartedly, offered for her, but that had been private and she had never confessed it to Mama or Papa. But when a marquess came in aristocratic state to formally ask for her hand — there was no hiding *that.*

A month ago, even two weeks ago, she would have gloried in such a proposal. She would have accepted Lord Embleton without an instant's hesitation and married him confident that his rank and position in society were all she wanted. But now, with Bertram, she had glimpsed the possibility of a different kind of marriage, one that had nothing to do with rank and everything to do with affection. With passion. With *love.*

She read again his letter, and found it strangely unemotional. The poem... yes, there was certainly some feeling in it, more than the letter, but still, it was... unsatisfactory. It was like Lord Brockscombe's kiss, pleasant enough but without fire. How could she marry him with no fire? How could she marry anyone with the memory of Bertram's kiss burning inside her? It was impossible.

Her father came to see her after a little while, pouring wine for them both and then sitting in Bertram's chair facing her across the desk.

"You do not seem very happy about this, Bea."

"It is such a shock," she said. "I had no idea."

"No? I confess I noticed no particular attentions from him, but you were always surrounded by Atherton and his cronies. That was where we expected your future to lie. Your stepmother was very hopeful of Atherton, but this is beyond her wildest dreams."

"Is it?" Bea said wanly.

Her father gave her a searching look. "I thought it was what *you* wanted, too. After all, you seem to have played him perfectly — not chasing him openly, like the others, simply treating him as a mere acquaintance, so that he cannot even see the game you are playing, and then sealing the deal with a kiss. No wonder he finds you irresistible."

"I was not playing a *game*, Papa, not with Lord Embleton! I felt sorry for him, that was all, and I thought he had no wish to marry at all, so I never even tried to attach him. And the kiss meant nothing, truly. How could I guess he would imagine my affections were engaged?"

"Do you dislike him?"

"No, not at all."

"Does the speech problem trouble you?"

"Oh, *no!* He is the most restful man to be with."

"He will not stop you learning Latin, if that is a concern. He cannot teach you himself, but he would engage a tutor for you."

"He told you that?"

Her father smiled. "I asked him. Bea, I cannot think you are overwhelmed by the prospect of being a duchess, for you have always had an abundance of confidence in your ability to take on any rôle. So what holds you back?"

"Papa, it is but a few days ago that I decided never to marry."

Her father shook his head, smiling affectionately at her. "I cannot believe you meant any of that, Bea. Marriage is every woman's ambition, surely, however much she puts a brave face on spinsterhood. For eight years now, ever since your stepmother came into our lives, you have focused all your hopes on marrying a man with a title. Are you truly asking me to believe that you have given up that ambition irrevocably?"

She was taken aback. If Papa did not believe her, what hope did she have of escaping this marriage? "Didn't you mean what you said? About wanting me to be happy and true to myself?"

"Of course! But you will be happiest within a contented marriage. The marquess has a sincere affection for you, and he will not chafe you, of that I am certain. You may learn Latin or whatever hobby takes your fancy, and be as true to yourself as anyone could be, as a marchioness. Bea, you said you wanted to be respected, and so you shall be — as the Marchioness of Embleton, and in time as the Duchess of Bridgeworth. Believe me, you will have all the respect you could wish for, and that will make me very proud. You will never get a better offer than this, and it will be disappointing if you throw away this opportunity for some frivolous reason. That is all."

The evening was endless. Mama was cock-a-hoop at the prospect of her stepdaughter becoming a duchess in the fullness of time, and although she was too proper to discuss the matter before the servants, whenever they were alone she exulted, and began making plans for the grand wedding that Bea's new status demanded.

Her father, by contrast, talked of everything *but* the presumed forthcoming wedding, and watched Bea uneasily. That, more than anything, brought home to her the gulf that had unexpectedly opened between them. She had thought they understood each other pretty well, she and her father. Always he had taken her side against Lady Esther's wilder ravings, and even when he was not minded to speak out, he had thrown amused glances at Bea, as if to say, *'Don't worry, I won't let her eat you alive. It is still the two of us against the world.'*

Now he had abandoned her, loading her with the weight of his own expectations, and walking implacably away. *'That will make me very proud.'* What daughter could hear those words and not want to obey the ambition behind it? But neither the marquess himself, nor his future dukedom, appealed to her, and she had no idea what to do about it.

She felt trapped, like a duck hiding in the long grass listening to the guns in the distance, hoping to escape notice, but knowing that, sooner or later, the beaters will come and she will have no choice but to fly up in terror and be shot down. Just another dutiful daughter of the gentry, falling, falling under the guns of society's expectations.

As soon as she had drunk her tea after dinner, she asked if she might retire.

"Of course, dear," her stepmother said. "You have an important day ahead of you, so get some sleep, if you can. It will be difficult, when you must be so excited. I have already asked Harper to press your new Indian muslin for tomorrow. It is a little fine for ordinary day wear, but for such a momentous occasion, one would rather do too much than too little."

"Thank you, Mama. Good night. Good night, Papa."

"Good night, Bea," her father said, looking searchingly at her. "If you have any concerns about this step, your prayers will bring counsel, I am sure."

"As well as the Sixth Commandment," her stepmother said smoothly.

"Yes, Papa. Yes, Mama."

Bea curtsied and escaped to her room, but there was no relief there, not in prayer nor in the commandments. *'Honour thy father and thy mother,'* indeed! As if she did not do so. As if she had not always done so. As if she did not *want* to be a dutiful daughter, and make her father — both her parents — proud of her.

But she also wanted not to have to marry the Marquess of Embleton, and it struck her now how odd that was. Surely every young woman wanted to marry, and to marry as well as she could, not just for her own sake, but for the sake of her entire family. She had no sisters to benefit from her ennoblement, not yet, but her young brothers would find their lives made easier by a duchess in the family. Her father could visit her at Bridgeworth and not be a despised outsider as he was at Marshfields. Even Aunt Betty and all the Newcastle cousins could visit, because she would be the duchess and no one could doubt her right to issue the invitations.

Yet that was no reason to marry anyone.

Harper came to help her undress, but instead of blowing out her candle, Bea propped herself up in bed and contemplated her dilemma. If she were to marry the marquess, she would please her parents, certainly, and naturally it would be gratifying to hold such high rank, but...

But what? *'Do not throw away this opportunity for a frivolous reason,'* her father had said, but what reason did she have? How could she possibly object to the marquess? Ralph, that was his name. He was sweet and gentle and kind, and there could be no conceivable objection to his person. And yet she did not want to marry him, and she knew the reason — he did not set her on fire. There was no warmth inside her when she looked at him. Not even when she had kissed him.

His poem! Perhaps his Latin verse, tucked away in a drawer of her desk, would engender the proper warmth in her. Sliding from the bed, she snatched up the candle and made her way in some excitement downstairs to the library, where the shadows danced about grotesquely. How odd the room looked, when so poorly illuminated! So alien and unlike its usual welcoming self. But she lit a candelabrum and sat down at her desk. Where was the poem? There it was. She began to read.

Almost at once, she saw the problem. As she sounded the words in her head, arranging them in what she hoped was the correct metre, it was not the marquess's voice she heard, or even her own — it was Bertram's. His clear tones filled her mind so that the marquess was driven out. All that remained was Bertram, and a Latin poem.

And there, deep inside her, was the warmth she sought. Even the thought of his voice made her smile and brought her great delight. What was it, this curious warmth, the fire that his kisses lit, the wonder of his touch? Then she remembered Walter and the way his face lit up when he spoke of Winnie... good heavens, was she *in love* with Bertram? Was that what was the matter with her?

But she had promised not to pursue him. She had given her solemn word and she would not break it, but she could not in all conscience marry the marquess while she was in love with another man. That was not fair to Ralph, not fair to herself and not fair to Bertram, who might one day come to love her, just as Walter had come to love Winnie. And just as Winnie had waited ten years for Walter, so Bea would wait for Bertram, without any real hope of success.

Still, she could wait... she could wait forever. She would dedicate her life to Latin and perhaps Bertram would one day turn to her in love, and perhaps he would not, but she would always be his friend.

Whatever happened with Bertram, however disappointed her parents might be, she could not marry the marquess. And with that thought, her confusion finally cleared. Blowing out all but her own candle, she returned on swift steps to her room, and calmly settled down to sleep.

27: A Betrothal

The whole house was in uproar by the following morning. Even the maid who brought Bea her early morning chocolate twittered and giggled, and nearly tripped over her own feet as she backed out of the bedroom. The prospect of a betrothal affected everyone. Except for Bea herself, who rose unhurriedly, and went to the library, as usual, only to be summoned back to her room by an irate Harper.

"I've to do your hair special this morning. Milady's orders."

Bea sighed, but there was no point in arguing. There would be a far greater argument later, so she would conserve her strength for that one. Occasionally she quailed, knowing that her father would be disappointed, but she could not marry the marquess and that was the end of the matter.

Meekly she submitted to Harper's ministrations, then endured breakfast with her parents, Mama dizzy with excitement and Papa inscrutable, watching her quizzically. After that, she was obliged to sit in the Gold Saloon, awaiting the moment when the marquess would return and her refusal would bring the wrath of her parents down on her head. But she was insistent on not wasting the whole morning on useless stitchery, so, despite her stepmother's protestations, she took a Latin book into the saloon with her.

Eventually, the distant sound of carriage wheels was heard, drawing nearer and then pulling up before the door. Mama had better control of herself today, so there was no rushing to the window. How amusing it would be if it were only Lady Strong or Mrs George Atherton or the Cathcart ladies! But no, for within moments the door was thrown open, and Hobbs was announcing the marquess.

He crept in, with Mr Franklyn behind him, and stood twisting his hands together, an anxious expression on his face. Clearly, Bea was not to be allowed to speak to him alone. It was better so, for that way her parents would know everything that was said and there could be no misunderstanding. It would have been dreadful to refuse him in private and emerge to find her parents full of congratulations. What an awkward explanation would then be needed!

But after bows and curtsies were exchanged, he said nothing, and it was left to Mama, equal to any occasion, no matter how delicate, to take charge.

"Lord Embleton, how delightful. Do come in. Beatrice is quite ready to accept your most obliging offer."

"Thank you, Mama, but I shall answer for myself."

A flicker of uncertainty crossed Mama's face, but the marquess moved slowly forward, as if mesmerised, his eyes fixed on Bea's. When he reached her, he gave a worried little smile.

"M-M-Miss F-F-F..." A quick exhalation. "Franklyn?"

"Lord Embleton, you honour me greatly with your proposal, and I am deeply sensible of all your many excellent qualities that would make you a wonderful husband. Your wife will be a most fortunate woman, and in other circumstances... if matters lay otherwise..."

Mama gave a tiny squeak of alarm.

Bea took a deep breath. "I am very sorry to give you pain, but I must regretfully decline."

"Decline?"

"Beatrice..." Mama began.

Calmly, she turned to her stepmother. "Yes, I know this is a disappointment to you and Papa, which is a great sorrow to me, but marriage is a matter that I can only decide for myself, with regard to my own inclinations... my own wishes... my own happiness. Lord Embleton, perhaps we could have been happy together... indeed, I am sure of it... but I cannot enter into marriage with less than whole-hearted enthusiasm, and at present I cannot do that. My interests lie in another direction entirely."

"I-I-I..." he began, but the thought was destined to remain unsaid, for at that moment, the door opened and Bertram walked in.

Even Mama for once was speechless, and for the space of several heartbeats they all stood as if transfixed, unable to speak or move.

"There you are, Bea," Bertram began with a wide smile, but then he noticed the shocked faces, and the stiffness of the tableau before him. His smile faded to bewilderment. "Embleton?"

The marquess's mouth flapped open and closed again soundlessly.

Into the void, the clock struck the hour, making them all jump. Twelve o'clock! Time for her Latin lesson, and now Bea took notice of the pile of books under Bertram's arm. With a squeal of pleasure, she dashed across to him.

"Have you brought it? The Virgil? I cannot wait to get started."

He laughed. "I have, but you are otherwise engaged, I think. I beg your pardon... I intrude. Shall I come back later?"

Lord Embleton crossed the room, and held out his hand to Bertram. "I s-s-see it all now. Con...g-g-gratulations, Atherton."

"Oh... um, thank you," Bertram said, shaking the proffered hand with a bemused expression on his face.

The marquess bowed meticulously to each of them in turn and walked with dignity out of the door.

Papa chuckled. "You are a dark horse, Atherton," he murmured as he followed the marquess.

Mama sighed. "Really, Beatrice, you might have mentioned this."

Then she, too, was gone, the door closed with a soft click and Bea was alone with Bertram.

"Whatever was that all about?" Bertram said, as Bea uttered a low moan of distress.

"Oh, of all the unfortunate things! Lord Embleton very obligingly offered for me and—"

"Embleton? Offered for you?"

"Yes. I kissed him, and he thought I was in love with him. Really, Bertram, you do not need to sound *quite* so astonished! Gentlemen have been known to offer for me once or twice before, you know."

"Of course! I did so myself, remember?"

"That was not real, though, was it?"

"What do you—?"

"Never mind that! We have very little time. There is the marquess's carriage coming round now. This mess is all my fault, Bertram. I refused Lord Embleton, of course, and—"

"Why *'of course'*?"

"—I made the mistake of saying that I had another interest, and then you walked in and they all assumed we are betrothed."

"Because you seemed so pleased to see me, I suppose." He chuckled. "But what are you doing turning down Embleton, Bea? I thought you wanted a title, and you will never be able to improve on his."

"What does the title matter?" she said crossly. "Who cares about a stupid title, anyway? I meant only that I have discovered *Latin*, and that is my great love now, but they have misunderstood everything. I shall have to explain, but—"

"No, wait a moment," he said, putting the books down so that he could rest his hands on her shoulders. "Why should we not be betrothed?"

"Because you don't want to!" she spat. "Honestly, Bertram, you have told me a thousand times that you never plan to marry, so stop being silly."

"Nor do you want to marry, do you? So we are in the same position."

"There you are, then."

"There is no need for us to actually marry," he said, laughing.

She stared at him. "What?"

"If we are presumed to be betrothed, or on the point of it, we can protect each other from unwanted suitors, and leave ourselves free to do what we want, without harassment."

Without harassment! That sounded so appealing that for a moment she was overwhelmed.

It was just at that moment that her parents returned, to discover them standing only inches apart, his hands on her shoulders, gazing into each other's eyes. If they had planned the pose as a means of convincing an observer of the existence of an understanding between them, it could not have been bettered.

"Ah, Beatrice! Mr Atherton! This is something of a surprise," Lady Esther said, her well-modulated voice level, but there was a hint of a chill behind it. Naturally, she would be disappointed that Bea was not to be a duchess after all.

"You could have given us a hint," Bea's father said, but his eyes twinkled at them.

"It was all very sudden," Bertram said smoothly.

"So it would seem," Bea's father said. "When do you anticipate making a formal announcement?"

"It is a shade difficult just at present," Bertram said.

"I rather thought it might be."

"The situation at Corland, with my grandmother so ill, and Walter so recently engaged to Winnie Strong... and my own father has barely begun to adapt to his own new position. It is best if we wait a little while."

"How very proper," Lady Esther said approvingly, brightening a little.

"Of course, of course," Bea's father murmured, but there was a gleam of amusement in his eye, as if he were party to some great joke.

Bea could not see it as a joke, nor could she understand why Bertram was so complacent about the situation. He should run a mile from any kind of entanglement with her!

As soon as an opportunity presented itself, she whispered in his ear, "Don't worry, I'll jilt you as soon as I can. I would never hold you to it."

But he only laughed, picking up his books and holding out his arm for her. "Latin, Miss Franklyn? Shall we begin our lesson?"

It was true that they sat either side of the desk for an hour, and it was also true that some Latin was spoken and written and even discussed. It could not properly be called a lesson, however, for Bea remembered nothing of it afterwards. Bertram made no comment, simply pretending that everything was normal, and Papa sat and read the newspaper, laughing occasionally when she mangled her grammar so spectacularly that even he saw the error. And then Bertram was gone, and she could not think, could not move, could not possibly find space in her disordered brain for a single word of Latin.

"I must say, Bea," her father said, folding his newspaper neatly, "you and Atherton are as good as a pantomime. I cannot recall when I was so well entertained. Whose idea was it?"

"If you mean this betrothal, it was his. I was set to tell you that it was all a misunderstanding, but he said it would protect us from harassment and we need not actually get married. Then you came back into the room and it all seemed to be settled. Papa, will you tell him it is all wrong? Because it is, isn't it?"

Her father looked at her thoughtfully. "Do you like him?"

"Bertram? Yes, of course I do."

"Enough to marry him?"

"He does not want to marry."

"Leaving that aside, suppose he came to you and proposed to you in the proper form, like the marquess... would you accept him?"

Bea felt trapped. This was one of those questions, she was sure, where there was no right answer, and whatever she said would be to her detriment. For a long time, therefore, she said nothing.

"Bea?" her father said gently. "You must have an idea whether you wish to marry him or not."

"Papa... I think I do... I might... *if* he were to offer. But you want me to make you proud, so—"

"Ah, that. I misunderstood you badly, Bea, and that must have made you unhappy. For that I am sorry. I can see now that you know your own mind, at least as far as the marquess is concerned. But Atherton is another matter. If you like him well enough to marry him—"

"But he does not wish it, and I promised him that I would not pursue him, so I cannot even think about it."

"Are you quite sure he does not wish it? For it seems to me that he likes you very well, and since this betrothal idea was his—"

"*No!* He has told me so many times that he does not want to marry, and I believe him, Papa. It may be that, if these lessons continue, and I am able to reach a degree of fluency in Latin, that he will look at me differently... perhaps. But I do not... I *cannot* depend upon it. And so you see why I feel uncomfortable with any suggestion of a betrothal between us."

"I understand that, but it was his idea to go along with it, and it did not strike me that there was any reluctance in him. You must know, Bea, that for a man... if he is a gentleman, at least... a betrothal is a matter which cannot honourably be broken. Bertram cannot withdraw, and yet he made no protest — quite the reverse. So do not be too hasty to conclude that he does not wish to marry."

"You think I should simply go along with it?"

"I do."

"He said we need never marry... and it would protect us from harassment."

Papa laughed. "And he is quite right. As the likely heir to an earldom, he is an object to every ambitious mama in Yorkshire, and your fortune has always attracted attention, not always of the right sort. So let this supposed betrothal stand. Your stepmother is very capable of conveying the right degree of vagueness to the business — an understanding, no thought of marriage just yet, his grandmother's imminent demise and so on — and if it comes to a sticking point, you may end it at any time you choose."

"Or whenever he wants to be free," she said thoughtfully.

"Precisely. But do, for pity's sake, pay more attention in your lessons, or all your good work so far will be undone."

He smiled at her with such understanding that she could not resist smiling back. "Oh, Papa, I do get into difficulties, sometimes."

"Of course you do. You are but one and twenty, and still a green girl in many ways. But whatever difficulties you may get into, be assured that I shall always be there to get you out of them... or to deal with the consequences. You are not alone in the world, daughter."

Impulsively, she jumped up and threw her arms around him. "Thank you! I think you are the best papa in the world."

"Which just shows how faulty your judgement is," he said, with a spurt of laughter. "There, now. You get back to your Latin, and I shall try to prevent your stepmother from throwing a grand ball to celebrate your unexpected betrothal."

***

Bertram left Highwood Place in a mellow frame of mind. He was betrothed to Bea, after a fashion, and if that could be left to run on for a while, there would be time for her to understand how well suited they were and come to feel the same attachment for him that he felt for her. She was not serious in her resolve not to marry, of that he was certain. And if her scruples brought her to attempt to end their betrothal, that would be his opportunity to tell her openly how much he loved her. Surely then they would be betrothed in truth.

His only concern was that he might not, after all, inherit the earldom, and he knew how important that was to her, no matter how much she denied it now. He would have to be honest about that. His mother's guest, Mrs Vaughn, was there as a potential new wife for Lord Rennington, and although that did not seem to be going well, his mother had other candidates to bring forward. One of them, no doubt, would suit a man as easy-going as the earl, and then the nursery at Corland Castle would be brought back into use. How strange that would be, to have a new Lady Rennington!

At first, he said nothing of his situation to his family, unsure of whether this odd betrothal was to be acknowledged publicly or not. But he quickly learnt from Bea that Lady Esther was telling all her acquaintances that Bea was shortly to be engaged, so he went to see his father in his study.

"There has been a development with Bea Franklyn," he said, sitting in the opposite chair to his father's beside the fireplace, and removing his spectacles to polish them.

His father marked his place in the book he was reading and closed it, removing his own spectacles with a smile. "A champagne development or a large brandy development?"

"I am not quite sure."

His father chuckled. "That sounds like brandy to me. I shall need one, anyway. Do the honours, will you, and then you can tell me of this development."

Bertram poured two brandies, and then related the whole story, hiding nothing. His father listened without interruption, and only the occasional raising of his eyebrows indicated his thoughts.

When the tale wound to its conclusion, he sipped his brandy, then set the glass down on the table beside his chair. "In my day," he said thoughtfully, "courtship was a straightforward business. One met a young lady, one fell in love, one proposed. One then found oneself betrothed... or possibly not betrothed, but one was left in no doubt as to which it was. This newfangled idea of covert betrothals that might not actually be betrothals is too modern for me. I should not like it very much. Why do you not simply go to the girl and tell her how you feel about her?"

Bertram laughed. "I shall do so, in time, but her situation is very unsettled at present. She has been raised by Lady Esther to view a title as the summit of her ambition, and she is only now realising the emptiness of that principle. Only a short while ago, she was engaged to Walter, with her future settled. I do not want to rush her into a hasty decision, either to marry or not to marry. It seems to me that she needs time to adjust to her new situation and decide what she truly wants. I hope it will be me, in the end, but if not... well, I can still give her Latin lessons."

"I suppose that is what passes for courtship in your head," his father said sadly. "Forget the Latin lessons, Bertram, just kiss her. If you want to win her heart, kiss her. A suitably passionate kiss will reduce the most resistant girl to jelly."

"That did not work at Landerby," he said crossly. "I kissed her and reduced *myself* to jelly, while she went off and kissed all my friends. And Embleton, seemingly, and reduced *him* to jelly, too. Kisses are not the answer, Father, not with Bea."

His father sighed. "Perhaps you are right. But one thing is increasingly clear to me — we all need to get to know this girl a great deal better. I shall ask your mother to invite the Franklyns to dinner."

28: An Evening At Westwick Heights

Bertram was deep in preparation for his next lesson with Bea one morning, when his father came into the library.

"Did you hear a horse on the drive just now?"

Bertram blinked, bringing himself back into the modern world. "Erm... horse? No."

His father chuckled. "You would not hear the last trumpet unless it bellowed right in your ear. A horse came up the drive and round to the stables."

"Oh? An interesting visitor?"

"No, an interesting horse. One we have been much wondering about."

"Catullus?"

"The very same, with John Whyte leading him. Shall we go and hear his story?"

"It had better be good," Bertram said grimly.

By the time they reached the stables, all the grooms had gathered around Whyte in an angry altercation. They fell silent when the Athertons appeared.

"Well now, Whyte, we have been much concerned for you and Catullus," Bertram's father said in pleasant tones. "We were sure some accident must have befallen one or other of you, but here you both are, safe and sound."

"There *was* an accident, sir, and I'm very sorry for it, for it were my own fault. It were no more than five miles from Landerby, and I'd taken it easy and stopped to rest Catullus, but he seemed frisky after that and so... so I..."

"Yes?"

"So I let him have his head for a spell, sir, and there was a toll-gate and... well, he were all set to jump it and I were trying to rein him in, and he just went, sir. Nothing I could do."

"You *jumped* him?" Bertram said, startled.

"Aye, sir. Never meant to, cos you've always said you never jumped him, but he just took it into his head to do it, and then, what with me trying to hold him back, he caught one foot on the top bar. He were all right, seemingly, not lame nor nothing, but I were that worried, sir, in case I'd done some real damage, so I never rode him after that, just walked him."

"Walked him? All the way here?"

"Aye, sir. At least... not here. I took him to me sister, out at Brigg's Farm, cos the pastern were inflamed and I dursn't bring him back here till he were right again."

"And you could not have sent us word, I suppose?" Bertram cried. "Morton has been all over the place trying to find you. We were worried about you!"

His father chuckled. "We even wondered if you had run away because you were afraid to face Captain Edgerton's questions on the murder of Mr Nicholson. You received a letter that the captain wanted to question you, and the next thing we know, you have disappeared."

Whyte's face was a picture of bewilderment. "Mr Nicholson? You thought *I'd* killed the poor gentleman? Oh, Lord! It weren't me, Mr Atherton, sir. I'd never *murder* anyone! I never had nothing to do with it, I swear."

"We know. It was Tom Shapman."

"*Tom Shapman?* It never were! He'd not harm a fly, Tom wouldn't."

"Well, he has confessed to the murder of Mr Nicholson, and is currently in York gaol awaiting the Lent Assizes," Bertram said.

"But... but he'll *hang!*"

"Precisely. That is what happens to murderers." Bertram turned to the head groom, who had been carefully feeling Catullus's legs. "What do you think, Morton? What is the damage?"

"He's fine," Morton said, sounding surprised. "Whatever treatment you gave him, Whyte, it seems to have worked. I can't even tell which leg it was that was injured."

"Tis this one, sir," Whyte put in eagerly. "Will it do?"

"Sir?" Morton said to Bertram's father. "What do you think?"

"It looks fine to me."

"I'm real sorry, sir," Whyte said to Bertram. "I'll collect my things."

"Whatever for?"

"I assume you'll turn me off... won't you?"

Bertram shrugged. "You got him back safe and sound, in the end. Next time, write to tell us what is going on."

Whyte laughed. "I never thought of that, sir. I'm a fool, aren't I?"

"No, just a lad of only sixteen. No one expects you to be wise to the ways of the world, Whyte, not at your age, and you did well to get Catullus and yourself home safely. That is something to be proud of. And now, there's a broom over there waiting for you, and a yard to be swept."

"Yes, sir. Right away, sir. Thank you very much, sir."

***

Bea was not sure what to make of the invitation from the George Athertons. Was it a recognition of her betrothal to Bertram, or merely a routine offer of hospitality, to be returned in a month or so when the George Athertons would dine at Highwood Place? Her stepmother took it as the former, and insisted that Bea wear one of her grandest London gowns for the occasion, something normally reserved for Marshfields.

With five adult children in the family, together with several visitors, the drawing room at Westwick Heights was already crowded when the Franklyns walked in. Mrs Atherton greeted them affably, and towed Lady Esther away to meet a friend of hers, newly arrived that day. Bea's father was immediately scooped up by Mr George Atherton. Bea herself was surrounded by the Atherton daughters, but they were of no interest to her.

Ah, there he was! But Bertram was looking bemused, with an unknown young lady on either side of him.

"Who are *they?*" Bea said.

"Who? Oh, friends of mine," Julia said. "The Pailthorpe sisters."

"They are very encroaching," Bea said, seeing one of them place a proprietorial hand on Bertram's sleeve. "He needs to be rescued."

So saying, she ploughed her way across the room to Bertram, elbowed one of the Miss Pailthorpes aside, and tucked her arm into his. "Did you think you could hide away from me, Bertram? Goodness, what a crush! I cannot remember when I last saw this room so full. Are there any more to come?"

"No, with your arrival we are all here now," he said, giving her a warm smile. "We have guests in the house, as you see. Bea, may I present to you Miss Pailthorpe and Miss Anne Pailthorpe. This is Miss Franklyn, our neighbour and my good friend. My *very* good friend. I am teaching her Latin."

The sisters exchanged a glance, then with one accord they marched away.

"Oh, well done," Bea murmured. "You got rid of them very efficiently. I have a question about that passage from *The Aeneid*, where—"

"No Latin this evening," he said, although his smile broadened.

"Oh. None at all?"

"Not one word," he whispered. "Tonight is for good company, although not so many that we become overheated, and good food, although nothing too rich or indigestible, and good music, although not so loud that it hurts the ears. Mother has taken every precaution for our continued good health, you understand."

"Your mama is all consideration," Bea said, chuckling. "And even if we do happen to become overheated, we shall not be allowed to open a window."

"Heaven forfend that the evening air should find its way to our delicate lungs!" he said. "One can never be too careful, for we are now into

September and autumn is upon us. You wrapped up well on the drive over here, I trust? There will be fur wraps and hot bricks available for you upon departure, and if you take care to drink some beef tea when you reach home, warm but not too hot, you may be tolerably confident of surviving the night."

She giggled. "Your mama is lovely, and if she worries over your health somewhat, that is easier to bear than some other matters a mother might concern herself with." Her eyes strayed to her stepmother, presently engaged in conversation with Mrs Atherton and her friend. Lady Esther wore her habitual expression of restrained polite interest, but Bea thought she detected something more. Was it possible that her stepmother was surprised?

They went in to dinner soon afterwards, and Bea found herself, to her astonishment, seated next to Mr George Atherton. Her stepmother naturally had the place of honour on his right, but Bea sat to his left, and wondered quite what she would find to say to him. Did he know about her betrothal to Bertram? And if so, was it a good thing or a bad thing that he singled her out for this attention? Was he hoping to discover some hitherto unsuspected virtue in her, or was he wishing merely to confirm his previous bad opinion? She was sure his previous opinion had been bad, for even her father, who loved her unreservedly, thought she was bumptious and unrefined.

There was a small delay in serving the food, since Mrs Atherton's friend, Miss Priscilla Hand, called for grace to be said.

"Of course, dear," Mrs Atherton said. "Silence, everyone! Carter, keep the soup for a moment. We are about to say grace. Hush, Penelope, dear. Thank you." Everyone bowed their heads. "Um... bless this food to our use, O Lord, and us to thy service. Amen."

The refrain rumbled round the table, and the footmen hurried forward with the tureens of soup.

"Oh, no, Jane! That is hardly adequate," Miss Hand said, her fingers playing agitatedly with the cross at her throat. "Perhaps Mr Atherton could bring the necessary gravitas to the occasion?"

The footmen were waved away again, and once more heads were bowed. Mr George Atherton might have had more gravitas, but he was just as brief as his wife.

"For what we are about to receive, may the Lord make us truly thankful. Amen."

The chorus of *'Amen'* was louder this time, with an air of relief to it, but Carter held the footmen back, watching Miss Hand.

"Oh, dear," she said, playing with her cross even more violently.

Mr Atherton sighed. "Perhaps, madam, you would care to take the task upon yourself?"

"Oh... far be it from me to put myself forward... but if you insist, of course. Lord, bless this food and grant that we may be thankful for all thy manifold mercies. Bless us with thy grace, and...'

Eventually, some interminable time later, an interval punctuated by someone's stomach rumbling loudly, followed by muffled giggles, the prayer ended and the soup was permitted to be served. It was barely warm by that time, but no one minded.

Under the cover of the rising level of conversation, Mr Atherton leaned towards Bea and whispered, "She used to be such a mischievous girl, too. Always in some scrape or other. Sadly, when her mother was widowed, she remarried a dean... or an archdeacon at the Minster, I forget which, and both the ladies caught a severe case of piety. There is no cure."

Bea laughed, and whispered back, "Is it infectious?"

He pulled a horrified face. "Heavens, I hope not! She is here for a sennight, at least."

After that, he turned his attention to his soup, and Bea did likewise, but she was a little intimidated by him, all the same. All the Athertons intimidated her. No matter how affable they seemed, there was still an air of inherent nobility about them which made her very conscious of her humble beginnings. If her betrothal were real, Mr George Atherton would be her father-in-law, and even though he was a mere gentleman now, in time he would very likely be the Earl of Rennington. When she had been betrothed to Walter, she had taken great care to be on her very best behaviour in the earl's company, and although she fully intended to set Bertram free before too long, she nevertheless wanted to look well in his father's eyes.

For the whole of the first course, therefore, she took care to mind her manners and be as ladylike as possible in all her actions, as well as her conversation. When offered a dish, she took only a delicate spoonful. When asked how she had enjoyed her stay at Landerby Manor, she replied that she had enjoyed it very much and everyone had been prodigious kind to her. When asked her opinion of the Duke and Duchess of Wedhampton, she responded that they had been most gracious and affable.

By the second course, she was beginning to be bored. Mr Atherton was engrossed in conversation with Lady Esther about family matters at Corland Castle, and Bertram, on her other side, was being monopolised by Miss Hand, who was talking about the Archbishop of York and some uninteresting clerical matters. Only Mrs Atherton's constant refrain of *'avoid the fish bones... take the greatest care with bones... please be cautious, for there are bound to be bones'* enlivened the table.

So when Mr George Atherton turned to her with twinkling eyes and said, "How are you getting on with your Latin, Miss Franklyn? Bertram tells me you are an excellent scholar," she was delighted to have a more interesting topic of discussion.

"He is too kind, and so patient with my silly mistakes. I do my best, but it is not at all easy. One may learn the regular declensions very readily, but there are so many irregular ones to know, and so many words the meanings of which vary subtly from one situation to another. But it is fascinating to me to use the words of people who lived so long ago. Do you not think so, when you read Virgil or Horace?"

He laughed and shook his head. "It is a puzzle to me how I raised a son who is so proficient in the language, for I lost interest in it many years ago, and Greek, too. English and a little French are adequate to most occasions, as far as I am concerned."

"You do not even like Horace?"

"Not even Horace can tempt me. It is a favourite with Bertram, I know, and perhaps with you, too. Did you not recite one of the Odes at Landerby?"

"Oh, yes! It was the most amazing fun! It was book three, number nine — do you remember it?"

He shook his head, but with a smile.

"It is so beautiful! I wanted to learn it for my own amusement, but Bertram persuaded me to recite it aloud when the duchess was having an evening of poetry readings. The words are so wonderful — they echo in my head, and leave me feeling... oh, I cannot even describe it. There is something so magical in the Latin poets, do you not agree? The way the words sound when they are spoken aloud. *'Donec gratus eram tibi nec quisquam potior bracchia candidae cervici iuvenis dabat, Persarum vigui rege beatior. Donec non alia magis...'"*

Mr Atherton said nothing, listening with his full attention on her, and since she addressed herself solely to him, at first she did not notice the effect her words were having. But gradually it dawned on her that the general conversation around the table had died away. She became aware of her own voice, far more resonant than usual, and the eyes of the company turned towards her. Her voice dropped into uneasy silence.

"No Latin, Bea, remember?" Bertram said, smiling at her.

"Oh... sorry. I forgot."

There was some laughter around the table, but Miss Hand was clutching her cross in distress. "You speak the language of *pagans!"* she hissed.

Bea raised her eyebrows in surprise. "Latin is the language of civilisation, ma'am. It is the language of poetry and philosophy and rational thought. The Romans established a great civilisation when Englishmen were still rolling in the mud. I am not even sure there *were* Englishmen then. The Romans built beautiful monuments and aqueducts and roads, they had laws and education and houses that were heated by warmth beneath the floor. They were great engineers."

"But so many gods! They were not Christians."

"Well, I hardly see how they could have been!" Bea said, with a spurt of laughter. "Julius Caesar was BC — before Christ. They could not have been Christians before the birth of Jesus Christ."

That brought another ripple of laughter around the table.

"The Romans converted to Christianity in the 4th century AD," someone said from the other end of the table, and Miss Hand was immediately distracted. Someone else pointed out the widespread use of Latin in the church, and although Miss Hand muttered about Papists, and the

Anglican church using civilised English, the heat had gone out of her protests.

The conversation became more general again, but Bea lapsed into miserable silence. When would she ever learn to hold her tongue?

Mr George Atherton leaned towards her, and said in a low voice, "No one could doubt your enthusiasm for the language, Miss Franklyn. I look forward to hearing the rest of the poem at some future date, with perhaps a less critical audience?"

"You are very kind, sir," Bea said miserably. "I am very bad at recognising the inappropriateness of my behaviour, and I apologise for it."

He reached across and rested his hand on hers. "It is not you who need apologise. In fact, I would go so far as to give you this advice — do not ever apologise for being yourself. You have not an ounce of artifice, and that is to be commended."

"Thank you, sir," she said, but she could see her stepmother eyeing her from across the table, and knew she would be receiving a reprimand later.

Well, she was used to that, but both Bertram and his father smiled upon her, so she felt the evening was not entirely a disaster.

29: Lady Esther Has A Plan

"Latin again, Bea?" her father said, the instant they had made their farewells and the carriage was rumbling down the drive.

"Never mind that!" her stepmother said. "Did you see *that woman?*"

"Which woman was that, my dear?" her husband said equably.

"Miss Hand. Do you know why she is here?"

"She is an old friend of Jane Atherton's," he said.

"Yes, but she is here for Lord Rennington!"

"Indeed? She is an old friend of his, also?" There was a puzzled tone in his voice.

"No, no! She has never met him, but she is here to *marry* him."

Mr Franklyn only laughed, but his wife tutted at him.

"It is no laughing matter, I assure you. It is a disaster for Bea. Here she is, betrothed — after a fashion — to the heir to the earldom, and now we discover that the earl is *not*, after all, going to remarry Lady Rennington. He is planning to marry again and have legitimate sons, and then Bertram and his father will be cut out. *That* is why Lady Rennington went away, do you see? Jane Atherton planned it all, the scheming witch, and of course Lord Rennington is such a weak sort of man he will do whatever he is told."

"I do not see that it is such a disaster," Mr Franklyn said mildly. "Bertram is heir to Westwick, after all, with an income of three thousand a year."

"But no *title!*" Lady Esther said despairingly. "I did not mind Beatrice refusing Lord Embleton... not very much, anyway, when I imagined she had an understanding of some sort with a future earl, but to turn down a marquess — a duke, one day — for a commoner, no matter his income, is beyond all reason. Fortunately, this betrothal is not yet publicly known. I have merely hinted to one or two good friends that we expect an announcement very soon, and it could as well be one as the other."

"Mama, what are you planning?" Bea said in some alarm. "I shall not marry the marquess, I assure you."

"No, no, although perhaps that could have been revived... but no. We must aim for the original target, I believe, and since the heir is now uncertain, it would be safest to look to the current holder of the title."

"You cannot mean—?" Bea cried in horror.

"Tomorrow we shall call upon Lord Rennington," her stepmother said triumphantly. "He will not look at this Miss Hand when you are in the room. In fact, he will not look at any of Jane Atherton's suggestions. All older women — some widows, even. Men far prefer youth and freshness." She chuckled. "I wonder it did not occur to me before. You will be the Countess of Rennington before the year is out, Beatrice, you mark my w ords."

Bea sat in appalled silence as the carriage slowly made its way through the night.

***

An hour of reflection brought Bea to a calmer frame of mind. She could not be forced to marry Lord Rennington, or anyone else, no matter how her stepmother schemed. Visiting him would do no harm, and it might even be amusing to observe Miss Hand's attempts to capture his interest.

But breakfast brought a difficulty. Her stepmother was early, for once, full of excitement about her new plans.

"I have drafted a letter for you to send to Bertram Atherton," she said, placing a paper in front of Bea. "You may copy it in a fair hand, just as it is. There is no need to belabour the point. He will understand."

"A letter?"

"Ending this betrothal of yours. It was never a proper betrothal anyway, and this way you will not have the awkwardness of an interview."

"But I shall see him later today for my Latin lesson," Bea said, with a sinking heart, knowing what was coming.

"*That* will all have to stop, naturally. Your father will give him the letter when he arrives at noon today, but we shall be on our way to Corland Castle by then. Everything is arranged."

"Mama, I am not going to marry Lord Rennington. He is old enough to be my grandfather."

Lady Esther laughed. "Not unless he was extremely precocious."

"Well, my father, then."

"What has that to say to anything? Such marriages are perfectly common in the higher ranks, and it is not as if the earl were in his dotage. He is still perfectly healthy, and a little stoutness is only to be expected in a man of his age. Really, Beatrice, you are become most ungrateful for the opportunities which come your way. You baulked at the marquess, and perhaps you are not quite the right person to be a duchess, for it is a daunting task, so I understood that, and you already had an alternative. But Bertram is out of the question now, so—"

"No, Mama."

Lady Esther pursed her lips, and tapped the letter. "Write it out in a fair hand."

So saying, she rose and left the breakfast parlour.

Bea read the letter in growing disgust. *'Dear Mr Atherton, Pray accept my good wishes for your health and future happiness, but I cannot marry you or accept any more Latin lessons from you. Beatrice Franklyn.'*

"Not even an apology," she said sadly. "She cannot seriously expect me to send this... can she?"

"There is no knowing what she expects," her father said with a gentle smile. "She is as adamant, in her way, as you are, but the question of a husband is a matter for you alone to decide."

"Not entirely," she said miserably. "It is also for him to decide."

"True. So why not use this as an opportunity to find out what he wants? You have always said that you intended to put an end to this betrothal, so here is your chance. Send this letter, exactly as it is, with no hint of softness about it. If he heaves a sigh of relief and disappears back to his books, you will know where you stand. But if he has any affection for you at all, he will try to win you back."

"Or he might simply accept his dismissal, assuming I care nothing for him. If only I could talk to him, Papa! If only I could explain to him…"

"Why do you not?"

"Because I promised! I gave my word that I would not set my cap at him."

"Then of course you must keep to that," her father said. "But remember, Bea, he lives just three miles away, and you will meet often. He rarely leaves home, so he will always be there. You have endless time to win his heart. All is not lost if you set him free now."

"It feels like it," she said glumly.

***

Bertram rode Catullus that morning, glad to have his own horse under him once more, and as fit and full of energy as ever. He laughed as he thought of John Whyte jumping him over the toll-gate and making a mull of it, the horse determined that he would jump and the rider trying to dissuade him. That never worked! Once a horse has taken it into his head to jump, he was best left to get on with it. All things considered, Whyte had done a good job to get him over the gate at all.

Jumping was not Bertram's style. He rarely hunted, for that reason, and even when he rode in the regular way, he was happy to open gates with the ladies. He had never been one for showing off. Not like Grayling! His face darkened when he thought of that man, who had peacocked about in front of Bea, and then retreated smartly as soon as he saw that her father was an expert swordsman, who would not hesitate to call him out if he transgressed. A libertine and a coward.

Why was he thinking of Grayling, anyway? Much more pleasant to think of Bea, and today's Latin lesson. He had chosen a poem about kisses for her to read, and perhaps that would give her a hint of the way his thoughts were running. Her kisses… oh, her kisses! If only he could have more of them. The memory of her lips on his haunted his dreams, and his waking thoughts, too. Catullus sensed the sudden excitement in his rider, for he increased his pace uncomfortably, and Bertram was obliged to rein him back a little.

The sun was still warm on his face as he rode, but he fancied it was a little cooler now, a harbinger of the coming autumn. Soon there would be piles of rustling leaves under the trees and an opportunity for long walks in the woods, where an ardent suitor might perhaps be able to snatch a kiss or two. No more excuse for languidly sitting about under parasols on the terrace. Not that he did much of that with Bea, either. His hour in the library with her was all he ever seemed to have. Still, an hour a day, even under Franklyn's watchful eye, was better than nothing. It was very much better than nothing.

He took Catullus straight to the stables, then walked back to the front door. Lady Esther was not a person who would approve of visitors arriving through the back of the house. Hobbs greeted him, took his hat, gloves and riding crop, but did not bother to announce him, for he was expected.

At first he thought the library was empty, for Bea's chair was unoccupied, and Mr Franklyn's also. Then he saw Franklyn standing by the window, his face expressionless.

"Where is Bea?" A moment of fear. "Is she unwell?"

"She is quite well, but the ladies have gone to call upon the earl. Did you not see the carriage as you rode over? They have only just left."

"No, I came through the woods, not by the lane."

"Ah. She left a letter for you."

He handed it over, and perhaps his face should have given Bertram a clue that it did not contain merely an apology for missing their lesson. Instead, he read it in horror, crying out in anguish, "No! What is she doing? I *told* her— Ack!"

Crumpling the letter in hands that shook with rage, he was too agitated to be still, pacing across the room, then back again.

"What does she think she is doing?" he cried again. "How can she do this to me? In a letter... in such words... so cold! Why would she not tell me to my face? I *cannot* accept this. I will not! I will not allow her to end things, not like this, not in a few miserable words that mean nothing to her, but pierce my heart like spears. She of all people should understand the power of words. But *why?* Why would she do this?"

"My wife has discovered that Lord Rennington is looking for a new wife," Franklyn said. "She has an idea that Bea might suit."

"What? Bea marry Uncle Charles? Impossible! She could not... she would not... that is... no! I must talk to her, make her see sense. When will she be back? I shall stay here until she returns and then—"

"They have only just left, and you have a fast horse," Franklyn murmured.

"Yes! Yes! I shall go after them. My horse! I must find my horse." Throwing open the library door, he yelled, "Hobbs! *Hobbs!* There you are! My horse, at once! Oh, never mind, I shall go myself."

So saying, he ran across the hall, wrestled the door open himself and tore round the house to the stables. The grooms had barely got the saddle off Catullus, but they raced to replace it. Bertram stamped up and down as the head groom meticulously tested the girths for tightness. Then he was in the saddle and away. He had forgotten his gloves, but there was no time to go back for them.

Catullus shot down the drive, almost as agitated as Bertram. Away in the distance, he thought he could just see the hazy dust cloud thrown up by the carriage. Highwood Place was three miles from Birchall, and the lane was rough and narrow. He had time to catch them.

Veering off the drive onto open moorland, Catullus found the track that ran parallel to the lane and Bertram gave him his head. Slowly, too slowly for Bertram's peace of mind, they gained on the dust cloud. Above the hedge that bordered the lane, the top of the carriage could now be distinguished.

It was at this point that the defect of his plan occurred to Bertram. The hedge ran along the edge of the lane all the way to the main road. There were no gates, even if he had time to open one. If he wished to intercept the carriage before it reached the all too public setting of Birchall village, he would have to jump the hedge, and in order to avoid crashing into the hedge on the other side, the jump would need to be at an angle.

His heart quailed but Bea was too important for him to back down now. He was drawing level with the carriage... he reached it... he was a little way past it... was that a slightly lower point in the hedge just ahead of him? Without hesitation he turned Catullus a little and pointed him at the hedge. Then he suppressed the fear that was screaming at him inside, and put all his trust in his horse.

They neared the hedge, Catullus adjusted his stride fractionally and then... then they were sailing majestically through the air.

Bertram closed his eyes and tried to remember what one was supposed to do when one's horse fell. Feet out of the stirrups? Was that it? What about the reins? Hang on or let go...?

Catullus landed neatly and galloped on down the lane. Bertram was so surprised, he almost forgot to rein him in. Then he turned and rode back more slowly to meet the carriage, filled with exhilaration. He had jumped the hedge! And survived! How astonishing.

The carriage drew to a halt in front of him, and Bea's head popped out of the window. At once, the memory of that insulting letter brought Bertram's rage boiling to the surface again. Slithering from the saddle, he strode forward and hauled open the carriage door. Lady Esther sat facing forwards, as unperturbed as always, but Bea cowered back in her seat.

"What the *devil* do you mean, writing me a letter like that?"

"Mr Atherton..." began Lady Esther.

"I am not addressing you, madam. Bea, you cannot possibly marry a man old enough to be your grandfather."

Inexplicably, that made Bea giggle.

"There is nothing funny about this! How dare you write to me in such terms — *write* to me, for heaven's sake! Well, I will not have it, do you hear me? I will not accept it. If you want to end our betrothal, then you must tell me to my face, do you understand? You can tell me, *to my face*, that you would rather marry an old man who only wants you to give him babies, rather than someone who will love you and cherish you forever. I will not have it in a letter, and such a cold, impersonal letter, too, as if we have not been friends for years and years."

"Mr Atherton," Lady Esther said faintly.

"Be silent, woman! I am talking to Bea. Oh, this is impossible! Get out, Bea."

He grabbed her wrist and pulled her out of the carriage, although she put up no resistance at all.

Lady Esther's voice was a mere thread. "Beatrice, I shall not wait more than five minutes for you."

"Very good, Mama."

Bertram marched her behind the carriage, out of sight of the interested coachman and the footman standing at the back. Catullus had wandered that way, and was contentedly grazing an enticing patch of grass on the verge. Bertram stalked past the horse and a little way down the road.

"Well?" he said, turning to her. "What do you have to say for yourself?"

"I have not the least intention of marrying Lord Rennington. That was Mama's idea, but it is an outrageous suggestion."

"Then...?" Suddenly, he was floundering. "So what is all this about?"

"Did you mean it? About... about cherishing me? Loving me?"

He nodded. All his loquacity had dried up, as if the words that had bubbled up so readily in his anger, had all now leaked out of his head. What could he say to her? How could he possibly tell her how much he loved her, how distraught he was to lose her, how unhappy he would be without her?

But then she smiled, and it was as if he had been wreathed in clouds and now the sun had emerged.

She reached for one of his hands, and placed it on her cheek. Then the other, so that her face was cupped in his bare hands. Now he was glad he had left his gloves behind. He smiled back, thinking that a man could drown in those blue eyes of hers, the colour of the sky on a summer's day.

He knew what to do next. It needed no thought, but it answered all the questions in his mind, and hers too, he realised now.

Bending his head, he kissed her.

It was not like the first time. Then, he had felt as if he were drowning, swept away by the turbulence of his own emotions. Now, it felt more like sailing a small boat across the water, the bow skimming the waves, the sails filled with air, the speed exhilarating. There were no words. Somehow, they were gliding above the words, in the realm where the meanings, the intent of the words, the very heart of them, rose to become pure poetry. Nothing existed, nothing mattered, apart from the two of them, their glorious united joy and their love.

When they parted momentarily, she murmured, "*Te amo.*"

"*Mea vita,*" he whispered back. And when other pauses arose, "*Mea lux... meum delicium... meum solatium... mel meum... meum corculum.*"

She giggled, and repeated each phrase and then kissed him again.

"Mama has gone," she said eventually.

Surprised, he turned. The lane was empty, apart from their two selves, and Catullus waiting patiently. "Oh. What shall we do?"

"I had better go home," she said. "Will you walk with me?"

He laughed. "I have a much better idea. We shall ride."

Her hand in his, he led her towards Catullus, who turned his head towards them and gave a whuff of greeting. With one swift movement, Bertram put his hands around Bea's waist and lifted her onto Catullus's back. She gave a quick exclamation of surprise, then giggled. He liked her giggles, he decided. Some girls giggled in a silly way, but Bea was never silly. He mounted behind her, and found to his great pleasure that a lady sitting sideways in front of him was perfectly positioned for kissing. For some time, therefore, they did not move at all, and it was only when Catullus reached down for another tempting mouthful that Bea giggled again.

"Home is that way," she said helpfully. "Just in case you have forgotten."

He laughed, pulled Catullus away from the verge, and set him to a gentle walk. And so they walked and kissed, and kissed and walked, his arms wrapped firmly around his love, and she seemed content to snuggle against his chest and allow herself to be kissed.

After a while, words seeped into his brain again, and he began to recite. " *'Quaeris, quot mihi basiationes tuae sint satis superque. Quam magnus numerus Libyssae harenae lasarpiciferis iacet Cyrenis oraclum Iovis inter aestuosi et Batti veteris sacrum sepulcrum...'"*

"What is it about?" she whispered, when he fell silent again.

"It is about kissing. One might translate it like this. *'You ask how many of your kisses are enough for me and more than enough. As great as is the number of the Libyan sand... or as many as are the stars... to kiss you with so many kisses is enough and more than enough.'* There is more, but that is the heart of it."

"Ohhh," she breathed. "How romantic you are. You should say everything in Latin. It sounds so much better."

"Very well. How about this? *Te amo, Beatrice Franklyn. Visne mihi nubere?"*

"Does that mean what I think it means?"

He chuckled. "It does."

"Then... *ero.* I will marry you."

And somehow, that seemed to require a great deal more kissing.

30: The Dower House

Bertram strode into his father's study, and leaned over his chair, unable to suppress the grin on his face.

"There has been a further development with Bea Franklyn."

His father laughed. "By the look on your face, this is definitely a champagne development. You proposed, I take it."

"I did, and she said yes. Or rather, she said *ero.*"

That made his father laugh even more. "Did you propose in Latin, too?"

"Of course. It seemed... appropriate."

"But Bertram, whatever happened to the idea to give her time to settle and so forth? I am not sure I like this mad rush to the altar."

"It was not my intention," Bertram said, hurling himself into the twin of his father's chair. "I was quite happy to let things run on for a while, but Lady Esther had an idea, so..."

"That woman! She will be your mother-in-law, Bertram. She will be interfering with everything you do."

"I plan to be very civil to her, and take no notice of her helpful suggestions."

"Yes, but Bea will— But never mind. I am pleased it is settled, and if Bea Franklyn is the woman who has secured your heart, then I make no objection. Shall we go and tell the rest of the family?"

It was almost the dinner hour before everyone was gathered together. Bertram's father told the servants to leave, and then said, "Bertram has an announcement to make."

Bertram cleared his throat. "I am very happy to tell you that Bea Franklyn has agreed to become my wife."

For a moment, there was silence, then they all began to talk at once. Lucas's voice was the loudest. "She is a leech, brother. Why did you not run away when you had the chance?"

"Lucas, I will thank you not to speak of my future wife in such terms."

"But *why*, Bertram?" his mother wailed. "You cannot bring a girl like that into this family, to take my place, to raise your children! It is unthinkable!"

"Why is it unthinkable?" he said gently. "I will admit, I thought so myself, once, but as I have come to know her better and grown to love her, I cannot imagine my life without her. She is all that is admirable— no, hear me out, if you please. She is open-hearted and kind and generous, and will make me a wonderful wife."

"She only wants you because she thinks you will be the Earl of Rennington one day," his mother said.

"No, she knows that Uncle Charles is looking for a new wife, and she has recently turned down a much better offer, although you must not repeat that."

His sisters nodded, but Penelope said robustly, "I cannot like her, Bertram. I am very sorry for it, and I will try very hard when she is my sister, but I cannot forget the horrid way she went after Walter, then dropped him when he was no longer of use to her, and then set about ensnaring you. Which she has succeeded in doing, and just because you appear to be happy to be ensnared does not mean that I like it."

"You are quite right," he said. "She has not always behaved as she ought, but a great deal of the blame for that may be laid at the door of her stepmother, who stuffed her head full of pretentious nonsense. Now that Bea has seen the flaws in that philosophy, you will find her far more likeable, I am convinced of it. Once we are married, and she has Mother's excellent example before her, she will go on in a more proper way, I am sure."

***

Bea existed in a bubble of happiness. Nothing could puncture her joy, and not even Lady Esther's obvious disapproval troubled her. Bertram came every day, and not just for Latin lessons. He took her to Westwick Heights, where his family was grudgingly polite to her. The betrothal was formally announced, the notice went off to all the newspapers and a succession of congratulatory visits kept Bea sitting in the Gold Saloon for hour after hour.

One of those who came was Eustace Atherton. "Bertram? You do realise he is never going to be an earl? Father is looking for a younger wife."

"I know. The title is no longer of any interest to me."

"Then why Bertram? He is too bookish a man for an energetic and lively girl like you, Bea. He will be shut away in his library, leaving you all alone."

"No, I shall be in the library with him, Eustace. He is teaching me Latin."

"*Latin?* Good God, you are in worse case than I thought, if he has drawn you into his dusty world of long-dead writers of dreary poetry."

She laughed. "If you think it is dreary, you have never listened to it, Eustace. Now, you must not be cross because I chose him over you. Wish me joy and be done with it."

His face cleared. "I do wish you joy, of course, but you cannot blame me for being a little bit jealous. My offer has been on the table for several years now, and while I understood Walter's attraction, Bertram is a different case. I do not feel, if we stood side by side, that he would outshine me very greatly. So why him, and not me?"

"I cannot explain it myself," she said, with a quick shake of her head. "You are everything that is desirable in a man and yet… I do not love you. It is unaccountable, is it not? Bertram is the most unlikely man in the world for me to be drawn to, and yet… it happened. One cannot choose who one falls in love with."

He laughed a little, but she thought it was strained laughter. "True enough. He is a most fortunate man, that is all I will say about it. But you will not want a long engagement this time, I suppose? Is it to be a special licence? Or banns? And where will you live?"

"None of that is even thought about yet, but Papa is making noises about the spring. He does not want us to rush into it."

"That is very wise," Eustace said. "After all, who knows what might happen? If you had rushed to marry Walter, you would have been left high and dry, now, with no prospect of the title."

"There is no knowing what may lie in the future for any of us," Bea said pensively. "I do not intend to worry about imponderables. I shall not rush into matrimony, since both our lives have been somewhat turbulent of late, but neither do I want a lengthy engagement. We shall see."

***

Into the haze of Bertram's happiness, practical matters would occasionally intrude. The Franklyns therefore arrived at Westwick Heights in state one day to talk formally about the betrothal. The ladies would discuss dates and wedding clothes and the exact requirements for the new carriage, while Bertram and the other men would talk about settlements.

But first the two families met in the drawing room to enjoy a fortifying glass of Madeira before the serious business of the day.

"Have you two thought at all about where you will live?" Mr Franklyn said.

"My dear Mr Franklyn," Lady Esther said smoothly, "naturally they will live with us. We have so much space to spare. They will have the Royal Apartments in the North Wing... or the Blue Suite, if they prefer the view on that side."

"No, indeed," Bertram's mother said. "Situated in a dip as you are there... most unhealthy. They will do far better with us here. The Dower House will—"

"Dower House? I was not aware that you have a Dower House, Mrs Atherton," Lady Esther said.

"Oh, yes. It was built... oh, seven or was it eight years ago now? Before you came here, Lady Esther, and it has never been occupied, and quite secluded beyond the kitchen garden, so you would not know of its existence. But there it sits, awaiting me whenever George should depart this world, or perfectly suited to a young couple just stepping out in life together."

"But does it have a proper nursery? Sensible attics? I cannot but think, my dear Mrs Atherton, that Beatrice would be much more comfortable beginning her married life in her own home, where she is at ease, and her own parents may take care of her."

"It is for her husband to take care of her once she is married," Mr Franklyn said firmly.

"But you will not want your only daughter to go away and leave you, would you?"

"It is in the nature of daughters to leave their fathers," he said mildly. "I have long expected it. You were perfectly happy for Bea to live elsewhere when it was Walter in the case. But why do we not go and have a look at this Dower House, and then Bea can tell us whether she would like to live there or not?"

It took some time to locate the keys, for it was years since anyone but the servants had been in, and that very infrequently. Eventually, they were found and the whole party donned wraps and coats and scarves against the dampness Mrs Atherton feared was in the air, and ambled across to the Dower House.

Bertram well remembered the house being built. There had been an ancient cottage on the spot before, but it had been torn down to make way for the elegant new construction. He had still been at Eton then, and already had one foot in the Roman world, but he had not yet lost the fascination with the practical elements of his own. So it was that the long vacation that year had been enlivened by watching the walls slowly rising, then the roof going on and finally a succession of carpenters, plasterers, painters and the like working on the inside. He could still recall the excitement when a carved marble fireplace was fitted or the swirls of a chandelier hung, and then there was the never-to-be-forgotten day when the kitchen range was manoeuvred down to the basement.

He had not been to the Dower House for years, however. The hedge around it had grown high enough to hide it from the world, and he had almost forgotten its existence. Now he looked at it as a possible future home, and saw it in a different way. It was still sparklingly new, the walls and windows untouched by the grime of soot, the stonework unweathered. The roof tiles were still uniform, and every chimney pot stood proudly upright, just as the builder had left it. But the house was smaller than he remembered.

Inside, the rooms were empty, with not a stick of furniture or a rug to be seen anywhere, only bare floorboards in stark contrast to the opulent decoration of the walls and ceilings.

Bea ran ahead, throwing open shutters, while Bertram followed Lady Esther from room to room as she muttered, "No proper hall… tiny parlour… small study… inadequate drawing room… hmm, dining room not bad, but no service stairs."

Bertram's mother was in front of her, but she turned round to say, "This house was designed for only one person, Lady Esther."

Upstairs were the same four rooms in the same proportions, and yet another set above that.

"So many bedrooms, in a house designed for just one person," Lady Esther remarked. "You must have anticipated having a great many friends to visit, Mrs Atherton."

"I am very sociable, it is true," she said. "I have many friends. However, my main concern was to have enough room for all the children still in need of a mother's care, should I be widowed early. It is fortunate that I made such provision, for now there can be no question of inadequate nursery space."

Lady Esther had no answer to that. The attics were pronounced tolerable. When they returned to the ground floor, the men went off to look at the exterior, but Bertram's mother said brightly, "The basements, Lady Esther? The kitchens are the heart of any house, are they not? I am sure you will be pleased with the range we had installed."

"Kitchens… yes," Lady Esther said vaguely. "But do tell me more of this scheme to find a match for Lord Rennington. How ingenious you are, Mrs Atherton. But perhaps, with my connections, I might be of some service in the enterprise."

Their voices drifted away as they descended the stairs, leaving Bertram alone with Bea.

"Oh, dear," Bea said. "Now that I am settled, Mama will start interfering with everyone else's matrimonial plans. Do tell your sisters to be on their guard."

"She likes to be useful," Bertram said easily, in too good a humour even for Lady Esther to irritate him.

"No, she likes to manage everyone."

Bertram laughed. "You must have the patience of a saint to have survived her ministrations for so long. But let us not talk about your Mama.

What do you think?" He took her hand and led her around the ground floor again. "It is very small," he said sadly. "Not at all what you are used to."

"The rooms may be a little smaller than at Highwood, but there are more than enough of them. The dining room will seat twenty, at a pinch, and we have ample bedrooms, so we can invite all your scholarly friends to stay."

"And plenty of room for a nursery," he said softly.

She blushed and nodded. "Would you mind very much if our first son is not named after you?"

"What did you have in mind instead?" he said, smiling.

"Horace, naturally. Horace Atherton... that sounds well, does it not? Look..." She led him into one of the rooms off the hall. "Here is our library. There are two windows, one for each desk. We can have bookcases on every wall. The globes will go in this corner, here, and beside the fire, twin sofas so that we can both sit with our feet up as we read Horace. How does that sound?"

"It sounds... perfect," he said, with a sigh, pulling her into his arms. She lifted her face expectantly, but he only sighed again. "Will you ever tire of Latin, do you think? Will you tire of me? I am so dull and ordinary and uninteresting, and you are so—"

"Brash? Bumptious? Uncivilised?"

"Animated. Full of energy. You make me feel *alive*, Bea. I was living half a life, to be truthful, with most of delights of the world passing me by. I preferred my books and the Romans to the real world, and never knew what I was missing, until you came along."

"But I was living half a life, too, until I got to know you. I dutifully sat with Mama day after day, aware that there must be more to life than painting watercolours very badly and my appalling needlework, but not having the least notion how to find it. I thought I would start to live *properly* when I married a man of high rank. You showed me that there is so much more to life than marriage. There is *Latin!*"

"That is what I am afraid of — that you will find all your satisfaction in Latin, and will not need me at all. Or perhaps it will be something else that captures your interest, and I will be left behind in Rome or Carthage or Troy."

"I shall always need you, Bertram. Do you remember the first time you kissed me?"

"Of course!"

"That kiss was... amazing. Magical. The duchess said that when you kiss the right man, something magical happens and you just *know* that he is the one, and it is true. When you kissed me, I knew. Although, being stupid, I had no faith in my own judgement, so I kissed Lord Brockscombe and then Lord Thomas, and they were not magical at all. And even then, I thought I ought to kiss Lord Grayling, just to compare, but you rescued me from *that* mistake. And slowly — oh, I am so slow sometimes! — I realised that *you* were the right man all the time, and I discovered that I loved you. So no, I am not *ever* going to leave you behind in Rome or anywhere else, and yes, I shall always need you. Whatever happens to us in the future, whatever we have to do or say or be, whether you become the earl one day or remain an obscure country gentleman, whatever life throws at us, we will face it *together,* side by side. Two people with hearts that beat in unison. And that is a promise."

Bertram's throat was too tight for words, but when the words dried up, there were always kisses. So he kissed her and held her tight and then kissed her again, and lost himself in love all over again.

THE END

The next book in the series is *Anger,* wherein the earl's daughter, Izzy, discovers her five year marriage to Lord Farramont is invalid, and wonders what might have happened if she had chosen differently. You can read a sneak preview after the Acknowledgements.

For more information, go to my website at https://marykingswood.co.uk.

Thanks for reading!

If you have enjoyed reading this book, please consider writing a short review on Amazon. You can find out the latest news and sign up for the mailing list at my website at https://marykingswood.co.uk.

A note on historical accuracy: I have endeavoured to stay true to the spirit of Regency times, and have avoided taking too many liberties or imposing modern sensibilities on my characters. The book is not one of historical record, but I've tried to make it reasonably accurate. However, I'm not perfect! If you spot a historical error, I'd very much appreciate knowing about it so that I can correct it and learn from it. Thank you!

Isn't that what's-his-name? Occasionally characters from an earlier series pop up, or are mentioned. Lady Esther Franklyn's father, the Duke of Camberley, approved the marriage of his daughter, the Lady Grace Bucknell, to George Skelton, the Earl of Brackenwood's heir, in *The Governess.* Lady Esther's brother, the Marquess of Ramsey, had a tumultuous romance in *The Betrothed*. Lady Harbottle, in *The Widow*, and the Duchess of Orrisdale, in *The Duke,* were also Bucknells before their marriages.

About the series:

Book 0: The Chaplain: a man adrift, dreaming of a home (a novella, free to mailing list subscribers).

Book 1: Disinheritance: a man freed, looking for a new purpose in life

Book 2: Determination: a man pursued, forced to outwit his adversary

Book 3: Anger: a woman alone, trying to choose a different path in life

Book 4: Secrecy: a woman neglected, scheming to secure her own happiness

Book 5: Loyalty: a man of dreams, torn between the past and the future

Book 6: Ambition: a woman thwarted, unswervingly set on making a brilliant debut in society

Any questions about the series? Email me at mary@marykingswood.co.uk - I'd love to hear from you!

About the author

I write traditional Regency romances under the pen name Mary Kingswood, and epic fantasy as Pauline M Ross. I live in the beautiful Highlands of Scotland with my husband. I like chocolate, whisky, my Kindle, massed pipe bands, long leisurely lunches, chocolate, going places in my campervan, eating pizza in Italy, summer nights that never get dark, wood fires in winter, chocolate, the view from the study window looking out over the Moray Firth and the Black Isle to the mountains beyond. And chocolate. I dislike driving on motorways, cooking, shopping, hospitals.

Acknowledgements

Thanks go to:

Allison Lane, whose course on English Architecture inspired me.

The Latin poets, especially Quintus Horatius Flaccus (or Horace), whose words enthused Bertram and his friends.

Shayne Rutherford of Darkmoon Graphics for the cover design.

My beta readers: Caroline Allenby, Penny Bennett, Charles Crouter, Kelly Darpinian, Julie Desbrus, Sharon Flaherty, Melissa Forsythe, Erica Hague, Donna Sue Holly, Corinne Lehmann, Leann McKinley, Tina Miles, Pat Oen, Rosemary Paton, Kristen Pinto-Coelho, Melanie Savage, Helen Schneble, Laura Sporcic, Wendy Stubbs, Carol Sturz, Jeanne Thomas, A Usami

Last, but definitely not least, my first reader: Amy Ross.

Sneak preview: Book 3 of The Chaplain's Legacy: Anger

STONYWELL, NOTTINGHAMSHIRE: JUNE

Ian, Viscount Farramont, woke at his usual time. He invariably woke at his usual time, wherever he was, whatever the season. He rose and dressed himself in his old clothes and went for his walk. At least at Stonywell, he could take the dogs with him. Their boundless energy and endless enthusiasm for yet another pile of leaf litter, indistinguishable from every other such pile, always lifted his spirits.

Not that he was truly downcast. How could he be, married to Izzy? But today she would leave him again for a visit to friends. So many friends, so many visits. Ian supposed he could go too, if he wanted, but Izzy never suggested it and he knew that these gatherings were often overcrowded. They might have to share a room, and he hated to encroach.

The exercise in the cool early morning air did him good. He disliked being in town, when he was forced to walk the streets. The Brook Street house was too far from any of the parks for easy access, and there was nothing uplifting about London's filthy streets.

Discarding his muddy coat and donning indoor shoes, he made his way to the one room in the upper part of the house where he could find lively company at this hour. Peeking his head round the nursery door, he was greeted with squeals of glee from his two daughters. Helena, the elder at four, was all Izzy — the same wiry form and vivid green eyes. Aurelia, just three, had Ian's more solid frame, his washed-out blue eyes and a touch of his red hair. Fortunately, there was enough of Izzy's dark locks to render it auburn.

Sweeping Aurelia into his arms, he said, "Now, what are you two mischiefs up to, eh? Or are you behaving yourselves today?"

"They're good as gold, milord," the maid said bobbing a curtsy. "No trouble at all. They never are."

At least they did not take after their mother in that respect.

"Will you read to us, Papa?" Aurelia said.

"No, play a game with us," Helena said. "I can play cup and ball for ages now."

"What is your record?"

"Twelve," she said proudly.

"Well, let me see if I can best you. I used to be a champion with cup and ball when I was... well, perhaps a little bigger than you are."

The toy was found, and Ian soon discovered that skills enjoyed at the age of seven or eight could not be depended upon at the age of five and thirty. It amused the girls to see him struggle, however, and he never minded being a source of amusement to them.

"I can see I shall have to practise. Where did this come from? It looks just like the one I used to play with."

"It might be, at that, milord," the maid said. "Milady took the girls into the attics yesterday and found boxes of toys."

"Mostly wooden soldiers," Aurelia said in disgust.

"And there were spiders. And dust everywhere," Helena said. "We had to change all our clothes, and have our hair washed."

"Still, it was kind of Mama to find some new toys for you."

"It was because Madame Marie broke her head," Helena said sadly.

"Madame Marie? One of your dolls?"

"The one with the strange gown that sticks out. Mama said she was French because of her gown, but yesterday I dropped her and she broke her head. Mama said she'd buy me a new doll next time she's in London, but she doesn't know when that will be, so we went to the attics to find another doll. But there weren't any."

"I have to attend Parliament next month, so I can buy one for you then," Ian said. "At least you have something new to play with while you wait."

After the nursery, it was time to submit to Wycliffe's ministrations and turn himself from his rather scruffy and dishevelled early morning appearance into a gentleman. Wycliffe had only one mission in life, and that was to transform Ian into a sprig of fashion, so that when he walked down St James's Street or danced at Almack's, heads would turn and everyone would be so dazzled by his sartorial elegance that they would all want to know the name of his valet. In this regard, Ian was a sad disappointment to him. Wycliffe had assumed that a viscount would want to strut a little, but

Ian had never had the least ambition to strut, and if asked, would not even be able to describe what such an activity entailed.

He was very glad to be properly and soberly dressed, however, as befitted a gentleman, wearing dark colours, clean linen and no jewellery beyond a signet ring and a single fob. Such a style had graced his father and his grandfather before him, and Ian could not for the life of him see why he should consider changing it.

"There, sir," Wycliffe said at last, brushing a final speck from Ian's coat and stepping back to admire his handiwork.

"Thank you, Wycliffe," Ian said gravely. "You look after me very well."

"It's a pleasure to dress a gentleman so imposing as your lordship," Wycliffe said with a bow.

Imposing. That meant tall with bright red hair, he supposed. Ian could never lose himself in a crowd.

Since Wycliffe was satisfied that his master was presentable enough to meet the world, Ian turned his steps to the highlight of his day — breakfast with his wife. Not that she had conceded the privilege easily, but it was a point which for once he had demanded.

"Why do you want to see me so early in the day?" she had said, pouting a little. "I shall not even be dressed, and I dislike conversation at such an hour."

"Izzy, I must know what you have planned for the day — whether you will be out for dinner, whether we are expecting company, that sort of thing."

"Mrs Worthing can tell you such things."

"I have no intention of asking the servants about my wife's engagements. I wish to hear them from your own lips, and breakfast is a convenient time to do so. We need not talk at all, apart from that, but I so rarely have you to myself, even when we happen to be under the same roof, that I must have one meal each day with no distractions. I insist upon it, Izzy."

She had surrendered gracefully, perhaps assuming that he would tire of the arrangement when he saw her déshabillé but he never had. Whether she wore a robe over her nightgown, her hair tumbled down her back, or her grandest ball gown, her hair piled on her head and crowned with jewels, she was just as beautiful to him. He never tired of her.

Thus it was that he made his way with eager steps to his wife's sitting room. It had never quite recovered from Izzy's first disastrous attempts at redecoration, and even though she had subsequently received good advice on the subject, and had even listened to some of it, the results had never pleased her. Every time she stayed at Stonywell, she had one wall or another redone, so that now four entirely different styles glared balefully at each other.

Ian had no interest in what was on the walls, so long as Izzy was there. She was late, of course. Izzy never could get anywhere on time. She joked that she would probably be late for her own funeral.

She had certainly been late for her wedding. Ian had stood in the chapel at Corland Castle, Izzy's home, as the minutes ticked away, so utterly terrified that she would not come that his legs would barely hold him up. At any moment, he expected a footman to come in with a note for him. *'Fooled you! There will be no wedding. Whatever made you think I would marry anyone like you?'* But miraculously, there she was on her father's arm, coming nearer and nearer. She stopped beside Ian and smiled up at him, and he had melted all over again, just as he had the first time he had seen her. Then Nicholson had begun the service, the words had been spoken and it was done. She was Lady Farramont. His wife!

Today, she was only twenty minutes late, still yawning, her eyes heavy with sleep. As always, his heart somersaulted at the very sight of her. Five years married, yet he was just as besotted as ever. Did it never get any easier?

There were no greetings. He had quickly learnt that, however loquacious she was at other times, at breakfast she was as taciturn as he was, completely calm for once. She sat, he poured her chocolate for her, she crumbled a piece of cake. Today there was nothing to say, for he knew her plans — she was going away to visit friends, leaving him alone once more. He waited for just the right moment to produce the purse.

"For your visit to the Cotterills," he said, as he placed it on the table in front of her. "Two hundred. I know they play high, and you will not want to refuse to join in. Besides, if you should happen to go into Lincoln, there might be something you want to buy."

"Thank you!" she said, pleasure lighting her face. "You are very good to me, husband."

He never knew what to say to her at such times. Some men managed it easily, the glib words falling from their tongues without effort, but he had never had the way of it. So he merely grunted and continued to work his way through a mutton chop. She turned back to her slice of cake, now reduced to an almost perfect mound of crumbs.

"Will you be sure to tell me where you are?" he blurted into the silence.

She looked surprised. "You know where I will be — at the Cotterills. Somerton Manor."

"Yes, but if you should decide to move on... go elsewhere... there could be news from Corland any day."

"Grandmama? I have seen her not a month since, and if she should die— Or are you talking about this ghastly business of the murder of Nicholson? Who would murder the chaplain, Ian? Who would go to his room in the middle of the night and hack him to death with an axe? It is quite unbelievable!"

"Your father has engaged people to discover the murderer. I was not thinking of that particularly, no. There are a number of issues which might arise for your father and mother. I need to know precisely how to locate you, should anything occur which you would need to know. All I ask is that you inform me if you decide to leave Somerton Manor."

"Of course," she said vaguely, her attention already drifting away.

After breakfast, Ian went to his library to begin work for the day. His cousin, Henry Farramont, who acted as his secretary, was already at his desk, head down, pen scratching across the paper.

"The Caswell papers are on your desk ready for signing, also the new leases, and I am just drafting a letter to Hillman," he said, without looking up. "Three personal letters for you." The head lifted briefly to catch Ian's eyes. "Still nothing from Corland."

"It could be weeks."

"True. There is a vestry meeting on Thursday to talk about the roads — again! But I can go, if you prefer. It is deadly dull stuff. The new curate would like to pay a courtesy call to introduce himself. I have tentatively made an appointment for tomorrow."

"How efficient you are, Henry."

Henry looked up and grinned. "I was well taught. Besides, I have to catch you while you are here. Whatever whim brought Izzy back from town so soon, I am glad of it, for it brings you, too. You will be back there soon enough to support that bill of yours." A hesitation, then he went on, "Izzy is off again, I hear."

"To the Cotterills, yes."

Ian heard the implied criticism in Henry's voice but chose to ignore it. It was one of the few points on which they disagreed. From the day Henry had arrived on the doorstep at the age of eight, his dark eyes filled with awe at the imposing scale of Stonywell, he and Ian had been the best of friends. The two boys had gone to Eton and Oxford together, made their first steps in society together, grieved together at age fourteen when Ian's father had died, and when Ian had come of age and gained control of his fortune, had learnt to manage the estate together. Not once had they fallen out, until the day the Lady Isabel Atherton entered their lives.

"She is too overwrought, if you ask me," Henry had said. "Likely to be firing off in all directions at the least setback, you mark my words. Too unstable a female for a steady fellow like you."

But Ian, deep in the throes of his first passion, could not be deterred. "She will liven me up," he said. "A wife as staid as I am would be dreadfully boring."

"Izzy will certainly never be boring," Henry had said. "You deserve better, Ian."

Ian violently disagreed, and since he had not yet come to regret his decision, the two cousins skirted around the issue by never mentioning it.

For his part, Henry had taken a different route, marrying early to a clergyman's daughter. They and their growing family had initially lived in Stonywell, but moved out when Izzy arrived, and now lived contentedly in a cottage in the village, although they dined at Stonywell more often than not.

The two men worked diligently for an hour or so, then Henry went off about his own affairs, while Ian settled down with an inner glow of pleasure to the accounts. There was something extraordinarily satisfying about columns of numbers, some added and some subtracted, the totals in perfect alignment. And at the bottom of every page, the line that read 'To Savings'. Sometimes it was only a shilling or two, sometimes several pounds, but every week there was something left over to increase his wealth and stave off the terrifying possibility of debt and bankruptcy and the loss of everything.

As he worked, he was aware of the signs of Izzy's imminent departure. In the hall, mysterious thumps and the mutterings of the footmen suggested that luggage was being assembled. Then Izzy's carriage, an elegant affair in bright blue paint with yellow wheels, was brought round. That carriage always made him smile, with its jaunty colours and the blue velvet interior. A great extravagance, but Izzy loved it and it was so much in tune with her character that he loved it too.

Izzy was late, needless to say, so the luggage was loaded up and still the carriage waited. But then something else caught Ian's eye as he glanced through the window — a rider, coming fast up the drive, although the horse looked close to exhaustion. The rider wore the livery of the Earl of Rennington, and Ian knew that the wondering was over, and it was not good news.

He went out himself to greet the rider on the drive as he slithered to the ground in ungainly fashion, stumbling and almost falling.

"Urgent message for Lord Farramont!" he called out, as Eastwood and two footmen rushed out.

Ian was there before them. "I am Farramont."

Holding his hand out, he waited as the man prised off his gloves and reached into a deep pocket for the letter. It bore Lord Rennington's wayward writing, and his seal. Tearing it open, Ian scanned it quickly. It was as he thought.

Folding it neatly and tucking it into a pocket, he said, "You did well to get here so quickly. John, show this fellow the way to the stables and see that he gets a decent meal inside him. He will need somewhere to sleep for a day or two." He turned back to the house, his long legs taking the steps two at a time, then striding into the hall, as the butler struggled to keep up with him. "Eastwood, I need to talk to Lady Farramont. On no account is she to leave this house before I have seen her, is that understood? You have my permission to hold her forcibly if she tries. Tell Wycliffe to pack for me. A trip to London for a few days, personal business so I shall not need anything formal. Ah, there you are, Henry. Library, if you please. Remember, Eastwood — bring Lady Farramont into the library as soon as she comes downstairs."

"The letter has come then?" Henry said, closing the library door on the servants scurrying about the hall.

"Yes, and it is just as Rennington feared. I shall go straight up to town with Izzy— Ah, I hear her. Quick, man, move the porcelain."

In the hall, Izzy was tapping her foot impatiently as her maid, Brandon, drew gloves over her slender, white fingers. Ian loved those delicate fingers, always in motion, always busy about something.

"Lady Farramont, I should like a word with you in the library, if you would be so good."

"Not now. I am in the most almighty rush to get off. Come on, Brandon! Do get a move on!"

"This cannot wait. There is news from Corland."

"Grandmama?" she said, suddenly alert.

"No, everyone is well. It is a different matter entirely."

"Then tell me here and now, while Brandon is dilly-dallying."

"The library," he said, in his most uncompromising tones.

Her eyes flashed angrily. "Really, Farramont! I truly cannot spare a moment. I shall be late for dinner as it is."

"I am quite prepared to pick you up and carry you," he said calmly.

The servants stood statue-like, pretending to ignore the argument. Ian gave them no thought. They were surely used to Izzy's ways by now. He held the library door open, just as Henry scuttled out. With an exasperated sigh, Izzy finally accepted the inevitable and strode through the door, swirling round to face Ian as he followed her into the room and quietly closed the door.

"This had better be good, Ian. If I have to spend a night on the road because of you—"

"It is not good. It is very bad, and when you have heard all, you may not wish to go to Somerton at all. Will you not sit down, Izzy?"

"Just tell me whatever it is and get it over with, for heaven's sake."

She paced up and down, and Ian automatically checked the room. The valuable porcelain was all on an unreachable shelf, the ink pots hidden away in the desk, important papers hastily tidied away. There were still books scattered everywhere, and the globes, not properly repaired since the last time, were vulnerable, but it would have to do.

"Your father writes with news of Nicholson."

"Has his murderer been caught?"

"No, not yet. It is not about the murder."

Izzy made a strangled noise in her throat. "Just tell me!"

"Amongst his papers was a letter from Winchester, suggesting that Nicholson had not been ordained there. Your father has made enquiries, and it appears that Nicholson was never ordained as a clergyman at all."

Izzy laughed. "The old rogue! I always thought there was something not right about him. So he has been sitting pretty all these years, has he, married to Aunt Alice, his feet well and truly under the table, and acting as our chaplain when he was not even a clergyman?"

"Do you understand what that means, Izzy? He was not entitled to conduct marriages."

"Nonsense! He married us, as I am sure you will remember. I think you were there at the time."

"Yes, he married us, but he was not qualified to do so. It means our marriage is invalid, Izzy. That is the law. A marriage can only be valid if it is conducted by an ordained clergyman. We are not married, and the girls are illegitimate. Now you must not panic about this, because we can set most of it right. We can go to town and get a special licence so the marriage, at least, will be on a proper footing. The girls... there is nothing to be done about that, but—"

"Ian, I know you have very little humour, but is this your idea of a jest?"

"I only wish it were. But if we—"

She was breathing heavily now, almost quivering as emotions boiled up in her. "That man has been chaplain at Corland Castle forever — since long before I was born. Of course he is ordained! How can he be chaplain otherwise?"

"I cannot say how it came about. It was your grandfather who engaged him. He must have taken Nicholson's word for it that he was ordained."

"And no one checked? You never checked, before we were married by some... some charlatan!" Her voice was rising now, and her pacing had diminished to angry twitches from side to side. "How could you do this to me? How could you expose me to the ridicule of the world? I shall never, ever be able to hold my head up in society again. To be... unmarried and yet the mother of two children — it is... Ian Farramont, you were supposed to shelter me from the world and keep me safe, and you have ruined me! You have taken everything from me — my very position in society is gone! I am no one!"

"Temporarily," he said, placatingly. "You will be Lady Farramont again in just a few days, as soon as we can get a special licence."

"But I am not Lady Farramont!" she wailed. "How can you humiliate me like this? I am nothing without my title. At least I still have my birth title. I am still Lady Isabel Atherton."

"No," he said firmly, for she had to be made to understand the enormity of the disaster. "No, because Nicholson married your parents, too. They are not married, either, and all their children are illegitimate. You are illegitimate."

Izzy screamed. With one delicate hand, she swept everything within reach from Ian's desk, so that they fell to the floor in a great clatter of books, the standish, the wooden boxes holding paper and the metal stand used to melt sealing wax. Then she screamed again. The terrestrial globe was next, kicked across the room by a daintily booted foot. The silver salver on the sideboard was hurled at the window, but fortunately fell short, then she toppled a small table heaped in books.

Ian waited patiently, ready to step in only if Izzy seemed likely to hurl herself through a window. He had learnt very early in their marriage to keep out of her way when these storms overtook her, as well as the wisdom of locking away decanters and wine glasses, and moving anything to which one was attached out of reach.

Eventually, she collapsed like a burst balloon, sinking to her knees on the floor. Then she lifted her head and howled in impotent rage.

END OF SAMPLE CHAPTER of *Anger;* for more information or to buy, go to my website at https://marykingswood.co.uk.

Made in the USA
Las Vegas, NV
04 June 2024

90700224R00215